BOOK FOUR IN THE COIN FOREST SERIES

CRIMSON SECRET

JANET LANE

Dreaming Tree Publishing, LLC
Littleton, Colorado, USA

Janet Lane

PUBLISHED BY DREAMING TREE PUBLISHING
P. O. Box 1070, Littleton, CO 80160-1070, USA

ISBN 978-1-945508-01-1

First Edition
Printed in the United States of America

Available on amazon.com and other retail outlets
Available on Kindle and other devices

DEDICATION

This is dedicated to my critique group, Kay Bergstrom, Denee Cody, Carla Gertner, Thea Hutcheson, Alice Kober, Steven Moores, Pam Nowak, Robin Owens, Cate Rowan, Peggy Waide and Jessie Wulf. They are gifted writers and amazing friends. We have shared our dreams, our words, our novels, and our literary lives. I am eternally grateful for their generous support over the years of my writing journey.

ACKNOWLEDGEMENTS

Thanks to Margaret Bailey, Kay Bergstrom, Denee Cody, Pam Nowak and Peggy Waide for their keen insights and observations. Thanks to my husband, John, for his patience and support. Thanks to Sherry Carey for her fresh eyes and encouragement. Thanks also to Dawn and Andrea for their deep love of books and their in-depth reviews of my novels.

Thanks to Jalena Penaligon for this and her other amazing cover designs for the Coin Forest series.

Thanks to Jan Gerstenberger for her support, and for the treats from the Kashgar Bazaar. They were, after all, inspirational.

Janet Lane

Kings. They wanted a castle for their riches.
An executioner's block for their enemies.
Good food, good women, good wine.
And above all, power.
　　　... The Assassin
　　　　from Crimson Secret

IRELAND

Dublin ●

Holyhead ●

Crimson Secret
ENGLAND

Denbigh Castle ⊠

Coventry ⊠

Kilkenny ●

● Redstone

Rewley Abbey ● ● St.Albans

Bath ●

London ⊠

Winchester ●

Sandwich ●

Coin Forest ●
Penryton ●　Christchurch ●

Calais ●

4

Prologue

A herring seagull swooped into Luke's face, an assault of wings and sharp claws. Luke swatted it and his rope ladder teetered thirty feet above the water. Luke grabbed the rung and tightened his hold, the stiff twining cutting his flesh. His grip failed and the rope snaked from his hands. Panic crippled him and his foot slipped. He wobbled like a stricken duck, right leg flailing.

"Hold still. Grab my hand." From above on the bridge, his cousin Degory reached for him. "You're all right. Step up to the next rung. Slowly. A little to the left and … there. You have it."

In all his ten summers Luke had never experienced such fear. He felt his trousers moisten and he avoided his cousin's eyes.

Deg laughed. "Don't worry. If you fall, so what? That's what we're here for. If you do, don't dive. Go in feet first and swim to the left like I told you. I'm going to let go now. Ready?"

Luke took a deep breath and let go of Deg's hand. What could be so hard about swinging from a bridge? Certes, it was a high bridge, higher, grander and longer than any Luke had seen back home in Somerset. Its graceful arches reached high, as if made for angels, as splendid as Wells Cathedral with its fine stonework spanning the length of at least four tilting fields.

He hoped Deg hadn't noticed his trousers.

His cousin, three years older, swung over the bridge and descended onto the other ladder, nimble as a mummer. They stepped down their ladders and settled on the last rung.

Deg started swinging, pumping his legs, leaning back until his arms were straight and his swing formed an aggressive arch.

A quick look up showed that the rope was still securely attached to the bridge. A cool thrill of courage shot up Luke's spine, and he ventured a gentle pumping of his legs. Far below, the river churned and Luke grew light-headed.

"Look up!" Deg said. "Get used to it first before you look down."

Luke swung, higher, watching the clouds and the bridge swing in and out of his vision. His uncle's home sat snugly at the end of the bridge, and the shops seemed to sprout like mushrooms on the deck of the bridge. "I'm doing it," he shouted. "This is fine!" His toes tickled at the bottom of the swing's arc and his heart soared at the top, the shivering, light sensation as wondrous as sunshine after days of rain.

Up and down, up and down, defying the seagulls that still swooped toward them, protecting their chicks. They gave up and flew back to the roofs and crannies under the bridge where they nested.

Too soon, Deg called to him.

How long had they been swinging? A moment, an inch of the candle, a bell's time?

"Time to jump," his cousin said.

New courage emboldened Luke. "Ready!"

Deg rose to standing. "It's simple. Don't jump until after you reach the top of your swing and have started to drop. Go feet first. Use your arms to stay upright. Don't let the current take you past the fisherman's docks. Got it?"

Luke blinked in the flurry of instructions. "Got it."

Deg nodded. "Do what I do."

At the highest point, Deg stepped off the swing and into the air, arms circling to keep his balance.

Luke tried to imagine what it must feel like to fall that far down in the air. Breathing became harder.

A splash. Deg's black head bobbed to the surface, and he swam to the dock. "Come on!"

"Hey, Turtle!" A harsh, raspy voice boomed from above the bridge. Luke turned, and the air chilled. His brothers, Philip and Christopher. They weren't supposed to arrive from Somerset until later this eve.

A familiar blanket of dread fell over him, worse than the seagull's wings, one that always buried Luke when in his brothers' company.

Philip grabbed the top of Luke's ladder and tugged on it, making it keel to the side. "What's the worry, Turtle?" he taunted.

"Scared to jump, Turtle?" Christopher asked.

The nickname pierced his skull. He would not answer them, would not feed their appetite at shaming him.

"Here, let me help you." Christopher pulled his dagger and started a sawing motion on the rope that held Luke's ladder.

Luke yelled. "No!" Fear surged, but he struck it down. He would not let them see his fear, ever again, after the barrel. Gritting his teeth, he kicked his legs forcefully, swinging high, and jumped.

Luke plummeted down, the rushing air whistling in his ears. His body tilted to the right and he landed crooked in the water. The river slapped him, a massive blow to his body that took his breath and rattled his neck.

He cut through the water like a cannon, the water pushing his tunic up over his head.

Finally he stopped sinking and an image came to him of a watery grave and hungry fish.

Up, must keep reaching up. Luke clawed to the light above, lungs burning. He broke through the surface, gasping, and struggled to the shore.

"Bad landing," Deg said from the dock. "You all right?"

Luke's skin was on fire and his neck hurt, but he admired Deg and didn't want him to think, as his brothers did, that he was afeared or worse, weak.. "Yeah."

"So was it not fine as I told you?"

Luke rubbed his neck. "Aye."

"Let's do it again."

Up at the bridge, his uncle had joined his brothers. Luke could imagine Christopher's smile, his mouth curved in cruelty. After what they had done to him with the pickle barrel, they could not be trusted. He turned to Deg. "Let's go again later. After they leave."

Chapter 1

21 years later
Somerset, May, 1460

Joya Ellington, second daughter of Lord and Lady Tabor, waved her hawking glove and bumped the bed where her friends slept. "Come, ladies. It's May Day."

Her friend, Camilla, stirred. "Not for two days."

"Aye, but you won't make me hunt alone, will you?"

From Joya's bed Camilla groaned, her blue nightcap flattened from sleep like a storm-tossed tent. "The sun's not even up. Be gone." She pulled the covers over her head and her crooked cap disappeared.

Beside her, Prudence sat up, her slender shoulders sagging. She held her head, her expression pained from yester eve's wine. "Off to the forest with a dozen men? You'll hardly be alone."

Joya turned to her table and pushed aside the heap of hair combs, rings and pins to reach the water bowl. Sifting through the scattered garments she found a cloth, moistened it in cool water and pressed it to Prude's forehead. "This will help. And don't make it sound so improper. I'll be with my father and my priest." She looked forward to hunting with her father, Lord Tabor. She would receive his warm gaze of approval when she captured a pigeon or two for the festival table.

"Your father, priest, and ten other men," Prudence said.

Camilla's blue nightcap reappeared. She tossed the covers aside and propped herself on one elbow, regarding Joya with a raised brow. "Dawn has not yet broken, but look at her."

Prudence straightened and turned to Joya. "She's a vision." She touched Joya's coronet. "Not one hair astray, and her gown," she said, touching it. "The finest wool, yellow as the sun."

A teasing smile broke out on both their faces.

Joya rolled her eyes. Now would come the chants. She withdrew and plugged her ears. "I can't hear you."

"Oh, yes you can," Camilla said. "Her gown, so bright." Camilla started the sequence.

"A sheer delight," Prudence spoke the words in a familiar sing-song pattern.

"So small, a sprite," Camilla said.

Prudence tapped her chin, thinking. "Um—a bird, so light."

"Eyes dark as night," Camilla said.

"A lovely sight!" They framed their grinning faces with their hands.

"Stop you now." This ritual of theirs left Joya walking a narrow course. Their affection showed in their eyes, but small needles of disapproval winked below the surface of their words. "I am but lucky that my mother is such a good seamstress." She whopped them with her feather pillow. "There is no crime in looking nice."

"Good," Camilla said. "By cause if there were, the reeve would be shackling you."

Joya steered the conversation from herself. "So Cam, you're wide awake now. Come join the hunt. Think of the men. This could lead to your wedding day."

"The men don't look past you," Cam said.

"I am not interested." Joya clutched Giles' betrothal ring, suspended on a chain around her neck. Her fiancé had died months before at Blore Heath, at the hands of the malicious, usurping Yorkists. She would never love again. "Ah, but you should be. George will be there." George, the young Lord Minton. Camilla had been casting sheep's eyes at him.

10

"Even he isn't worth getting up in the dark for." Cam snuggled back under the covers. Joya grabbed for Camilla's leg and missed. "Hmm, I could strap your ankles to a horse and haul you out."

"Don't try me." Camilla bundled her legs beneath her and growled. "I have teeth. Good teeth. Now be gone. Anon."

Prudence swept an assessing gaze over Joya's gown. "And change that gown before you go out in all that mud."

Joya smoothed her hand over her skirt, full and flowing to allow free movement on her horse, the sleeves snug so she could efficiently handle her goshawk. She opened her mirror to check her coronet, bright with woven flowers and a yellow scarf. *One can never be too pretty.*

Prudence held her head. "Enjoy yourself." She laughed, a soft undercurrent of affection lilting her voice and warming her eyes. "What am I saying? You always do."

Joya planted a quick kiss on her cheek. "Thank you, Prude. Remember the games later at parish. Be there on time." She reached across and rocked Camilla's hip. "And you, Sleepy. I'll tell George you said good morn."

Camilla swatted her hand away.

Outside, Joya hurried through the bailey in the pre-dawn grey, heading for the mews. Father Jeffrye and her father waited with his knights by the drawbridge. Her brother's hound, Seven, sat between them, panting, ready for the hunt.

Sir Peter, short in the saddle and long in the tooth, turned an eye on her. "Late. So like a woman." His words taunted but his eyes lingered in admiration.

Joya raised a brow. "Early. So like a man." She waited for the men's laughter to die down and smiled at Peter. "We shall see if you can hawk like a woman."

"Or if you can hawk like a man," Peter answered.

"Do not bait her, Peter. At hawking, she will win," her father said, regarding her with affection.

"For me, she has already won." Peter's voice held suggestive undertones that drew more laughter.

11

Joya shot him a warning look. She enjoyed the hunt, had always been comfortable with the knights and their teasing, but she would not tread on the path to romance. Ever again.

She quickened her walk. This would be a good day. She and Diana, her prize merlin, would impress her father and provide food for the May Day feast.

She hurried to the mews, still feeling Peter's gaze on her. He had position, good humor and the wisdom of years, but he was not Giles. She still ached for him, felled by the maggot-brained Yorkists.

Giles would have turned twenty-two this month. She took a fortifying breath and ducked to enter the mews. Inside the squat hut her merlin, Diana, paced on her caged perch. She danced from side to side in excitement, a splendid bird with her white head, gold-ringed nose, and proud bronze and black-feathered chest.

From outside came the sounds of a trumpet and horses. Several men greeted her father. Diana's head jerked toward the rumpus. Joya positioned the hawk on her leather sleeve, hooded her and hurried outside.

A contingent of five men under King Henry's standard lingered on horseback before her father and his knights. "Spread the word," their leader said. They left, passing over the drawbridge.

Joya approached her father. "What word?"

"York. Word from Calais is that he and Warwick are returning."

"Again?" York and Warwick had escaped to Calais, and Warwick had returned after Christmas and stolen several ships from the king at Sandwich. Queen Margaret had effectively exiled them in Ireland. It all meant more war, more deaths. An old, familiar fear echoed from the past and Joya swallowed hard, fighting the nausea that rose from the mention of Yorkists. *We should have killed them all at Ludford.*

"Traitors," Peter said.

12

"They don't dare travel this far inland, damn their souls. If they do they'll rue the day they stepped on my land," her father said.

"They've been condemned." Not that it helped. Being attainted by Parliament hadn't stopped their five-year campaign to unseat King Henry.

"We're to be watchful on the highways, especially to the north," her father said.

The threat of war made the sky seem darker. Joya's skin crawled and she yearned to slap the Yorkists for the hateful bugs they were and feed them to the river snakes. She lifted her chin. *A pox on them. Bastards, all.* She posed a serene smile. She would not let them spoil the day. "Let's hunt, then, and provision our tables for May Day."

Joya handed Diana to the cadger. He added her to the six other hawks on the cadge and shifted it securely on his hips. Subdued, the hunting party headed for the woods.

By mid-day, the morning chill and dampness had burned off and Coin Forest was fresh with spring. The streams ran clear and tiny white flowers winked on tall stems within the high grasses. Pine needles carpeted the forest floor, releasing their fragrant resins as the horses crushed them on the trail.

Peter and the other men had taken their saker falcons west in search of grouse. Joya and her father had chosen to hunt at their favorite clearing a few miles away. They walked with their horses while Seven sniffed, looking for the opportunity to flush some game. Diana perched on Joya's protected arm, the goshawk on her father's arm.

In the companionable silence Tabor drank mead from his flask and passed it to her. She took a drink, stoppered the flask and positioned the strap over her shoulder.

Seven's tail straightened. He lunged toward a thick bush.

Three coneys burst from the cover, long ears flat, running in hell-bent haste in all directions.

"Ho! Ho!" Her father shouted to his goshawk. He unhooded and released the bird, mounted his horse and followed Seven and the hawk.

The sounds disturbed a bush full of flickers and they fluttered from their cover. "Het! Het!" Joya cried out and freed Diana from her hood and released her. Wings spreading almost a yard wide, she took to the air in a soft jingle of her bells.

Joya mounted Goldie and they followed Diana, ducking the low branches and thick brush. Their movement flushed a family of hares and more pigeons. Mud flew from her horse's hooves, splashing the hem of Joya's gown. *No matter. Must stay with Diana.* She could already imagine the look on her father's face when she returned with some plump birds.

She reached another clearing and a large pond, thick with lily pads. At the water's edge Diana pranced, mantling her prey. Joya dismounted, tethered Goldie to the low branch of a sprawling oak and approached her bird. "Good girl," Joya praised, trying to peer through Diana's wings to see what she had caught.

Behind her, Goldie huffed and pranced, trying to break free. "It's all right, girl," Joya soothed.

Diana continued to cover her prize, protecting it. Joya spoke softly and approached her, respectful of her sharp beak and claws. With a swift movement she hooded the bird, lifting her away to reveal the bird's prize: a fat vole. "Oh, Diana," Joya said, keeping the disappointment from her voice. "Very nice, my lady. Very nice." Joya opened her hawking bag, unhooded Diane and gave her a treat. The vole would not do for their May Day table, but she bagged it any way. The stable cats would be pleased.

Behind her Goldie still paced, skittish. "There now, girl," she said, approaching her horse. "What's vexing you?"

Her palfry strained her reins, eyes widened.

Joya lowered her gaze to the horse's legs. Behind them the muddy shoreline was churned by the hooves of many horses, the deep imprints filled with water. Unseen earlier in her rush to tend to Diana, blood glistened in the pools.

Fear tingled her neck and the ground beneath her shifted. She was alone. How distant was her father?

She met the white-framed eyes of her frightened horse and followed her gaze to the left. Visible by a wild rosebush at the base of the giant oak was a bloodied arm.

Crimson Secret

The pool of blood beneath the body was as large as a soldier's shield, and his face—early twenties, she guessed—had taken on a grey tinge. His armor had been stolen, all but his greaves. The man had expired.

What if there are more? One step back, then another. On her arm, Diana crouched to spring.

I haven't tethered her. She reached for the bird.

Goldie gave another sharp tug on her reins and the branch broke. The horse bumped into Joya, knocking her off balance. She fell in the mud, arms outstretched to break her fall.

Diana fell off her arm and rolled. When her hood fell off, she flew to a high branch.

"Diana!"

But the hawk was hunting again and flew off, bells jingling.

Joya crooned to her horse. Calmly mounting her, she reined her to follow the hawk. Something caught her eye again, an object near a group of diseased trees. A pair of boots and legs by a fallen tree.

Stay, or go? *My hawk. But what if this one's alive?* She would check. If he still breathed, she would assure him she'd return, get Diana and find her father. She pulled her dagger. *If he tries to harm me, I'll defend myself and escape.*

She swallowed the stone in her throat and approached.

There were no signs of blood on this man. He was a few years older than the other man, fine lines settling around his eyes. His powerful brow line suggested much contemplation or deep study, and clearly by his clothes he was a nobleman. New mustache and beard growth shadowed his face. Hair the color of sand, nice jawline, thin face, high-set ears that brought attention to a fine, sensitive mouth. No helm or breastplate. She kept her distance, dagger drawn, poised in front of her chest. "Who are you?" As soon as the words passed her lips, her heart jumped to a dizzying beat. Why waken a sleeping bear? *Where's Father?* She stepped back a safer distance. Hands shaking, she pulled her hunting horn from her belt and blew hard. Her father would hear her and come.

The injured man hadn't reacted to her. She tried to walk away, but decency held her. She approached, caution tensing her muscles, dagger still drawn as she knelt beside his head. "Don't move," she warned, "Or I'll kill you." She placed her hand beneath his nostrils.

Moist air blew rhythmically against her skin.

His face was thin, and beautiful. Like a soft breeze his breath awakened sensations that had long been sleeping, and she was acutely aware of his masculinity, his power. She should leave him, but she could not. She tapped his forehead and received no response. Slapped his face, nothing. Finally she rolled his head back and forth. "Wake up!"

He stirred and groaned, holding his head. His eyes opened, blue, compelling. A thrill not unlike that of falling jolted through her core.

"Here, drink this." Her voice shook slightly as she offered him her father's berry mead, but he waved it away, rolled over and threw up.

"Who are you?" At his misery she softened her voice. "What happened?"

"Highway men," he said. His voice was heavy, shockingly deep and masculine. It stirred something inside her, something pleasant. His beard reflected a few days' growth, not yet shameful. Inexplicably, she wondered what that new growth should feel like under her fingertips. While worry lines creased his light skin between those icy blue eyes, his mouth lacked any lines that suggested he ever smiled.

She thought to look around again. "How many of you are there?"

He coughed, avoiding her eyes.

Apprehension stiffened her back. "How many?"

"Only the two of us." He hesitated. "Is he alive?"

"Tell me your name. Now."

"Bonwyk. Lord Penry."

She had heard the name. "Baron?"

"Aye."

"Somerset?"

16

He avoided her eyes again. He struggled to stand, shaky on his feet.

She pulled back, brandishing her dagger. "I'm sorry. Your friend is dead."

His brows knit together and his eyes closed for a moment. He opened them, put his hand out, palm toward her. "I will not hurt you." He took a step, and his knees buckled. He fell back on the ground, fainted.

He may be dying from unseen injuries. She lowered her dagger and lifted his collar to see any evidence of his coat of arms. A pin— she turned it and jerked her hand free, the badge too hot to be touched. It was a rose, a white rose.

White rose, symbol of Richard Plantagenet, Third Duke of York, the miscreant who sought to steal the crown from King Henry. White rose, symbol of greed and murder, the force behind the battle of Blore Heath, where Giles and two thousand others died defending their king.

A wave of nausea assaulted her. Bloody nails. Her softness for him, her concern for his injuries fled like morning smoke, and fury churned her stomach. *Swine. A Yorkist.*

She rose quickly. *Let him die.*

In the distance a horn sounded, two short, three long notes. Her father. She released a shaking breath. Her father was coming back and he would deal with this traitor.

A flurry of movement surprised Joya.

Lord Penry jumped to life. He batted the dagger out of her hand, gripped her shoulders, covered her mouth. She screamed into his hand.

"Quiet," he barked. "You will come with me. Be silent." His blue eyes had darkened, his jaw pulsed with determination, and he poked an exotic dagger into the soft skin under her chin. He blocked her right arm with his body, lean, muscular as it pressed her against an old oak. "Understand?"

Stupid girl. She chided herself for her distractions with him. *Here, alone in the forest. Stupid, stupid.* The weapon and his menacing presence paralyzed her. She could not reach her own dagger, now lying useless on the ground. The wind stopped swirling through the pines. The birds ceased singing and she could not breathe.

The swine Penry, who had appeared close to death moments before, now loomed over her, vibrant, strong, commanding. He reached to retrieve her fallen dagger and fumbled at her gown, finding her purse. With a quick motion he used her dagger to cut the purse cord and bound her hands with it. Her fear took wings to heights greater than her hawk had ever seen.

"Let me go!" Joya's heart hammered in her chest. *Hurry, Father, hurry!*

"When I'm safely away I'll release you." He grabbed Goldie's reins and slung Joya onto her horse. "Where's your saddle?"

The question stirred her Roma blood and she glared at him. "I don't need one when I hunt."

He looked to the heavens and back at her. His hair tumbled onto his forehead and he cast a determined gaze at her. "Then we shall ride without one. Don't do anything foolish." He swooped onto Goldie, leading her away from the clearing and into a dense thicket of trees.

Joya struggled in the prison of his arms. He had tied her hands tightly, and the cord cut into her wrists as she gripped Goldie's mane for balance. "You're hurting my horse. We're too heavy for her."

"You can't weigh seven stones, wet. She'll be fine," he said, his voice curt, indignant. He guided Goldie through the dense undergrowth, weaving slightly for balance, clearly not accustomed to riding without a saddle.

"You'll be gutted when my father catches you. He's an Ellingham, you know. Lord Tabor."

Penry grunted. "The one who wed the Gypsy. That explains your lack of saddle. And your skin."

"You won't have any skin left when he's through with you." Self-conscious, she shifted her weight. Her skin bore evidence of her mother's heritage, but also of her father's. "I have Spanish blood."

"M-hmm," he said, smugness deepening his words. They neared a series of fallen trees. "Hold on."

Goldie picked her way around debris that cluttered the trail. They cleared a large, long-dead tree that sprawled across the forest floor, overgrown with moss and mushrooms. *The mushroom tree.* A familiar area for Joya that held mysteries and legends her father had told her. She noted the sun's position, hoping desperately to keep some reference point so she could later find her way back. If she could escape. Goldie pounded over the trail, taking them farther and farther away.

"My father heard my signal. He'll catch up with you," she said.

He did not respond, and she heard no sounds of pursuit, only the swish of branches as they snagged her gown, the fine wool by now in tatters and drenched in mud. The ribbons of her coronet fluttered in her eyes, stinging them, mocking her morning efforts at beauty. She rued her crippling stupidity. *One can never be too pretty, Joya. Especially when you're an imbecile who allows yourself to be abducted by a maggot-brained Yorkist. Yorkists, known to murder on a fancy.*

At her parish Joya had heard the knights speaking of the Yorkist cruelty after the Blore Heath battle, how they chased the king's soldiers who fled the battlefield when defeat was certain. One mob carried their blood thirst into the tiny abbey of Inton, snatching the hapless nuns from their beds, raping them, stripping the abbey of their wine and fish, and running three nuns through when they tried to save their sacred bowls and chalices. And now she was at the mercy of one of them.

A bell's time later, they had covered much ground and still Joya heard only silence behind them. Somehow Lord Penry had managed to elude the entire Coin Forest hunting party, and they had emerged from the forest into an area of hills and meadows dotted with the occasional herd of ewes and cows. The open ground brought fresh hope that she would be seen by someone and rescued.

But Penry was armed and clever, avoiding roads and settlements.

They approached a wide river and he slowed Goldie, paying special attention to steep river banks.

Floating logs littered the river's waves and churning water suggested depth and a dangerous current. On the other side of the river, a thick growth of trees crowded the bank and a chill whiffed down her spine. If they entered there, she would never be seen or heard of again. She shuddered. "Don't try to ford here," Joya said.

"I don't need your help," Penry said. "I know every route between here and London. We'll cross there." He pointed to a distant bridge.

As they drew nearer to the bridge, its details became clear. Joya studied it with hope, scanning the bridge for a hermit shack. Hermits often occupied bridges, collecting tolls. Mayhap he was a young, strapping hermit who would note her distress.

But the bridge was sad, dilapidated, with no shack and no hermit. Tears of frustration stung her eyes. Goldie clumped onto the heavy boards and the wood gave way. Two large cracks sounded as unseen wood beneath them splintered. The timber beneath them shuddered. Goldie whinnied, backing up.

Penry reined her horse. "God's pains," Penry muttered. "It's a bad deck, or worse, the piers."

"We can't cross," she said.

Penry dismounted, climbed a support beam on the bridge and tied the reins high where she couldn't reach them. "Stay here." His eyes speared her. "Don't do anything stupid."

Joya's neck heated all the way to her ears, wishing sorely for her stolen dagger. "You've come this far. Let me go now."

He ignored her and tugged again on the tied reins. Satisfied, he strode to the middle of the bridge and bent down, looking for something.

"What are you doing?"

"Checking the piers." He kicked the wood, testing, muttering more to himself than to her. He had probably concluded she was, indeed, stupid. "Rot, but it's only superficial. Should be sturdy enough to bear our weight." He walked six feet away, then

20

several feet more, dropping on his stomach to look beneath the bridge.

Behind them, hoof beats of several horses became audible. Joya jerked around, saw a group on horseback approaching. She couldn't be sure because they were at least a half mile away, but that had to be her father, her priest and Peter and the rest of them.

Wary, she looked to Penry. He was almost hanging off the side of the bridge. He heard the horses, met her gaze.

She bit her lip. This was her chance! If she could get off Goldie and run, it would be enough delay for her father to reach her. But her hands were tied, and it was a long jump off the horse. She wouldn't be able to get her balance and would fall, and he could pick her up and stab her for her efforts.

She eyed the bridge's railing. She could slide off Goldie that way, land on her rump on the railing and it would be an easy slide down to the floor of the bridge and she could run before he knew what happened.

She'd run toward the horsemen, screaming and dancing like St. Vitus on an anthill. They'd rush to her aid.

In some remote part of her brain she heard a voice warning her it might not work, but what choices did she have? The forest on the other side of the river loomed. He would violate her, leave her to die. The vultures would find her, pick her bones, her face—the grisly stories haunted her.

She thought all this in the tiniest fraction of time. Penry was rising to his feet, urgency in his eyes.

It was more than she could bear. Swinging a leg over Goldie's back, she took her chance, pushing hard off her horse so she could reach the wooden rail.

Penry scrambled to his feet and bounded toward her in large strides. "What in hell?"

She landed on the rail with a crash, pain spiking up her hip. She swung her feet between the rail cogs, trying to gain grip on the cogs and keep her balance.

Penry's arms reached for her, but Goldie was between them.

Her feet slipped off the cogs and flew into the air. Off balance. Falling. She cried out, flailed, but couldn't grip the railing.

Penry's eyes darkened. "God's blood, girl. Your hands!"

Her legs scraped against the rail and she slipped off into the air.

His face, wide-eyed and furious, grew more distant. Joya felt the sickening sensation of falling, falling backward into the swiftly running river below.

Chapter 2

The lame-brained girl! Could this day grow worse? First highway thieves killed Durken and stole Luke's best horse. Now this. He ripped at the lacings on his boots and glanced toward the advancing horsemen. They wouldn't reach her in time to save her, and if he saved her, they'd catch him and find his plans. Damn. He wrenched his left boot free and pulled at the lacings on his right boot. Now there she was, hands bound and falling off the bridge. Her rescuers would be too late. The Parrett River was swollen, clogged with trash and whirlpools.

He freed the second boot. She had hooked her bound hands over a log with broken branches. Smart.

Her ells of skirts floated and she bobbed like a fat yellow duck, but now she was as good as chained to that log. Dangerous.

"Help me!" Her cry sounded wet as the cold water took her breath.

Her horse jerked madly on its reins. Luke cut it free and cast another glance at the approaching men.

And back at her.

He would be captured.

But if you don't, she'll die at your hand.

Ballocks! He held his head, splitting in pain from the attack.

Damn, damn, damn. He stepped up on the rail, took a deep breath and jumped.

The water sliced into him, bitterly cold. He gasped, oriented himself and swam downstream after her yellow, half submerged skirts.

Approaching a log jam, Luke swam in place, pumping his arms and legs as hard as he could to avoid getting trapped in the treacherous tangle of deadwood. Summoning a burst of power, he pulled a log free. He swung an arm onto it and hurried after her. By now her skirts had disappeared, and her flowered headpiece had fallen over her forehead. Terror widened her eyes. He reached out to her. "Turn to me so I can free you!"

Her purse string frayed easily with his knife, and he released her hands. He stored the knife, keeping a firm grip on the log.

She wrapped her legs around him, pulling them both under. Luke had anticipated that and taken a deep breath. Water filled his ears and turned the world green. A sharp piece of debris stabbed into his side, but he held firmly to the log. The river churned and tossed them, and Luke was reminded of the Redstone River, of daring jumps off the swing. Their biggest enemy would be panic. He held her to him to give her comfort and kicked forcefully to the surface.

Her gurgling gasp told him she had taken in water. The burden of her skirts had to be heavy, so pronounced was the panic on her face. She wrapped her legs tighter around him, and he couldn't move.

They continued to drift with the current, treacherous with spring flow and fallen tree limbs.

"What's your name?"

"Joya." Her teeth chattered.

"Joya, let go of my legs so I can get us to shore. Trust me." Dizziness began to overtake him, and fear visited. He had spent much of his strength surviving the highway attack and getting them this far. They may both drown if he didn't get them out soon, before his strength ebbed.

With a sharp glance she released him.

Panting from the effort to keep them upright, he finally saw an opportunity. "See that? He gestured to the bank with a toss of his head. "It's not so steep. I'll grab branches. Pull us out. Keep your head down. Protect your eyes."

He swam closer. An opportunity came, a few branches from the trees above with space for them to get out. He grabbed a sturdy branch with one hand, holding her securely with the other.

The current slammed them against the bank. Branches scraped his face. Fighting a wave of alarm, he opened his eyes. He could see. The branches had not blinded him. Relieved, he dug his toes into the bank, but it was slick, soft. "Dig your feet in," he told her. "Try." They managed to get a first foothold, then another, but the bank was steep and they kept sliding.

Small stars winked in front of him, obscuring his vision. Such a foul way to die. The duke was expecting him at Christchurch, counting on his report. He thought of his brothers for the first time in months. This was his death day.

Something slapped Luke in the face. A rope. "Here. Take this." High above, a tall man dangled a rope. He couldn't see the details of his face, but it would be a good wager to say it wasn't friendly.

"Father!" Joya's voice rang with excitement, confirming his fears.

Devils. Dreading the consequences, Luke grabbed through the stars and took the very rope with which they would probably hang him.

Joya reached for her father and he pulled her from the river. She collapsed, sobbing.

"Joya. Dear," her father said, holding her close. As if through a pillow she heard harsh shouting from Peter and the other men, and Lord Penry's deep, angry voice in reply.

Her father broke the embrace. "I heard your signal and came quickly, but you were gone by the time I arrived. He must have— what happened?"

Joya told him how she had approached Lord Penry to see if he still lived, how she had discovered the white rose, and how he had surprised her.

Her father crossed his arms, and a muscle flicked at his jaw, a familiar, unwelcome signal to Joya. "What is it?"

"Careless. Approaching a stranger, alone. We taught you better." He spoke softly, his voice devoid of anger, but his words stabbed her with shame. She had failed. Disappointed him. Could he see her weakness, guess her mistake at having been distracted by Penry? She could not meet his eyes.

* * *

Joya rode with her rescuers, headed home. They had been traveling for two hours and the mid-day sun shone grey through the growing clouds. An erratic breeze whipped around her.

They emerged from the forest and Joya shuddered. She was cold. Wet. Her yellow gown, now soiled, bunched in muddied shreds over Goldie. Her hair hung in stringy knots over her shoulders and petals of the spring flowers had fallen from her coronet into her face. She had lost one of her white calfskin boots in the river, and the other was caked with mud. She had fallen as far from pretty as she could without slashing sword and dagger at her person.

Joya tightened her legs against Goldie but the warmth didn't travel to her chest. It was far worse inside. Her heart wavered, bruised beneath her ribs. Instead of pleasing her father with a few good birds and coneys, she had mindlessly placed herself in harm's way.

She had failed to exercise the caution her mother, Sharai, had taught her.

Repeated lessons, she reminded herself, her gloom deepening. "This is serious," her mother had said, over and over again. You're small. There are bad men out there, at the market, on high street, at the fairs. Bad men who will try to hurt you, steal you, sell you." Her mother had given her her first dagger at ten summers and taught her how to avoid capture, how to defend herself against men much larger than she by using her size, her flexibility, her speed, her teeth, her dagger.

26

Today she had possessed her dagger, but allowed herself to be distracted by this – this Yorkist, allowed him to catch her by surprise. The hunting day had been ruined by her idiocy. Like some brainless moppet she had fawned over Lord Penry. He had probably peeked through his lashes while feigning a swoon and seen her casting him sheep's eyes. She shivered in shame at her failure.

She tried to dismiss her misery. It could have been worse. Lord Penry could have held her for ransom and cost her family what small fortune they possessed to buy her freedom. At the least she was still alive. She would find a way to redeem herself. She must.

As they neared home her mood brightened. The blanket of clouds had broken and it had become warmer. Coin Forest Castle sat in a valley painted with the special green of spring. The fields had awakened, dotted with livestock and yeomen homes that gradually gave way to larger merchant houses and the village. She knew the castle's lines as well as well as she knew herself. It stood tall and rectangular, built from the stones of local quarries and roofed like a French chateau. A sliver of sun escaped the grey sky and streaked the brown stone lighter. They bypassed the village and passed the small church. On the right, the hill came into view where she and her older brother Stephen had raced their greased sleds on the grass so many summers ago.

They crossed the large moat and passed the oak tree where Kadriya used to feed her birds. Past the stone curtain Joya looked up to the wooden elevated walkway where her mother had almost perished during a siege.

Home. Joya wiped her eyes. Twice today she had been sure she'd never see it again. Twice she'd thought herself doomed, certainly in that horrible river. She patted Goldie and her heart ached with relief. She was alive. Muddied, ugly and shamed, but home.

Beside her, Lord Penry – she'd learned his name was Luke – rode with her father on his destrier. Now it was he whose hands were bound. He met her gaze, and she was taken again by his presence. She remembered his strength as he'd supported her in the river. The concern in his blue eyes, his patience even in the face of her brainless leap from Goldie to escape. He could have taken her horse and avoided capture, but he had sacrificed himself to save her.

She would have given him a smile and expressed her gratitude, but she had heard what they found in his boot—plans confirming he was a spy and enemy. She had seen him hesitate to save her from the river, and now his blue eyes looked past her, flat, unreadable. Joya bristled. He thought her stupid and didn't give a lick whether she lived or not. He had correctly assessed the situation: capture was imminent, and had she drowned with bound hands he would have been tortured before death. Saving her was merely the practical thing to do. She shook the wisps of gratitude away. He was the king's enemy and deserved whatever he received.

She reined her horse away from him, and her father took Luke to the west entrance that led to the gaol. She was glad to be free of his presence. The queen would decide his fate.

Two bells later, Joya soaked in a hot bath in her chamber.

"More hot water, miss?" Effie, her chambermaid, paused, bucket raised, waiting. The young girl was shy as a deer but efficient and friendly.

"Thank you, no. It's perfect." Joya slid deep into the tub.

The door to her chamber opened and Camilla hurried in.

Prudence followed. She walked as she usually did, her arms folded across her chest, as if protecting her heart, her back bent sideways at a slight tilt, a young crab making her way toward her goal. To protect her feelings, Joya would never directly ask her friend of it, but she suspected an early injury. That didn't explain the arms, though. Perhaps she was always cold.

"By the saints," Prudence cried. "I can't believe what happened to you. And he saved you from drowning." She cocked her head. "Did he kiss you?"

Joya held the soap to her chest. "Have you been tipping mead? I almost died."

"We were at the parish church helping with the firewood baskets, and we heard," Camilla said. "We stopped by the gaol to see him."

"Effie, that will be all for now, thank you." Joya gave her maid a gentle smile of dismissal, and she left.

Joya turned to Camilla. "You saw him? And?"

"He's hale. Doubtless tricked you with feigned injury so he could take you away for ransom," Camilla said.

"He's comely." Prudence gave a slow smile. "Finely made. Eyes like the pools in Bath, so blue."

An image came to Joya of his eyes, so intense as he held her in the swift current. His soft breath on her face, the cleft in his chin, the pronounced curve of his upper lip and how it had felt to have his strong arms hold her during the long run with Goldie to the Parrett River. A cool current of caution brushed her neck and she jerked up, sitting straight, arms braced on the sides of the tub. What was she thinking? He was bold. Dangerous, determined to destroy England. "He's the enemy," she said, pumping up her anger like venom to protect her from her own addle-brained weakness toward him. "He's a maggot-brained Yorkist."

Camilla raised a brow, a gesture that seemed to say that Joya had not the intelligence to think clearly. It was one of the few things about Camilla that annoyed Joya. "What?" Joya demanded.

"I do believe you are smitten," Camilla said.

Fear rose like a stone in Joya's throat. Camilla had seen it, her strange confusion about Lord Penry. How evil could she be, thinking such thoughts? Saints drinking the ale barrel dry! If her father heard about this… She lashed out at Camilla. "How dare you presume to know what I think?"

Camilla rolled her eyes, ignoring Joya's anger. "It's good you're finally able to recognize a fine young nobleman when you see one."

Prudence laughed. "Aye. We get you wed, Joya, and the men will look at us for a change."

"Wed! My father would have my head." Joya's father was deeply loyal to the king and Queen Margaret. Last year, Margaret had spared Joya's brother, Stephen, from the chopping block during a trial for treason.

"Lord Penry saved your life," Camilla said. "He could have run. Stolen Goldie. But he stayed to save you. He saved your life and you don't give a whit that he's been imprisoned? 'Tis an outrage that they keep him in gaol. Like some common thief."

Joya bristled. "Don't let my father hear you speak thusly." She pointed a dripping finger at Cam. "He's a stinking Yorkist. I wish I'd never found him."

"Ah, but Joya, they say he's a bridge builder," Prudence said.

Ah. That explained his thorough inspection of the bridge.

"That he knows all the major roads in England," Prudence continued. "They found plans in his boot, plans about York's men. He's a member of York's army. Your father has already sent a messenger to the queen. Had you not found him, Margaret would not have been forewarned."

Camilla tapped Joya's nose. "Yes, you should be glad you found him." She rose and signaled to Prudence. "Let's leave her to her ablutions." She smiled crookedly. "And her wicked thoughts about Lord Penry."

Joya cut through the water with her hand, splashing Camilla.

Camilla stepped aside, too late. She laughed, a throaty ha-ha-ha, as if she were really saying the word repeatedly. It sounded forced but amusing at the same time, always welcome at a festival and always causing a tickle behind Joya's heart, and she couldn't resist joining Cam's laughter.

Cam brushed her gown, a twinkle in her eye. "Consider this, my friend. Your handsome Yorkist can fetch a pretty ransom for the crown. And who knows? Lord Stanley switched sides twice, once from Henry to Yorkist, and back to the Lancasters. Margaret pardoned him and welcomed him back in her flock. Why not your Lord Penry?"

"He is most certainly not 'mine.'" Still, Cam's words struck a chord. Joya had forgotten that Margaret had exhibited a rare patience and generosity toward those who once sympathized with York. She nodded.

"Oh, and Lord Combwich defected, recall that?" Pru said. "And my uncle told me that Margaret pardoned seven noblemen who abandoned York at Ludford, last October."

Camilla waggled a finger at Joya. "Use your charms. You could change Lord Penry's mind, too. Now, what could you do to convince him to defect to Margaret's side?" She smiled broadly. "And wouldn't your father be proud of you if you could do that?" With a smug smile she joined Pru at the door and they left.

Chapter 3

The next morning broke under a clear sky. "Look at all the people," Joya said. "And it's hours yet before the bonfires." Joya, Camilla, Pru and Father Jeffrye entered Ilchester, a market town in the hundred of Tintinhull, County Somerset. It had been a short five-mile ride to the town, which straddled the borders of Coin Forest and the neighboring village of Faierfield.

Camilla reined her horse to follow, smiling broadly. "Winter lasted for ever. Finally, it's time for Beltane!"

"Not until tomorrow," Joya said, knowing today was as important as May Day itself. Beltane, a three-day celebration to welcome spring. It would be held here in Pru's village. Tonight there would be feasts, music, fresh ale and dancing. On the morrow, the old would sleep late and the young women would rise early to dally through the forest with the young men. They would collect flowering branches, and one lucky man would spy the perfect birch tree that would become the Maypole. One lucky woman would be named Queen of the May. And tongues would wag of what may have happened all that time the maids and men lingered in the shelter of the trees.

Joya wore her green brocade gown. Delicate circles were woven into the fabric, down the bodice and over the skirt. The special weave had caught her mother's eye at the Winchester Fair. It reminded her of the rings in Tabor's coat of arms, green on green, the Ellington colors. Sharai had sewn it into a form-fitting gown that befitted a day of celebration. Yet an edge of sadness dulled her happiness at wearing it.

Joya's eyes misted. Ever since her father pulled her out of the river, odd sentiments had plagued her. She wondered that she could be amazingly happy and frightfully sad at the same time. Life had become precious, as had her family, her friends—but another sensation had settled in, one of vague fear. Diana had been found and returned at dawn, and instead of the joy she had expected to feel, she had burst into tears. She drifted in a whirlpool of feelings more erratic than the Parrett River.

And she kept seeing blue eyes, hearing a resonant, deep voice, and sensing trouble.

They dismounted and tethered their horses by the river Yeo. The temporary stables were crowded with wagons and people from the neighboring villages.

Across the stone bridge a steep stone stairway led to the top of the hill and the elegant Woodborne Parish Church. Originally built as a monastery, it had been converted to their parish church and perched with its new tall tower atop a high hill. The sweeping view went on for miles over the fresh green velvet of fields and trees.

"Fleur de Lis," Camilla said. Indeed, the churchyard was bright with hundreds of iris, tall purple heralds of spring. "And *daezeseye.*" She picked a couple of daisies and wound them in her hair, the white pleasing against the dark blue of her gown.

To the east, shelters of oiled canvas had been stretched between trees for the hundreds who had come for the celebrations. Baking bread sweetened the air and the grounds buzzed with activity. Tables were placed near the outside kitchens and on the south side, men were building a wooden footing for the raising of the Maypole.

Joya had spent the last mile of their trip scolding herself. She must stop fretting about her father's displeasure and about Camilla's ill-conceived suggestion to woo Lord Penry to the Queen's side. *Think of your responsibilities.* She was in charge of scheduling the mummers and Morris dancers. She would keep the games and entertainment flowing smoothly through the evening's bonfires and dances.

The vicar, Thomas Dollyn, greeted them with his round cheeks and warm manner. Where Joya's priest, Jeffrye, possessed a dark countenance, Father Thomas's presence made the church light up during prayers. He embraced Joya. "My child, God has spared you and brought you home to us." He patted her arm. "Be generous with your prayers of thanks." He turned to Camilla and Pru. "Ladies, we could use your help in the misericord. Dame Edith is inside, waiting for you."

Joya waved to her friends. "See you at nones. Or before if you can get free."

They left and Joya proceeded with Father Jeffrye through the parish grounds, looking for her entertainers. She found them tuning their instruments on the side lawn. Her three dozen mummers and dancers were scattered near the cemetery, some on stools, others propped on a stone wall that kept the sheep out.

Father Jeffrye shot a disapproving gaze at them, his disdain for music well known.

Oliver, Ilchester's wiry, grey-haired butcher, repeatedly played a single note on his recorder while the others tried to duplicate it on their instruments.

Her brother Stephen plucked on his gittern, adjusting a tuning peg for each string. He stood tall, like their father, but his black straight hair, his brown eyes and walnut-hued skin were like hers, from their mother's Gypsy blood. He had recently married and he and his wife, Nicole, were expecting their first child. They lived in Faierfield, a neighboring holding.

He noticed her, strode forward and folded her into his arms. "I heard what happened. God's wounds! You could have drowned."

She accepted his affection but wilted from embarrassment. "He caught me off guard."

Her brother's eyes narrowed. "Give me time alone with that Yorkist scut. Binding your hands and pushing you in the river. I'll give him what he deserves."

"No, Stephen. He didn't push me. I jumped."

"Of course you did. You were terrified. He'd be dead if I had my way. If he comes near you again, I'll…"

"He saved my life."

Stephen's lips thinned. "I'll kill him. Ransom or no, he'd better not touch you again."

"He's in the gaol. Queen Margaret will be pleased, and that's the end of it." Joya changed the subject. "You're pale." His forehead was warm to the touch. "Are you ill?"

"I've been better. Not enough sleep. I worry about Nicole, with the babe so close. Mother's herbs are helping."

At the mention of her mother, a soft ache formed in Joya's chest. She yearned for the comfort of her mother's wisdom and humor. Surely Joya's problems would not be so large if she could talk with Sharai about her feelings, so rampant and mixed after her ordeal in the river. "Will she be coming back home soon?"

He tugged a strand of her hair. "I'm sorry. I'm sure you miss her, but Nicole is suffering from fear for the babe. I'll be leaving early, though. I don't want to be away from her for long."

"Binnie is there. I'm sure he's tending to her, too."

Stephen tilted his head, watching her. "Binnie's at university. You know that."

She pressed her hand to her forehead. "Of course. I don't know what's wrong with me.

"Given your ordeal, 'tis understandable. Any way, I only came because Nicole insisted I do. She would make my life miserable if I didn't."

Joya managed a smile. Nicole, Stephen's wife, was spirited. "Smart man, you are." She returned to her duties and gave her brother and the other musicians colored bands and ribbons. "Wear these on your right sleeves tonight." At their lack of response, she turned to Oliver. "Would you please remind them why it's important?"

"The ribbons match the small flag poles at the high table. Yellow flags will be raised when games are on, blue for jugglers and mummers, red for strings and harps."

"And you'll tie the matching ribbon on your instrument to identify it as yours," Joya said. "When you're not playing you can check it in at the table by the rood screen and Dame Edith will see they're kept safe. This way there'll be no stealing of instruments like last year. Understood?"

They nodded.

"I'll be at the head table during supper if you have any problems," Joya said. "Don't trouble the priests or the vicar. I've promised them all will run smoothly."

The men returned to their instruments, but her brother still looked troubled. "You came to play," she told him, "Stop worrying and play your favorite song."

Stephen laughed. "You know me too well." He strummed his gittern, the melody teasing and familiar. Recorders and flutes joined in and Joya started humming.

"Come on, Joya, sing for us," Oliver said.

"Yes, sister. Take your own advice and sing your favorite song."

The music transitioned into the chorus, and Stephen cocked his head, encouraging her.

"Not by myself, I won't." Joya grabbed Camilla and Pru, who had escaped from Dame Edith. Holding hands they danced by the corner of the stone wall under the fragrant apple blossoms. Joya sang the chorus, "The rising of the sun and the running of the deer, the playing of the organ, sweet singing in the choir."

Father Jeffrye scowled in disapproval. Joya gave him her best smile and kept singing. How he could remain so dour on such a pleasant day mystified her.

Camilla and Pru sang the second chorus. The vicar arrived with the gravedigger and a half dozen of the church helpers. They joined hands, making a larger circle, and sang lyrics that told of the cycle of life. Joya pawed the earth, mimicking the deer in spring. Stephen's pleasure with his gittern, the smiles on her friends' faces and the earth, soft and moist under her feet warmed Joya's heart.

The Morris dancers lifted their reindeer antlers in front of their heads and joined the circle.

"Father Thomas." Father Jeffrye's voice interrupted, cold and angry as he strode to the vicar. "A word." His tone gave no indication that his position as village priest was inferior to Father Thomas' position as parish priest. Father Thomas remained gracious, though, and followed him. They huddled at the corner of the stone wall, close to Joya and her friends and spoke under the music.

"Dancing." Father Jeffrye spit the word. "The bishop has ordered there be no dancing. We are to bury Beltane and offer prayer and devotions. No heathen worship, no going a-maying. No games. No eggs."

"Jeffrye my friend," the vicar said with a gentle smile. "The young will do what they do, with or without us. To be glad for spring is not shameful."

Camilla pulled Joy and Pru closer. "His face is so sour a pickle would be sweet. I hope I never get old and angry like that."

"Maids gadding in the forest with men, that's not shameful?" Father Jeffrye harrumphed. "And wearing green gowns!"

"What's wrong with green gowns?" Pru asked.

Joya turned to her. "He's being sarcastic. Green, what your gown becomes from lying on the grass," she lowered her voice. "On your back."

Pru's brows remained furrowed, uncomprehending.

Joya rolled her eyes. "While your lover shoots the bolt." 'Twas a crude expression for coupling, but Pru finally comprehended and covered her mouth, already spreading into a wide grin.

Joya and Camilla laughed.

"…and I say you should forbid dancing, Father Thomas. Or…"

"You'll contact the bishop? Do so if you must, my dear friend."

"I am not your friend."

"The bishop knows my position." He placed a hand on Jeffrye's shoulder. "If you choose not to dance, we will not plague you."

Father Jeffrye stormed toward Joya, his brows drawn in anger. He grabbed her wrist. "We'll not linger here. We're returning home."

"Home? I'm overseeing the musicians and mummers," Joya said. "I'm staying."

"You will come with me now."

"I'll be with her," Stephen said.

"You're leaving early for Faierfield," Father Jeffrye pointed out.

"I'm eighteen," Joya said, unwilling to be pulled away like an errant child. "I've reached my majority."

"While here you are my ward," Father Jeffrye said. "You are unwed. Still a maid, and you have not deported yourself properly. Your father trusts me to protect you." Father Jeffrye pulled her aside. "Think you that I cannot hear? That I miss the profane words you utter, words of sin and fornication that bring you and your friends to laughter? Even as a child you shunned your studies. You prefer the tongues of gossip to dutiful conduct and piety."

Would that she could muzzle his harsh judgments. Joya watched his finger wagging, so like a horse's tail at sunset, batting flies. The image brought a smile to her lips.

Which did not go unnoticed by Father Jeffrye. The priest's eyebrows melded into a deep frown. "You failed miserably at letters and disappointed Sister Issabel. From what I just witnessed here, 'tis easy to understand. You lack industry, and you have lost your modesty. I shall return you to your father before you lose more than that."

Joya's spine stiffened at the reminder of her weaknesses, but she held her tongue with the thinnest of threads. She would not anger her father by publicly challenging the gnarly old priest. And well she could not, for she could never escape the shadow of Sister Issabel's condemnation.

She embraced her brother. "Godspeed, Stephen, and Godspeed to Nicole." Gathering Pru and Camilla to her, she whispered, "I'll be back before the egg toss." Smiling past her anger she took the owly priest's arm and they walked back to the stables to get their horses.

Peter joined them for escort. She swung onto Goldie and paid close attention to her reins to avoid Peter's longing gaze, and they left the merry melodies of Ilchester behind them.

At Coin Forest, Joya found her father in the stables, brushing his horse down after returning from Faierfield where he had visited her mother.

Joya approached, running her hand over the well-worn wood of the stall.

"Why aren't you at Ilchester?" he asked.

"Father Jeffrye," she said. "I was committing the sin of dancing, so he brought me home."

Her father laughed. "He gets more grim with every year."

"Save me from him. Please."

He still takes great pride in his illuminations," her father said. "I'll get him busy copying one for me today, and he'll be too busy to worry about you." He tweaked her nose lightly. "We can be back there by supper."

Joya ventured the next subject. "How's Mother?" She had been proud of Joya's ability to defend herself in spite of her size. She had to have been disappointed that Joya had let her guard down with Lord Penry and been abducted.

"Hale. And Nicole is taking a clear broth now."

"Thanks be."

"It's your mother and her herbs." Pride thickened his voice.

"Did you tell her—"

"About Penry? Yes." He stretched, holding his side. "She might have cracked a rib hugging me when she learned you were safe."

Joya twisted her sleeve. "What did she say?"

"She said to give you this." He handed her a small package.

Back in her chamber, Joya excused Effie and sat alone by the dying fire. Her mother's package was thin, half a foot in length. She unwrapped the white linen and found a necklace fob that smelled suspiciously of duck fat and ashes, one of her mother's spells for safe travel, she guessed. She continued unwrapping and found her mother's dagger.

* * *

Later, Joya crossed the bailey, heading for the mews. She passed the outside ovens where Maud, the head cook, supervised the baking of dozens of meat pies. As a new arrival from Hungerford many years ago, she'd had fiery red hair. It was now thinning and faded, but her eyes remained bright and hale.

"Joya!" she cried, hugging her, and Joya became lost in Maud's magnificent bosom. "I about popped my peplum when I heard what befell you a'hunting. Thank the saints you made it home safe." She lifted Joya's chin. "You're looking tired, sweetling. And hungry." She stabbed meat from the fire and waved it in front of Joya's face. "Sausage? Made the way you like them."

Joya accepted it, giving it an appreciative smell. She bit through the crisp skin and the flavor of the meat burst, rich with juices and butter and extra nutmeg and salt. Her favorite of all, even over mortrews. She closed her eyes, savoring it. "Perfect."

Maud leaned forward. "I saw the filthy soldier."

"Who?"

"Lord—what's his name? Embly? The pig Yorkist who almost killed you."

Joya straightened. "Penry. He saved my life, Maud."

Her eyes narrowed. "He stole you away. Bloody traitor. I had to follow orders and brought him bacon and barley bread this morn. If it was up to me I would have brought him eight-day porridge green with mold. And he's cold as a winter draft. Barely spoke a dozen words."

"What did he say?"

"Asked to be left alone."

"Alone? What an unnatural request." *Did he ask about me?* Joya dared not let the words pass her lips.

Maud fluffed Joya's flowing sleeve. "Not everyone's like you, Missy. You like to fly with the flock, always have. From the time you could talk, you've never been alone."

He must not have.

"Any way, this Lord Penry. Full of himself, full as a tick, he is." Maud's eyes narrowed. "Queen M will have him drawn and quartered. That'll be the sight."

At the thought of Luke being tortured, Joya swallowed convulsively. "He could have escaped but he chose to help me." Her emotions swirled. "You've told me many times how my father saved your life."

Maud's mouth softened into a gentle smile. "Aye. I was fourteen and if not for your Da, I would have been done for."

"You're thankful, yes?"

Maud's brows rose. "I would die for him. I told him, too, he needs me, I'll always come when he calls. Him or Sharai, they know that."

"So you can understand how I am thankful to Lord Penry. I do not wish him to be tortured."

"He's an enemy to the crown, and your Da is loyal to the king, always has been! It would grieve him beyond words to hear you speak thusly. Penry is a Yorkist," she hissed.

Joya thanked her and walked away, her legs and heart heavy. Peter had talked of Penry—Luke—on the ride back to Coin Forest. He was from a village not far from Coin Forest, but Penry didn't participate in court or local matters. Prudence heard he carried important information about York, and maps. That York was coming soon and Salisbury, too, as the king's messenger had predicted yester morn.

She was touched by Maud's gratitude toward her father for saving her life, even after twenty years

Luke had done the same for Joya, and at great personal cost. Now imprisoned, he faced the wrath of people loyal to the king, people like her father, like Maud. They would cheer his death, and she hadn't thanked him for such a sacrifice.

His selflesness didn't change who he was—a Yorkist, after all—but it imbued him with honor. Dignity.

Camilla and Pru's proposal could work. She could express her gratitude in the most sincere of ways by saving his life in return. If she could convince him to change sides, he would be spared and appreciated for the hero he really was.

Of a sudden her next step was clear, a higher purpose than merely convincing her father she could be more than a common dolt.

She looked back toward the mews. She would see Diana later. This could not wait.

Her leather slippers settled into the descending stone steps, made concave from wear through centuries of use. She passed the storehouse, the treasury, down a narrow hallway to the dungeon. Untouched by fire or sun, a persistent mold clung to the steps, an earthen smell no amount of scrubbing could dislodge.

She pressed her hand against her heart to settle it. Composed, she reached the guard's table, manned by the captain's son, a short man of twenty years with massive forearms. Martin had also been Giles' best friend. Since his death, he had been especially protective of her.

"Martin."

"Mistress Joya," he said, eyes widened.

"I have brought a poultice for Lord Penry. For his wounds."

He hesitated. "Don't you think …"

"It's all right. Stay at your post and I'll call for you if need be."

"Keep him at arm's length." Martin swung the heavy door open. "Penry. You have a visitor."

Martin turned to Joya, brows furrowed. "Call if he so much as breathes crooked. I'll be right here."

Heart throbbing in her ears, she entered the dark chamber.

Chapter 4

A fire burned in the corner fireplace, too small to dispel the chill and stale rot of old rushes. She and Stephen had played here as children, taking turns at being the prisoner and the executioner. She viewed it now through older eyes, a place where one could languish and die. But her father used the gaol rarely, and he loathed the practices of humiliation, starvation and torture.

Other than the rushes, the chamber held no smells of filth or disease. Any night pots had been removed, and no vermin moved in the shadows.

The gloom gave way to a grey-tinged vision of the chamber.

Pitch burned in a single wall sconce, fouling the air with its acidic smell. Spider webs laced a pair of chains anchored to the wall. Luke sat on a stool by the fire. The light bounced off his features, now further shadowed with early growth of a mustache and beard. His light brown hair split in furrows, as if he had run his hands through it in exasperation. A lock of it broke away from the rest, brushing his eyebrow. A wisp of defiance, a reminder of his unpredictable temperament, vulnerable one moment, possessive and conquering the next. Firelight flickered in his eyes, revealing midnight blue.

At sight of them a thrill chased through her, and she twisted one of the yellow ribbons of her coronet. "I had to see you."

He said nothing and rested his hands on his knees, the chains binding them clinking as he changed position. An angry scratch slashed across his cheek, running dangerously close to his eye. She remembered the dense growth at the river's bank, and his warning to close her eyes to protect them. He had risked his sight to grab the branches to save them. He coughed, a dry, short cough and his mouth tightened in a line of ill temper, insolent, as Maud had said. He was a man immersed in treachery and plans that spelled death to the red rose, her people. Her father's people.

He raised his chin to meet her gaze and it became suddenly difficult to breathe. Was it hostility that dwelled behind that gaze, or arrogance? A sliver of fear?

The chamber remained still with his lack of greeting, his lack of invitation, his lack of any verbal acknowledgment that she had come to this dark, dank place to see him.

She should leave but her commitment to help him held her firm to the reeds and stone. *He must think me a total idiot. Say something!* But her tongue lay thick and limp in her mouth, and his presence hummed in the air between them. She approached one slow step at a time, watching his face for a response that didn't come.

He coughed again and raised his chin, his eyes questioning. "What?" His deep voice clashed against the stone walls, startling her.

"I came to thank you."

"For what?"

"Saving my life." She looked for a place to sit and found only the fireplace hearth, black with soot and charred wood, so she remained standing. "To your detriment." She waved a hand, indicating the gaol.

"Indeed. And now you have thanked me, you may leave."

His words slapped her. "You needn't be so short."

"I don't relish your company. The last time I was in it I almost died, and now I most certainly will."

Echoes of her conversations with Stephen and Maud reminded her of his plight. He was hated, his life threatened. "I did not cause your predicament," she said. "Look you at your collar and the color of your rose. You brought this on yourself by taking arms against your king."

He splayed his hands in front of her in protest. "I have never raised arms against Henry."

She noted his hands, free of callouses with long graceful fingers, more like those of an artist than a knight or a builder. "You don't look like a bridge builder. What do you do?"

"I have no issue with the king," he said, ignoring her question. "York has no issue with the king, either."

"You oppose the Queen. It's the same thing."

"Hardly. Given the choice of the throne or England's safety, she has chosen the throne. She will cause England's downfall, mark my words."

Joya's back stiffened. Margaret was hated by many, cursed for being French and for her admirable strength and determination to save the throne for her son, what any good mother would do. "The prince is the legitimate heir. What you're doing is treason."

He turned away. "You've thanked me, condemned me. Now leave."

"That's it? I disagree so you dismiss me?"

"I dismiss you because you are not the cleverest of girls. In fact, you are quite dim-witted."

Heat flashed up her neck. "What?" He had stripped her of her defenses, seen straight through to her failings. Of a sudden she was that hopeless child back in the dreary chambers of the abbey, the girl who couldn't learn, who struggled against the scorn of Mother Issabell and the sharp sting of her willow rod. She regarded his blue-eyed arrogance. Would that she could choke him with his chains.

He turned to face her. "Only a simpleton would throw herself into the river when her hands are bound."

She wanted to strike back, but struggled instead to catch her breath. "How dare you."

"Only a dolt would fail at escape and later ask her captor to help her."

"You vile man. You were the only person there. You would have me drown, waiting for a friendly face?"

He leaned toward her. "Your judgment today was highly suspect, so if you think you can convince me that the Queen cares a whit about England, save your breath." Impassioned, he stood and swung his fist in the air. "I'm a knave. Enemy to the king and the church and all that is good. I'm in chains and you're safe. Now go." He turned his back to her and sat facing the wall.

Anger flashed its way up to her ears. "I don't like being called stupid." She knew she was, had lived in shame ever since Mother Issabel's public proclamation of it, and his flagrant affirmation of it was cruel. "You got yourself in this fix and you have the gall to blame me. And I was stupid, yes, stupid to come here and thank you for anything. And to think I brought a poultice for your wounds." She tossed it into the rushes. "They all hate you here, and yet I bothered to check on you. My brother would have you killed, too. Well." She reached speechlessness for a moment and another wave of anger overcame her. "You can rot in here. They can draw and quarter you as Maud says. There, see? I'm getting smarter."

He didn't respond, waited for her to leave. But how could she? She had come to save him. Damnation!

She wanted to thrash him, as so many others did, but they hadn't seen him rescue her, hadn't felt the surging relief and gratitude when, after her skirts had yanked her under the water, he had pulled her back onto the log. And now, curse him, something in the stiffness of his back, in the rigid set to his shoulders spoke to her. It was as if he had thrown a curtain of anger between them, and now it fell in a disheveled heap, revealing his position, his peril.

She felt a pull to him, and reached past her anger and his arrogance. She touched his shoulder, hoping to comfort him. "I came to help."

He took her hand, his touch warm. His nails were well groomed, his skin soft next to hers, and the connection overwhelmed her.

He turned and stood, chains clanking.

Startled, she withdrew her hand.

He took her in his arms, his blue eyes dark, dangerous. His jacket carried the scent of the river, green and sweet with damp hints of fish. Abandoning modesty she pressed against his chest, relishing his heat and nearness.

He raised her chin and covered her mouth with his. He crushed her to him, one hand behind her neck, the other at her back. It was an assault, as if his emotions had been chained, too, and were suddenly loosed.

She gasped and returned the kiss. Her passion, long buried, erupted with an urgency she had never before experienced. She swam in the fluid passion of the kiss, welcoming the heat of the depths, clinging to him as much as he clung to her.

A creaking noise sounded.

Luke tensed suddenly and ended the embrace.

The sensuous fog slipped away.

"Joya." A masculine voice barked.

Martin stood in the doorway, scowling and clutching his club.

What madness had possessed her? Her hands fluttered of their own will, tidying the folds of her gown. "Godspeed," she said to Luke, unable to meet his eyes. She dragged her feet one in front of the other and followed Martin out the door.

Martin slammed the door and homed the bolt, leaving Luke framed in the small barred window.

"May God return you to your senses." Martin said no more, but his widened eyes spoke of shock, disapproval, warning.

She turned. "It's not what you think," she whispered.

Martin nodded deferentially. "Of course it's not." Still his voice held a dark edge.

"This has been a trying day," she said.

"You almost met your death," he said. "And it's because of that man in there, I remind you."

"I haven't forgotten," she lied. "But I have reason to believe Penry can be turned to the queen's side."

"Like that?" Martin tipped his head in the direction of Lord Penry, skepticism pinching his features.

"Please say nothing of this to my father."

"I'll not risk my position to abet a traitor." He returned to his post, giving her a pointed look. "Nor should you."

* * *

Joya walked past the parish church in Ilchester, looking for her friends. She and her father had arrived after the egg toss, missing most of the games. Such things meant little to her this night. Her life had become littered with uncertainty. She stayed her distraction to check on her musicians. The time for stories and poetry had passed and now red ribbons fluttered on the sign post, signaling the musicians to play drums and tambors and gitterns, lively carols for dancing. All was in order. Her father had finally left her side, and Joya made her way to the main green in the gold cast of daylight's final rays.

She found Pru and Camilla by the dancers. Camilla fluttered her hands and giggled, a change from her usual brash and cool manner. George, Lord Minton, stood by her. Tall and broad-shouldered, George often won in the lists and was usually the first one picked for football teams. Camilla's favorite. He greeted Joya and leaned down, whispering something that made Camilla giggle again. Hand in hand they left for the dance circle. Pru stood at her usual crooked angle, arms folded across her chest in spite of the hot fire, and she rolled her eyes. "She acts like a loon when George is around." Her words struck home for Joya. Hadn't she herself been acting like a person possessed, throwing herself at Luke? She did unthinkable things, thought outrageous thoughts when in his presence.

Pru regarded Joya. "What's wrong?"

Joya felt exposed. "What do you mean?"

Pru tilted her head. "You had the strangest expression just now. And where's Father Jeffrye? If he sees you here by the dancers he'll haul you home again."

"He's such a cranky rooster," Joya said. "He's stuck in his church back home. My father put him to work with illuminations, thanks be. He can punish the parchment instead of me."

"Well. While the cat's away, let's play." Pru guided her past the ale barrels to the small enclosure tended by Ilchester guards. "Try my uncle's strawberry mead," Pru said. "It has a staggering kick."

Joya unclipped her flagon and handed it to her and Pru returned it, filled with the fragrant drink of honey and fruit. Joya took a sip, and it was as if she swallowed a sweet shot of fire. "Whoo, that is strong, and flavorful."

They left the bar and stopped to watch the dancers. "To spring." Joya raised her bottle.

"And love." Pru tapped her bottle against Joya's, the metal clanging. "Methinks I know who will escort Camilla in the woods on the morrow." She turned to Joya. "But poor you." She gave Joya's arm a gentle squeeze. "Guess you'll be a-maying with me since your man is stuck in gaol."

"He's not my man," Joya said. "And he's no longer in gaol."

Camilla returned from the dance circle. "What? Did the handsome spy escape?"

"I reminded my father that he is a nobleman, after all. He agreed to give him run of the west tower. It's heavily guarded."

"Mmm, this works well for our plans." Camilla took Joya's flagon and drank heartily of the mead. "Sorry, I'm thirsty. All that dancing. Say, this is really good." She drank the rest and handed Joya the empty jug.

"So, tell," Pru said. "Did George ask you? About tomorrow, a-maying."

Camilla smiled broadly, all sign of her giggles gone. "What do you think?"

They laughed.

"Ladies, I need a word with you." Joya led Camilla and Pru to the west side of the church, where a less populated bonfire roared. They settled on a bench near the rectory. After a quick look to be sure there were no eager ears near, Joya lowered her voice. "I saw him."

"Ooh." The firelight danced in Camilla's eyes. "Tell us. Tell us all!"

Joya revealed what Luke had said to her, his anger at her for throwing herself in the river. His rudeness, how he ordered her to leave. She omitted the part where he called her a dim-witted dolt. That was the last thing she wanted her friends to think of her.

Pru's mouth twisted. "He sounds awful."

"He's upset," Joya said. "Who wouldn't be? He's in chains and faces death. I did want to throttle him, though."

"So you left him to stew in his own juice? I would," Camilla said.

"There's more." Joya needed to make sense of what had happened in that gaol, and between Camilla's sensibility and Pru's sensitivity, they might be able to help her understand what had happened. She told them about their embrace.

Pru's hand flew to her neck. "Sweet souls," Camilla said. "How was it? The kiss, I mean."

Joya trusted them, but had a hard time finding the words. She could say it was a shock, which it had been. She could say it made her feel more alive than she had ever felt before, as if she were floating, falling through the air—that flutter before landing onto a soft mound of hay. But all that sounded like a giddy minstrel's song. She could be honest and admit that Luke's kiss had set her on fire, that she had never felt such intense feelings with Giles. And how realization of that had brought a deep shame.

"Come on," Camilla demanded. "Tell us."

"I could not pull away."

"More," Cam demanded.

"It was ...fierce." She gestured to the bonfire. "Hotter than that."

"Ooh. And?" Pru asked.

"I didn't want it to end." Joya took a deep breath and let it out. "Ever."

"Sounds wonderful," Pru said.

"So why do you look so miserable?" Camilla said.

"Because of who he is." She fingered the ring on her necklace. "He's not Giles. He was my only one. I felt comfortable with him. With Luke I feel…" Joya struggled for the word. Threatened? Out of balance? "Tense."

"Giles is gone," Pru said gently.

"Besides, Luke is old," Joya said.

"Mature. And a nobleman," said Camilla.

"Dangerous." Joya picked at her purse string.

"Exciting," Pru countered.

"He's a condemned traitor."

"Nothing you can't handle," Camilla said. "Remember the plan. Convince him his loyalties are ill-placed."

"But his opinions are cast in stone. You should hear him."

Camilla laughed. "It was only one kiss. See how he feels after three."

What had first seemed to be a good idea—entice him to return to Margaret's fold—now seemed cumbersome and ill-planned. Still, he had revealed his honor in the river. He had sacrificed his freedom to save her. "What if I fail?"

"You won't." Camilla put an arm around Pru and the other around Joya. "You have us."

Joya freed herself. "Do you know what my father would do if he knew we had kissed?" Joya released a shuddering sigh. "He made me promise I would not see him."

Camilla gave a sly smile. "Well, we know how far that will go."

"No. You don't understand. I have never lied to my father. Never! Now I've promised him, I can't see Luke."

"Verily." Camilla's voice lilted and she and Pru laughed.

Joya turned away, letting the fire warm her right side. Her friends could be glib because it wasn't their father they were discussing. And they were different. Camilla had a toughness about her, an independence that shielded her from the sting of displeasure, that needling pain that came when she disappointed her parents. Pru had to shed some of her shyness or she would never experience such passion in the first place. And Pru always did as she was told.

What Joya's father thought of her mattered. He could always be relied upon to favor her—provided she did not overstep the boundaries of behavior he deemed acceptable. It had been easy to navigate while she was a little girl. As she grew into a woman, though, that boundary began to shrink, to become more and more confining. She learned, in embarrassing moments of reprimand, not to shout her opinions on matters of court. And he valued loyalty. Joya would never defy her father, for that would break the gentle thread of his favor. "I will not see Luke again."

"Good even, ladies." A male voice sounded behind them, and Martin, the stout gaol guard, approached.

Joya's stomach fell, and she spilled what was left of her mead. Had he seen her father? Told him?

He met Joya's gaze with a deliberate one of his own. "I would have a word with you."

"Of course, Martin," she said. "And you may speak here, with my friends. We have no secrets."

Chapter 5

Martin watched the girls scoot closer to each other on the rectory bench. Not what he needed tonight, he thought ruefully, the daunting task of talking sense into not one but three women. He turned to Joya. "You are treading on dangerous ground here." Martin spoke with urgency, but remained respectful. Joya was a noblewoman, a God-fearing maid, and his late friend Giles' fiancée. Her ordeal at the river had unsettled her, or she would never have behaved with such disgrace. Her father would handle Lord Penry, in a way that pleased the queen.

Had Tabor seen his daughter's lewd passion with York's spy ... Martin shuddered. "You persuaded your father to release him. I have no choice but to tell him what you did. He needs to know what transpired in gaol."

"You will not." Joya's voice wavered, revealing her fear.

Martin had second thoughts. Maybe he could harness that fear to keep her away from Lord Penry. But Martin couldn't watch her every move. *No. You must look out for Tabor. Get Joya under control and put Penry back in chains.*

The arrogant bastard. Taking advantage of Tabor's kindness when the garrison would prefer to hang him. Over fifty Coin Forest men had perished at Blore Heath, among them Giles, and Martin's own father. The few survivors had told of the heinous cruelty Salisbury and his men had wrought on the queen's troops. Penry deserved to die.

But Joya had intervened and now the knave had run of the west tower, free to gather more information to use against Margaret.

Small fingers encircled his forearm. "Martin."

He looked squarely into the eyes of Prudence Meaker. Prettiest girl of the three, her hair the color of fresh-cut oak, curled around the ribbons of her coronet, her brown eyes wide-set, shining in good health. She always carried herself with her arms to her breasts, a manner most called peculiar, but it charmed Martin, who likened the posture to that of a small bird protecting her treasures. Dainty Prudence, who never broke into conversations like a thoughtless bull, as Camilla did. No, Prudence always arrived on a soft breeze, as she did now, her touch like a whisper on his arm. "I must have a word with you," she said.

She led him several yards from the fire. "You are a fine-looking man," she said boldly. Even as she uttered the words, a crimson crept up her neck, flushing her skin. Her cheeks glowed in the soft light of sunset.

He struck his ear, testing it. He couldn't be hearing correctly. Prudence, always shy, quiet, being so bold.

"You are stronger than most men, but you control your temper. There's honor in that. Lord Penry is sour and disagreeable, I've heard. Not much to like about the fellow."

"We need to kill him."

"We know something about Penry," she said, her voice gentle, sweet. "Knowledge that can be of good use to Tabor. To the queen. We …" she paused and lowered her delicate lashes, and they brushed against her skin like fans. She looked up and the sun's last rays lit flecks of gold in her eyes. Martin leaned closer, absorbing the smell of her skin, warm with a hint of flowers.

"Please." Her eyes widened. "Give us two days with him. I will watch Joya. Make sure she doesn't … ah … get too close to him again."

He considered her proposal. Well, she was the sensible one of the three. Joya, strutting like a peacock, always stirring things up, and Camilla, loping along with her knowing smiles and brash laughter—there wasn't a rule made that Camilla didn't mind breaking. But lovely Prudence was out of line. He couldn't have them...

"You can trust me." The flush still lingered on her cheeks, but her eyes were direct, sincere. Her glance shot downward to her hands, still clutching his arm, and she released him. "Pray forgive me for being so bold." She lowered her eyes. "Please. We have reason to believe we can turn him."

"I don't believe it."

She met his gaze. "Only two days. I'll be with her every moment."

Drinking the heady spell of her closeness, he wanted to please her, but he needed to protect Tabor. Ah, but what could two days hurt? He would get the captain to double up on security so the traitor couldn't slip away. He took her small hands in his. "Two days. Only for you."

* * *

After the bonfires that same night, Joya followed Peter and another guard as they escorted them during the short ride back to Coin Forest. Joya reigned Goldie to the left to make room for Camilla and Prudence and together they passed the Coin Forest orchards. Early blooming apple blossoms perfumed the air and the moist earth, stirred from the horse's hooves, released the musky sweetness of spring.

From Joya's saddle rose the tantalizing smell of smoked sausage, a treat she would give to Effie and her family. The aroma of the links mingled with that of the sweet earth and brought memories of springs past. A sense of heightened wakefulness came over her. This spring was different. Luke was in her castle now.

Luke. The trees whispered his name.

Joya looked past the drawbridge, past the ancient oak tree to the castle and the west chamber where he waited with his blue, blue eyes. She wanted to tell her friends of the sweet feelings he stirred in her, but an unusual wish for privacy kept her silent. "So, Pru. What did you say to sway Martin so quickly?" She spoke quietly, though the guards were deep into their own conversation. "I vow, you blushed so much, you almost swooned."

Pru gave intense attention to her reins, avoiding their eyes.

"Come on, tell," Cam said. "What did you say to him?"

Pru hesitated. "That he could count on me to make sure you don't see Luke alone."

"No, no, we mean what did you say to make him smile like that? Martin never smiles. Well, rarely." Cam rode closer to Pru. I can't see in the dark. Are you blushing again? You can't really be interested in him. He's only a guard."

"He's the captain's son. He will be knighted."

"You've given thought to this." Surprise animated Cam's voice. "But he's so serious. Not like George at all."

Pru laughed. "And I'm not at all like you, Camilla."

"So, Cam, what about Lord Minton?" Joya asked.

"George? He has hairy arms … and great lips."

Joya and Pru laughed.

"And he licks his lips, in the corners of his mouth, when he's nervous." Cam grinned. "I told him he had a nice tongue, and that he could put it to much better use."

"You didn't. Cam," Joya said. "I vow, you're brassy!"

"What?" Pru asked, reining her horse closer. "What was brassy about that?"

Cam pulled her horse to a stop. "Really, Pru. You've seen the bulls with the cows?"

Pru looked at them, her face blank. A moment passed, and her mouth dropped. "Cam!"

Joya and Cam laughed.

"Ladies. Don't lag," Peter said. "Stay with us."

They drew up closer to the guards, maintaining enough distance for private conversation.

Joya turned their conversation back to Cam. "When George wasn't licking his lips for you, I saw him whispering something while you were dancing. What did he say?"

"He likes my gown. See, I told you I needed to wear the green one. And he said he's been thinking about me all this past fortnight," Cam said.

"Yeah. Doubtless thinking of your great lips," Joya said.

"And he knows precisely how to use his," Cam said, laughing.

"Pru, thank you for speaking to Martin. When he saw us kissing, his jaw fell, I can tell you. He was Giles' friend. What he must think of me."

"He worries about your father's standing with the queen," Pru said. "I'm sure he doesn't deny you happiness. It's been a long time since Blore Heath."

"Only seven months," Joya said.

"Verily, but still a long time," Pru said.

"A Yorkist," Joya said. "I couldn't believe it was me in that gaol, either. I'm ashamed. But I can't think clearly when he's around. If I have an urge to see him again, stop me!"

"Oh, child," Cam purred. "From the look on your face right now, it will do no good."

The castle came into view, the village snuggled outside the stone curtain like a cape, shimmering with tallow torches and oil lanterns. But the village was hushed, mainly populated by guards at paced intervals as the women approached the bridge into Coin Forest Castle. Irwin's Inn was empty, bereft of the usual whores' laughter and playful taunts. Only Irwin and his wife were there, sitting quietly by the fire.

"Like a graveyard," Joya said

"Most stayed at Ilchester. George did, too." Camilla said. "We'll need to leave early so we don't miss the songs."

"You'll need to leave early so you don't miss George," Joya said.

"Oh, he'll wait for me." She laughed. "Or I'll find him. There's no tree big enough that can hide him."

The guards allowed them to enter, and Prudence led the way to the stables. "Of course he'll wait," Pru said. "His cone is red, red, red."

Camilla guffawed at the crude reference to George's passion. "Pru! There's hope for you yet."

"One thing's sure," Joya said. "This will be one morning we won't have to drag your sorry bum out of bed."

"You'll be up before the cock's crow," Pru said.

"Certes," Cam countered. "And you won't sleep a wink thinking about Martin." She sang his name a couple of times for effect.

Pru said nothing, but a slow smile pulled at her mouth.

In Joya's chamber they washed and cleaned their teeth with Sharai's mint leaves. "Here, Effie," Joya said, handing her chambermaid the package of sausages.

Effie sniffed deeply. "Pork sausage. You're so good to me, my lady. Thank you," she said. "My family thanks you, as well." Smiling, she set the package aside and helped them lay out their gowns and coronets for the morning.

The girls pulled the curtain aside and fell into the bed.

"I can't believe it's almost here. May Day," Camilla said. "I wonder who'll be crowned Queen."

"And who'll find the maypole tree," Pru said. "I hope Martin asks me to help him."

Joya laughed. "Do birds sing in the morning? Of course he'll ask you. He probably looks like you do now ... wide awake, staring at the fire, dreaming of you."

Pru gave Joya a sheepish smile and turned over. The fire dwindled. Conversation died, and Camilla started snoring.

Joya lay awake, watching the moon through the open curtain of her bed. May Day meant naught to her. She inhaled deeply, acutely aware with each breath that Luke was two doors away in her brother's former chamber. She had noticed, when they passed it, that the fire was burning high. It had not been banked, which meant he was probably not going to bed yet. Was he owl-like with his habits, staying up late, she wondered?

Sleep evaded her and Joya quietly climbed out of bed and slipped into her chemise and a robe. As she turned the bolt, a hand stopped her. Pru.

"Privy?" Pru asked." We have our chamber pots."

Joya considered lying and rejected the thought. "No."

"Then get back in bed."

Joya hesitated.

"You asked us to stop you."

"I'm going to check on him. See if he needs anything." It sounded lame as she said it.

"I promised Martin. And you promised your father," Pru added.

"He saved my life. I need to return the favor, and if I can turn him he can be an asset to the queen."

"Don't be scandalous. It's late. Do this in daylight."

Joya felt invisible chains on her arms, weighing her down. Her stomach suffered a peculiar fluttering. Desperation pulsed through her limbs. She had to go to him. "I can't wait." She removed Pru's hand from the bolt.

"I don't understand you," Pru said. "Wait until daylight."

"You're right. I don't understand me, either, but I must go."

Joya slipped out the door.

Pru stuck her head out into the hall. "Be back in the shake of a lamb's tail, or I swear, I'll come fetch you."

Freed, Joya approached Stephen's room. Her blood pulsed in her ears, and each breath was a trial. *What's wrong with me?* A raw restlessness emboldened her.

When Luke was near, he stirred her senses. Even now, knowing she grew closer to him with each step, he affected her.

Soft snoring sounded from ahead, and Joya turned the corner that led to the west hallway. A guard slept, failing to hold his post. He leaned against the wall, reeking of mead, sprawled on the bench.

She slipped by him and reached Stephen's door, scarred with deep scratches from Stephen's sword play when he was a child. It was slightly ajar. She couldn't knock and risk waking the guard. Putting her hand on the door, she opened it slightly. It creaked, unsettling her, but she forged ahead anyway, driven by a need to see him.

Inside, the fire crackled, the room comfortably warm. His opened garderobe door revealed a few of Stephen's clothes that still remained there.

"Lord Penry?" she ventured.

A hand gripped hers.

Joya gasped and turned.

Martin drew her close and shoved his wide face into hers, mouth tight, his brows drawn in a judgmental scowl. "What in Hades' fire are you doing here, alone?" His lowered voice had a rough edge to it.

Joya cringed at what he knew and what he suspected. She licked her dry lips, feeling very young of a sudden, very naughty, very exposed.

"Well?"

Thoughts lost all form and rattled around in her head. Finding no excuses, she returned his scowl. "'Tis no business of yours." She fought to keep the nerves from her voice, to take him off balance with her scorn.

"Perhaps you'd rather tell Lord Tabor." He pulled her out in the hall.

"No. No. I was…wakeful and walking, and saw the fire in Stephen's room and wondered…" She faded into the futility of her defense. "Well, never mind. I'm back to my chamber with Cam and Pru." She pulled free and before he could chastise her further, she hurried down the hall toward her room.

At her door, she looked farther down the hall and noted firelight coming from the solar, late as it was. And a man's soft cough that had become familiar to her. Luke.

She entered her chamber and closed the door.

Pru slipped from the bed and approached silently. "That was quick. What happened?"

Joya pressed a hand to her heart, trying to still it. "He wasn't there. Martin saw me."

"Oh no. Joya! He'll think I let him down."

Pulling the door open again, Joya slipped away from her. "I'll find him. Explain."

"I promised him."

Her impulsiveness was hurting her friend. "Don't worry," Joya said. "I'll fix it."

Confirming the hallway was empty, Joya proceeded to the solar.

Chapter 6

The hallway was cool and quiet, the guard at his post, still snoring softly.

The worry lines on Pru's face had driven home to Joya how much Martin meant to her. She and Pru had been friends since Joya could remember—she was almost as close to her as her sister, Faith. Joya had failed both Martin and Pru.

And what was she doing now? Was she seeking out Martin to help smooth things over for Pru? No, she was following Luke's voice to the solar. She shook her head at her own stupidity.

As she neared the solar, her father and Luke's voices grew clear and her curiosity flared at what they might be discussing.

Staying in the shadows, Joya peeked in.

A fire shed a ring of light, and a half-dozen candles burned on the massive table where her mother sewed during the day. Ells of colorful fabric stood on end in the corner, and the table now held a chess set, over which her father and Lord Penry were hunched. They sat across from each other, deeply engaged in the game and their conversation.

Luke had cleaned up. She had seen his face muddied and caked in blood in the forest, had seen it wet, dripping and determined in the river, and stubbled and bloodied in the gaol. He sat at the table now, clean shaven, washed, his hair shining and groomed, a lighter shade of brown than she had thought.

His usual scowl had vanished. The sharp planes of his thin face had softened, more relaxed as he regarded his chess pieces. They were drinking a bottle of her father's reserved wine, stoppered with the oiled cloths of the Benedectine monasteries in Burgundy.

She took full advantage of her shadowed shelter and studied him.

His face was handsome, complex. Firelight shone on the surface of his blue eyes. His regal nose, ever so slightly off center to the right, divided his long, thin face. His ears, positioned high, made his face seem longer. He had shaved, but left some of his recent facial growth—the beginnings of a mustache accentuated the sensual curve of his upper lip. Oh, she knew what those lips felt like, how they tasted...

What was she doing? While ogling Luke, she had unknowingly slipped further into the room, still in the shadows, but the door was now several feet away, and she hadn't announced her presence. If they caught her snooping in the shadows, she would faint from the humiliation of acting like a gawking loon. But there was no shelter to take. She sank slowly to her knees, hoping to sneak out so she could re-enter more graciously.

Luke advanced a chess piece and her father leaned forward, resting his chin on his hand, studying the board.

"So. You build bridges."

"Yes."

"My Fritham overseer came to us from your village. He knows of your work on the Harrold bridge, and the new extension you built on the Stour. Word is, you're accomplished at your craft."

"Thank you."

Joya warmed to her father's praise of Luke. If they could save him, he would be a most suitable match for her, a landed noble with a fine reputation. Fresh hope made her light-headed of a sudden.

Her father straightened. "It appears you're involved in a very large project now."

Luke kept his gaze on the board. "Yes."

His responses were short, curt. From the shadows Joya took comfort that Luke was about as conversational as a wall with her father, too.

Tabor cocked his head and regarded him. "Your father and I spent some time together at court, especially during the tax session in Calais. I was sorry to hear of the fire, and his passing. His, and your brother's."

"Thank you."

"It must have been a sudden blow for you. Not only did you lose your father, but your older brother at the same time. You had established your reputation as a bridge builder, but suddenly you were heir to your father's holdings and responsible for Penryton."

"It was."

Tabor's mouth puckered in annoyance. "Your family has long been loyal to the king. What led you to change?"

"It wasn't sudden."

Her father rose and began to pace, a sign of impatience Joya had known since her childhood. "We have the plans we found in your boot," he said. "You were going to meet with York. When?"

"You read the plans."

"God's nails, Penry, you know it's all in code! What are you and York scheming in Sandwich?"

Luke said nothing.

Joya looked back at the door. If she could inch her way toward it, she could enter normally and join the conversation, help her father as he tried to talk sense into Luke and sway him to the king's side. Still on her knees, she bobbed a couple of steps toward the door.

Tabor slammed his hands on the table and leaned on them, towering over Luke. "Speak the truth. You've joined York to rout the king from his throne."

Luke gazed at him, cool and deliberate. "Yes."

"You won't live long enough," her father growled. He stood and looked her way. "And Joya. Are you a young child of a sudden? Haunting the halls in your robe? Get off your hands and knees and come out of the shadows. It reflects poorly on you."

Aghast, Joya rose.

"From what Martin says, you have a strong interest in Lord Penry," her father said. "Come hither, and you'll learn more about him."

A fresh scowl creased Luke's forehead.

Joya approached, walking through the heat of embarrassment. "I'm sorry, father, I—"

"You were inspecting the underside of the table, I'm sure," her father said. "Looking to clear the spider webs?"

Luke and her father laughed.

At my expense. Shamed, Joya's face heated so that it threatened to melt right off her shoulders, and she met her father's gaze, silently cursing his ill-timed sense of humor.

"God only knows you've always been curious." Tabor's eyes narrowed. "I've had my talk with Martin," he said, his voice sharp. He turned from her. "Penry, you're yet young. Impressionable. Your loyalties have been swayed by half-truths. There's still time to save yourself. Help your king, your queen—"

"Margaret is what's wrong with England. You're blinded to it because she spared your son."

"Stay your tongue!" Joya blurted. Her brother had been wrongly accused of treason and spared by Margaret. Stephen was her hero, a fine man with a spotless reputation of honor. "He was innocent!" His humiliation and near death at Blore Heath—that and her deep respect for Giles dashed all affection for Luke. "How can you presume to know anything about Stephen? You didn't fight at Blore Heath," she guessed. "Where were you when five thousand good men died for our king?"

Her father held up a hand, silencing her, and turned to Luke. "Do not dare suggest that my son—"

"Is it not true?" Luke challenged. "Did she not spare Stephen from charges of treachery?"

"Yes, but—"

"So she spared him. But everyone knows Stephen was no traitor, was he?"

"No, he was not. All know of his loyalty. His integrity." Her father's eyes had turned dangerously dark.

"So she spared him, which cost her nothing, and gained your lifelong loyalty. Quite the self-enriching trade, wouldn't you say? Margaret is loyal to nothing and no one but her own cause. We have no king. She is the one who has usurped the throne, not York."

"Enough of this!" Tabor slammed the table, and chess pieces tumbled to the floor. "You seem bright, but sadly misinformed. You're taking a treacherous path. King Henry is pious. Generous. He established the very college where you studied! He—"

"He's infirm, Tabor. We need a king, not some Frenchwoman who cares naught for England, one who hires French mercenaries to kill our own people and pays them for their services by letting them raid our treasuries. Our queen," Luke sneered the word past curled lips, "convinced her addled husband to give away our lands—Normandy, and Burgundy fell because of her. She cares only to seat her son on the throne." His eyes narrowed. "A son who may not even be the king's issue!"

Joya gasped at the blasphemy. Oh, Margaret would have his head.

His profanities echoed in the solar, raining guilt on his shoulders. He seemed now to carry the pall of death. Gone was the spell of his blue eyes, and she saw him fading before her, his end imminent.

Luke shifted on the bench and gave Tabor a pointed look. "You will not sway me."

The silence grew. Her father's gaze remained fixed on Lord Penry.

"Then you will die, young Luke, for those are your choices. Die, or beg forgiveness. Pay Margaret the fine she'll demand for your treachery. Join us. Help us defeat this threat to our king."

"If she would but step down from the throne that is not hers – stop dragging the king from battlefield to battlefield, King Henry could rule when clear-headed. When not, York is willing to serve as Protector. When Henry dies, York would inherit, and we would have a strong–"

"I've heard enough." Tabor leaned forward, the chess game forgotten. "Joya, you've seen with your own eyes that this man is our enemy. No amount of your charm is going to change his mind. Stay away from him."

Luke turned to her, an expression of surprise and recognition in his eyes. "Ah, so it was a concerted manipulation." He leveled a glowering look her way, lids dropped in an assessing gaze. "And methought you liked me." He used outdated language to taunt her, his voice, low and edged with amused disdain. It cut through her feeble attempt to salvage dignity from the moment. Her heart sank.

"Penry." Her father interrupted, shaking his head. "Your brothers have sent word. They've heard from the queen and they're coming tomorrow. I'll show them your plans. Mayhap they can open your eyes to the truth."

Luke's mocking smile faded, and in its place grew an expression of thinly disguised dread.

As he did so frequently, he turned away.

* * *

Dawn came in Ilchester, chasing the night shadows away and revealing hundreds of young men, clustered in small groups by the graveyard. Loud and boisterous, they taunted each other with predictions of who would find the perfect tree for the maypole, and wagered shillings on who, under the forest's protective canopy, would steal a kiss from the maiden of their dreams.

Hovering near the church, the young women wore gowns of vivid reds and oranges, yellows and blues. Coronets and flowers peeked out from their braids and tresses, their eyes fresh as the spring air. They laughed softly in their groups, tossing their hair, their smiles coy, here and there an occasional sigh as they caught the eye of their favorite young man. A lift of their shoulders, a twirl of their skirts told of their interest in joining them for a walk in the forest to find the brightest flowers … and perhaps the perfect maypole.

Joya walked through the tall grass, brushing the morning moisture from the green blades, the dew running in small rivulets down her hands. She thought of tears and quickly chided herself for gloomy thoughts. Still, she could not summon any excitement for May Day. She looked down absently at her gown—she'd slipped into a tan gown, simple, a plain linen. It would do. She wouldn't be dancing today. She wanted only to apologize to Pru and go home.

The heady scent of honeysuckle filled the air. Wispy clouds swirled in the pale blue sky like maiden's hair loosed in the wind, and each secret smile and sensual, sideways glance between the men and women pierced her spirit. It reminded her of the way her mother and father had always been toward each other, sharing warm affection, united by an invisible thread of love in all they did. Joya had seen it when her father whispered in her mother's ear, in her mother's soft smile. She saw it between her brother, Stephen and his wife, Nicole, a flash of passion in her brother's eye at Nicole's touch.

Giles had stirred warmth in her, and a connection grew between them during their time together. No intense pleasures, though. She had hoped they would become so with time, but Giles had died before it could.

Now, like some evil punishment, Joya had felt this pleasure with the deceitful Yorkist. Why not with noble Giles, and why with the dishonorable Luke? It haunted her, the way he looked at her, the way his arms had held her, protected her in the river. The way he had crushed her to him, covering her mouth with his. Heady and intoxicating, it had made her yearn to enter that wondrous world, made her hope she could share such joys with him.

So foolish. He had led her into that breathless place, only to scorn her later and judge her stupid. He had dismissed her in her father's presence with a cruel, sardonic smile and cold, distrustful eyes.

Now she saw only Luke's self-destruction.

More girls passed, seeking their special man. She spotted Cam by the graveyard. She had shed her crusty exterior and given

George a smile so gentle it lit her eyes and pinked her cheeks, something Joya had never seen from her coarse friend.

This should have been a pleasant day, a day of teasing both Cam and Pru about their affections toward George and Martin, a day when Cam and Pru would sing-song as they always did, and tease her about her softness toward Luke.

She had hoped he could be here. Had entertained rosy thoughts about flowers and embraces, hot kisses under the cool protection of the trees. Stupid. Foolish. As if her father would have released him from the castle. As if Martin would stop his campaign to keep them separated. As if those kisses, that passion they had shared in the gaol, were real.

It had only been real for her.

Now she hated him, an unrepentant traitor who would soon die, and deserved to. Her heart ached with the loss of that which she had never possessed, and bitterness that the man she found most attractive was no more than a sickness, a tainted fruit that would only make her ill.

From the graveyard fence, the knight Peter met her gaze, his eyes full of hope. He started walking her way. She gave no thought to courtesy but spun on her heels and walked into the church. Surely there was some task for which she could volunteer to avoid him.

Inside, Joya spotted Pru in the north transept, stacking bread baskets. Seeing her, Pru froze, holding her basket mid-air. Her eyes lacked warmth, and she dropped her gaze and returned to her task.

"Why did you leave without me this morning?" Pru and Cam had hurried away from Coin Forest, not waiting for Joya to join them in the ride to Ilchester.

"I don't crave your company of a sudden," Pru said.

"I'm sorry about Martin. Where is he? I'll apologize to him, too, explain that it was me, and you tried to keep me away from Luke."

"I haven't seen him. He's avoiding me, thanks to you. I doubt my word will ever hold water with him again."

"Pru, I'm sorry."

She was considerate enough to come close and whisper. "You left the safety of the hallway and entered his chamber in the middle of the night. What were you thinking?"

"I didn't think. It's hard to think with him. I—"

"You said you'd talk to Martin, and you didn't. You left me to explain why I didn't keep my word to him."

"Where is he? I'll tell him now."

Pru crossed her arms and backed away. "Pray leave. Leave me alone!"

Cam joined them, her face still flushed. "What's wrong?"

"She's what's wrong," Pru said, her voice soft to avoid a scene, but cold. "I've disappointed Martin, and it's her fault."

"Yes, Joya, what was that about?" Cam asked. "Sneaking into Luke's room? That's not what we planned. What a dumb idea."

Joya interpreted her criticism: you're stupid. An echo of Luke's appraisal. She blanched at the accusation. Albeit true, it stung, and anger flared. "I said I'm sorry." She wagged her finger at them. "This was your idea, you know. I was clear on it; he's a Yorkist, but no, you two goaded me into trying to get him to switch loyalties." She glared at Pru. "Fine. I don't care if you talk to me or not."

Cam looked at her with fresh eyes. "Say, are you sick? This is May Day, and you're wearing that old gown? It's pilled, and the hem is worn."

Pru looked up, blinking. "And your hair!" She turned Joya to the side. "Did you comb the back?"

Joya self-consciously ran her fingers through the tangles in her hair. "I don't care. I don't care a whit. And you don't have to pretend with me; you don't care, either. You don't care to know about last night. Martin's version of it is more important than mine." To her horror, Joya felt tears betray her. She brushed them away.

"What happened, Joya?" Pru's voice had softened. "Come on. Let's take a walk, away from curious eyes." She gave a pointed glance at the musicians gathered nearby, who were staring.

70

Joya brushed her hand away. "I'll try to mend it for you with Martin. But curse your plan about Luke. He's determined to die. I hate him. Hate him. The sooner he dies, the better."

"What did he say to you?" Cam asked.

Joya waved her away.

"Well, forget him." Cam tipped her head toward Peter, who lingered, painfully obvious, by the nave. "Now there's someone who's shown his loyalty to your father and the king his entire life." She shrugged her shoulders and grinned. "Why not? He would crow with delight if you joined him to hunt for the maypole."

She dared not glance Peter's way. She knew the look he would have in his eyes—needy, desperate, fragile as a leaf, and if she showed any interest in him at all ... she shuddered. "I'd rather not." A vision of blue eyes assaulted her again, and she caged her face in her hands. "What's wrong with me? I hate Luke. He's arrogant and stubborn." He thinks I'm stupid and now he thinks I'm cheap and manipulating. "But he's still the only one I want to see."

Chapter 7

From the narrow windows in the solar Luke had been observing all the morning activity in the bailey. The last few days had been trying—all the people, the prodding and snooping. The quiet of the solar was a welcome change.

Joya's meddling friends had left early with several other people. The guard said they were headed to the parish church in Ilchester for May Day celebrations. Later, Joya had left with a large party, and the bailey had become quiet.

Morning became afternoon and Luke still stared, thinking how futile it would be to try an escape. The guard Martin was always watching him, his eyes cold, distrusting. Drawn from his thoughts by a commotion at the gate, Luke peered out the window of the solar and saw them. His three brothers, striding across the bailey with Lord Tabor.

Luke's thoughts scattered like tadpoles. Pain, humiliation, fear, loss. His father's and brother's deaths had thrown his once-strong family into a state of confusion. He watched his surviving brothers approach.

Searching for a weapon, he found only a collection of fabrics in the corner, and they hadn't trusted him with a knife for his mid-day dinner. He clenched his teeth, fighting the urge to flee, a useless thought.

He centered the large table and positioned himself between it and the window. The more distance between his brothers, the better.

"He must be in here." They burst through the door, self-righteous and impatient.

First came Christopher. The frustrated third-born was barrel-chested, short and sturdy, a fine soldier, quick with the sword and brutal in battle. Humfrye came next, more like Luke, tall, muscular without brawn. Often vague with the truth, he spun schemes that offered the most benefit to him. Hugh entered last, the youngest, self-indulgent and lazy as the morning breeze, happy in whatever lap of luxury he encountered. Tabor would have a hard time getting Hugh to leave the comforts of Coin Forest.

The table served its purpose and Christopher stopped in front of it. "So." He cocked his head and raised a brow. "Lucas. 'Tis been a long time, brother."

As children, Chris had been much larger and stronger than Luke. He had always used it to his advantage, humbling and frightening Luke as a young boy. The other brothers had found it amusing enough to add their own punches when they could. During his time at university, Luke had come to realize the extent of his vulnerability, all those years ago. Still, spiders of disgust and long-ago fear scrambled up Luke's spine, remembering his brothers' cruelty.

Though Luke had since caught up with his brother's height and weight, Chris still postured with power and insolent challenge.

"Good morn." Luke wouldn't give them the honor of addressing them by name.

"You know why we've come," Chris said. Humfrye and Hugh stood behind him, letting Chris speak for them.

"Tabor informed me," Luke said.

Chris stood taller, making his broad chest larger. "Have you lost every kernel of sense you may have ever possessed?"

"Ah, the same old song," Luke said, stretching a smile he knew would irritate his younger brother. "It's as if no time has passed since last I saw you."

Chris's eyes narrowed. "We thought you were building bridges, gaining honor for the Bonwyk family. Instead you've been plotting against Henry. Bloody nails, Luke! Knights with no colors sneak about in the village. Spies, asking for you. Word travels. No one speaks to us at parish, and I've not received an invite to tourney for six months."

Luke hooked a thumb on his girdle. His disgust leaked out in his stiff smile, but he cared not. "You've always been most concerned about your standing."

"Hell's torture, yes!" His brother said. "What is a man without good standing? Not that you care. You're willing to toss it in the fire, along with us."

"You send no word to us, only to William on matters of husbandry," Hugh whined. "William controls the treasury since you left. We can't buy supplies, food."

"It appears you haven't missed a meal recently," Luke countered, giving a pointed gaze at Hugh's stomach. "What's amiss? Wine cellar running low? Or did you already drink it dry?"

The Bonwyks had been like any other noble family, possessed of good lands and titled. Philip stayed at Penryton while their father prepared him for the duties inherent with his eventual title. Luke and Christopher followed their own interests. Christopher has chosen the excitement of competition at tournaments, and Luke had left to study under the master bridge builders in London. As their mother faded away from a lingering illness, the walls of Penryton swallowed Humfrye and Hugh, and they had never found interests beyond the manor.

Then Philip and their father died and left the Bonwyks splintered. Philip, first-born and heir, lost his title at the grave. In an instant, Luke had leap-frogged from second born son into the title. By that time, Luke had grown a thick, defensive skin and had no use for his brothers. Bridge-building became not only satisfying but a good excuse to avoid them.

Chris glanced at Tabor and shook his head. "We've come all this way to help you."

"Why bother," Hugh said. "He never could think beyond his rivers and models."

"Father would rise from the dead if he knew what you're doing. Have you no shred of honor left?" Chris asked.

Luke laughed. He'd once wilted before them, but he'd been through so much since leaving Penryton. The pointed insults no longer stung. It was as if a curtain had been raised and he could see through all their threats and admonitions.

"Those messenger pigeons fly both ways," Luke said. "You've been perfectly content living off my land. Have you once tried to contact me?"

Luke had maintained frequent contact with his steward, William, regarding manor management. "William tells me you were quite comfortable demanding more funds, but not once have you questioned him about my safety or well-being."

"And where were we to send our notes of concern? We didn't know where you were."

"William has always known. But this is about more than your comfort, or mine," Luke said. "Have you ever had a cause, Chris? I mean, a cause higher than your next tournament, or which ladies' skirts you'll raise?"

Luke walked around the end of the table, stopping in front of Humfrye and Hugh. "How about a cause that benefited more than yourself, Humfrye? And Hugh, how about a cause that required work? And sacrifice? Not because your king or your clergy or your family think you should, but because you know, deep in your heart, that it's the right thing? Don't try to pretend to know what I'm thinking, because—"

"By cause you're clearly not thinking, Turtle." Humfrye slapped Luke with the old pet name. "You can think things ten times over, and still never hit the target."

"Enough," Christopher said. "We didn't come to fight. We came to save our holdings."

"My holdings," Luke corrected. "Mine. I'm heir to Penryton, not you," he glared at his brothers in birth order. "Not you, and not you."

"Really, my Lord?" Chris had dropped the veneer of civility he'd raised for Tabor's sake, and his face knotted into a sour expression. "Well, be stubborn like this and you won't ever be returning to the head table, because your head—" He closed in on Luke and beat his forefinger on Luke's chest at every other word, "will be rolling in the mud for treason."

Luke's gut tightened and shadows of his childhood roared in his ears. He pushed his brother back. "Don't touch me. Don't ever touch me."

Chris's eyes narrowed, but he retreated enough for Luke to breathe. He pulled a parchment from his cloak and thrust it in Luke's face. "Here's what your simple-minded thinking has brought you, brother."

Luke noted the seal of Henry VI, his name vivid in the wax.

"Think you're so clever, do you? You can read well enough, but let's see if you can sort the meaning of the words. Read the title below this seal!"

"I know the point of it. It's Latin. *Henry, by the grace of God, of the French and of England, King.* But he didn't send it."

"Are you blind? It's his farking seal!"

Luke leveled a gaze at him. "Margaret uses his seal. Like she uses his armies. And I see you've broken the seal. What a surprise."

"Sodding read it."

Luke unrolled the parchment. Despite his outer bravado, his hands went numb and he almost dropped the missive. The message revealed his brothers' concerns.

One thousand pounds. One thousand. The wretched queen was fining him one thousand pounds. An exorbitant sum. It would bankrupt him. He thought of York and Warwick—their cause, the importance of their task. He had taken it on with open eyes, knowing he was risking everything, but the numbers, written in the artistic flourish of an accomplished scrivener, stabbed his eyes with their sheer significance.

"What say you now, brother?" As if Hugh had ever known the value of money, as if he had ever earned a shilling in his life. He raised his chin, priggish and satisfied.

"Believe your eyes, you scut!" Humfrye shouted.

"How in Hades will you pay this?" Chris's face had turned red.

From the corner of his eye Luke saw a flash of long black hair and a tan dress. Joya. God's nails. She was supposed to be at May Day celebrations.

He turned his attention back to the parchment and regarded them. "It's addressed to me. Private business which does not involve you. I will handle it as I may, and our time is done here. You may leave."

"So you can put your head on the block and forfeit our holdings? By hell, we will," Chris shouted.

Tabor had at some time entered the solar. "Listen to them, Luke. They're your family. They're here to help you."

"Indeed? Have you heard them offer funds to help pay the fine to save Penryton, where they all live? I appreciate your hospitality, Lord Tabor, but this is not your affair."

Like an overspent candle in the sun's heat, Humfrye's face had melted into a mask of pure contempt. "Turtle, Turtle," he crooned.

At hearing their demeaning pet name for him, Luke's throat constricted. It would always be associated with dark terror. "Yes, you boot licker?"

Humfrye's face darkened. "Turtle, you always get so confused. Nothing has changed. You're neck-deep in trouble. You will pay her. You have no choice. After you do, we'll not have funds for our horses this year, and we'll scrape by to seed the fields, and because of you we'll struggle to store the buttery for winter, but you'll pay."

"And you'll by God beg for Margaret's forgiveness and help our family regain our position," Chris stormed. "Or by my faith, you'll see the bottom of that barrel again," he grabbed Luke by the throat, "you pignut of a brother."

Fury filled Luke's veins. He seized Chris's thumb, jerking it back forcefully. He heard the snap.

Chris cried out in pain and released him.

Luke drew a fist and struck him in the jaw. Seeing him fall felt exceptionally fine.

"God's blood, Turtle!" Humfrye intervened, eyes wide. "What's wrong with you?"

"Not a thing." Luke struggled to get the words out. "At least I have the ballocks to act on what I believe."

"Pigeon shit." Chris choked out the words past the pain, holding his thumb. "You only support your own selfish needs."

Luke's heart was racing, and his blood itched to strike him again, and again, and again. "Don't call me Turtle," he growled at Chris. "I'll kill you the next time." He wiped the blood from his hand, shaking out the sting.

Luke noticed the shock on his host's face. "My apologies, Lord Tabor. We're not on good terms." He regarded his brothers. "You've had your say. Now get out."

"I'm sorry, Lord Tabor." Chris wiped the blood from his chin as he left. "We only wanted to help."

Humfrye approached cautiously. "You must save Penryton, Luke. If she takes it back, she wins. You lose."

Hugh touched his arm, his expression disturbingly grave. "You'll lose everything."

* * *

After Luke left, Joya's father caught up with her on the stairs. "It's good you saw him like this," he said, his mouth thinned as he shook his head. "In case you still harbor any interest in him."

Joya held a hand to her breast, still startled by what she had just witnessed. Unable to endure the May Day festivities, she had returned from Ilchester and followed the angry voices up to the solar, only to witness the explosive violence of the man with the piercing blue eyes.

"You must keep in mind that he is the enemy," her father said. His eyes softened. He brushed errant strands of hair from her face, tucking them behind her ear. His hug calmed her, though it was delivered with hesitance and an awkwardness that had come between them since she had grown into a woman. Joya wished for that moment she could return to the little girl she once was, greedy for his bear hugs and the tickling fall of her stomach when he tossed her in the air until she squealed with delight.

Joya rested her head on his chest.

"Daughter." It was all he said, his voice rough with emotion. He tapped her nose and gave her a crooked smile, shaking his head in masculine dismissal as he left the solar.

Feeling the weight of his disapproval, she walked the length of the solar, where Ellingtons of the past roosted in their heavy frames, forever locked behind their dusty portals. She approached a rendering of a tall, stout man with a thick, black mustache, the grandfather she had never known. Carston Ellington, killed when Joya's father was about her age. He frowned down at her as if disapproving of her, as he had disapproved of her father. What a sad tradition they shared.

Her father's older brother, William, sat in the next frame. He had died along with Carston during the siege. Their father had favored William. Perhaps Joya's father had forgotten how it hurt to be a disappointment to one's parent. Perhaps he failed to notice the pain in her eyes when he was short with her, when he didn't understand how difficult the choices could be. Had he ever been young and uncertain or had he breezed past all of life's obstacles?

He had communicated his hopes for her many times. Marry a respectable man, comport herself as a lady, draw no negative attention to their family, and serve Queen Margaret with unquestionable loyalty in all cases.

His expectations had never concerned her. Until now.

She walked to the window, chilled from the night and now bearded with condensation. The room burned from the tension and discord.

After the argument, Luke had stormed off toward Steven's chamber, and his brothers had settled belowstairs in the great hall, their conversations dark and muffled.

Luke hadn't noticed her. Joya picked at the pills clinging to the old fabric of her gown. She hadn't known him long, but they had come close to death in that river. That, she thought, revealed much about a person.

He had shown no violence toward her when he stole her from the hunting party, only urgency and grim determination. And only concern when she had stupidly thrown herself in the river. It would have been understandable if he had become angry when he had been rewarded for saving her life by being chained in the gaol, but he had remained stoic. Resigned to die.

The man she saw with his brothers was a different person.

"I'll kill you," he had threatened to the very brother who had traveled forty miles to help him.

She retreated to her chamber with a niggling sensation of having missed something, some snippet of conversation that might explain his sudden fury at his own kin.

* * *

In her chamber, she collapsed on her bed and drifted into a sensuous dream.

"Hold on. I'll get us to shore." Luke's strong arms held her in the churning water, and she felt his stubbled jaw on her neck. His muscles tensed against her back as he anchored her to the large driftwood.

She struggled against the purse strings that bound her hands, unable to break free. His arms created a cocoon of safety, easing her panic.

With the magical swirl of dreams, the river water vanished and a field of early spring daisies and clover tickled her toes through her sandals, fragrant and warm against the awakening earth. She and Luke were in the woods outside Ilchester, walking together. All around them, laughter and intimate conversations floated through the air as other couples combed the woods, searching for the maypole tree.

With a hand to her waist he pulled her closer and nuzzled her neck, sending tingles of excitement to her breasts. She drew a breath and pulled him down for a deep kiss that caused ripples of desire.

He pointed to a tall, symmetrical tree with a gently tapering trunk, taller than Father Thomas's tithing barn and straight as Fosse's Way. "There it is," Luke said. "We found the Maypole."

They threaded their way through the ribbons, and his hands held her waist. He led her in a graceful dance, wrapping her in a yellow ribbon, her favorite color. His eyes, blue as a day's end sky, were heavily lidded with desire, and she answered the invitation in his eyes, surrendering to his beribboned web.

He pulled her close, whispering in her ear. "I will follow you, Joya, but you must first love me."

She kissed him. He plunged his hands into her hair and undid her combs, and her hair fell onto his shoulders, black against his skin.

They were nude, in bed, and he was stroking her breasts. Chains rattled, and she remembered his plight, and the chains disappeared. "Oh, Luke," she sighed, kissing him again. "I love you already."

Their tongues danced, his mouth sweet, arousing. "I love you. I am yours."

"My little Angel. Joya."

Joya awoke to a familiar female voice. She saw someone before her, much shorter than Luke. Her eyes adjusted, and the form sharpened into a beautiful woman, her long, black hair bound, silver at the temples. She wore a blue travel cloak. Dark eyes watched her from under thick lashes, and a gentle smile revealed even, white teeth against her dark skin. She took up only a small portion of the bed, her body like that of a richly plumed bird, small but strong and hale.

"Mother!" Joya threw her arms around her. I've missed you so. She traced her gently lined face, still comely at 47 summers. "I thought—"

"I know. I should be with Nicole, and I cannot stay long, but I saw a sign. An omen."

Her mother read signs in the weather, the lakes, and any and all creatures. Spun from the strands of her Gypsy legacy, she had been known to cancel a trip if she witnessed a spider repairing its web. "What did you see, Mother?"

"An owl, falling from the sky with no apparent injury, in full daylight. It landed in the bailey just after we received word of the Bonwyk brothers' visit. Eyes wide, she shook her head. "It foretells disaster. I came to warn your father, but after what he told me about your behavior with Penry—I'm here to warn you."

Had she talked in her sleep? She hugged Sharai. "Is Nicole better?"

"A little, but I have to get back to her. She's so worried about the babe and the birthing. Though she knows better, the curse still haunts her dreams. But I had to see you, *Ves' Tacha.*" Her mother pulled the covers from her. "And what are you wearing, today, day of days?" She pulled pills from the fabric on the sleeve. "This gown isn't fit for the stables. Come. Let's get you ready for supper." She led her to the garderobe and studied the gowns hooked to the wall.

Her mother pulled one at a time from the pegs, a blue gown, an orange one, a moss green with pleats. "Ah, this one." She held up a gown the color of raspberries, smiling broadly. "Remember when we found this fabric?"

Memories misted over Joya, warming her. She and her mother were so different. Joya couldn't sew a straight stitch, and bless Sharai, she couldn't sing harmony. Her mother preferred life within the walls of the castle, managing Coin Forest and Fritham as well as any steward, keeping track of supplies, food and wine stocks, all but field and crop cases. Joya loved the outdoors, hunting with her father, and travel, dances and parties and people. She wasn't smart like her mother, so she enjoyed more physical activities.

They shared one great passion, though, and it drew them close. They both loved fashion. Sharai created the designs and nimbly sewed them. She and Joya relished the fabrics and shopping the fairs and markets for them. Between her mother, who dressed her fine as a princess, and her father, who savored the admiration those fashions drew, Joya could never be too pretty.

"I remember," Joya said. Hugging her through the deep red fabric. "Southampton." Joya touched the delicate chain at the shoulders. It stirred sweet memories.

Her mother helped her out of the worn gown and slipped the red damask over her head.

Joya smoothed the skirt, admiring the deeper red swirls over the lighter red. "It's beautiful."

Her mother attached and laced the sleeves. "I could not believe what happened to you hunting. How you let your guard down."

"I was careless," Joya said. "Thank you for the dagger."

"We almost lost you, sweetling. And now this ... this Lord Penry, and your ... unseemly conduct with him." She tilted her head to the side, as if trying to peer under the brim of a hat so she could better see Joya's eyes. "Sneaking into his chamber, without escort? Eavesdropping on your father?"

"I was waiting for them to finish so I could announce my arrival," Joya began, knowing how feeble it sounded. An idea came to her and she saw her mother as an ally. At a young age, Sharai had been sweet on Lord Tabor. His mother refused to accept Sharai and arranged a marriage for Tabor with an earl's daughter. Surely her mother would remember the agonies of love denied; she would convince her father to rescind his order to stay away from Luke.

"You and Father had your struggles when you first met. You recall, Mother, how hard it was?"

Her mother buttoned the lower sleeves snug to her wrist. "That was different. You, my daughter, were caught in an embrace in the gaol. He plots with York. With Yorkists." She repeated it, eyes widened.

"I need to talk to him, get him to return to King Henry's side. He has secrets, yes. If we can get him to tell Margaret what York plans, we can—"

"He saved your life. You're confusing valor with true affection."

"He's a nobleman from a good family. He's a bridge builder."

"He is a traitor."

"Father doesn't believe we can change his mind. He doesn't understand that it's the man I care about, not his principles."

"Ah, but my sweet daughter, a man and his principles are one and the same. Do not forget this."

"I have good judgment; you've told me that many times, Mother. I sense that he's a good man."

"And you would be able to judge this in the few hours you have shared with him?" She waved the thought away with her small hand and cupped Joya's cheek. "You must visit the rainbow mist."

"Oh, Mother. That's a child's poem."

"It's a spell. It strengthens your vision, child. Say it now."

Joya looked into the depths of her mother's brown eyes, dark with an intensity that none of the other mothers in Somerset possessed. Her mother liked to say she didn't create spells, but rather wished harder and more effectively than other people. Could it be that Joya had only to wish harder?

Joya took a deep breath, released it and recited the rainbow spell her mother had taught her as a child.

> *Deep in your soul you'll find the hue*
> *Lively colors that lead you to*
> *Birdsong sweet and rose's thorn*
> *With trials and truth you'll be reborn*

"You must turn to it, *Ves' Tacha*."

"I did. I saw the colors, but there's this pain, this yearning."

"Colors? You saw them?"

"This morn." Joya had found the quiet, sensed the spirit, seen the soft green. "A distant flash."

Her mother rested her hand on Joya's heart. "You will find the harmony."

"It doesn't come from some spell. Your harmony came from my father."

"No, Joya. It comes from inside me. Search your heart. Listen."

"Please don't speak in your riddles, Mother."

"Like a jewel, love has many faces. Some sparkle but are dangerous. I sense the feeling you have for this man is the same."

"I can help the queen."

"That would be a very good thing to do, Joya, because we are beholden to her. You must support Margaret, not your own secret dreams."

"What mean you?"

"You spoke aloud."

"What?"

"In your dreams."

"Nay."

"Yes. You have pined too long for Giles, Joya. You have been too long without a man's affections. You have known Lord Penry but two days, yet you profess your love for him in a tortured, breathless voice."

Abashed, Joya studied her hands.

Her mother cradled Joya's face in her small hands, her voice tender with love but her words unyielding as stone. "I am in agreement with your father on this. I, too, forbid you to seek him out." She tilted her head and shot a determined gaze her way. "Stay away from Lord Penry."

Chapter 8

"Where to next?" Prudence, short as a sneeze in her unadorned blue gown, positioned her horse downhill for an easier mount. She gained the saddle and perfected her posture, her left arm poised like a protective wing over her chest.

Joya had chosen a vivid green silk gown for their outing, one that hugged her curves and blossomed from empire darts into a generous, fluid skirt. Green, her family's colors, for she felt closer to her family since she had withdrawn from Lord Penry.

She absently braided Goldie's mane, considering their options in the bright midday sunlight. She had been riding with Pru, Camilla and the old knight, Hugo. They had passed the Maypole, and Joya thought of Lilla, an armorer's daughter who had been crowned the May Queen. Joya had missed all the celebrations while lost in reverie over the sullen, selfish Lord Penry. Whatever had possessed her?

A week had passed since that embarrassing night in the solar with her father and the family argument between Luke and his brothers. Joya's self-imposed love spell had lifted and she had returned to the daily pleasures of springtime—hawking, music and friends.

They had finished a mid-day meal in the oat fields, deserted by the farmers as they left their planting to take their midday naps. Crows scoured the furrows, digging for seeds and avoiding the young boys who chased them, throwing stones. Camilla and Hugo had picked their favorite boys and wagered which ones could kill the most birds for an evening stew. Now they rode toward Stephen and Nicole's village, Faierfield, following the Ten Mile River on their way home.

"Let's ride to the overlook before we go back," Joya said. It afforded a majestic view of the fields as far as the eye could see, many filled with ewes. "Maybe we'll see some new lambs." Lambing season had begun and Joya loved seeing the tender babes with their endearing, wobbly first steps.

Hugo mounted with a grunt, grumbling about the coins he had lost to Camilla over the wager of which boy would bag the most birds.

They approached a turn of the Ten Mile River and Joya spied a man sawing wood on the Halfway Bridge. He wore loose work clothing and high boots. His movements were compact as he guided the saw, unhurried and precise. He was tall, but not as tall as her father, and . . .

A fluttering tickled her stomach, and the air grew heavy. She had successfully avoided him in the great hall and the solar, but now, twenty yards distant, his presence affected her. "Who's on the bridge?" Joya asked, already knowing.

"The Yorkist traitor," Hugo said. "I should run the knave through, but your father warned us to do no harm."

"He's loose?" His hair, light in the sun, called up memories of its silky smoothness when wet, the fine hairs on his neck as she held on to him in the water. She swallowed, her throat tight of a sudden. "What's he doing?"

"Lord Tabor decided he might as well put the traitor to work while they're waiting to hear from the queen about what to do with him. 'Twill be good to see his head roll. Until then, he's fixing the bridge and he won't go far. He's been forbidden a horse, and see, there's Peter and a couple of other knights guarding him." He pointed to the men, fishing a stone's throw down the river with a clear view of both Luke and the bridge. "One misstep and he gets shackled, though. Lord Tabor doesn't trust him any further'n a frog's hop. And your mother's given us our orders about you." His face tightened with a priggish expression that hinted at his displeasure that Joya had befriended Luke.

She turned to him and the face that lived in her dreams, the unexpected sight of him as enjoyable as a French wine at sunset. They must cross the bridge to reach the overlook, and that would bring her closer to him. Her commitment to avoid him vanished in the soft breeze that came up from the lazy river below. "Is the bridge passable?"

"Yes. It's only routine work," Hugo said.

"Then let's go," Camilla said. She raised a brow at Joya. "You lead the way."

Joya shook her head and led Goldie to the back, behind Hugo and the girls.

Camilla laughed and urged her horse into a run, clattering up to Luke. "Lord Penry. Fancy seeing you out here, in the fresh air."

"Good morrow," Luke said, not breaking the rhythm of his saw. His clothes were of simple, loose-woven flax, brown and ill-fitting on his muscular frame. The sleeves of his tunic were pulled up, revealing his bronzed forearms, muscular and covered by soft hair that shone in the sun.

The scent of fresh wood shavings greeted her. The water beneath the bridge rushed against the pilings and made her heart hurry, summoning memories of safety in his arms.

"I'm Camilla. Remember me? Last time Prudence and I saw you, you were in gaol. In chains," she added wickedly. "Things seem to be looking up for you."

Luke coughed softly and ignored her.

"And I'm sure you know why." Camilla laughed and rode past him.

"Now, Cam." Pru passed, and Hugo approached Luke and drew his sword, pointing it within an inch of Luke's back. "Traitor." Hugo's voice lowered, hoarse with contempt.

Luke neither shrank from nor turned to Hugo, but kept to his work.

Joya wedged Goldie between them. "Not very civil of you, Hugo." She deliberately omitted his title, a slight to make him aware of her displeasure. "He is a Bonwyk, helping with this bridge. Sheath it," she said, gesturing to his sword. "Lord Penry is our guest."

Hugo laughed. "A dead one if he doesn't pay the queen her due. He can fool you, Joya, but he can't fool Margaret."

"My, but the day is burning," Pru said, watching Joya closely, "Let's be off now."

As they approached the end of the bridge, Luke spoke. "Joya." His voice held no sign of a question, only an even intonation of her name.

Joya pulled Goldie's reins. "Yes?"

"A word with you, if you please."

Joya swallowed a dose of dread and curiosity. He had never called her name or sought her out. He was a handsome, heart-stopping curiosity, but they shared no common loyalties or concerns. The queen would soon crush him if she couldn't pull his military secrets from him. Joya avoided the pull of his blue eyes. "I have had quite enough of your words, Lord Penry; we have nothing—"

"There is one thing," Pru interrupted, her voice unusually crisp. "I believe Lord Penry needs to make arrangements to return some of your belongings, lost during your hunting trip?"

Joya peered at her. "What?"

Pru angled her horse close to Joya. "Your dagger. He took it from you," Pru whispered.

"It could be anywhere—"

"You're in the company of knights and friends, an opportunity to visit with him without being improper. Hear him out," Pru murmured. She raised her voice. "Of course, Joya. We don't mind waiting for you. We'll go down to the river and see if the men have caught any fish yet."

"Yes, I could use a little rest," Cam said, trotting her horse down the bank where the knights kept their eye on Luke.

The bridge now empty of all but the two of them, she dismounted and turned expectantly to Luke. "Yes?"

He finished the log, a perfect cut, and placed it on top of the others, skidding it carefully until its end was in precisely the same position, forming an edge to the pile so perfect it could have been one piece of wood.

His jaw worked, as if he were chewing tacks. He picked up a new piece of wood and positioned it on the saw rack.

Joya shook her head in frustration, "You've asked for a word. Say it now."

No furrow split his brow, but his mouth was tense. Not with anger, nor urgency or passion, all of which she'd seen in abundance each time they had met previously. All she saw was a beautiful man, frozen in his tracks, covered in a shroud of uncertainty.

She softened her voice. "Luke?"

He gave great scrutiny to the stitching on the side of his boots. "I must needs tell you…" Scratching a line into the wood with his knife, he paused.

Sensing his discomfiture, she gestured at the wood and saw horse. "What's wrong with the bridge?"

Relief swept across his face. "I'm shoring the supports," he said, confident of a sudden. "This is a simple bridge, one span at this point in the river, so no intermediate supports are needed. Only the abutments, but they have been compromised by rot and the current, over time …"

He saw her smile and his words died away. "I have been rude to you. Harsh." A full minute passed, but she would not help him with this. It was of too much import to her.

He looked in her general direction, eyes darting the slightest bit, as if wary to meet her gaze. "I'm sorry for that."

His blue eyes finally settled on her, and she saw his sincerity. "Thank…" She cleared her throat. "Thank you."

"What did your friend want you to discuss with me?"

"Oh. Prudence. She wants you to return my dagger."

"I fear it was lost in the river. If I'm ever freed, I will replace it."

She preferred not to look into the shadows of his future. She also preferred not to look at Peter and the other knights staring at them, so she walked off the bridge, down a small slope on the bank that afforded a small privacy. She sat on one of the support beams that jutted out from the earth, and he joined her, sitting a respectful arm's length away.

Silence enveloped them. She didn't have to ask if he had responded to Margaret's demand for one thousand pounds, or if Margaret had sent any further messages. From overheard conversations she knew the answer to both questions: no. The impasse could only mean further trouble for him, death likely.

"Thank you for what you have done for me. Speaking to your father."

"You saved my life. 'Twas the least I could do."

"I doubt you would have jumped in the river, had I not stolen you and your horse from the hunting party."

"Where were you taking me?"

"I would have delivered you safely to a church. I sought only an escape."

"And Goldie? My horse?"

"I might have had to borrow her for a time."

She knew the depth of his convictions now and dared not revisit his loyalties, so she remained silent.

"I wanted to apologize before I … leave."

Joya cringed at his pause. "Leave" served as a thinly veiled reference to his execution.

He could have just as easily left her to drown. Regardless of his decision to support York, she sensed a basic goodness in him.

"What will you do?"

He didn't respond.

"Your brothers told my father that you have the funds to pay Margaret." Surely he would not forfeit all of his family's holdings.

Silence hissed in her ears. There remained no words to be uttered, no hope or solution to be found, but she could not leave him. For some unspeakable reason, she felt a connection. The sound of buzzing broke the quiet, the pleasant business of fat honey bees, their transparent wings whirring.

A large field of spring flowers hugged the riverbank, sweetening the air with their fragrance. Dozens of bees and butterflies flitted among the blooms, and under the bridge, two butterflies flew in a dancing figure eight pattern.

Luke's full, sensitive mouth spread into a small smile as he watched them. "Wood butterflies."

She wanted more from him, more pleasure on his face, more words. She could smell the wood chips clinging to his tunic, and the tang of his sweat. She followed his gaze to the butterflies, dark brown with orange spots. The common butterfly had never looked so beautiful to her before.

"Look at the male," he said. "See his black eye spot? How big it is? That means it's going to be a hot summer."

"How do you know? That it's a male, I mean."

"Because his flight is more graceful."

She felt her smile vanish. "How can you say that? They fly the same way."

"And," Luke continued with a deliberate gaze, "He is the more beautiful one."

Affronted, she stood and met his blue eyes. "What? Why, that's the—"

He raised his hands, palms facing her, and laughed. "No, no. It's the female," he said. "I said it in jest."

Jest? She was left speechless.

"I had to," he said, standing. "You looked so sad."

She averted her gaze. Did she wear her heart on her sleeve so much? She gave him a crooked smile, trying to recover. "Besides, you can't tell which one is male or female. They're probably both female."

"No. Look closer. See the one with the darker underside? That's the female."

"Of course." She straightened and raised her chin in challenge, her gaze never leaving his. "And she is glorious."

He reached out to her, clasping her wrist in his big hand, somewhere between a caress and pure possession. His blue eyes sharpened with that look of hunger that she'd seen in the gaol. His intensity seemed to open a door to his soul.

Her legs grew weak, and she leaned into him, closing the distance between them.

She melted into his arms, and it was happening all over again, the weakness, the dizzying burst of heat melting her resolve.

Joya heard movement on the bridge. With difficulty she pushed away and walked up the bank. She would not let the knights know what they had shared.

As she reached the deck level of the bridge, a woman stood, silk gown flowing gently. She held the reins of a familiar horse.

Joya stopped. "Mother."

Sharai led her horse over the bridge and hooked Joya's arm. "Let's walk."

At a safe distance, her mother turned to her. "Joya, you put me beyond words. You've always been such a good girl."

"I still am, Mother. I did not come here seeking him out. We needed to cross the bridge."

And gaze into his eyes, and embrace him.

"Remember, I heard you speaking as you dreamed of him. I forbade you."

"Of all who know me, I would think you would understand. Do you remember when you first met Father?"

"Joya, he was my life's great love. This man is wrong."

"Did you not tell me how wrong it was for you to hold such strong feelings for a nobleman? How you hated them? "

She took a deep breath and twisted her earring. "Yes, but he was no Yorkist. No traitor. He—"

"And didn't Etti see how you felt about him, and did she not help you spend time with him?" Etti was the old Gypsy – the Rom – who had taught Sharai how to support herself by dancing at the regional fairs. She had also shrewdly contracted Sharai's seamstress services to Tabor so they could be together.

"It was a business, my sewing," her mother objected. "A contract."

"Do you not see how I feel about Luke? Not so different from what you felt for Father."

93

"He is dangerous. That's what is different. I fear him." Shari touched Joya's arm, slid down and held her wrist. Her eyes were wide, moist. "I almost lost Stephen to the block," she said. "Do you know what it would do to me if I lost you that way?" She closed her eyes. "This isn't about gazes and kisses. This is life and death, and you are getting too close to him."

Joya met her mother's eyes, and the bronze face that she so dearly loved. "He is a good man."

"You cannot save him." She cradled Joya's face in her hands. "I will find a spell to help you."

"Mother, no. Go back to Stephen's. Help Nicole get better. I will take care of myself, mama. I do not need saving."

"Oh, but my sweet daughter. You very much do." She kissed Joya's forehead, sealed it with her thumb, plucked a hair from her scalp and hurried away.

Luke watched Lady Tabor embrace Joya and walk to her horse. The sense of doom settled on his shoulders again. The Ellingham family was fiercely loyal to Queen Margaret, and it was apparent that his presence caused Lady Tabor anguish. Lady Tabor cast a look Luke's way, her gaze cutting through the distance between them. She joined her knights and they rode off toward Coin Forest.

Luke ignored the hard stares of the knights. His closeness to Joya was stirring hostilities, to be sure. But he couldn't stay away from her.

What was it about her? Her body was the stuff of dreams, certes. The hint of honeysuckle flowed from her black hair, and her eyes, a rich maple in the night. They kindled the oddest urges – to kiss her eyelids, to run his lips across her long lashes, to fall into those eyes and suck her lips, plump and ripe as berries. From the moment he first saw her, when she fell to the ground and rested her lush breasts on his chest, checking his breathing, he had not been able to find his own.

What had happened to his mind, that he would flirt with her like some rascal at court, teasing her about—of all things— butterflies? What had possessed him?

She had been so sad. He could not imagine why this spirited, exquisite creature could care for him. He had stolen her horse, insulted her. But he felt it on his skin, in her soft breath, in those wide, gloriously expressive eyes, in the way her lip trembled. He had only thought to apologize for his behavior, and had managed instead to dredge up yet more of it, grabbing her like some braying mule.

He resumed his sawing.

Now he would never make the rendezvous point, never join forces to defeat Margaret and restore peace and order to England. Hell's fire, he probably wouldn't make the summer solstice before Margaret relieved him of his head.

He worried about his brothers, as angry as that made him. He was nothing to them but the brunt of their jokes and cruelty, nothing but a threat to their security and positions in Penryton. Their prestige was of more import than England's future.

Luke rubbed his face with his hands. Why did he continue to care for such ne'er do wells as his brothers? Why did he feel so drawn to Joya, a forbidden woman? Mayhap he was so devastated with the certainty of his coming death that he had latched onto her as a diversion? Having reached the end of his days, did he see new hope for a happiness that had always eluded him?

He tossed his saw to the bridge deck in disgust. What angered him most in his life were the condemnations of his father and brothers, and it appeared at the moment that they had been right all along. He was ineffectual, powerless and dense.

That may all be true, but he owed York the truth. He must get word to him.

* * *

In Ireland, Dublin Castle rose before Richard, Duke of York, taunting him. The pitched torches stood like sentinels, lighting the gateway and reminding him of another castle, the one that held the throne that was rightfully his. He should have taken it after Blore Heath, but decisive victory remained elusive, and

Parliament remained painfully neutral. Exiled in Ireland, York could only watch while Margaret stripped his properties. He shifted in the saddle and turned to his eager second in command, Simon Wagg. Wagg had big ears, a hint of his character, for the young man didn't seem to let any conversation continue without his presence. He was reading a messenger's missive. "Was Penry successful?" Lord Penry was overdue to have arrived at Christchurch.

Wagg crumpled the parchment and slipped it into his tunic. "Nay. He was arrested."

"Sod it." York shoved his opened palm at Wagg. "Give me the message." Wagg had proven himself clever and capable, but he possessed a raw edge of ambition that worried York at times.

"Pray forgive me, Your Grace," Wagg said, hastily smoothing the parchment and handing it to York.

It was as he had said. Penry had been placed under arrest at Coin Forest, under the care of one of Margaret's most loyal barons, Lord Tabor. And the queen had fined Penry a thousand pounds.

"God's nails. If he pays that large a fine, how in Hades can Penry continue supporting us?" He shook his head. "I grow weary of the queen's good fortune." York stretched, trying to find comfort in his tunic, which seemed to have shrunk. He was gaining weight again, losing his fitness. The middle of May—he would turn forty-nine in September. The crown owed him over thirty-eight thousand pounds, funds he had advanced in the name of King Henry over the years. He wanted repayment, but the harlot Margaret had spent it all to destroy her enemies, mainly him.

York needed to retire Henry without killing him and take the throne. Lord Penry was a secret and vital part of their plan. York had sent reinforcements for him, but not in time. "How can she continue to be so godrotting lucky?" He fisted his hands, wanting desperately to choke the power-hungry life out of her.

King Henry had lost his mind, wandered aimlessly, speechless for over a year. How could he possibly have sired the son Margaret delivered after seven barren years of marriage?

True, he had bouts of intellectual clarity now and then, but they were unpredictable and for brief bits of time. He needed to be relieved of his position and allowed to live out his days in peace. That wouldn't suit Margaret, though. She dragged her husband like a puppet from battle to battle so she could put her bastard son on the throne when Henry finally died.

"Do you think they found it?" York asked.

"The plan?" Wagg said. "Nay. Not the real ones, at least. They found what we wanted them to find." He referred to the misleading plans Penry had carried.

York prayed their attack plan would work. "Are the Irish troops ready?"

"Yes," Wagg said, "I sail with them on the morrow."

"Excellent." He and Warwick were preparing what would be his most organized attack against the royal forces.

Warwick. Richard Neville, Earl of Warwick, the wealthiest and most powerful nobleman in England. If their plan worked, it would break Margaret's grasp on the royal army, unseat the feeble King Henry and restore order and dignity to England. This would be the coup de grace that would end the festering division and lawlessness of the realm, left floundering since Margaret managed to convince Parliament to remove York as Protector five years ago.

The plan was daring. From France, York's brother-in-law, Salisbury; Warwick and the Earl of March would sail from exile in Calais to Sandwich, on England's east coast.

From Ireland, York's ships would sail into the English Channel and release a thousand Irish troops near Christchurch. Lord Penry would repair a bridge that would enable the Irish troops to travel quickly to London, join Salisbury's six thousand troops and crush Margaret's ragged mercenary army. York would ascend to power, retire Henry and exile his foul French queen.

"We need to free Penry," Wagg said.

York nodded. Penry, an odd man whose voice held an influential power, possessed a strong conviction that fired men's loyalties. Were he not so reclusive, he would have made a fine commander. York had seen it for himself when Penry was last in

Ireland with them. With just a short, impassioned speech, Penry had managed to recruit hundreds of Irish to travel with Wagg to England and fight the queen.

"Wait." Wagg slapped the saddle, startling his horse. "I have a plan."

Wagg was building a reputation for military cunning. "What do you propose?"

"Take advantage of Margaret's reputation for cruelty and revenge."

"That sounds good," York said. The queen had been known to kill some of her own commanders on the field who did not bow to her will. "How?"

"We'll take the Bonwyk treasury. All will believe it's for the thousand pound fine Margaret assessed Lord Penry."

"A thousand pounds." A fortune. It could strengthen his troops.

"Penry's treasury is likely more, much more," Wagg said. "He's known to be frugal, not at all like his brothers. Some say his coffers hold treble that."

Three times. Wagg was offering a key that could unlock three thousand pounds, held by an imprisoned nobleman who would lose it to Margaret, any way. It could buy the new, light German armor for his commanders. And provisions to sustain a march long enough to reach London with well-fed troops.

He met Wagg's eyes, bright with the rewards of his idea. "You, my friend, are clever beyond words."

"Then we must make haste," Wagg said. "We need to get several knights under King Henry's banners to Penryton … before Margaret does."

"Tempting, my friend, so tempting," York said, "But no. I have been patient this long. I am making progress in Parliament. I'm loathe to betray Penry after his support, and contrary to Margaret's claims, I am no thief."

Wagg visibly stiffened, but did not gainsay him. Good. But York made note to keep on eye on his zealous young commander.

Chapter 9

The assassin and his fourteen mercenary knights approached Penryton, a quiet, crenelated manor. Featuring none of the impressive towers and artistic flourishes of more prominent demesnes, this was a big, staid structure, grey with age and hungry for improvements to its grounds and roads.

It rose from the hill on which it sat with a curious elegance. With its sturdy curtain walls, the old fortifications had probably offered good protection for the Bonwyks over the centuries.

The village lay at the manor's feet, a village neither poor nor wealthy, several dozen homes and merchants—the usual blacksmith, butcher, blood letter and alehouse. As they approached, the acrid smell of pitch mingled with the tantalizing aroma of searing meats, roasts on spits and fresh baked bread. The sun had set, and the people were ready for supper, games, and more than a few tankards of ale.

But the assassin wasn't here to play, or eat, or drink. Wagg's orders had been specific: take the treasury, transport it forthwith back to Wagg, and anything else of value was spoils. That suited him fine. He had learned early to put himself first when pandering to the whims and demands of royalty. One privileged whoreson king was as stained and cruel as the next. They wanted a castle for their riches, an executioner's block for their enemies, good food, good women, good wine. Above all, power. And as soon as one learned to cater to the royal's tastes, the current king would get his head lopped off and another one would be coronated with pomp and accolades. Same in Spain and France as here in England. He would follow orders, collect his fee and move on.

A gaggle of prostitutes gathered in front of the tavern, threadbare dresses moistened to reveal their nipples. His groin responded, but he resisted. Time for that later.

The whores looked to the banner he was carrying and started chattering. It featured gold lions rampant and *fleur de lis*—King Henry's banner. Henry the Sixth—the English possessed no imagination when naming their kings. The banners meant royalty and royalty made the whores smell wealth. They responded with seductive poses and motioned their welcome to him and the knights who followed behind him, also carrying the royal bearings.

Peasants appeared behind them, asking questions of his men. They had, of course, been ordered to ride in silence.

They approached the portcullis, making no announcements, but their slow trip through the village had created an advance notice to the manor, and they were received immediately. Why would they not believe the banners and livery? Any man caught impersonating royalty would suffer torturous execution by stretching on the wheel.

They climbed the steep slope, gained passage at the gatehouse and inner fortification curtain and entered the bailey.

Three men stood at the main entrance, flanked by six mounted knights. The assassin assessed them based on the information given to him by Wagg. High boots, good leather, cotehardies of good fabric—had to be the brothers. Tall and muscular—had to be Christopher. The other, more slender—Humfrye. The third was shorter, lilly-skinned, with arms thin in their sleeves, thin but for his stomach sporting a paunch already. He must be Hugh. With his straggling chin hairs, he resembled a goat. One who spent more time at the tables than on a horse. The third, fourth and fifth born sons. Poor bastards. He had orders for all of them.

"Let's talk in the hall," the assassin said. He addressed the Penryton knights. "You will wait here with the queen's troops." The assassin's men formed a wall, blocking the Penryton knights' path to the manor. He took four of his paid knights with him, but there would be no sword raised against a royal guard this night. The assassin quite enjoyed the invincibility the stolen uniforms had given him.

The Bonwyk brothers proceeded to the great hall, nervous in their furtive glances to each other. Good reason to be afeared; their older brother had offended Queen Margaret, the king in skirts who currently ruled England.

The assassin silenced his inner pity. To succeed, he must fortify himself. He hummed in his head as he always did, distancing himself from their dread, so he barely heard their words as they spoke them.

In the hall, he produced a writ. He opened it, held it out to them, but would not release it from his hands. "It's a writ of attainder. For failure to pay the penalty assessed by the crown to one Lucas Bonwyk, Lord Penry. The queen has sent us to claim his holdings and remove his treasury." The assassin read it loudly, intending that the cluster of guards and manor folk all heard the pronouncement and abandoned any hope of interfering. This was, after all, a royal matter. Any insurgence meant instant death or, worse, torture.

The brothers protested, as he knew they would, denying knowledge of the treasury's whereabouts. The middle son Humfrye grabbed for the writ. The assassin pulled his dagger and stabbed him in the chest.

Christopher lunged toward him and the assassin turned to face him head on, sword raised. The assassin's knights pulled their swords and aimed them at Christopher's head. With effort, the brother contained himself.

When Humfrye breathed his last, the remaining guards and witnesses in the hall shrank back, clustering by the fire.

The assassin sensed a sudden movement to his left and grabbed for the short goat brother but he wiggled free, darted behind a pillar and ran away. Screaming incoherently, he disappeared into the buttery.

Sending one of his knights to capture the goat, he turned to the tall, sturdy one. "Let us look for the storehouse," he said. He signaled Paul, his first knight. Paul struck Christopher with a club and punched him in the gut. He crumpled, and they dragged him down the steps to the lower chambers. He had a rough idea where the armory was. They'd check there first. He sent four other knights into the upper chambers. They were not leaving without the treasury.

The wine cellar was impressive – 20 racks, each with 64 slots for wines, only three racks filled. Sign of a new austerity, perhaps? Christopher babbled about his brother, Luke, how secretive he was to them, how Luke had never revealed the treasure location to them.

The assassin shut out the fear in the brother's eyes, shut out the protests, the fervent vows. Must ignore any emotions from the condemned ones. To feel for others' plights meant certain failure.

Two hours later, they still had not located anything of value. Oh, several books. They had cut the chains securing them in the library and taken those, and the best wines, of course. He had run one of his own knights through when he found him coupling with a chamber maid. He would not tolerate neglect of duties. The maid was comely—he would see her later.

Once he realized Chris wouldn't reveal the treasury location, he killed him—no brother was to be left living—and they searched for the fat little goat. He was nowhere to be found.

Frustrated, he located the mews, took the four best falcons, took eight good horses, set fire to the stables and left. They could sell the horses, tapestries and silver, but Wagg wouldn't pay a single farthing if they were found out. They had best quit the village while the peasants still thought they were Margaret's men. They'd ditch the king's livery and get the hell far away from Penryton before dawn.

* * *

Joya entered the great hall. It was midday, with light streaming in the two large windows. Meagon's red curls framed her freckled face as she supervised the half dozen maids at the large trestle table. Trays of dried rosebuds mingled with other trays of dried rosemary and orris, the chopped wood-like roots of iris flowers. They created a pleasant fragrance cloud that filled the cavernous room. Other trays on the next table held small bags of colorful silks and ribbons with which to tie them.

Aye, that's the way," Meagon said with the same voice of easy authority her mother, Maud, possessed. "Put the old herbs in here." She demonstrated, tossing contents of the spent sachets into a large bin. "We'll be giving those to the parish."

The women washed the old sachets, while others stuffed the clean ones with fresh herbs for the storage chests and bed linens. They worked in a line, each performing their assembling tasks.

At the other end of the hall, women scooped up the soiled rushes and swept the floors of bones and waste from a fortnight of dinners and suppers and begging dogs.

Yet more women balanced on scaffolding above the fireplace and doorways, sweeping the stone walls and tapestries of accumulated dust and soot.

All would be made fresh and clean for the queen's arrival. She had not yet told Tabor when she would come, but it would be soon, and the castle would be orderly for her arrival.

The dust blended with the pleasant fragrances. Joya's nose tickled and she sneezed.

She missed her mother and worried about her increasing fear for Joya's safety. Not having her here—much as she knew Stephen and Nicole needed her—made Joya wish all the more for her presence. The discord brought a strain to Joya. She wished to please her parents but when it came to Luke, it was as if all stores of her obedience had been spent, and she could no longer do their bidding. Not if the cost was letting go of Luke.

She had stored each memory of the time they had shared at the bridge—his smile, the pleasure in his eyes, the playful teasing about the butterflies. Her heart had nigh burst when he held her. It was as if he were the sun and his warmth had burst from the horizon and reached the depth of her bones. She needed the feel of his skin on hers, of his lips on hers, of his eyes on her, a need that left her constantly off balance when he wasn't near. With every breath she took, from the moment she wakened until the moment she lay down to sleep—yes, even in the dark she felt his presence and ached to be with him.

She looked at the stairwell leading to the solar. Perhaps he was there. She must see him.

She lifted a box of candles at the end of the table. "These ... I'll take these to the solar," she said.

"Thank you," Meagon came closer. "I took him his dinner earlier. He's up there," she whispered.

Joya should suffer some degree of embarrassment at wearing her heart on her sleeve. She might just as well have written it on her forehead, "Mad in love." Joya had gone beyond reason, and no longer cared.

Martin was guarding Luke. She felt frost in the air as she passed him.

She found Luke in the solar. He faced the light of the window, his back to her, bending over something at the table. He turned, revealing his profile, with that slight dent in his forehead. Small sticks rested in a pile to his left. He selected one of them and worked at something concealed by his back.

She stopped just past the entrance. "Forgive me for intruding," she said. "I have fresh candles."

He stood and faced her. His lean legs were covered in brown hose and he wore a dark brown girdle. His vivid blue tunic lit his blue eyes. There was an eagerness in them that she had never seen before, a new comfort and welcome, and his smile sent a shiver of wanting through her. "And I have something for you." His voice stirred her, rich and inviting.

She approached him, unaware of her feet touching stone as she crossed the room. Her heart grew light as feathery lion's tooth seeds floating in the air. Finally, she stood before him.

"Here. Let me take that." Luke's fingers touched hers as he relieved her of the box of candles. A gentle fire whispered across her skin wherever he touched, so exquisite it took her breath.

104

He slid the box on the table and turned back to her. "The rain kept me from working on your father's bridge, so I ... I made something for you." He lowered his lashes, a demure gesture that further stole her heart.

He hid something behind him. She tried to peek.

"Let me explain first." He took a deep breath, and she sensed the importance of the moment. "I learned to love bridges as a young boy. Pathways—rivers, roads, highways, the narrow trails animals make through the forests—they all fascinate me. Bridges create new paths."

He reached behind him and presented a small bridge made of delicate sticks of wood.

"Everything about a bridge is good. When I build a bridge, I reach out into the air, into the space between separate bodies of land, and I unite them. I create a new path to somewhere."

"It's extraordinary," Joya said. "And you made it."

He smiled. "From nothing, I create a support structure— then the deck. It can be that simple, or larger, it can become an advanced study in grace—elegant arches, anchored to the earth with sturdy abutments."

Joya watched the faraway look in Luke's eyes, vibrant blue in their passion. His vision. He had opened the door for her.

The model, just smaller than a man's shoe, featured those graceful arches he had mentioned. He handed it to her with the reverence one would offer his heart.

Joya held it, surprised at how light it was. She raised it, looking above and below it. How his man's hands could have created something so small and detailed—she could not imagine. "There are houses on it."

"Aye. It's a residence bridge. Merchants have their shops on it. People live in its houses."

"I ... thank you," Joya said. "I'll treasure it."

"It's just a model. I'd like to show you the real bridges I've built."

She swallowed. "I would love that."

Joya lifted her face for his kiss, heart pounding.

The door creaked all the way open. Martin entered and stood just inside the solar, arms crossed. His eyes were narrowed, disapproving, and he made it clear in his stance that he would not afford them any kind of privacy.

Luke straightened and slanted a look of challenge at Martin, quickly replacing it with an amused smile. Taking her hand, he withdrew a proper distance and brought it to his mouth. His lingering kiss melted the bones in her hand. "Godspeed, my lady. I've enjoyed our visit."

"As have I," Joya said. Body humming, she carried her gift into the hallway, giving Martin a curt nod as she passed.

* * *

Early the next morning, noises woke Joya. A watchtower horn sounded. Visitors. Who?

Armor, metal scraping metal.

Her braiding had come undone during a dream; she brushed the loose hair off her face and acclimated herself. The green silk drapes—her bed. She parted them. Her chamber was still shrouded in the dark silver that precedes dawn.

Outside her window, the drawbridge groaned as it was engaged. Chains clanked as it lowered.

The sound of a few horses approaching, maybe four.

Men's voices.

She had seen Luke at the bridge each of the last four days, had eagerly anticipated seeing him again today. She glanced toward her ablutions table where she had placed the model bridge he'd built for her. Still there, reminding her of his talent, but the urgent sounds outside stole the growing hope she had for his future.

They had come for him.

She flung her covers aside and spread the curtains, punching her arms into the sleeves of her night gown. Throwing on an outer tunic, she rushed without shoes past the solar and down the wide staircase to the great hall.

Outside, the air was moist, the earth fresh. Droplets of condensation clung to the railing. The dew-laden grasses soaked her feet as she ran through them.

"For God's sake, let us pass." A male cried out, his voice scraping hoarsely at the edge of reason. "I must needs see my brother, Lord Penry!"

Relief wilted her, relief that royal troops hadn't arrived to execute Lord Penry, but alarmed that Luke's brother had been driven to raw fright.

The drawbridge gears reversed, and the deck descended to meet with the banks of the moat.

Hugh, Luke's pasty-faced youngest brother, rushed past, his face twisted with fear. He reached the steps, halted his horse and met her father. Hugh gripped Tabor's arms, pulling at his sleeves. They spoke a few words and disappeared inside.

Joya ran through the bailey, vaguely aware of the small stones pummeling her bare feet as she raced up the steps.

Above stairs she found Luke, her father, Hugh, and Tabor's first knight, Fritts Greenlea. Martin and several other guards had gathered at the top of the stairs, too curious to resist eavesdropping, too respectful to come closer.

In the solar, Tabor had seated Hugh and given him a flask of ale. Hugh gulped it in one tip. "I came straight here from Penryton. As God is my witness, Luke," he spoke through labored breathing, evidence of his forty-mile race to Coin Forest. "They came after midnight. Must have been thirty royal knights."

"From Covington?" Joya asked.

Luke glanced at Joya. " How many knights came, Hugh?"

"Thirty!" Fritts said.

"Well, could have been twenty," Hugh corrected. "They arrived without prior announcement, and it was dark—they arrived like thieves—no herald, no courtesies."

Luke grabbed Hugh's small shoulders and turned him so they faced each other. "Was William there?" Luke asked. "My steward," he said to Tabor.

"Nay. He was at his wife's birthing, at the midwife's, in the village," Hugh answered.

"Why was she at the midwife's? Midwives travel to the laboring mother's home."

Hugh's face reddened. "She should have been in confinement, but the babe came early. Her waters spilled while she was in the village." He stumbled along. "They didn't wish to move her."

"Did the knights identify themselves? Whose were they?" Luke asked.

"That she-devil, Margaret's. They presented a writ from her. Humfrye tried to read it and they ran him through. He's gone." Hugh glared at Luke. "We told you. We warned you, but you turned a deaf ear. And now," he swallowed hard, "they also murdered two of our knights, no protocol, no chance. They pulled our arms and bearings from the bridge, the towers, from the great hall."

"You must be mistaken," Tabor said. "Did they wear royal livery?"

"Aye. They came to raid the treasury," Hugh continued.

"Take a breath," Tabor ordered. "You're claiming the queen's troops attacked Penryton?"

"God's blood. Yes. They took Father's sword collection, the books. The spices. The tapestries—and still they weren't satisfied. They demanded Christopher tell them where we stored our coin and jewels. He told them the truth. 'We don't know,' he said. 'Luke has never trusted us with that.'" They slit Christopher's throat, Luke. Slit his throat and while he was gasping for air, the bastard shoved him to the ground like a slain boar. Chris is dead, too." Hugh's voice cracked.

Luke uttered a string of oaths. He looked to Joya. "Do you not see now? This. This is the Margaret I know. When she's not recruiting men and giving out silver swans to her recruits."

Joya shook her head. All she had heard of Margaret, throughout her life, had been the struggle of a devoted wife fighting for her husband's right to the throne, fighting for the right of their son to inherit his birthright. "She would never do this."

"She cares naught for England or her people," Luke said.

A rain of protests fell from the stairwell, guards shouting allegiances to the queen and proclaiming the queen's innocence.

"Silence." Tabor closed the door. "Were they royal guards? You must be absolutely sure before accusing our king and queen. Were the knights in royal livery? Did they wear the king's colors?"

"Red as the blood they drew," Hugh said. "Lions on their chest. Royal killers."

"What did the writ say?"

"Failure to pay the fine, a writ of attainder. That they were there to reclaim your holdings and collect the treasury."

"Did they give you a chance to renounce York's cause? To pledge your faith to the queen?" Tabor asked.

Hugh spit, his face distorted with disgust. "Murderers, all. The leader—a churl, low-born by his speech—he waved the writ in front of us, but didn't let us see it. He demanded the treasury, and all we did was tell him Luke never told us where it is. That's all! God's blood, he even killed one of his own knights before he left Penryton."

"That's the kind of men Margaret recruits." Luke gave a pointed look at Joya. "No wages because she's wasted the royal treasury. Instead, she gives them license to raid."

Luke approached Tabor. "They have brutally killed all but one of my family, Lord Tabor. Please give me an escort of two knights. I assure you we'll go forthwith to Penryton. I must needs bury my kin and fortify my lands."

"You can't fortify them. Margaret has claimed them."

"So you agree. She killed my brothers."

"She would not do that without warning. She would have sent word to me."

"Mayhap she doesn't give a whit about you," Hugh shouted. "Mayhap she'll take your holdings next, and we'll see how strongly you defend her after that."

"You've been scared witless, Hugh. You don't know what you're saying." Tabor slashed his hand in the air. "Silence. All of you. Penry, Margaret has ordered me to keep you here, and I will.

I support my queen. I don't believe she did this. We will learn the truth."

Joya's heart faltered. In light of what happened, her father would keep Luke here, waiting for certain death, without a chance to bury his family? Surely there was time for Luke to pay Margaret's fine before her henchmen came to place Luke on the block.

"Father!" Joya grabbed his arm and walked with him to the cabinet where he stored his maps and court papers. She lowered her voice, showing respect. "His family has been murdered, by Margaret's own men. Surely you will give him a chance to bury his family. Luke can still pay the fine. That and an apology and he'll be freed."

"Would that your mother were here to help you see, Joya. You try my patience with your loyalty to him. You heard for yourself the hatred he holds for Margaret. He refused to respond to her writ, and now he has caused his brothers' deaths. You think he will now embrace Margaret's cause?"

"I think he should have a chance to think through it. He has only now learned of it. Please. I'll—"

Her father's mouth thinned, and he pulled his arm free. "We are beholden to our king and queen." He ground the words out one at a time, his voice stormy. "You will stop meddling. You will step back now, and be the perfect example of an obedient, loving daughter."

His words pierced her heart. "I have always loved you."

"Show it now," he said. "Respect your family. Not this traitor, and the danger he brings to us."

He gave her his back and returned to Luke. "I am deeply sorry for your loss, Lord Penry. I will keep you and your brother safe here, at Coin Forest. I strongly urge you to send word to the queen and make arrangements to pay your fine. Time is running out for you." He leaned in, giving Luke a decided gaze. "Save yourself." He gestured to Hugh, whose brow was wet with perspiration. "Save your brother, and save your father's lands."

"Fritts, please escort Hugh and Lord Penry to their chamber. Post a fresh guard every two hours."

Fritts signaled to the men to join him, and they left the solar.

Tabor turned to Joya. "Margaret will judge our loyalty by how we help her with this." He gave her a sad smile. "A blind man could see that this is hard for you, but I'm relying on you. Your family—everyone in Coin Forest is relying on you to stand with us on this."

He took her hand, turning her to face him. "This is of critical import to England. His bloodline is good. He comes from a good family, but he is a professed enemy of the crown. He holds secrets that threaten King Henry's life. Nothing—please listen to me, nothing you can do will help him." He kissed her forehead. "Your bridge builder will choose his own fate."

* * *

Joya walked through the field of purple iris blooms, listening to the occasional birdsong from the awakening trees. How, she wondered, could such beauty surround her at a time of such pain and uncertainty? She passed the maypole, now void of the colored ribbons, and stopped at the crest of the hill where the Woodborne Parish Church sat amid a field of white daisies. Far below the hill, the mid-day sun shot fingers of light onto the fields and trees that stretched to the horizon, an endless carpet of spring. The earth released the rich aroma of new growth, but dark storm clouds were pressing in, warning of heavy rainfall.

And danger. Distressed after Hugh's terrible news and her father's pointed reminder about loyalties, she had traveled to Ilchester right after mass.

She absently smoothed her hand over her moss green gown. The precision of the tiny pleats at the bodice, so predictable, brought her comfort. Would that her life could be so manageable and orderly. The moss green gown did not lift her spirits as she'd hoped. It was still lovely, though, a style that had to have challenged Sharai's patience with a needle. The bodice was covered with tiny pleats, with a panel of diagonal pleats that traveled below her breasts, set off with clusters of white buttons at the neckline and wrists.

During her time with Luke in the solar—his gift to her, his kiss—he had revealed his passions. Their visits at the bridge over the last few days had revealed things about him, as well. He was a precise man, the way he stacked the wood, and more than a jot stubborn and rigid. He possessed a sense of humor, and he cared for his brothers in spite of their hostilities.

With time to think, Joya recalled the way Christopher had attacked Luke and kindled the hostilities; Luke had only reacted.

Beyond their differences, though, they were his brothers. What pain it must have been for Luke to hear how they had died such wrongful deaths.

Doubts still lingered about their murders. The brothers were loyal to the queen. Could the queen be so callous? She shook her head, unable to accept Hugh's account of that night.

Luke was a good man. He was wrong to believe in York, but he was moved by a deep love for England.

Luke challenged her long-standing beliefs with difficult questions. Why did Joya and her family always refer to Queen Margaret, and not King Henry? Did that not prove that Margaret had already taken the throne for herself, leading the king's armies, recruiting the king's men, depleting the royal treasury? Killing loyal men? Did that not mean that Henry, mentally infirm, fading for months at a time, had already abdicated the throne to her, when he should have abdicated it to the rightful heir, the Duke of York?

Such thoughts hurt her head. The nun's condemning words echoed. She had been too stupid to learn to read when she was twelve and now, much older, she still struggled to find answers to difficult questions. Quick-witted men like her father, clever thinkers like her mother—they could see past the puzzling array of facts, and they had concluded that their queen was well-intentioned and good for England.

Now, doubts visited, and guilt burdened her as she started doubting her parents' judgment. Until now, Joya had never created more than mischief. Her family was the fire of her life, offering light in darkness, warmth to chase the cold, fuel to heat her chamber and sweeten the great hall with life-sustaining meats and breads.

She planned to openly defy them.

Her heart pounded so hard in her chest that it became difficult to breathe.

If she didn't act, though, thoughts of Luke's fate terrified her. What would Margaret do to Luke? Torture methods flashed in her mind, weakening her knees. Mutilation. Getting broken on the wheel. Drawn and quartered.

And what of her? If she succeeded with her plans, her head may roll. Mayhap in front of her mother's eyes.

She had reached the church steps. She pressed the latch and opened the front door.

Inside, Pru, Camilla and George sat at the collection table. Camilla had impressed upon George the barbaric manner in which Margaret had killed Luke's brothers. She had reassured George that his part in their plans was very small and would have no repercussions for him, but he could save the Bonwyck brothers' lives—whilst gaining great favor from Mistress Camilla.

Pru had been easy to recruit. She held a soft spot for Luke, and being the romantic, she was horrified to think that Luke would be killed after Joya had become so fond of him. She, too, had been angered by Margaret's brutality.

At her father's order Peter had accompanied her here, and his presence had given Joya an idea. She would create a sense of calm. Through Peter, she would convince her father that she had stopped meddling and become, once again, a dutiful daughter. If her deception worked, she would free Luke.

Joya took a chair at the table. To mislead Peter, she must appear sure of herself. It was vital that he believe what he heard them say. And he would hear, because after a few furtive glances and carefully staged whispers with her friends, she knew he would eavesdrop.

"What are you planning?" George asked.

"Wait." Cam closed the door and checked the window. "Where's Peter?"

Hopefully in one of the many nearby alcoves, spying. "I sent him to the village on an errand," Joya said. "We have time." She took a deep breath and proceeded. "My father sent word to Margaret. She'll be here on Monday." She turned to George and did not lower her voice. "We're going to help Luke and Hugh escape before Margaret arrives."

"At Coin Forest? You jest," George said. "It's crawling with knights."

"Just listen," Joya said. "I'm thinking past midnight on Saturday would be a good time. It will be crowded. Lord and Lady Onslow and their household will be there. The Westchester musicians are coming and the hall will be crowded with merchants and townfolk. The gatehouse will be busy watching all of them traveling back and forth from the village."

"What guards are scheduled Saturday night?" George asked.

They discussed ways they could distract the guards, and considered using the tunnel to free Luke and Hugh.

Joya snapped her fingers. "I know where the keys are kept. During the music—that's when I could get them."

"I don't like it," George said. "Tabor's knights are disciplined, and he's no one's fool."

"I have to say the same, Joya," Pru said. "Someone could get hurt. If we're trying to avoid more bloodshed, this is not the plan."

"How about this," Cam said. "Why don't we petition Margaret for leniency, and point out that she's already taken Luke's treasury?"

"Why would she listen?" Joya asked.

"Because she needs us to fight," George said. "Between Coin Forest, Faierfield and Ilchester there are at the least fifty knights to fight her battles. Find a way to delicately remind her that she shouldn't be murdering men who are loyal to her."

"Talk to your father," Pru said.

"But what about my plan?" Joya asked.

"It's ill-conceived," Pru said. "Trying to free Luke—well, it's dull thinking, Joya."

Joya's neck heated. She knew it was said only for effect, but it cut too close to her heart.

"I'm sorry," Pru rushed on. "I don't want you to be hurt. And you surely don't want your father choosing between you and the rest of his family, and his holdings."

"We're not criminals," Cam said. "We're your friends. We can't draw a sword or—"

"Speak for yourself, Camilla," George said.

Camilla gave him an impish smile. "Well, we women can't draw a sword or fight." She sobered. "Forget about this. Trust Tabor to handle Margaret."

Joya paused. Now she would back off the plan, loudly and clearly enough that Peter would hear it and relay it to her father. They would think her friends talked sense into her, and they wouldn't suspect anything."You're right. It won't work. I was foolish to think it could."

"I understand your concerns for the Bonwyks," Camilla said. "I'm loyal to King Henry, but we mustn't forget, Margaret is French, and you know how they are."

"Remember Agincourt," Pru said.

Camilla laughed. "You weren't even born yet."

"But we know the stories," Pru insisted. "The French are brutal. They think all can be solved with their swords. We need to remind Margaret she's in England. Ask your father to impress that upon her."

"You're right, Pru," Joya said. "Let's forget all this, and I'll talk with him."

"Now, Joya, that doesn't get you out of your invitation," Cam said. "Let's go to Pru's and wait for Peter to return. Then back to Coin Forest for music and some of Maud's boar's head soup."

As they left the church, Joya spotted movement in the bushes by the cemetery. A sideways glance at George and her friends confirmed that they had seen it, too.

Chapter 10

Two days later, Joya and her friends cleared the hill toward the Halfway Bridge. The horses nickered amiably in the high grass. It was midday, and above, a thin sun begged through a flat cloud layer. Joya reined Goldie to a stop and removed her travel cape. She wore a gown the color of the setting sun, an orange fabric that had caught her mother's eye at the Southampton market. Joya had selected the amber necklace her sister, Faith, had made for her because it matched the gown so well.

Beneath the simple bodice, her heart skittered. Her hands were so moist the reins slipped in her fingers, her armpits damp. She chided herself silently. *What's wrong with you? You have the perfect plan. Luke gets saved, no one gets hurt, and no one will know what you did.* An ingenious plan, remarkable that she had thought of it.

Below the bridge the Ten Mile River wore a feathery collar of weeping willows, their leaves still bright with spring green.

Cam tilted her head, looking into Joya's eyes. "Scared?"

Joya swallowed hard. "If it weren't my own family at stake, it would be easier. There'll be no going back. What are you doing, coming with me?"

Cam laughed. "I wouldn't miss it. You'll be beholden to me forever."

"It's a sound plan at first glance, but things could go awry. Cam? You can still go back and not do this."

Cam looked away, staring into the thick stand of trees to the left. "Loyalty. It's expected of us. For that we get to live in peace. We're not murdered on our own land for a transgression we had no part of."

"It's wrong," Joya agreed.

"Margaret has stepped too far with this," Pru said. "It's one thing to fight for the throne, and it's another to kill innocents."

"Luke is stupid to defend York," Cam said, "but I understand his opposition to Margaret. I didn't before, but now I do. Besides, she's French. England's throne should not hold French leaders. At least York is English."

A tingle crawled down Joya's scalp all the way down her back. "You support York?"

"I didn't say that. I'm saying King Henry should sit on the throne, but if he can't, we don't need some Frenchwoman sitting on it."

"Pru, it's not too late for you, either. You can go back."

"No. I can't support what's happened. Let's get Luke away."

Joya cleared her throat. "If it fails, run your horses as fast as you can back to the castle. Tell them I slipped into a wild spell and lost my senses. Save yourselves."

"Joya. Let's not get maudlin," Cam said. "The plan is good. We'll all be victims. They'll never suspect." She scanned the woods to the left, lingering on the small yellow bush they'd discussed earlier.

"I've been watching it, too," Pru said. "George isn't here yet."

"He will be," Cam said. "You can count on him. Your plan is sound, Joya. I see your father trusted Luke to finish the bridge. Looks like Peter believed what he heard at the church. He must have told your father we were no threat."

Thank the Lord, Joya thought. Luke was at the saw rack, working alone again, but today he was more closely guarded. Twenty feet downstream, Peter, the old knight Ralph, and two other knights sat on the grass, eating their midday meal. They had brought only breastplate armor, which remained tied to their horses. They didn't expect trouble.

117

"You're brave," Cam said. "Lead the way."

They rode down to the bridge. Luke had removed his tunic, baring his chest. Joya gaped, unable to take her eyes off him. He had continued to shave the growth from his jaw, but kept the shadow of a mustache. His brown hair was wet with sweat, strands of hair fused and scattered above his eyes. Beads of moisture glistened at his temple, and the sun lit his eyes to an impossibly deep blue. His pulse throbbed at the base of his throat. He was alive.

Of course he's alive, Stupid. Gather your senses.

He avoided Joya's eyes, looking somewhere between her and Cam. "Good morrow."

"Good morrow," Joya answered, her body humming at the sight of him.

An awkward silence followed, and Cam dismounted. "I see they've let you out again. I'm surprised they'd trust you."

"We don't," shouted Peter from a few feet away on the riverbank. "That's why Tabor sent us along." He pointed a finger at Cam. "And why his brother is still under guard in the castle."

Cam and Pru looked to Joya. They hadn't expected that. Fah! How could they get Hugh free?

"I wanted to finish this for Tabor before I leave." Luke's deep voice touched her, a rich, deep melody that made it hard to think clearly.

Joya looked instinctively to the small yellow bush. Nothing white was visible yet, the signal George would post to let them know he had arrived. Had he been delayed? Her heart skipped. Caught?

She freed the leather sack from Goldie's saddle. "We brought refreshments for you." She spread a blanket on the bridge deck and placed cold meats, cheese and bread on the oilcloth. With enthusiasm she presented a large red bowl and made a big show of it, holding it up in the air. "We have a special treat. Roasted apricot seeds. All the way from Burgundy."

"By Gosse!" old Ralph exclaimed from downstream. "Might we have some, too?"

The seeds were a delicacy, and an indulgent one. Sharai hoarded them for holidays and special guests, and she'd split a seam when she found them gone. But they were tempting enough to distract the men. Joya opened the lid and poured them ceremoniously out of the bowl into Cam's and Pru's hands. "These seeds are so good," Joya said. "I'll bring some over to you and your men, Peter, after we've had our fill," Joya said.

Cam popped some in her mouth and crunched. "Mmm, salty."

"Nutty. Delicious," Pru said through munches.

"Would you like some?" she asked Luke. He slipped into his tunic, took a modest amount and settled on the blanket with them. "My thanks." He took one at a time, wordless, but his eyes closed as he chewed. Through all the nervousness, Joya fought a searing need to be close to him.

After carefully counted minutes, Joya started the final part of her plan. Hands shaking, she leaned forward, concealing the bowl from Luke's view. She secretly gathered a half dozen seeds and nestled them in her left hand. With her right hand she unstoppered a tiny vial of oil and poured its contents into the red bowl with the rest of the apricot seeds. In a series of smooth movements she stirred the seeds with the empty vial then slipped it into her boot top, and stood.

She lifted the bowl with her right hand and, careful to keep the dry seeds safe in her palm, hiked her skirt with her left hand to better navigate the uneven ground to reach the knights. Giving another special smile to Peter, she raised the bowl. "I saved some for you."

At her arrival, the knights rose hastily to honor her. She waved, indicating they could settle back down on the grass, and she offered Ralph the seeds.

Ralph picked a single seed from the bowl, the delicate gesture from his big, calloused hands amusing.

"Make free of them," Joya said. "We've had our fill."

Ralph plunged his hand into the bowl, spilling some, and the other knights cursed him, scrambling to pluck them from the tall grass.

"Here, Peter, before they get them all," Joya said, pouring the last dozen or so into his hands.

"My thanks. You're good to us," Peter said.

She studied his face. He looked as if he would eat her up along with the seeds, and she fought to keep her smile intact. If he suspected anything, he was hiding it well. "So Peter, what are the plans, do you know? Have Lord and Lady Onslow arrived yet?"

"They're to arrive after noon. They'll stay a sennight."

And Margaret would arrive on the morrow.

The Onslows' visit was well timed. Not only good friends of her parents, they were frequent guests of the queen. Their presence would be a good reminder to Margaret that Joya's family was part of a small circle of her most loyal subjects. Arranging her skirts to protect herself from ants, she sat near Peter. "Have you heard they're bringing Catherine Bradshaw with them? She's played several times for King Henry. They say when she plays the harp, it sounds like the music of angels. And with Margaret coming at the same time—so much excitement."

"You sound like an angel when you sing," Peter responded. He continued complimenting her voice, and the harmony she and her brother Stephen lent to the parish hymns. The words blended one with the other into a verbal soup, incomprehensible, so hypnotized she was by the way he rolled the seeds in his hands while he talked. Her teeth hurt from clenching them as he lifted a seed to his mouth, only to continue talking and drop his hand back down to his lap again. He moved on to a discussion of the Onslows and the three pigs they would butcher for the feast.

Joya casually raised the dry seeds she had stored in her hand, retrieving one seed at a time with her tongue, drawing it into her mouth, chewing and moaning with pleasure to Peter's rapt attention. Finally her seeds—and what she hoped was a convincing demonstration of the wholesomeness of the seeds— were finished. If she lingered any longer with Peter, it would be awkward. She rose, straightening her skirts, forcing her gaze to the river. When she looked back, Peter had popped three seeds into his mouth. He sucked the salt and oil from the seeds and crunched noisily.

Relief made her want to dance; instead, she methodically straightened her skirts. "We'll need to get ready for tonight. We'll be on our way."

"Thank you for sharing," Peter said. "And perhaps tonight," he added, lifting a brow, "you'll wear your red gown."

Joya's eyes widened at his audacity, and Ralph and the other knights laughed.

Back at the bridge, Luke had already returned to his work, and Pru and Cam glanced at her, questions in their eyes.

She nodded slightly and sat back down, portioning the meats and cheeses so they would last.

They fussed with the cheese, cutting precisely, their movements rusty, almost creaking as they bided time. Cam stared at the yellow bush, her face tense.

Joya looked, too. A breeze ruffled a small patch of white on the yellow bush. George had arrived.

Luke straightened and lowered his voice. "What goes here? Why do you all keep looking behind me?" He turned and looked at the woods behind him, and back to Joya.

Downstream, the men had grown quiet. Ralph had lain down.

"It's working," Cam whispered.

Joya jerked her head to the right. Ralph was supine on the grass, hand thrown over his eyes. The other two were prone, but Peter remained upright. "Joya," he called, his tongue thick and slow. He dropped to one elbow.

Luke followed her gaze. "What happened? What's wrong with them?"

"We're freeing you."

"What? What did you do to them?"

"Don't worry," Joya whispered to him. "It's the apricot seeds. They're coated with an herb for sleeping."

Luke pulled back. "By the saints!"

"It's all right. Your seeds were not coated. My mother has used this herb many times. She gave it to Nicole for morning sickness." Joya pointed to the yellow bush behind him. "George is there. He's brought a horse for you. You can go."

"What mean you?" Luke's wide-eyed look was not what she had expected.

"You're free. You can go home. Bury your brothers. Claim what's left of your estate and go where Margaret can't find you."

"Nay. Nay!" He grabbed Joya's shoulders. "How long does the spell last?"

"It's not a spell. I told you. They're herbs. They will sleep a few hours—two, maybe three. You may be home before they wake. George has provisions for you—clothes, better boots, food. You need to go now."

"Joya," Peter called again. Holy Virgin. He was groggy, but awake. The fool hadn't eaten enough seeds. She turned to Luke. "You must go."

"God's nails, how? Think you I would leave without my brother?" He paced, eyes darting, considering possibilities. "'Tis done. We can't undo it. We'll need to send for help. Tell your father about the seeds. They're foreign. Tainted, and you didn't know it. You'll apologize."

"Luke, lower your voice," Joya whispered. "Peter only ate a few. See there, he's still awake."

"Exactly, but we can explain it away. You foolish girl—girls. Why did you do this? If word gets out, your father will have no choice but to punish you."

"She did it for you, you dumb goose," Cam said, striking his arm. "You'll be dead in two days if you stay, then what good will you be to your brother?"

"Nothing will be solved if I run in disgrace. I've already lost my holdings. My brothers will have a proper burial—even Margaret will have the decency to allow that."

"You need to get far enough away to be safe," Joya said.

He straightened. "I am a Bonwyk, not some common criminal who would hole up on the continent. England is my home."

"Time is running, Luke. You must—"

"Have you thought what this will do to Tabor? What will he say when Margaret comes for me? Will he risk himself to save your life? Yes he will, because he's a good man. He will die for your—for this reckless betrayal."

His face grew red, his eyes narrow. "Stupid girl! What gave you the right to speak for me? Do I look like such a coward to you?"

He looked handsome. Virile. But her last glimpse of him would be of the back of his neck, under an executioner's blade. "No," Joya shouted. "You don't look like a coward. But you do look much better with a head on your shoulders."

He spun away from them. "I'm going to help Peter now. Take your horses, your friends and your foolish ideas, and go. I'm staying here."

Cam grabbed a board from Luke's flawless wood stack and hiked it high. "No you aren't, you ass." She swung it fiercely into the side of Luke's head.

Luke's legs buckled, and he fell to the ground.

Joya gasped. "What have you done? Cam!"

Cam bent to his face. "He's breathing. He's out, but probably not for long. What a stubborn man." She tried to stifle a smile that tugged at her mouth, and failed. "And he does look much better with a head on his shoulders." She started giggling in spite of herself. "Much better," she repeated, her laughter growing into noisy, beastly snorts.

Pru joined her with her soft, tittering laugh.

It was contagious. After the last hour, laden with worry about their apricot seed ambush and whether they would get caught red-handed, they had succeeded in conquering a handful of experienced knights and one blustering bridge builder.

And Luke still had his head. It made no sense, but it was mightily amusing. Joya laughed as well, her giggles bubbling like an untended stewpot, overflowing, making her gasp.

They continued laughing, and tears formed in Joya's eyes.

Hoofbeats sounded, and George arrived with two saddled horses. "What goes here? What has overcome you all?" he asked. "What happened to him?" He gestured toward Luke.

"He's an idiot," Cam said, her laughter fading. "He refused to go. Stubborn as an old cat."

"And why is he still awake?" George asked, pointing at Peter.

"He didn't eat enough seeds," Joya said, subdued. "I don't think he can ride. I don't know how long he'll be sluggish like that."

Peter's arm slid in the grass, and his head fell to the ground.

George dismounted and embraced Cam. "What can we do?"

"We've gone too far to turn back." Cam's voice lacked its usual bold edge. She rubbed the palm of her hand repeatedly on her skirt as if to clean it. "We have committed treason."

They looked at each other, and the fear in her friends' eyes paralyzed Joya. She dropped her gaze to the river and a net of silence fell over them. The ceaseless bubble of the tumbling water should have soothed her, but the ill-starred rescue, the danger into which she had pulled all of them, lightened Joya's head. The sound of the water swirled into her memory—the shocking cold when she had plunged into the water, her hands bound and the powerful fingers of current pulling her to her death. She reached for Luke's wooden workhorse to steady herself, yet still the river warned her that time continued to run.

She yearned to go home, to safety. "We could leave them all here," Joya said. "Go back to the castle, like Luke said. Tell them it was bad seeds…" Weakness settled in her veins, and her hands trembled as she touched the growing bump on the side of Luke's head. His head…

Their laughter had not chased away their fright. She could not watch his head roll. "He must leave before Margaret gets here." Joya stood and turned to George. "Do we have rope?"

"No."

It was Joya's turn to pace. She pulled at her hair and gritted her teeth at his cursed stubbornness. Her plan was supposed to be a gift to him, the gift of his life, and he was supposed to have been bold and clever and grateful. It would have all looked like an accident and somehow all of this would blow over. No one would have been hurt—the men would recover quickly, there would be no beheading—everything would have been good eventually.

Luke lay sprawled where he had fallen, looking peaceful and innocent. He had crashed into her life and nothing was the same. She looked at the road back home to Coin Forest. How could she go there now? Peter was awake enough to remember—and tell—all. They couldn't feign sleep, couldn't pretend the seeds were corrupted and had made them all fall asleep, that only Luke had not been affected and had mysteriously escaped. All excuses were lame. She couldn't go home and face her father.

"Fine." Her voice sounded old and harsh to her own ears. All was lost, except Luke. "Tie him to the horse." She raised her gown, reaching under for the linen. She bit into the fabric a few inches above the hem and ripped four strips free. "Here." She tossed two to George. You bind his hands, we'll do his feet and load him onto the horse. Get him secure."

Once he was trussed tightly, George turned to her. "He was supposed to ride away, free, while you pretended to recover from the seeds." His gaze stayed fixed on Joya. "Who's going to ride with him?"

Joya straightened, too committed and too guilty to return home. "I will." As the words passed her lips a vision assaulted her, one of herself walking to the block and facing her executioner. A vision of her mother, witnessing the last moments of her life.

Cam stepped forward. "I will ride with you. I'm not going back there."

Pru stepped forward. "I will ride with you, too, Joya."

"Can they trace the horse you brought for Luke?" Joya asked George.

"Only if they're thorough," George said. "I bought him from an innkeeper way over in Foxton."

"Can you slip back to Coin Forest unnoticed?" Joya asked George.

"Peter has seen him," Pru said. "He can't go back."

"Here we are," George said. "Let's all go while we still can."

"Where to?" Joya asked. They hadn't considered this. Their plan had been to simply send Luke on his way.

"Certes not Penryton," Cam said. "They'll go there first."

"Not Ilchester, either," Pru said. "They'll go there to look for Cam and me."

"Winchester," Joya said. "My sister, Faith, will help us."

"That's too far. It would take a week to get there." Cam shook her head. "The rest of my family is almost all the way to London."

Pulse pounding in her temples, Joya thought of someone. A beautiful woman, not family, exactly, but close. Joya had known her all her life. She was bright and resourceful, and she, too, had been in trouble in the past; she would understand. Married to a knight in good standing with the church, should they need to seek sanctuary. To reach her was only a day's journey.

"Kadriya."

* * *

"There's Cerne," Joya said. In the bowl-shaped valley below, the moonlight turned the small village a light blue. It was so late that all the fires had died but those on the city walls. Joya shifted in her saddle. The hills surrounding Cerne were difficult for horses and riders alike.

"It's small," George said.

"Yes, mainly merchants that supply the monks, and the usual herdsmen and tillers," Joya said. "And there's the abbey." At three stories tall, it dominated the valley.

"Dreary," Cam said.

"It's pretty in the daylight," Joya said. "Golden. Its stone was quarried from Kingston." Two bells rang out. "Matins," she said. "We should make it to Kadriya's before dawn."

Prudence rode behind her. She yawned again and Luke, riding next to her, remained silent. His head had to be pounding from Cam's blow. He had cursed and threatened them when he had first awakened, and they had ignored him. After a few miles Joya relented and released him, all but his hands, and she kept his reins. She stayed deaf to his pleas to be released. He remained too eager to face Margaret's wrath, but Joya would avoid that for as long as she could. She had compromised her reputation, her standing—in truth, her head—to save his thankless soul; she wasn't about to let him return to his death.

Five miles past the abbey, John and Kadriya's small country manor came into sight, bringing fond memories of childhood trips. "There it is!" The tension in her shoulders vanished, and her heart swelled with affection and a deep sense of belonging. Her bones ached from neck to feet, she could smell the hours of fear and horse sweat on her gown, and her stomach growled with hunger, but they had made it to Kadriya's.

"Nice estate," George said.

Dogs barked, announcing their arrival, and lights bloomed in the windows.

"The horse stables have been expanded, I see," Joya said. "Kadriya boards horses and tends to the sick ones." She turned to Luke, her dagger poised. "Give me your hands."

"You would release me now?"

His public condemnation of her as stupid still stung, and she was losing her patience with his indifference to his own death. "You will dismount. You'll not take this horse as you did Goldie. Promise me that and I'll release you." Joya dismounted and gave Luke's horse's reins to George.

"I will not steal your horse." Luke dismounted and presented his bound hands.

His eyes lacked any warmth.

This man was difficult. Joya had upended her life to help him, and he was nothing but deeply affronted. "If you choose to run on foot back to Coin Forest, I won't stop you. But methinks it will be much smarter to accept food and rest here before you hurry off to your beheading."

Three men on horseback rode to the gate. "Who goes there?"

"It's me, Joya. I've come to see Kadriya."

John Wynter rode out to meet them. He was first knight at the abbey and as tall as Joya remembered, tall and barrel-chested, with light brown hair turned white at the temples. After introductions, they entered the manor gate and tethered their horses.

An older couple appeared, bearing a torch, and the long-haired woman ran toward them, braided hair flying. "Joya!" Kadriya wore an orange robe with white trim. The green of her eyes shone in the torchlight. Fine lines that weren't there before etched her face, but her teeth were still white and her skin was as light as Joya remembered, still smooth and fair.

"Ves' tacha!"

My beloved. Joya's eyes stung at the word of endearment. Kadriya hugged her. "What's amiss? Sharai—"

"Is fine," Joya finished, "and Tabor and everyone is fine." Loath to bring bad news, her smile faded. "I—we—are in trouble."

John's eyes narrowed. "What kind of trouble? Has someone died?"

"Aye, men from Penryton—you don't know them," Joya said. "It will take some time for the telling, but we have done nothing like that."

Joya introduced George and Cam, who stood together, hands held. She introduced Pru and turned to Luke. "And this is Lucas Bonwyck, Lord Penry."

Kadriya looked him over, turned to Joya, and raised an eyebrow. "I see."

Joya blushed in the torchlight, and Kadriya smiled. "Come in. You're all most welcome. Matthew," Kadriya turned to the older man, "please stable their horses. Now, come in and let's hear your story."

A series of sharp cries came from the hallway as they entered. There on the upper stairway stood a short, hairy imp of a creature, white-haired, jumping up and down and poking his hairy arms through the railing. He wore a red patterned diaper.

"Prince Malley!" Joya had been too distraught to wonder if the little monkey would still be alive. He screeched non-stop, holding his arms out to her.

Joya lifted her skirts and ran up the steps. She held his head in her hands, scratching behind his ears. "Prince Malley. Good boy. Good little boy."

Prince Malley moaned softly and chattered.

"How sweet," Pru said.

Cam shrank back. "Does he have fleas?"

"No more than our dogs," Kadriya said.

Prince Malley leaped to her shoulders, wrapped his big feet around her waist and stroked Joya's face. He snuggled his head into her shoulder.

She danced with him. "I missed you, too, Prince Malley."

Luke looked up at her, his blue eyes dazed. He was the only one who remained untouched by the monkey's affectionate greeting to Joya. Mayhap he was still groggy from the blow to his head, or thought he was having a very strange dream.

John Wynter nudged Luke with his elbow. "He's a hairy little screamer. He's all right, but don't let him sleep with you or get near your horse."

Two boys raced from their chamber. "Aunt Joya!"

"Sam! Robert!" They resembled their father, and perhaps their grandfather, as well. Kadriya's mother had been with a fair-haired nobleman from Southampton. When she died Sharai had taken Kadriya in as a little sister.

Joya shifted Prince Malley to one arm and opened the other to the boys. "You're taller than I am now." She had to reach up to hug them.

They told Joya about their horses and the sheep they were raising.

John watched them with pride. "Do you need my help, Joya?"

"We may need sanctuary. Do you think the abbot will help us if we do?"

"I'll speak on your behalf should you need it." He paused. "I meet with the abbot after lauds. I need some rest before I leave. I'll see you all for the midday meal." He and Kadriya shared an intimate glance and he took the stairs.

Kadriya sent the boys back to bed. She showed Joya, Pru and Cam their chamber, giving the back chambers to Luke and George. Later, she called them to her hall, where she offered them each a tankard of ale and a large platter of meats and bread. "Eat. You can't think on an empty stomach."

After the food vanished, Kadriya scooted closer to the table. "Let's hear your story now. Are you running from someone?"

Joya picked up the monkey, who had been waiting for them to finish their breakfast. "This is difficult. We are in big trouble, Kadriya."

"You can tell me all. I understand. I have had my share."

"With the abbey, I remember." Of a sudden Joya realized their experiences were similar. Over a decade ago, Kadriya had defended a man accused of stealing, which angered the abbot. "I defied my father ... and Queen Margaret."

Kadriya's hand went to her throat. "How?"

"I'll understand if you want to send us on our way. We do not want to bring trouble to your door." Joya explained Luke's loyalty to York, Margaret's huge fine, and Luke's brothers' brutal deaths, omitting her growing affection for Luke, and that moment of passionate kisses in the gaol.

Cam and Prudence stepped in with details from time to time, but George and Luke remained silent.

Kadriya's expression revealed little. Occasionally her green eyes would widen with shock, and when Joya described the apricot seeds, Kadriya lost her composure and gasped.

"Joya's plan was sound." Cam defended her, and Joya's heart swelled at her friend's loyalty. "Until this id—until Luke," Cam corrected, "refused to leave Coin Forest. Had he left, none would have been the wiser."

Luke's eyes narrowed and he shot forward, gripping the table. "By the light of heaven! You dare to dismiss this as a midday feast gone bad? None the wiser? What of the queen? What of Hugh, still detained and soon to face her? And by this deception I have become a fugitive."

Cam slammed the table with her fist. "Uttered like the thankless, ill-mannered ox you are. You can't see all she's sacrificed—"

Prince Malley jumped up from Joya's lap, emitting a series of short cries and pulling his fur.

"Cease!" Kadriya said. "Brawling will not solve this, and you have upset Prince Malley."

Joya apologized, soothing him. "If we can rest for a few hours, Kadriya. If you can spare, we need funds to travel. And I would seek your counsel on what we should do next."

"You needn't leave." Kadriya glanced pointedly at Luke and Cam. "So this is your plight, Joya." Kadriya ticked off points with her fingers. "You have angered the queen. You have defied your father. You have risked his friendship with the queen. You have risked your family's holdings. You have involved your friends in an act of treason. You have worsened the plight of Lord Penry, here, and you have soiled your reputation and now risk your own execution. Have I missed anything?"

Joya stroked Prince Malley's fur, blanching under the damning facts. "No."

Kadriya patted Joya's hand. "You must have faith. I was as desperate as you that one time, and I found a way. You will, too."

Kadriya stood. "You all look exhausted. Go abovestairs and rest. We'll break our fasts at nine bells. Prince Malley will stay with me." She took the monkey. He chattered in protest, but she held him firmly and started up the steps. "I trust you will be staying, Lord Penry."

Nodding, he gave her a tight smile. "You have my word."

Chapter 11

During their pre-dawn ride to the abbey, Luke took measure of the man riding beside him, John Wynter, first knight of the abbot and Kadriya's husband. Tall. Muscular, big legs and chest—must have weighed sixteen or seventeen stones. Luke would want Wynter on his side in any battle.

Luke's head throbbed, an insistent pain to the right of his eye. It had been Camilla who had struck him, of course—always needling him with her brash comments and horse-like laughter. His back ached from being tied on the saddle, and the side of his neck was stiff from bumping against the stirrup bar.

But he wore clean clothes, smelling fresh from the sun, loaned to him by Wynter, and they had broken their fast with bacon and bread. Wynter had been as generous as Tabor.

But he needed to contact York. He had to know by now of Luke's aborted trip to Christchurch and his arrest in Coin Forest. Did he and Salisbury know that Margaret had found his notes?

Margaret would pursue him. Once he hired guards to accompany him, Luke would hurry to Christchurch. He could only hope to find York and Salisbury there. Darkness was lifting, and the sky had turned golden to the east. They would arrive at the abbey after first light at five bells.

"You support York," Wynter said. It wasn't a question.

Luke didn't want to get on Wynter's bad side, but he was not ashamed of his loyalties. "Yes." He went on to explain why. The more people he told, the more people who might think more carefully about the harm Margaret was doing, and stop her before she destroyed England.

"I'm sorry for the loss of your brothers," Wynter said. "I find it difficult to believe that Margaret would do that."

"Had you heard my brother's account of it, you would believe it," Luke said.

"If you're to seek sanctuary at Cerne Abbey, it would be best if you avoided accusing her of murder in front of the Abbot. He's loyal to King Henry."

"I will avoid accusations," Luke said.

"The abbot and I have been friends for many years. We served together in France. He has been good to me. I owe him much."

"I will not cause any trouble. I give you my word. I need only summon funds and hire guards. I hope to be granted sanctuary, along with Joya and her friends. My conscience will be settled knowing they won't suffer for having tried to help me." He shook his head. "It was such a foolish, senseless thing to do."

"Kadriya told me about the seeds. It was a clever idea—incapacitate four knights without killing them, provide a horse for your escape, and present a credible excuse for Joya and her friends afterwards. But Joya has always been good with people. They flock to her, and she understands even the most sour, difficult people."

Like you. He didn't finish the thought, but Luke felt the insult sting as it hit. Over the years, Luke had grown accustomed to being misliked. As far back as he could remember, he preferred being alone with his own thoughts and projects. People mistook his ways as being cold and judgmental.

"Joya has stayed with us many times over the years," Wynter continued. "To Kadriya and me, she is like a sister. When it's time for her to return to Coin Forest, my sons are sad for days. She can chatter like Prince Malley, and she sings like a nightingale."

Angry as he was with her, Luke had to admit that Joya was comely and charming. He had no defense against those big brown eyes of hers, how they grew heavy-lidded with a deep hunger that matched his own. The way she carried herself, breasts high, her movements smooth as a breeze, her hands expressive when she talked, flying like those butterflies at the bridge, dancing in the air. Her hair, thick and smooth in his fingers, straight as a blade and always sweet, the fragrance of lilacs in spring.

Wherever she was, other people gathered. She attracted people like ants at the table. Luke shuddered. Groups of people sapped the strength from his bones and made the air hard to breathe. Joya thrived on people, the more the better. That part of her troubled him, and it was a big part.

But when it was only the two of them, she was tempting, exciting. He lusted for her as he had never lusted for a woman before, but the two of them were like sugar and vinegar. Darkness and light.

"Did you hear me? Luke?"

Startled, Luke turned to Wynter. "What?"

"I said, if you're so certain Margaret's men killed your brothers, don't you have one lick of appreciation for what Joya did for you? She freed you from Coin Forest so you can do whatever it is you have to do, even if it means treason. For you, she has risked all. She has been forced to leave her home and family. She may die for her actions."

Wynter reined his horse and faced him, his blue eyes—lighter than Luke's, and cold. "I'm fond of Joya. She's a generous woman who seems to care for you, but I can't see why. It sickens me that your only comment about all she's done for you is that it was a foolish, dumb thing to do."

Heat spread up Luke's neck. Wynter was right. "I'm sorry to appear ungrateful." He rode on, burdened with the truth with which Wynter had slapped him. "I—am not comfortable talking of my feelings. I am responsible for her plight, for the plight of the others. I didn't ask to be rescued, but because of me, their lives are in danger." He looked to the sky and back. "It's a favor I can never repay. It's a problem I have no way of solving. It makes me angry." *And I have been blaming her. It's easier.*

Wynter offered no consoling words, and they rode on in silence. Finally, Luke faced him. "If I succeed with what I do for York, my brother will be released. Joya and the others will be deemed heroic. If I fail, they will all be punished. Severely. I know this."

"Good," Wynter said. "Or I would have to hit you on the other side of your head." Wynter's expression was serious. "I would lock you in the abbey until you reveal your plans against the king. I will recommend this to the abbot."

"Lord Tabor has been gracious, and Joya saved my life," Luke said. "I vow to you, I will die if need be to succeed at my mission. It's all I can do."

"You can consider that there are always more paths than one. Joya didn't save you, only to have you die. I think the lady has other plans for you."

Luke inhaled deeply and exhaled, unsteady. Yes, he feared that, too.

* * *

Luke wended his way through the village market. He had met with the abbot, who had granted Luke's request for sanctuary. They would all travel to the abbey on the morrow. So long as they stayed there, they would be safe from Margaret's troops and any retribution they might have planned.

But Luke would not be sequestering himself within the abbey walls. This was his chance to end Margaret's run, to free not only Joya and her friends, but the whole of England.

Using the abbey's messenger pigeons, Luke had sent one message to an abbey in Dublin to eventually reach York, and another message to a parish near his uncle to be delivered to Luke's money changing merchant. He would issue a bill of exchange to repay Wynter. The bill would allow Luke to pay for provisions for himself and the three guards he had hired.

Once again he sent a prayer of thanks skyward, relieved that he had not stored his funds at Penryton. Margaret's thieves had stolen his household treasures, but having his life funds stored elsewhere had spared him major losses. Before tomorrow's daybreak they would leave for Christchurch, some thirty miles away.

Cerne was small, but its market was bustling. Luke's skin crawled as he moved through the crowd. There had to be hundreds of people here, something about a local celebration and a bishop's visit, Wynter had said. The crush of faces thinned the air, and Luke's throat constricted from a sense of imprisonment.

He fought through it and remembered his purchase list. Crates of the abbey's beer stood in neat rows. Good though it was reputed to be, Luke would pass on that. He needed his guards sober and capable of reaching York post haste. Instead he sought dried meats, grains and lard, beans and cheese.

Nearing the poultry pens he saw her, a flash of jetstone black hair and red fabric.

Joya. She and Kadriya stood in front of a tailor's shop, measuring for garments.

Joya spied him and waved, her butterfly hands flitting through the air.

Wynter's words haunted him. He would control his anger at the situation and try to let her know he appreciated what she had done for him.

Her beautiful body was concealed in an ill-fitting gown that dragged on the ground. As he neared Joya, sensations assaulted him. His heart hurried, as if he were running a race, and he felt lighter of a sudden, a shudder of desire tightening his loins. He fought to contain a smile.

Too late, he saw from the abundant smile she gave him. "I missed you this morn," she said.

And I, you, he realized. "Wynter brought me along to the abbey," he said.

"Good morrow," Kadriya said. "Did the abbot receive you?"

No secrets appeared to exist between Wynter and Kadriya. Luke felt exposed. "Yes."

As Luke closed the door to further chatter, Kadriya turned her attention back to the tailor.

"What did he say? The abbot," Joya asked. Her beautiful face became strained, and Luke sensed her vulnerability. She had placed herself in such peril for his benefit.

He took her hand. It nestled in his, small and warm. What was he doing, lifting her hand and kissing it, in the presence of all these spying strangers? Her skin tasted sweet with roses. "He offered you sanctuary."

Her hand lingered in his. "For Cam and Pru? And George, too?"

"Aye."

Joya released a little squeal and threw her arms around him, hugging him. "Thank you. Thank you, Luke."

She pressed herself to him, all softness and breasts and firm stomach and thighs and something sweet and floral, and a wave of pleasure washed over him. "You are welcome." He wished to say more, but the crush of people all around them made it hard to breathe.

Kadriya turned to them. "I'm going to be a while getting clothes for all of you for your stay at the abbey. I have your measurements, Joya, and I'll order two skirts for you, tunics, and three gowns. I'm meeting John, but not for another hour or so. Luke, please escort Joya back to our manor."

"I will see to her safety," Luke said.

"Oh, and mayhap you can stop by Ridge Hill, Joya, on your way. And see the lake. You always love going there. Be back before sunset."

Time alone with her. The roasting meats suddenly smelled sweeter, the breads fresher. "I have only to order bread, then we can go."

He hurried back to the food market, rushed through the selection, and returned. He would make peace with Joya before he left for Christchurch. He would not lose control and kiss her again. She had saved his life, and deserved more than to be ravished by a man with death on his shoulders.

He calculated the time he would have with her. A gift. A warm spring day, and not much past two bells. Seven hours and sunlight, and Joya.

Luke and Joya traveled on the busy southwest-bound road that followed the River Cerne. They reined their horses to the side of the road to accommodate traveling merchants as they headed for Cerne. After they passed, she led Goldie back on the road and they continued.

She rode on Luke's left side, and could see the large bump by his temple. He did look so much better with a head. She smiled at the memory, the laughter her friends had shared along with the fear. So much had happened, so quickly. She had surprised herself by succeeding with the apricot seeds. Now he was here with her. Only the two of them. The thought warmed her like a fine, honeyed wine.

And Kadriya. She had sent them on their own for the good part of a day. Well, no surprise. Joya could not hide her attraction to Luke. Kadriya had likely felt sorry for her, and given her some time with him.

He said he was going with them to the abbey tomorrow, but she sensed he would be gone on the morrow, off to change England by joining York. Joya didn't doubt that Luke would die if he stayed. She was equally certain he would die if he left, but she could not see him in gaol again, even if it was within an abbey. This would be the last time she would see him. She would not linger on that, though. He was with her, now. No chains, no guards, no others. She would think of a way to thank Kadriya.

At Dickley Hill they left the main road, taking a secondary path that led past Hill Barn and into the steeper hills. By the time they reached Ridge Hill, they met no other merchants, and the homes and farms became more scarce.

"I remember riding here for the first time," Joya said. "After Kadriya's wedding." Joya, Faith and Stephen had come with their parents to see Kadriya's new home. "Kadriya was so beautiful. She had been in so much trouble, and the abbot forgave her because she helped find the chalice—" Joya checked herself. The abbot had forbidden all of them to speak of it. "Well, any way, Kadriya is brave. And quick-witted."

Luke smiled. "Like someone else I know."

"Who?"

"Your friend, John Wynter, pointed out that I found no value in what you did for me at the bridge, freeing me. " He cleared his throat. "I believe I told you it was a stupid idea. Wynter pointed out that, on the contrary, it was quite clever."

Joya hesitated. It had ended so poorly, and his tongue could be so harsh. "Are you mocking me?"

He shook his head. "No. I was wrong, and I—"

They rode through a break in the trees. A lake came into view and Joya abruptly reined Goldie to a stop. "Look."

Ahead fifty yards, Crystal Lake nestled at the base of heavily forested hills. They approached its shallow end, where it lived up to its name, clear to the bottom and strewn with driftwood debris to the right. It dropped off some twenty feet out, becoming deeper, where the wind rippled the surface and the sun turned it to shimmering gems.

This lake had claimed Joya's heart from the first time she saw it. It was no meager little fish pond, muddy and murky, no treacherous river with hidden whirlpools. Every visit had brought sensual delights – the warmth of the shallow water, the firm lakebed under her bare feet and farther out, the refreshing depths, cooler, peaceful and invigorating. "This is it." She clapped her hands together. "Isn't it grand?"

"'Tis beautiful," Luke said.

"Most of times the dock is busy, but the fishermen are all at Cerne," Joya said. "The bishop is scheduled to visit the abbot, so they combined markets this week. The abbot is displeased that they celebrate, but it's a boon to the fish trade and an opportunity to sing. And dance."

"I prefer fresh air. And quiet."

"Then you'll like where I'm taking you. This way." She led him around the left side of the lake to a point at the edge of the dense forest, stopping at a large boulder. Chiseled deeply in the stone was a large, sideways oval with a dot in the middle.

"What's this?" Luke asked.

"The Evil Eye," Joya said, deepening her voice . She dismounted by the stone and tethered Goldie in a protected field of grasses. "You know the Gypsies—their mystery and magic. They say that many years ago, old Theodore Fiske—he owned the fishing docks back then—and his brother, Sigaer, found this big stone when they were clearing trees for the new docks.

"Men from Dickley Hill said that long ago, Gypsies had camped here. The Gypsy King was stabbed in his sleep, so the Gypsies called the stone from the depths of the lake, and placed it here. They cursed the land, and they burned their king's body on a boat, along with his treasures. The gold sank along with the king, to the bottom of the lake."

Luke dismounted and tethered his horse next to hers. "Hogwash."

"'Tis true that Gypsies burn their dead. And their tribes are led by kings."

Luke's eyes blinked rapidly for a moment, pleasing Joya. She enjoyed weaving a spell with Gypsy tales she'd learned from her mother. She widened her eyes and continued. "A group of fishermen gathered at this very spot one night, and much ale was downed. They lit a fire at the base of the Evil Eye stone, and warned that any man who dared pass the stone would suffer a painful death. Theodore and Sigaer laughed and relieved themselves on the stone. They accepted the challenge—and they passed the Evil Eye, into the forest. Right here." She moved to a point to the left of the stone. "The men called to them, but they never answered. Dawn came, and still no sounds or signs of them." She paused for effect. "The next day they found Theodore's hood floating on the surface of the big lake. But no trace of them was ever seen again." She slowed her voice and reduced it to a whisper.

Luke frowned at her, still uncertain.

"Boo!" She raised her arms high at the same time she shouted.

Luke jumped.

Joya laughed and ran into the forest, past the Evil Eye stone. "Fooled you!"

She paused to look back. Luke stood watching her, head cocked to one side, and started after her in a full run.

She held Kadriya's long gown high, freeing her legs, and maneuvered through the underbrush, pine needles soft under her feet. There was no path because the Gypsy legend and the unusual, carved stone, combined with other mystery stories over the years, had frightened everyone away.

She reached the clearing she remembered, a branch of the main lake, where she and her brother, Stephen, used to play as children.

She slipped behind a thick bush, removed her boots and pulled her hose off, placing them neatly on a moss-grown rock. She unlaced the sleeves and sides of Kadriya's gown and pulled it down past her hips, her excitement evident in her shaking hands. Her mind tangled like so much rope as she thought through what she was doing.

Nothing more than what you've already done with him. You went for a swim together. This time, the only difference is that you won't be scared for your life.

"But your gown," her inner self protested.

"Not mine," She answered to herself. "It's Kadriya's, and I can't travel with soaking clothes. Besides, I'm wearing a chemise to my knees."

Luke caught up and stopped. "Where are you?"

She stepped free from the bush, holding her red gown. She met his blue eyes, and her bravado melted. She swallowed. "Wading. Pray join me."

He backed away, but his lids grew heavy. "'Tis not meet. Not at all meet."

Not proper. Not safe. "There is no one here to judge." She folded the gown neatly and hung it on a branch. "I'm only proposing that we wade."

His eyes grew dangerous. "How deep?"

A streak of wildness assaulted her. "As deep as you dare." The words slipped out of her mouth, bold as a siren, and she felt

141

her neck heat. *What must he think of me?* But she had run out of caring what he thought. He had been abrupt and judgmental and disapproving of her from the start. She had grown accustomed to it, and enjoyed the exasperation that now tightened his lips. "Come on. Are you afraid of me?"

He bent down and unlaced his boots, devoured her with his blue eyes. "Any sound man would be," he said. Still, he took another step toward her.

She laughed and ran into the water. Dipping her hand, she drew up a handful and splashed him. "Come on."

She waded in to her knees and enjoyed the view as he removed his tunic, baring his chest. He left his chausses on, and she could see the shape of his manhood straining against the thin fabric. It sent flashes of heat to her core. Aware of her feminine power, she continued her flirtation, feeling daring and naughty and free.

Spying a dried pod flower that stood on thick stems above the water, she plucked a handful. "Let's play a game."

He waded toward her, stopping six feet short of joining her. "Another tale?"

She smiled. "No, although I enjoyed that one. Didn't you?"

He raised a brow. "Oh, yes. You're quite the jester."

She laughed, feeling tickles in her stomach. It was only the second light-hearted moment of amusement she'd shared with him. "Let's have a race. I learned it from my brother, Stephen. Here are yours. They're ships." She handed him three. "And here's mine." She pulled the dried stem and petals from them and placed them on top of the water. "See how they float. And see that big rock, about twenty feet out" she said, pointing to it. "That's where we finish. Whoever gets there first with all three ships, wins."

"Wins what?"

"A kiss." Her heart faltered as the words passed her lips.

His voice deepened more. "That's a very dangerous prize, Mistress Joya."

She gave him a smile that barely contained the desire that was humming through her body. "Only if you win."

"And if you win?"

She struggled for a breath. "Then it will be very dangerous for you, Lord Penry." She laughed, got on all fours in the shallow water, and started blowing her pod-ship toward the rock.

"No hurry," Luke purred, his deep voice smooth, vibrating into her core. "I'll give you a head start."

He launched his own pod ships. They were light and unsteady in the water. They could not be rushed. Experienced with the game, Joya steered her ships better and gained an early advantage.

She grew light headed from all the puffing, but she was determined to win. They eventually entered water deep enough that they could no longer rest their hands on the bottom, but had to balance and blow the ships.

"Watch out, Joya. I'm going to win."

She heard a splash and turned.

Luke had employed another means of propelling them. He placed the heels of his hand in the water and pushed, creating two waves. His ships zoomed forward on the small waves he'd created.

"No fair. You can only blow your ship home," Joya said.

Luke laughed, a rich, deep sound. Water dripped from his freshly shaved jaw. His face was transformed. No longer the tight-lipped judge, his eyes were laughing now, his broad smile revealing mischief and straight white teeth. Could this be the same man who had brow beat her, the same man who often looked as though he had lost his last friend?

"Too late to change the rules now," he said, and returned to his wave-making.

Joya blew harder, a mistake that made the little pod boats tip over. She righted them.

"Ah, no fair touching them," Luke teased.

She had been so distracted when she told him about the game, she had forgotten to establish all the rules.

Luke's boats were leading hers by at least six feet.

Joya tried to mimic Luke and create waves, but the ships kept falling over.

The last of Luke's three ships sailed to the rock, and it was over.

"Yes!" Luke raised his arms in victory. "And now for my prize." He lunged toward her.

Joya cried out and abandoned her ships. She turned to escape, but the water was chest high and difficult to wade through. Thrills shot through her stomach as he pursued her, both of them splashing wildly.

Her legs slogged through the water, slow as a snail, while her heart pumped faster and faster.

He caught up with her before she'd run two yards. He tackled her. They fell and sank together to the bottom.

Joya surrendered to the water.

Luke lifted her out and she squealed.

He laughed, an undeniably masculine blend of power and delight. It rumbled from deep in his throat as he turned her to face him.

He towered over her, brown hair shining in the sun, lake water dripping, tiny beads of moisture on lashes over blue, blue eyes.

She looked up at him, expectant, heart beating wildly.

He cradled her face in his big hands and lowered his face to hers.

His mouth was wet and soft on hers. Her legs went weak and she sank into the water.

His hands went to her waist and he lifted her high, let her slide down the length of him. She slid over his chest, his trim waist, and the considerable hardness of his desire as he cupped her bottom close to him.

She wrapped her legs around his hips, moving against him.

He groaned and claimed her again with a kiss, his tongue impatient, invading.

His heat penetrated her thin chemise.

Sliding upward, his hands skimmed her hips, her waist, and cupped her breasts. He ended the kiss and gazed at her from his wet lashes. "You are the most beautiful woman," he said. "I lose all thoughts but those of you."

He sucked her lower lip and kissed her again.

Sin, sin. She returned the kiss, threading her fingers through his hair, caressing his scalp. *And should I sin too much, I shall surely go to heaven.*

She touched him under the water, his shaft hard under the thin fabric of his chausses.

He tried to pull away. "I cannot deflower you."

"You won't," Joya said. "We were only days from our wedding when Giles went to battle. We said our vows secretly. And consummated them."

He caught her meaning, and inhaled sharply. "Forsooth?"

She nodded.

"I can make no promises. No vows."

"I know." She pulled him to her, kissing him deeply.

He grabbed her bottom and rubbed her against him. "By the saints. By the glorious, sweet saints I have dreamed of this." He kissed his way down the side of her neck, trailing more kisses on the tops of her arms. He moved to her breasts and suckled them.

She gasped at the pleasure.

He pulled her chemise up to her waist and his fingers traveled between her legs. Touching, stroking. His thumb stroked her, applying pressure, sliding into her.

She was on fire in the cool water, feeling his hot fingers inside her. She opened her legs, inviting more. Clinging to him.

He pushed against her, sliding himself into her folds, and drove into her, hot and slick.

Gasping with pleasure, she wrapped her legs around his waist. This was the man who had taken her breath from the moment she first saw him, the man who had invaded her dreams, made a small bridge for her, insulted her, and saved her. He had surprised her, disappointed her, and excited her more than any man she had ever known.

Joya threw her head back. Luke fondled her breasts, kneading her nipples until she cried out for more. Water swirled between them, and she pulled him to her, thrusting her tongue into his mouth, moaning as he stroked inside her.

Her core, hot and fluid as the water around them, and pressure. Passion she had never known drove her to new heights, and a pulsing urgency that made her at once aroused and desperate. She clung to him, needing more of him, more, more, and she moved against him faster, seeking something unknown but so intense she could not breathe.

He felt it, too, and answered her thrusts.

Water churning, she shuddered from the delicious tremors that overcame her.

Chapter 12

Her head rested on his shoulder, and he twirled a lock of her hair around his finger.

They had hung their clothes on tree branches to dry. Luke had checked on the horses and returned with a travel blanket, which he spread on a sunny patch of grass near spring flowers. "This is pleasant. Here." He caressed the length of her arm. "With you." His deep voice sounded like music in the quiet.

Pleasant, he said. Like a good game of chess. She smiled to herself. He was so reserved with his emotions. After what they had shared, his word was bland, but the look in his eyes said so much more.

"Would that we could stay here forever," she said. An occasional bird sang, a squirrel scolded, and a breeze made the trees whisper, but she could not take her eyes from his face. He met her gaze with a tenderness she had not seen before. His relaxed features softened the angles of his face, and his smile was fluid, almost lazy. This was a Luke she had never known before, a sensual, sated man, comfortable in her arms.

"What are you thinking about?" she asked.

"How much I like to win." His smile widened. "Can we race again?"

"Only after I explain all the rules." Her fingers skipped over his flat stomach.

He laughed, catching her hand, and knowing he was ticklish made her laugh, too.

"Losing has its advantages," she said. "But I look forward to winning."

She told him about the games she, Stephen and Faith had played as children. They had made home-made slides from winnowing baskets saturated with duck grease. They rode them, sliding faster than the wind down the grassy hill by the church. They would practice with the bow and arrow targets for entire days, or spend lazy summer days catching caterpillars, and her parents would decide who had the best collection.

"I like seeing that playful side of you," he said. "I love that part of you. Most of times you seem so delicate, so serious in all your finery. I was surprised." He traced the curve of her ear. "Your gowns—they're more beautiful than those at the king's court."

His words echoed in her head. Did he just say there was something about her that he loved? She basked in the warmth of his compliment.

"Thank you. My mother sews all my gowns. Her fingers are so nimble, she can sew silk over rosary beads so that you never see a single seam. 'Tis my good fortune. My garderobe is filled with her designs."

"So you dress to please your mother."

She laughed and shook her head. "We both enjoy shopping for the fabrics, a special time only for the two of us." Thoughts of her mother shone like sunshine in Joya's heart. "I'm proud of her. 'Tis dear to me to wear her gowns. My father and brother are also pleased with her talent. They wear the finest doublets, with a perfect fit, in spite of their height." She nuzzled into his shoulder. "Pray tell me about your father. Did he have your blue eyes?"

"Aye."

His silence told her she'd reached the end of that very short road. "Did you play games with your brothers?"

"My brothers and I would hold races, too," Luke said. "We'd use frogs, crickets, snakes—anything that moved," he said. "Humfrye loved to fish. He could turn every nibble into a bite, and he always knew where the big fish were." He smiled. "And Christopher, he could throw rocks like a cannon. His arm was so strong. He used to win all the games at festivals. No one could come close to him. We used to race with barrels in the bailey…" His smile died, and that hooded, protected look came into his eyes, shutting her out.

"You used to race barrels," she said, prompting him to return to his story.

He took a deep breath and exhaled. "I can't believe they're gone." He looked toward the lake. "We had our differences, as you saw that morning in Coin Forest, but they were my brothers. My father had five sons, and now he's gone, and only Hugh and I are left."

"And your mother?"

"She died when I was seven."

"I'm so sorry," Joya said, dismayed that their talk had lead to pain and loss. "Hold me." She wrapped the blanket around both of them, snuggling next to him, in contact from head to toes. "Hold me and know that I care for you. When it comes to you, I'm shameless. I can't stay away from you."

"'Tis my good fortune, I assure you." He traced a finger across her lips.

She kissed him, soft at first, and deeper as she sensed his awakening passion.

"Joya." His voice thick, he turned her away from him and pulled her close, her back nestled against his chest. Stroking the side of her breast as light as a whisper, he kissed the side of her neck. His hands traveled to her waist, and he kissed his way down her back.

Fresh desire licked its way to her core, and she pressed closer to him.

His chest warmed her, heating her blood.

Her skin tingled as he trailed his hand over the swell of her hip. He cupped her bottom, stroking the sensitive skin until she squirmed. He slid his hand between her legs to tantalize her further.

She turned to face him. The fire in his eyes melted her, and his firm lips slid wet and warm against hers so she could feel nothing but the sun and the pulsing desire between them.

His musky scent held a trace of lake water and grass, and his hair, thick between her fingers, was still damp.

He would be gone on the morrow, and he saw no future for them, but her heart melted from the intensity in his blue eyes, and she opened to him.

He loved her then, slowly, tenderly. They joined, becoming one, and a renewed passion raced through her veins. His rhythm quickened and slowed, a sensual dance inside her, lifting her higher, higher. The ground under her seemed to spin, and she held him closer. He moaned and clutched her bottom, driving deeper. The turbulence of his passion overwhelmed her, and she gasped for relief. Finally she abandoned herself and cried out as shivers of delight pulsed through her.

Joya awoke to his kiss.

She snuggled into his shoulder, refusing to open her eyes. She had slept in his arms. She wanted to return to sleep, to this special dream.

He laughed softly. "Wake up, little butterfly. Come back to me."

'Twas no dream. It was better than she had dreamed. She opened her eyes and pulled his face down for a kiss.

"This day is special to me. I will never forget it. Never forget you."

She put two fingers on his lips. "Shh. Let us speak naught of the future."

"I must tell you this, though. I enjoy being with you. When I see you, my day is brighter. Always."

Warmth poured from his words to her heart. "And I, you." Behind him, the sun had slipped below the tops of the trees. She tried to swallow the knot in her throat as they approached the time of their parting. "When I'm not with you, I think about you. I worry for you."

"What you did for me at the bridge, that was brave. I told you at the time that it was a stupid thing to do, but I said that because I was angry. Angry at the danger in which you placed yourself and your friends, only to help me. It was too dear a sacrifice."

"You saved me in the river."

He kissed her again. "I thank you for helping me, and I'm glad you have sanctuary. I can't stay long, though. I must...leave."

"I know, defeat Margaret. I can't believe she killed your brothers," Joya said. "There has to be some explanation."

"You heard my brother. Think you he lied?"

"No. No. Only that it doesn't make sense."

His muscles tensed against her.

"I'm sorry, Luke. The truth will come out."

"I'm sorry for you when it does. Your faith will be crushed." He softened his voice. "I will leave on the morrow. I will never forget you, Joya."

"You will come back," she said.

He traced her mouth with his finger. "My days are few. I have nothing to offer you. I like working alone. Living alone." He turned away. "You would wither and be unhappy with me."

She turned him to face her. "But today. Here. What we've shared—"

He kissed her hand. "This day. You. It will remain always here." He took her hand and placed it over his heart, and she could feel its strong beating.

His eyes were soft with sorrow.

Her throat constricted, and she had to break from his gaze to avoid tears. Composed, she met his gaze again.

"I must go. I am good as dead. I cannot claim you, but I promise, I will help defeat Margaret, and you will all be released and exonerated." He placed his hand on her heart. "And I vow, I will help save England for you."

* * *

Joya rose before the sun and struggled with the lacings of Kadriya's gown. Her body still hummed from the passion she and

Luke had shared at the lake the day before. Today would be difficult. She would ride with Luke and her friends to the abbey. She shivered. Months may pass before she could escape its walls.

"Here, let me help," Pru said. Facing an uncertain future at the abbey, they all had suffered a restless night. Cam had sneaked into George's chamber some time past midnight, and Pru and Joya had fallen asleep in the midst of worries that the abbot may be as joyless as Father Jeffrye.

Pru worked fast, the laces shushing through the eyelets. Securing the neckline, she sucked in a breath and her fingers stilled.

"What is it?"

Pru didn't respond.

"Well? What is it?" Joya repeated.

"I—did you take your necklace off?"

Joya's hand flew to her neck. "No." She felt for it on the back of her neck, but it wasn't there.

Gile's betrothal ring. She had worn it ever since he had given it to her, months ago.

She met Pru's gaze. "The lake." She and Pru had talked into the small hours of the night, and Joya had told her of the boat race, and hinted at the pleasures she and Luke had shared. She shook her gown, but no chain, no ring fell out. "Sweet heaven, I must have lost it in the lake."

She dropped to her hands and knees, checking the floor. "It's gone." She thought back, re-tracing her steps. "We were splashing so much. It might have been when I took the gown off. I was in a hurry …" Her face heated as recognition lit Pru's eyes.

She hurried on. "It could have been worn thin at the hook and broken there, or during our ride back home."

"We can go back to the lake when we ride to the abbey," Joya said. "I can find it."

Pru touched Joya's shoulder. "It's gone, but you will always have the memories."

"But it's to honor Giles, his sacrifice, I—"

"He would want you to be happy. How do you feel about it now, as we speak?"

Joya tried to put words to the fresh sense of loss, the scarred wounds suddenly fresh and painful. "Wretched."

"And how did you feel yesterday, at the lake?"

"I can't talk about that now, knowing I lost Giles' ring."

"Yes, you can. How was it at the lake, with Luke?"

Joya closed her eyes, felt the moisture as it traced its way down her cheek. "I felt light. Happier than ever before in my life. I had moments when I thought of how it must feel in heaven."

Pru gave her a gentle smile and hugged her. "Giles loved you. He would be glad to know that you have found such happiness." She released Joya and finished securing the gown's neckline. "We have a busy day today, no time to think any more on this. We're off to the abbey, and we'll want to be sure to thank Kadriya for helping us. We'll need to pick up our clothing at the tailors in the village." She shook Joya by the shoulders. "And you need to cheer up and think of seeing Luke again after your special time yesterday."

Luke. He would leave her today. The floor seemed to sway beneath Joya's feet. He would meet with York. Again her throat tightened at the grim thought that she may never see him again.

Their time at the lake had been wondrous. Watching him leave today would hurt. Her shoulders grew heavy of a sudden, with a weariness of the constant worry for him. Save England for her, indeed. What transgressions had she done in the past to deserve a man who thought he could singlehandedly save England?

Her mother was wrong. It was not to be that Joya would be a happy bride, wife and mother. Giles had been killed in battle, and Luke Bonwyk, Lord Penry, the man who had stolen her heart, would lose his head trying to save England for her.

"Are you ready, Pru?"

"Almost." Pru placed her slippers into her travel bag.

Joya lifted her bag and walked toward the door, each step an effort. To have shared such love, followed by bitter disapointment, had drained her.

Luke was doomed. And she couldn't help him any longer because she was going to be in what amounted to a cell, locked in an abbey with an army of monks.

Pru turned toward her, a look of surprise on her face. "Did you hear that?"

Joya raised her head, feeling rusty. "What?"

"A herald." Pru's eyes widened and she opened the door. From belowstairs, Prince Malley shrieked. "Someone's here," Pru said.

George and Cam appeared from the hall. "Visitors," George said. "Half a dozen knights."

"Your father," Cam said.

Joya looked out the window, but it faced away from the bailey. "Are you sure?"

"Green flag with three rings and a sword," Cam said. "It's him."

They clattered down the steps and outside, where Tabor was dismounting by the stables. The earthy smells of grasses and soil filled the morning air, and the early morning dampness made her hold her arms to her chest. "Sir John. Mistress Kadriya." Tabor glared at Joya.

Her heart faltered. Always hoping for his approval, she knew she would receive none on this day. She had betrayed and shamed him.

Kadriya rushed forward to embrace him.

Tabor returned the greeting and pulled back. "Godspeed. Thank you for sending word. I, too, have news." He turned to Joya and her friends. "Where's Penry?"

"He must still be abed," George said. "I'll fetch him."

"Get him down here posthaste." Tabor turned to Kadriya. "We must talk."

"The hall?" Kadriya asked.

"Lead the way," Tabor said.

Joya followed her father as her friends lagged behind, uncertain whether to follow and too curious not to.

In the hall, tension spread, a consuming web of unease that snared them all. Joya's skin tingled as all eyes flitted from her to

Tabor in curiosity. Joya fought to maintain her composure. She had attacked his knights, defied him by aiding the enemy.

She reached for her father with the smallest of gestures, but something in his eyes restrained her. He stopped, squeezed her hand, and moved on in silence.

The tables had been stacked by the wall. Tabor dragged a bench to the fireplace, scattering the rushes that covered the stone floor, and sat facing them. Wynter took one bench, and Kadriya took the other.

"You'll be relieved to know…" He looked across the hall to where Joya, Pru and Cam stood. "Joya, sit you next to Kadriya." Joya complied.

"You'll be relieved to know that all of my knights survived. Not without pain or embarrassment. Apparently the only one seriously injured was Lord Penry." Tabor glared at Cam and scanned the hall. "Where is he?"

George appeared, pushing the heavy wide door open. "He's gone."

Joya's stomach seized. *He left me.*

"Gone?" Tabor repeated.

"Along with his horse and guards."

"Guards? Who gave him guards?"

"He procured his own. At the abbey," John Wynter said.

Tabor grimaced in disbelief. "You let him?"

"He sought—and was granted—sanctuary at the abbey," John replied. "Joya and the others were granted sanctuary as well."

"So he is at the abbey."

"I think not," George said. "The guards at post early this morn said they saw him heading toward Crete Hill."

"South," Tabor said. "Away from the abbey. And John, you didn't suspect for a minute he would leave?"

"Having been given sanctuary? No. And forsooth I didn't think he would ever leave Joya's side."

Joya looked at her father and her neck heated all the way up to her ears.

Tabor stood and paced, a sure sign for Joya that he had reached the end of his temper. He took two more passes, kicked the fireplace and launched his tankard into the fire. "God rot it!" He took a deep breath and turned to Joya, his expression thunderous.

"Margaret did not raid Penryton or kill Luke's brothers. Her troops did not attack there, either. She knows nothing of it. She's deeply sorry it happened, and she is furious with you, Joya, for setting a known traitor free. She bids you return—Luke included—back to Coin Forest. She's prepared to reduce his fine. But now he has sauntered off, carefree as a squire to the fair, to meet York." He gestured at Joya's friends, their backs pressed against the wall. "You believed the worst, and didn't trust your queen. She showed compassion and generosity to you, and now I have to go back with this news."

He turned to Joya. "Since you're so close to the traitor, where do you suppose he went?"

Her father's eyes were wild, and she flinched. "I don't know. He told me he would see me this morn."

"And you believed him."

He scanned the room, sweeping Kadriya and John as well with his anger. "You all believed him."

* * *

Luke hurried up the spiral staircase to the Christchurch tower, resisting the urge to sneeze as vapors from the pitch torches assaulted his nose. He emerged from the stairwell into a cold mist at the landing, and one of the most beautiful views in Devon. Dusk had thrown her wide cloak over the harbor. Tinges of purple still lingered in the growing darkness.

The harbor stretched out before him in grand display, the inlets curving below like an elaborate kell being formed under a monk's pen.

Lights flickered from the dozens of wharf side cottages and, in the outer rings of the harbor, docked boats floated, their lights bobbing with the movement of the channel.

"Lord Penry." Wagg, York's young commander from Ireland, sat at a table with Lord Harmon, a commander Luke had met in Ireland. But where were York and his allies? Wagg rose and approached him. His large eyes drooped at the corners, and his unfortunately large ears stuck out from his head like a bull terrior's. His young, sturdy body carried him well, though, and his eyes were filled with intelligence. He shook Luke's hand firmly. "Godspeed."

"Godspeed."

"I'm pleased to see you," Luke said. In truth, he would rather have seen York. Though Margaret had confiscated all his lands and ordered his death, York was safe in Ireland. He was no doubt frustrated to be exiled, but the duke enjoyed the support of its people. The Irish Parliament had twice protected him from Margaret's attempt to capture him in Dublin. Like so many others, the Irish had come to hate the grasping queen and were solidly behind York in his bid for the throne.

Why wasn't York here? To Wagg he said, "When did you arrive from Ireland?"

"Two days ago. We had to be watchful. The queen has her spies about."

Wagg placed a hand on Luke's shoulder. "We were outraged to hear of your brothers' deaths."

His sympathy pierced Luke's heart anew with a terrible sense of guilt. Had Luke not aligned himself with York, his brothers would be alive. But yes, it was Margaret's doing. And he would see her humbled, nay, destroyed. "Thank you."

"Another shameful incident of Margaret's brutality in the name of the throne," Wagg said. "However did you escape her in Coin Forest?"

He thought of Joya. "A good friend's bravery. I'll need your help in being sure she's protected, and her family's name cleared. She's currently claiming asylum at Cerne Abbey."

"Of course. All our supporters will be richly rewarded."

Lord Harmon approached, wearing his age in stooped posture and a limp. "Lord Penry." He shook his head. "Never thought we would see you again."

"Nor would we have, had we not acted," Wagg said. His smile was compressed, smug.

How could Wagg have been involved? "You helped me?" Luke asked. "How?"

Wagg shook his head. "What's important is that you're here. York has some directives for us."

"I thought he would be here," Luke said.

"He's been delayed." Wagg approached a table and rolled out a map. After a cursive scan of the tower he lowered his voice. "There have been several changes in our plans."

The map he unrolled detailed the south of England, encompassing the Irish Sea and the English Channel.

"York and Warwick plan to sail the Channel to Calais. Your Irish troops are due to arrive here from Dublin within a few days."

"Forgive me," Luke interrupted. "But I won't lead the troops."

"Sorry." Wagg held up his hands. "Poorly worded. We know you're not a commander. You'll accompany the troops. Originally, you would all have gone north to repair the bridge."

"Yes," Luke said. Margaret's troops were marching toward that area, preparing to take York's Denbigh castle. Luke was to have repaired a critical bridge that would allow York's men to more quickly intercept them.

Wagg's mouth spread in a satisfied grin. "From my sources in Coventry we have learned that Margaret has changed her route. She's headed to the east coast."

"We have benefited greatly from your spies," Lord Harmon said. "That, and your experience."

Luke raised an eyebrow at the groveling fool, fawning over a superior half his age, trying to better his military position. Such posturing was yet another reason Luke chose to avoid people in general, leadership appointments specifically.

"Thank you, Harmon." Wagg turned to Luke. "Margaret is now planning to attack Sandwich instead. Rout the Yorkists when they arrive from Calais."

Alert, Luke leaned forward. The most direct route to Sandwich would take them to Redstone, where Luke's uncle and cousins lived, where he had spent many of his summers. He recalled when he was ten, when his brothers had tried to cut his swing. Worry for his family began to mount.

Wagg returned to his map. "York and Warwick will eventually reach London." Wagg pounded his chalk on the map. "And Margaret wants to reach London, too. To do so, she'll have to cross the Red Bridge." He marked the location. "We'll be ready for her."

Luke's heart stuttered. Wagg had marked his uncle's bridge.

"You'll be there ahead of time," Wagg continued. "The bridge has five spans. You'll have time to compromise the bridge at midway."

Luke grabbed Wagg's arm, stopping his vicious chalk strokes on the bridge. "You realize it's a residence bridge? There are shops. Homes. Families on it."

Wagg jerked his arm free. "Unfortunate. But necessary. Hear me out. You'll advance the Irish—"

"I helped recruit, but I'll not lead the troops," Luke said. "I made that clear from the beginning."

Wagg waved his objection into the air. "We know, we know. We have a couple men in mind. The Irish will challenge, and Margaret will have no choice but to answer if she's to proceed south. She'll relish it, actually, because they will outnumber us, as they did at Blore Heath. Once they've populated the bridge—and it will accommodate over fifty cavalry—you'll rip it out from under them, and we'll annihilate them."

Wagg made two bold strokes with his chalk, creating an "X" on his family's bridge.

Quiet roared in Luke's ears. His role in all this was to repair a bridge to hasten York's travels. Now it involved destroying his family's bridge and killing families and royal troops. "No."

Wagg raised his droopy eyes. "Perhaps you miss the good fortune of all this. A quick victory at the Red Bridge and you'll save thousands of lives. It will be an end to all the fighting."

"I won't be a part of it."

In a dramatic move, Wagg held up the map and shook it. "We need you. You know the bridge. Its design, its strength, its weakness. This war has been raging for five years, and Margaret shows no signs of quitting."

"I'm a bridge maker."

"England's best. And you hold England dear. That's why York sought you out. York is counting on you. I am counting on you. England is counting on you. Do you not wish to end the plundering and lawlessness? Do you not wish to end the killing of innocent people like your brothers?"

Luke's chest burned from a raw, primitive grief. He could never undo the events that caused their deaths, but he could avenge them by stripping Margaret of her power so she could do no more harm. As he had so often told anyone who would listen, to save England, Margaret must be stopped.

But the Red Bridge. His uncle's bridge. To defeat Margaret, would he be forced to destroy it?

Chapter 13

"Thank you," Joya said, shrugging out of Kadriya's overly long red gown.

"We're all so relieved to have you home again." Effie's voice was soft as she helped Joya out of her chemise. Her grey eyes studied her. "You look awearied. A good night's rest will help."

The trip from Cerne Abbey had been tiring. Her body, this morning thrumming from her time with Luke, had long since cooled and she faced a new truth. Luke was gone.

Camilla, Pru and George had left her father's traveling party at Ilchester. The remaining miles had stretched forever. Lord Tabor rode with his knights and Joya remained locked in an invisible cage of regret that she had caused the deep worry lines marring his face. They had finally arrived in Coin Forest to a subdued village and household. Margaret and her troops were gone, along with Lord and Lady Onslow and their household.

Now the sight of her home tightened her throat—the church, the ancient oak where Kadriya had fed her doves, the hill and memories of sliding with Stephen—all had been a balm to her soul, and she was prepared to sink into the soft pillow of home.

But all had changed, and she had caused it. Peter manned the gate. He had opened it slowly and stared at Joya, his eyes wounded, bearing no trace of his former ardor and admiration. His lack of warmth silenced her and stole her smile.

She had been acknowledged by a perfunctory glance from the guards. In the castle, Maud, Meagon, Martin, and the kitchen maids gave her a cool welcome. Their eyes held a reserve that had never been there before, as if Joya were a stranger on her first visit to Coin Forest. Her plan to free Luke had seemed innocent because no one was physically injured, but it had placed the knights and servants at risk of losing their homes and positions in Coin Forest. She had betrayed their trust.

And it had all been for naught. Had Joya not intervened— had Luke been here, the queen would have arrived and asserted her innocence of having killed Luke's brothers. Margaret may have pardoned him. Reversed the fine. Luke would have spent time with her, seen her compassion and goodness, and he may have shifted his loyalties back to the crown.

Now, she would never know.

Joya washed the dust and grime from her arms, and bathing revived her. She was finally alone with Effie and she could find out what had happened during her absence. "So you saw the queen, Effie? Did King Henry come, also? And Prince Edward?"

"The king and prince remained in Coventry. Margaret arrived alone. I helped prepare Lord and Lady Tabor's chamber for her. She is dainty, and very beautiful. Her travel gown was a bright blue, with tiny ruffles of white lace at the hem. It was cool and smooth in my hands when I hung it to air. She was patient, and kind to me." Effie wiped spilled water from the table top.

"Did she see Hugh?"

"Aye, in the hall, not privately. She expressed her sorrow at Hugh's brother's deaths, and the attack on Penryton. She had no part of it."

"Your mother was here," Effie continued. "And Lord Tabor and the queen and Lord and Lady Onslow stayed late in the solar."

"Did they speak of me?"

Effie gave a knowing smile. "Some of the kitchen and buttery maids… hmm, happened to be belowstairs, outside of the solar. It was a warm afternoon so the windows were open. Her grey eyes sparkled. "Meagon may have climbed the wall a bit to better hear. Your name was spoken, along with Camilla and Prudence." Her smile faded. "And Lord Penry."

"And they said…?"

"Lord Tabor spoke of your virtues. He mentioned that Lord Penry had saved you from drowning, and your loyalties might have been … compromised. The queen received his comments graciously, and …" Effie paused.

"And what?" Joya asked.

Effie studied the stone floor. "She became angry."

Dread seeped, cold and rancid, into Joya's bones. Her plans had failed. She had sewn virulent weeds in her mother's garden, and they would spread like a plague and kill all the good plants. And there was nothing she could do to right the wrong.

Effie said no more. Her expression remained quiet and gentle. It conveyed deference, but held an edge of warning.

Joya spent the night tossing and reflecting. Her father was steadfast in protecting her, yet all she could think of was protecting Luke.

He's years older than you. A baron. What can you, a stupid woman, do to protect him?

Her thoughts grew desperate. Could she enlist Hugh's help? No, it was too late to help him.

Conversation from the guard towers rose and drifted down to her chamber. She shuttered the windows, but opened them again when the air had grown stifling. When the bells rang for Matins, she heard her father's voice near the baking ovens outside the kitchen, his voice and Maud's.

Maud's skills transcended her job as head baker. Few discerned that her bawdy manner concealed her cunning, and she often served as Tabor's ears in the kitchens and halls. What were they discussing at this early hour? She checked the sky. The sun would be up soon, and the bread would be in the ovens and baking. The women would be free to gossip, and less observant. If she could avoid those at early mass, she may slip by unnoticed and listen from outside the baking kitchens.

Joya slipped into her tan dress. It was old and worn, but the sleeves were still attached so she could more easily dress without waking Effie to help her. She crept silently down the steps, over the stones, out the door.

To prevent fires and minimize smoke, the kitchen rooms were built outside the castle. Most of the women congregated at the tables in the preparation room, where the risen dough was formed into loaves in the moist heat. Her father, Maud, and another woman were in the smaller room with the ovens. Maud was in the midst of describing Margaret's knights and guards, making note of their physical prowess, the width of their chests, and their lower body features. The venting windows were too high to see inside, but Joya could envision Maud, her large melon breasts jiggling and threatening to pour out of her strained chemise. Her red hair, frosted white at the temples, had likely become tightly curled and wet from the heat.

Joya heard baskets being stacked and the scrape of the large spatula as Maud scooped the baked loaves out and slid them on the cutting boards.

"Here's the last of this batch."

She heard the sound of soft shuffling from the other kitchen, and murmured grumbling from Maud's helper.

"Fast on your feet there, and get those cut. Time's a wastin'," Maud said.

A screeching sound suggested Maud was cleaning the brick shelves with the ash scraper. A young woman hurried out with filled baskets, her dress soaked down the front and back from the extreme heat.

"She's gone. We can finish talking." Her father's voice, lowered, meant only for Maud, but clear enough for Joya to hear. "What makes you think so?"

"It were the tall knight, the one who announced her grace," Maud said. "Said they would leave at first light the next morn, and they did. That's when he told them."

"Tell me exactly what he said, word for word."

"Beggin' your pardon, my lord," Maud said, "but I can't. 'Twas me daughter Meagon who heard. They don't pay me no

164

mind no more. I'm so old, and my merry maids have dropped lower'n my belly button." She gave a laugh, and Joya could imagine Maud grabbing her breasts and lifting them to her neck, as she was fond of doing to shock a stuffy knight or two. "But Meagon, she can flash those big eyes of hers and smile, and they feel it in their hose, I can tell you, I've seen 'em. 'Twas Meagon who heard them talking. Said he's been riding his high horse on a lucky saddle, but that he wouldn't live to see the next full moon."

"So they're going to follow him?"

Him? Joya pressed closer to the hot stones, trying to hear all.

"To the coast," Maud said. "Holyhead."

Holyhead. A major port in Wales, on the Irish sea.

"Are you absolutely sure, Maud? Is Meagon dead certain?"

"Surer'n the sun rising, my lord. I made her swear to her first born, and she had no problem."

"I'm grateful, Maud."

"I'd bleed for you, Lord T., I would."

"No need for that, Maud. It's late," her father said. "Let me know if you hear aught from the shipbuilders when they pass through."

"Yes, my lord." Oh, and one other thing," Maud said. "They said he wouldn't live long enough to deliver his secrets to York."

Maud left the small kitchen and Joya hurried from the ovens to the well, crouching and pressing against it so Maud wouldn't see her. She hurried through the thinning darkness, back to her chamber, Maud's words echoing, "...deliver his secrets to York." Despite what she had said, Margaret and her troops were hunting Luke.

* * *

The morning sun broke from the horizon, spilling shafts of light on the stairwell. What Joya had learned eavesdropping had destroyed any chance of sleep. She descended the steps to the ground floor, grateful for the excellent fit of her own blue gown after days of wearing Kadriya's long one. Her steps were quick, driven by a new urgency. She must find a way to help Luke.

Janet Lane

Her mind raced. She knew not one soul in Holyhead to whom she could send word, but she knew someone who might.

Hugh.

Belowstairs, a modest fire was already burning, chasing the morning chill.

At the east side of the hall, Lord Tabor was holding conference with his steward. Outside, Lady Tabor, back from Stephen and Nicole's now that they had recovered, was tending her gardens. Her mother's steps were sure as she paced out the rows, marking where to plant. She would have some sharp words for Joya about her apricot seeds. Joya hurried out before her mother noticed her.

The bailey shouted with activity, the clink-clink of the blacksmith's hammer, Meagon's laughter as she scattered last night's leftovers by the garden, and the chickens and ducks squawking and fighting over them. In the distance, the knights grunted, swords singing as they practiced in the lists.

Maud oversaw the kitchen maids as they tended large cauldrons in the bailey and the pleasant aroma of chicken stew filled the air.

Joya found Hugh as he was leaving the church. She kept a respectful distance until Father Rannulf and Hugh finished their discussion, then approached Hugh. "Good morrow," she said.

Hugh looked no better rested that she, his walk slow, eyes shadowed and worried.

Joya teetered on the edge of an emotional roof, churning inside, yearning to find Luke herself and tell him that Margaret was considering reducing his penalty payment.

If he returned willingly.

She almost laughed. 'Twas time to stop dreaming. That was as likely as the sun shining through the night. Words from her mother's poem whispered to her: *with trials and truth you'll be reborn.* The truth. Luke would no more willingly submit to Margaret than he would have willingly bent to his brother's demands, all those years ago. The sharp thorns of truth wounded her.

Hugh took her shoulders, steadying her. "What's wrong?" He was a sparrow of a man, thin arms and legs and a sagging

166

belly. He resembled Luke only in coloring and the same blue eyes. They reminded her of Luke, which calmed her. She would remain steadfast. So long as he lived, she would keep faith. "I'm fine. Have you learned of Luke's whereabouts?"

"No. Didn't expect to." He stopped at the fence by the archery targets, watching the squires practice. "We were never close."

"I gathered that when you and your brothers visited," she said. "I'm sorry for the challenges your family has faced with all this."

"It's nothing new," Hugh said. "We always fought— Christopher, Humfrye and I—but I never thought I'd lose them. Never thought they'd be murdered." His eyes shone with moisture and he looked away. "I was sure it was Margaret. But when she came here with her priest and her men, she denied any wrongdoing."

Martin had told Joya about the royal knights' proclamation. The men swore oaths before Father Rannulf, and told the priest and Tabor about the attack. Fourteen royal guards had been found, ambushed and killed, near Exeter. Their horses and livery had been stolen. Whoever killed those guards also raided Penryton and killed Luke's brothers.

"It wasn't Margaret," Joya said.

"So, who killed them? And why?"

Joya shook her head. "I'm sorry. I don't know. What will you do?"

"I'm free to go, but I have no funds. Penryton is laid bare." He punched a fist into his open hand. "God's nails. I need to help him. I think I know where he is. I need to get there."

Joya's throat constricted. "Where is he?"

He lowered his voice. "I heard them in the solar. They're looking west, but I think he's headed north. I know where he'd go."

"Can you summon your knights," Joya asked. "And find him?"

Hugh fell silent for a time. "I have no funds for travel."

Joya took a deep breath. "If I provide funds, will you take me there?"

Chapter 14

Her father's hands cradled Joya's, their warmth and gentle touch calming her. His dark eyes studied her, reaching into her closest heart for truths she was afeared to share.

The solar was quiet in the late hour, the great hall below emptied of food and drink, the servants sleeping. She had summoned him with hope, even knowing their family's precarious position. After the troubles she had caused him, she despised herself for asking him for favors. He deserved more than a dim-witted daughter who had not the sense to manage her own affairs.

But she had lain with Luke, given herself to him, and their passion had joined them as surely as the earth takes the sun to her breast each night. Luke was in her mind, in her skin, in her heart. She could no more forget him than cease breathing.

Would her father help? He should refuse her and lock her in her chamber, for if she failed to convince Luke of Margaret's good heart, Joya's actions would bring nothing good to her, her family or Coin Forest.

"Why, Joya," he asked, his voice soft and wondering. "In light of all the trouble he has caused, why do you persist? We have tried to help him, but he has refused. He has chosen his path."

"He doesn't know that his brothers' deaths weren't Margaret's doing. He has been carrying a fresh hatred for her that isn't deserved. I need to tell him. Help him see the Margaret we see, the queen we know."

"Why you can't see is the puzzle. He chose York, long before he met you. All you can do is delay his death by a day or so. Is that worth risking all?"

"She is compelled to try." Her mother's gown rustled as she entered the solar and seated herself opposite Joya at the table.

Her father released Joya's hands. "You support her on this?"

"Not at all," Sharai said. "Her emotions went unchecked while I was at Stephen and Nicole's. I wasn't there to help her while there was still time."

"Help her do what?"

"She has seen too deeply into him. You said yourself he's from a good family, and he's a good man. A good man who has made a very bad decision. And you know how Joya is."

"What does that mean," Joya asked. Would they berate her lack of good sense, as Sister Issabell had done?

Her mother released a sigh, the kind of sound she made when hours of trying produced no progress. "You always see blue sky through the rain. Why can't you see danger, Joya? Luke may be a fine man in other ways, but his choices have been deadly."

"I need four knights. Two," Joya amended. "Luke needs to know all the facts. If I tell him, and he still decides to support York, I'll give up. I don't want to support my queen's enemies. But what if he learns that the queen will reduce his penalty? He will accept. She will gain vital information about her enemy. Luke will shift from traitor to hero." She took a breath. "Will you help me?"

Her father sighed, shaking his head. "No."

Joya's heart fell.

"*Ves' tacha.*" He released the endearment with a sigh.

Joya's eyes stung, and she swallowed with difficulty.

"The hope in your eyes makes this a trial. I must protect you from yourself. You will go to your chamber. You may not receive guests, other than us. Your meals will be brought to you. All until Luke is arrested."

Her mother straightened and her hand fluttered to her neck. She gave her father a loaded glance.

He turned to her, brows raised.

"I'm loathe to gainsay you, my love," she said, her voice soft, her eyes apologetic. "But was this not the problem we faced with your mother?"

Tabor's jaw dropped for a moment. His mother had evicted Sharai from Coin Forest to keep them apart. "My mother was considering what was best for Coin Forest," he said. "It's not the same."

"Which is why you banned her and sent her to Fritham?"

Her mother's reasoning kindled fresh hope for Joya. "That's right. Grandmother put Mother's life in peril so you sent her away."

"The only way your life will be in peril is if you follow him," her father said.

"Think, my lord," her mother said. "Would our lives have been happier had you obeyed your mother?"

Joya waited for his reaction. Had he obeyed his mother, he would have sent Sharai away and wed Lady Emelyne, the earl's daughter.

Her mother's voice dropped to a whisper. "You chose me."

Her father read her mother's eyes. Her hands were steepled as in prayer. He turned to Joya, studying her face in the thick silence. He opened his mouth to speak, stopped and collected himself. "I forbid you to leave, Joya." With a final solemn glance at each of them, he rose from his seat and quit the solar.

Her mother cradled Joya's face. "My daughter. Whatever happens, you will bear witness that your father forbade you to go. You will have no escorts from us. You will not tell me you are leaving, but you will take Hugh, who is also anxious to join his brother. The two of you will be escorted in the dead of night by Luke's knights, those who escorted Hugh here from Penryton."

Faeries danced in Joya's stomach. She should be afraid for all the things that could go wrong, but elation overcame her, and she hugged her mother. "Thank you."

"But there's a price. There is—"

"—always a price," Joya finished her mother's old saying about favors. "Pray tell, Mother."

"I ask only one thing from you. You must promise me, Joya." Her mother waited.

I will see Luke. Her mother was known for her hard bargains, but for the chance to see Luke, Joya could not refuse. "Yes," she said, feeling faint from excitement. "I promise."

"Take a pigeon with you when you leave, and one day—one day, Joya, not two—one day after you leave, release the pigeon to come back home with word of where you're going. That will give you time to convince Luke, if you can. If you cannot, your father will come to bring you back home. And when he arrives, you must promise me that you will return here and give up this hopeless quest."

"Father will not bring guards to arrest Luke?"

"I cannot speak for him."

Joya's neck stiffened. "That means he will."

Her mother swept her comment aside with a gesture. "Luke has proven himself adept at avoiding capture. And if he persists with his support of York, I have no doubt you'll tell him your father is coming, so he'll have advance notice to flee."

"That's two promises," Joya said, "Send a messenger pigeon, and come back home."

Her mother's brows shot up and she cast Joya a "don't-anger-the-skunk" look.

Then her countenance changed. She smiled and opened her arms to her daughter.

Joya fell into them, relief weakening her knees. "I'm sorry, Mother."

"My sweet, sunny Joya, how I love you. Yes, two promises." Her smile turned sad. "You are my witty, cunning girl. Your judgment was flawed in defying the queen and freeing Luke. I fear for your safety, but what's done cannot be undone. I will share my secret." She lowered her voice. "I admire your courage. You felled four knights, without swords, in the light of day." Her smile grew warmer, with an eyebrow raised in amusement. "But you owe me for two pounds of roasted Belgian apricot seeds."

* * *

Joya traveled with Hugh and two knights. Fosse Way proved to be the most direct route to the Red Bridge. They lost one day to heavy rains, and another half day to find a saddler to file that same uneven spot on the saddle that afflicted Goldie. Finally the Red Bridge came into view. It had been over a sennight since she had seen Luke. Her skin was needy for his touch, her eyes hungry for the sight of him. So much in need for him, she refused to consider that Hugh may be wrong. Luke had to be here.

She studied the elegant lines of the bridge and her neck tingled. "It's the bridge Luke made for me. The model." The sunset bathed the weathered wood, giving it a glow. "But it's not red."

"The village is Redstone," Hugh said. "Named after a red vein of rock in those hills. They quarried enough for the church, and used the rest for the bridge's base and piers."

Joya dropped her gaze below the bridge to its base. Five arches and four sturdy piers supported the bridge, and large red stones protruded above water level, so like the small model Luke had crafted. The model bridge was stowed in her travel bag. She had not been able to leave it behind, for it was an intricate work of art he had made for her.

The bridge whispered to her, secrets she wished she could understand about the man with eyes bluer than the color of the sky. This was it, the structure that had inspired a young Luke to invest his life in bridges. Hugh had told her of the summers they had spent here with their uncle and cousin, Degory. She had seen bigger bridges—London especially—but such bridges had been surrounded by the brawn of thousands of dwellings.

By contrast, a bustling but smaller town framed the stately Red Bridge as it united the rolling hills. The town gave way in both directions to miles of crops and grazing animals. The bridge took center stage, a tidy street of buildings above the water, surrounded on each bank by homes that sprouted like mushrooms on the riverbanks. It spanned well over a hundred yards. The river had cut deep banks on each side, and the bridge's arches reached some thirty feet above the fast-moving water.

Luke's bridge.

A church and a handful of other buildings perched on the south side of the bridge, like any high street, minus a green. A matching number of buildings had been erected on the north side.

"Our Uncle Benjamin lives there." Hugh pointed to a three-story structure next to the church. "He's the mayor."

"How far is Coventry?" Joya asked. In response to growing tensions in London, four years ago the queen had moved the royal court into the Midlands.

"Fifty miles," said Mace, the older of Luke's knights. Mace wore more stitches than a Christmas duck, nasty white scars that meandered down both arms and one side of his neck. Over the years of battle, he had lost his Christian name and become known for his skill with the weapon of the same name.

Just fifty miles—Margaret's that close. Mayhap she could arrange a meeting for Luke. But how could Joya be sure Margaret wouldn't arrest Luke, and there would…

The younger blond knight cleared his throat. "We should follow them," he said.

Brought back from her thoughts, she glanced ahead. Hugh and Mace had almost reached the bridge. Joya spurred Goldie ahead to catch up with them.

Mayor Benjamin Bonwyck, the sign read, black letters on white. It swung in the evening breeze. Music floated in the air, the sounds of dulcimers and gitterns, men singing and lively conversation.

"Hugh!" An usher greeted him with sympathy in his eyes and a firm grip on his shoulder.

"Michael," Hugh said.

Michael grasped Hugh's thin arm, tapping it gently. "I heard about your brothers. May God rest their souls."

Hugh teared up and recovered. "Thank you. Please, Michael, tell me that my brother is here."

"He is, yes," Michael said. "He'll be glad to see you, very glad. I'm sorry, but we're in the middle of an appreciation dinner tonight for Lord and Lady Thorpin. They pledged funds for a new marketplace. Come in, come in."

Hugh introduced Joya and the Bonwyck knights.

"Welcome." Michael ushered them in. "Hugh, go on up to the study. We'll have your bags sent up for you." He apologized that they had missed dinner, but dancing would soon begin on the bridge deck in front of the house.

Inside, the chamberlain offered to take Joya's travel cloak. She shrank back, surveying the guests. The men were dressed in subtle colors, but the women wore brightly colored silks and taffetas in styles that were popular several years ago, but gowns, none the less. She glanced down at her dark blue travel suit, a good Florentine serge but a workaday wool fit for horse riding, not dancing. "I'll keep the cloak, thank you," she told the chamberlain with an apologetic smile.

An elegant older couple approached and Joya saw the family resemblance. Luke's Uncle Benjamin was tall—of course, everyone was taller than Joya—with the family blue eyes. His white hair revealed age, but his posture and movements suggested vitality. He wore a wool doublet with two forgiving pleats to suit his expanding middle.

"So you are Lord Tabor's daughter, Joya. Godspeed, my dear. I'm afraid this will be a busy evening after your travels." He introduced her to his wife, Emma.

Joya apologized for arriving uninvited. She should have been more gracious, she knew, but she couldn't help looking over the mayor's shoulder, searching for Luke. Her heart stuttered madly in her chest. She had taken such chances to be here. Would he not greet her?

She turned her attention back to the mayor.

175

"... but you don't want to hear about roof supports and markets." He pulled her aside and lowered his voice. "You must know that Luke would not tolerate all these people. He's on the deck with his cousin, Degory. My wife and I are deeply thankful for your help in freeing him from Coin Forest. We are shocked that he has allied with York. We're committed to changing that. I implore you to further our cause. Degory has been talking sense with him, as well."

A group of men approached, looking expectantly to Benjamin. He nodded to them and raised his voice. "You must be tired after all those miles, my dear. Pray join us after you've settled. Emma will show you to your room."

Joya thanked him and followed Emma upstairs. As the music faded on the next level, Joya glanced back down the stairs. Who were those men, and why did the man with the sagging eyes stare so brazenly at her?

* * *

An hour later, Joya admired the view outside her window. Looking down made her toes tingle, for the river sparkled far below, reflecting the torchlight on the bridge. The house protruded from the edge of the bridge, far enough that it seemed she was floating high above the water.

She patted her throat and took a breath. Emma had loaned her one of her daughter's gowns. Below a deep neckline, darts hugged her curves in a dusty pink silk that shimmered against her skin. Emma's maid had lifted Joya's hair in combs and it fell in black swirls against the pale, delicate fabric. She fussed with the neckline again, uncomfortably shy, as off balance as she had been at her debut at King Henry's court, years ago.

Luke. She would see him now. She grew lightheaded; surely the bodice was tailored too snugly.

A side door led to the outside deck, which featured a railing that bordered the length of the bridge.

Hugh stood, leaning against the railing, his skin paled by a darker complexioned young man with broad shoulders who

176

stood by him. His blue eyes suggested a relative, and Joya guessed that this was Luke and Hugh's cousin, Degory.

A third gentleman with well cut clothes stood by the railing. His hose was fine, his boots laced high and precise in black metal gores. His black damask gipon, trim to his chest and topped by a firm, high collar, shone in the pitch lights under his freshly shaven face. His hair, shining and neatly combed above that small, indented scar on his forehead. He turned and his eyes met hers, rich blue in the darkness with an excitement he couldn't conceal and a sense of possession that shot darts of desire into her core.

Luke.

She drank in each detail of him, dizzy with relief that he was safe. Alive. Here.

"Joya." It was all Luke could say. Hugh had told him she was here, but the simple knowing had ill prepared him for the sight of her, her dark, rich skin, her luminous brown eyes, her black hair, her breasts, high and full above a dainty waist and elegant, beautiful hands.

She had frozen. Like a deer poised to flee, she watched him.

He strode to meet her, hand extended in welcome, proper when instinct demanded that he instead sweep her into his arms and crush her to his chest, covering those supple lips with his own. He couldn't resist taking hold of her shoulders and slipping into those dark, lovely eyes. That she had come to him and brought his brother to him was a gift. That she continued to risk her reputation and safety for him was torture, however. The more she sacrificed the worse he felt, because he was tainted and condemned, and he was loathe for her to share his penalties. But he was happy beyond words to see her. "My guardian angel." As the words passed his lips, he realized she was, in some ways. "Thank you for bringing Hugh."

Degory appeared at Luke's side. His cousin appeared to have entered a trance, his mouth open, eyes wide. "Prithee introduce us, Luke."

Could his cousin have looked more foolish? Casting sheep's eyes at her like a green young man, with no attempt to cover it. Annoyed at Deg's daftness, Luke sighed and introduced them.

Joya proved most gracious, overlooking Degory's stumbling attentions. They talked at length about living on a bridge, where Emma kept her root garden and where the chickens were kept.

This bridge. My bridge. Degory had merely lived here. Luke had learned the bridge's strengths, its secrets. And Joya—he had learned her secret passions. His chest tightened in a most peculiar manner and Luke fought a curious impulse to hoist Degory over the railing and into the river.

Chapter 15

Luke fidgeted, wishing Degory would retire for the night. When Luke was young, Degory had been his hero, the one who had taught Luke how to swim the river's currents and whirlpools. He shared the secrets of how to recognize the best times in the evening for catching the biggest fish. Degory, two years Luke's senior, had grown up on a bridge, had been around people more, and had learned much about travel and gold, and girls. Deg had taught him many things for which Luke's father had no time because his father's priorities properly rested with Philip, his heir. Degory had shown Luke the subtleties and necessities of life.

But Deg had not prepared Luke for a woman like Joya. In truth, one could not be prepared for such an abundance of color, of deep passions that swamped him like the foaming surfs on Ireland's West Coast.

Deg wore all signs of being enamored as well. He had seized upon Joya's interest in the bridge and over the last two hours had exhausted every topic about it.

"I must needs speak with Joya now, Deg," he said.

Degory continued to gaze at Joya.

"We have matters to discuss," he told his cousin, raising his voice a notch. "Privately."

His cousin turned to him, and at last recognition lit his eyes.

Taking Luke's pointed cues, Deg bid them good night and left to join his father.

179

Luke took Joya's hand, and the touch of her small fingers sizzled up his arm. "Let's walk the bridge." Off the north end of the bridge the stables had quieted for the night, and Simon waved from the guard house. The church was dark, as were the haberdasher shop and the goldsmith's house.

They walked the deck, the hollow sounds of their footsteps on the wood a faint music from his childhood memories.

A breeze brought the smell of the river, of fish and the rich earth of summer.

He nestled her hand into the crook of his arm, a most natural feeling. Her breast pressed against him and he remembered her thin chemise, shimmering with lake water, clinging to her lush breasts, her nipples taut under the fabric.

Turning her to him, he took her face in his hands and looked into her eyes, where he saw a depth of emotion and welcome he had never imagined. He covered her mouth with his, and her soft lips moved against his. Heat lashed him, and he fell into a desperate need to have her close to him.

He kissed her ear, her neck, the top of her breasts. She moaned and offered herself to him. He wanted to fall to his knees and take her with him, love her on the deck of the bridge, but he would not ruin her.

Summoning control, he forced himself to pull back. He would never have expected her to affect him thusly. He was loathe to send her away, but he must.

Wagg's news changed everything, but it was so drastic a change from York's original plans that Luke had immediately sent word to him in Dublin. He understood the need to adjust the plans because Margaret had changed hers, but in the original plans, he would have repaired a bridge to hasten movement of troops. In the adjusted plan, he would destroy a bridge to kill the king and hundreds of soldiers. Mayhap York did find it necessary to sacrifice hundreds to save thousands of lives and end the fighting, but he needed to hear it from him directly.

In the meantime, he must keep her and his family from danger. "I am glad to see you." Indeed, words could not do honor to the feelings she stirred in him. "Thank you for bringing

Hugh, but it's not safe here for you. You must leave on the morrow."

"Were it not for me, things would have been simpler for you. You heard from Hugh, I'm sure, that Margaret came with her troops to Coin Forest."

"I did."

"A sennight ago, while we were in Cerne."

"Had I still been in Coin Forest—you saved my life. And here you are, now. 'Tis hard to believe you possess such boldness. Surely Lord Tabor didn't agree to this visit."

She lowered her gaze. "It is most certainly against his order. But my mother…" She paused. "My mother understands how I feel about you."

"Why would she allow you to sacrifice your reputation?" A complicated stew brewed in his mind. He had hoped that what they shared was based on genuine affection rather than a family struggle of wills. Young women were known to ruin themselves to avoid an arranged wedding to a loathesome man. He wondered, too, if her actions were those of a too closely guarded daughter. But they had shared their passions at the lake, and she had traveled all this way to see him. And what of Lady Tabor? Surely she could not approve of her daughter favoring a traitor. His thoughts veered into the Gypsy path of magic and dark secrets, and Joya's story of the Evil Eye.

"Luke, are you all right? You look absolutely ill of a sudden."

"Your mother agreed? To your coming here?" More unsavory thoughts came to him. Kadriya had suggested that Joya show him Crystal Lake, back in Cerne. And he had been the fool, thinking it was merely a stroke of good luck, having hours alone with her. Had Kadriya been helping Lady Tabor offer up her own daughter to Luke as an opportunity for Margaret to spy on him?

Joya's eyes grew wide, as if Luke had said she had two heads. "Oh, my no." She shook her head vigorously. "She's not pleased about it." She tilted her head, regarding him. "Oh." Her eyes cast down again, in thought. "Oh." A frown wrinkled her forehead. "What you must think of us. What you must think of me." She pushed him away.

"No. No, Joya. That's not what I was saying." *What am I saying? Egad, I'm denying something I never said. Can she read my mind? It's not true. It's not true. Is it?*

"Oh, yes it is. I see it in your eyes. You don't trust me. You don't trust my mother! Of all the reprehensible, insulting things you could think. After all I've sacrificed for you. After all my father and mother have suffered because of you. Because of my defense of you. Because I love you." She struck him on the chest with each word, her dark eyes vivid with anger. "Well, I don't any longer. I can't love a stupid man, and you are stupid, stupid, stupid if you think I'd lay waste to my life like I have, for personal gain with the queen."

He had thought that back in gaol when he met her friends, sharp-tongued, horse-laughing Camilla and tittering little Prudence. It was an insult, but not as bad as the one he'd been thinking. He warded off her blows, realizing anew that as trying as it had been to have Joya Ellington as a friend, it would be much more hazardous to have her for an enemy.

"As for my mother, she happens to believe in true love. Something you, clearly, will never understand. She gave me this one chance to talk sense into you. Your uncle told me tonight, he's trying to talk sense into you and get you out of this York plan. We're all trying, but you choose to suspect me. And my mother." She gathered the skirts of her sparkling gown and marched back toward his uncle's house, her steps short and thumping, punishing the wooden deck.

Luke ignored the warnings blaring in his head and pursued her, snagging her arm. "Wait. Surely you can see that—"

"I see all right. I see now why you always prefer the company of one—yourself. You trust no one, you think of no one but yourself. How you are affected, not how others are."

"It's for the others that I'm with York. The years York ruled as Protector were good years for England. The years under Margaret have been bad. Simple."

"Ah, so simple, even I should be able to understand it?" Joya shoved her face into his, nose to nose, eyes flashing. "Here's the rest of the 'simple' truth. Margaret came to Coin Forest to lighten

your fine and spare you. The raid on Penryton was a deception."
She had leaned in so close he could feel the heat of her words.

"Hugh doesn't believe her, either."

"But you must. She had nothing to gain from such brutality.
She could have claimed your lands, sent your brothers packing
and beheaded you, all before breakfast."

She was right. He stood, unable to think further, unable to
speak.

"Margaret wants the throne for her son. What do you really
know about York?"

"I could tell you again, but you don't believe me."

"Nor do you believe me."

A stony silence settled between them.

"My mother gave me one day with you." Her anger had
faded, her words dull with resignation. "After that, my father will
come to escort me home. Will he tell Margaret where you are?
Probably. Unlike you, he's loyal." She spun away from him again
and strode to his uncle's porch.

"Wait, Joya."

"No." She hurried into the house.

In his chamber, Luke paced. The evening had gone badly.
After all she had done to help him, he had offended her. Who
knew what she was thinking? If he guessed incorrectly at what
had offended her the most, she would be angry with him for
thinking, not one, but two or more insulting things about her and
her family.

Yes, this was why he kept his own company. He had
successfully avoided such confusing, tangled bonds in the past.
How much easier to laugh over tankards with an alehouse
woman, pay her generously and bid farewell after a good romp
under the covers.

But Joya's eyes shimmered for only him. She had opened her
heart to him and he would never be the same again. He could not
return to that quiet place that offered peace but no Joya.

Life had become progressively more dangerous. Had Tabor
summoned Margaret? He recalled Joya's casual mention of his

beheading, and rubbed his neck. Every gesture she made to help him seemed to instead force him into a more perilous position.

Three soft knocks sounded. She donned a robe and opened the door.

Luke slipped in. "Sorry. I need to talk with you."

"Say it quickly. This is improper."

"I'm sorry. All are asleep. 'Tis very late." His uncle had given her the best guest chamber, the one facing the east. She would see a beautiful sunrise on the river in a couple of hours.

She lit a candle from the small fire and settled at the table.

The quiet near hummed in his ears. He cleared his throat, despising social intercourse. "I meant no insult to you or yours," he began. He scratched his nose, and his neck needed attention, so he scratched that, too. "It has been awkward for us from the beginning. I don't understand why you've been so helpful. I have done naught but disrupt your life and cause damage to your standing."

She did not respond.

"I need to know if you have told Lord Tabor where you are. I don't doubt his loyalties for a moment, and if he knows, Margaret knows, as well, and I will need to leave posthaste." He paused. "Please."

She still said nothing, and Luke hesitated, wishing to gain his balance. "Does he know?"

"I will send word tomorrow."

Luke calculated. That meant he had three, mayhap four days. "Thank you." Afraid to sit lest he fall off the bench from lack of grace, and loathe to leave when there existed such tension between them, Luke remained standing.

"You thought that my mother was using me to spy on you."

It was an accusation, not a question.

"It makes sense. First Kadriya sent you away with me, without escort, for several hours. And your mother allowed you to come all this way—against Tabor's order—to see me again."

"I knew you weren't listening. Did you not hear what I said outside? My mother knows I care for you."

184

"And how can you? You don't know me. We met a fortnight ago. My family's been murdered. I'm without lands and funds. You said I care only for myself. I did not seek you out. Why do you care?"

She took his hand in her small ones. "I tried not to. I'm not foolish. Most of times."

Raising her hands in his, he kissed each one. "You are beautiful, the woman of any man's dreams. How could I be deserving of your affections?"

"I told you I tried to stop." She pulled him down to her for a kiss. It was soft and dainty, the touch of a butterfly's wing against his mouth. Her tongue slid under his lips, met his tongue, and slid deeper.

He kissed her chin, her forehead, her hair. He lifted her up above him, as he had in the lake, and let her slide down the length of him, her body soft and her hips and stomach and breasts massaged his body, setting him on fire.

He swung by the door, latched it, and carried her to the bed. They fell gently onto it. "The lake," he spoke into her hair, lifting the beautiful black locks from her shoulders, up above her head, where it cascaded like swirls of ink in water. "I was loathe to leave you after the lake. You're in my dreams. You're there when I close my eyes." He kissed her again, lingering, a sweet melting of the body as he heated up for her again, his body straining. "I will love you so much that you will remember that I think of you with every breath."

"Joya." He helped her out of her robe and chemise. He raised her arms and kissed them all the way up to her hands. He held them as gently as he would a dove, kissing them, licking the tender pads between her fingers. "I love your hands."

Her sharp intake of breath when he sucked her fingers was satisfying, but he wanted more sighs, more excitement.

He caressed her shoulders, following his fingers with more kisses. He rolled her over to expose her beautiful back and kissed down each bump on her spine, each rib, and down to the dimples below her waist. He trailed his fingers lightly on the beautiful swells of her bottom. She gasped and he hardened, clenching his teeth at the pleasure it brought him to hear her love sounds.

She raised her bottom to him and his fingers trailed between her legs, finding her sweet folds, wet with desire. He stroked her until she panted, and slid his forearm between her legs, rubbing her in long, smooth strokes. She cried out and trembled, and he could stand it no longer.

He turned her over and rubbed himself against her opening, delighting in the smooth wetness and the wild look in her eyes, the way she clutched his neck and tried to climb up to him.

He drove into her, and closed his eyes, seeing the fire behind his eyelids as she stroked him with her body.

She grabbed his bottom and moved wildly below him, a dance of desire he had never known before.

She said his name, a kind of cry, and he shattered. He thrust inside her deeply, withdrawing, entering, feeling the velvet and friction, until he could feel and say no more.

When he could next register thought, she was kissing his face and stroking his back.

"Now you know," he said.

"Know what?"

"How I feel." Surely after what they shared, she knew now.

"Tell me, please."

He rubbed a finger over her lips, swollen from their lovemaking. "You know."

"You can't say it?"

"You know I can't." The warm glow left him, replaced by frustration. "You know how it is between us."

"You know I'm no spy?"

"Yes."

"Then we've made progress."

He smiled. She was beyond beautiful, and she was his. It pleased him and scared him, but it would scare him a great deal more if he were forced to put it into words.

"Will you at least consider that Margaret had nothing to do with the attack on Penryton?"

"I cannot."

"What would it take for you to believe her innocence?"

"She is too protected. It will never come out."

"You refuse."

Pre-dawn light started slowly stealing the darkness. He would need to go soon so he wouldn't be seen leaving her chamber. "What would you have me do?"

"Meet with her."

He thought of York's amended plans. He'd meet with her, all right, if she decided to lead the royal troops to fight York. Luke would meet with her right here, and stop her from getting across this bridge and to London. "I might."

Her eyes widened. "Might what?"

"Meet with her."

"Forsooth? Oh, Luke, I'm sure ..."

Her words faded because hatred raged in his ears as he thought of his brothers, dying at Margaret's bidding. This time, it would be her turn.

* * *

Later that morning, Joya finished her brief message and released the bird. Her mother would be angry with her for sending it late, but she honored her promise. She would have all day with Luke, another opportunity to get him to meet with Margaret.

He had encouraged her, agreeing to meet with the queen. She included that in her message home.

Degory was at table when she returned. He greeted her with enthusiasm and mentioned a visit to the village.

"I would like that, thank you," she said. "And Luke, can he join us?"

"He left," Degory said. "He said he'd be back for dinner."

Degory held the front door for her as they left. "The streets are still muddied," Deg said. "Better to ride and protect that lovely gown. 'Tis a most unusual shade of red."

Joya ran her fingers down the double princess seaming that defined the bodice. "Thank you. It always reminds me of red wine in the morning, that lighter color."

They rode down the high street, past the church and green. The sun peeked through a break in the clouds, making the water sparkle as it splashed from the miller's waterwheel. Pigs snorted enthusiastically as they snouted through their scraps, and a baby's cries sounded from one of the marketplace stands.

"Redstone is an old Roman town," Degory said. "A stone axe and some flints were found by what is now the mill, and Roman coins have been found on the riverbanks. Parts of the river are too narrow to handle ships, but it accommodates small ferries and boats, and it's close to Fosse Way. It's a market town but has never received license for a fair." He reined his horse off the road to a large brick building lined on the outside with large barrels.

A rich, sweet smell intensified as they neared the building, the aroma of malted barley and yeast. "Millith makes a great potage," Deg said. "Step carefully by those barrels."

Inside, more barrels lined the left wall, and long tables allowed a narrow aisle that ended with a table laden with pitchers and jugs. The air was moist and fragrant with boiling meat, grains and herbs.

A serving girl greeted Degory and brought them each an ale and trencher of meat. Joya pulled her knife from her girdle and speared a chunk of the meat. "Delicious." The house was near empty, just another table occupied at the far end. "Have you had any success with Luke?"

"Nay. He's entrenched. He's always been that way." Deg talked between bites. "It's not just me, or you. He's been that way since I've known him. You should have seen him and his brothers fight."

"I did. Dreadful." She cleaned her knife and returned it to her girdle, frustrated once more. "There must be something we can say that will convince him."

"You don't know Luke. He closes his ears and his mind. His brothers used to call him Turtle for the way he would draw in to himself, disappear just like a turtle."

"I heard them call him that. Luke threatened to kill Christopher if he called him that again."

Deg stared at the line of barrels. "There was one time. Luke was really young, and Philip and Chris were trying to get him to do something." He studied the big beams overhead as if trying to pull down the memory. "I can't remember what it was they were trying to force him to do, but Luke refused. They called him Turtle and spied a rotted pickle barrel. Luke was strong, but not strong enough to fight the two of them. They stuffed him into the barrel and slammed the lid shut. He still has a scar on his forehead from it."

"Why didn't you stop them?"

"I wasn't there, or I would have. Humfrye told me. He thought it was amusing. They rolled him around in it for a while, and then just left him until someone discovered him."

"He must have been terrified. He could have died."

"Humfrye said there were spaces between a few of the staves for air." Deg paused. "Please don't mention it. I never told Luke I knew. I only mention it so you know how stubborn he is."

A sense of powerless outrage flared, making her breathless. "How long?"

"What?"

"How long was he locked in that barrel?"

Degory ran his hand through his hair. "I should not have spoken." He licked his lips. "I don't know."

Chapter 16

Luke entered the Redstone Changing House. After greeting the guards, he followed James Swift into the counting room.

A cat greeted them and jumped on a high shelf. His head had grown out of proportion to his body, mayhap one full size too large. He was all white with a touch of black on his ears and tail. He studied Luke with large eyes that seemed to glow.

"Your cat?" Luke asked.

James smiled. "Florin. My wife named him."

Luke laughed. "After a coin. Clever, considering your course of life."

"He's worth at least two shillings, too," James said, gesturing Luke past a large table. "He's a good mouser, but he has strange eyes."

Luke glanced again at the cat. His eyes glowed gold, almost pulsing and cutting right through Luke. He tried unsuccessfully to conceal the shiver that crept through his shoulders.

"Some people get unnerved and think he's been taken by the devil, so we keep him inside most of times."

James was born for a life inside, too, sheltered from nature's challenges and aggressive men. Taller than Luke but half his weight, James was a grass blade of a man, with long fingers meant to handle thin coins and vellum notes. His dark brown hair had receded past his ears, taking his eyebrows along with it. He secured the door lock and pulled a panel aside to reveal a bank of safe cases where funds, notes and valuables were secured.

Luke settled at the table in the middle of the room. Privacy walls had been built on three sides of the table.

"I was sorry to learn about your arrest. Didn't think I'd see you again." James shook his head. "And your brothers—God rest their souls." He pulled two sets of heavy chains free from the row of the cases, grunting as the chains slithered through the vertical door handles. He unlocked the cabinet in the middle of the top row, numbered 22. Releasing the covered drawer, he slid it onto the table. "I'll secure the door. Ring the bell when you're done."

Once alone, Luke unlocked the lid and took stock of its contents. He had long ago transferred a large portion of his funds to an account here in Redstone. His bridge projects took him far from Penryton for long periods of time, and his meetings with York required frequent travel—and contributions.

'Twas Luke's good fortune that his steward, William, was so competent—Penryton thrived under his management—and that Luke had secured his resources here. Had he not, Margaret would have stolen all he owned, in addition to murdering his brothers. Having verified the total in coins, bars and notes, he removed all the contents and rang the bell.

James returned and Luke gave him a list of names and amounts to be drawn into notes. To James' credit, his features remained still as a passion player's mask as he reviewed the list of substantial numbers. He unstoppered the ink and began issuing them. "Thank you for helping us." James kept his loyalty to York secret to protect his business—and his family, since both were located in Margaret's stronghold area in the midlands. He advanced funds in a widely cast system that included areas as distant as Dublin and Calais. "I have a message for you." He offered a parchment.

Luke focused on the sealed missive. He accepted it, looking closer. The wax seal was not York's, but a white "W."

James discreetly returned to his notes, and Luke turned away and broke the seal. *Meet me on the morrow in Abington, at St. John's*

Hostel. We have your material. The Luck of the Irish is with us now. The Irish troops were on English soil. The plan was unfolding. Ice settled in Luke's stomach. "Your material," Wagg had written. He had procured the blasting gunpowder.

He heard a voice nearby. James. "... so wherever you're going, Godspeed."

It was James' cautious way of asking where Luke was going.

"'Tis all unsettled now," Luke said. Forsooth, he did not trust anyone with his personal business, and besides, avoiding details would protect both York and James. He would leave the Red Bridge, but he would return. To destroy it, along with the building in which he and James were now sitting.

James slashed his pen across the paper, scowling. "It would please me greatly to see Margaret's head on London Bridge. Hers and that bastard son of hers."

James was more than an enemy of the queen's—he was a seething enemy. When Margaret was last in Gloucester, she had found herself short of horses and raided James' son's Wharton home of his horses and all his lifestock. For her cause, which his son was supposed to have been proud to have provided.

"I respect the king," James said. "He's pious and generous when he's well. But as long as he's alive, Margaret holds England in her fists. York should have killed him rather than taking him hostage."

James spoke of the Battle of St. Albans, when the Lancaster troops were defeated and they left King Henry under a tree, so confused he didn't know where he was. York spared the king, returned him to London where he placed him under constant and courteous guard. York served as the king's Protector, much to Margaret's fury, for several years, years in which York had righted England and restored order and safety.

"York must have been tempted but, had he killed the king, the boy you call a bastard would have been crowned."

"Aye, another child king, this one owned by Margaret. You're right. Nothing would have changed."

"Keep heart, James. York's gaining ground with the people," Luke said. All but stubborn holdouts like Joya's family who were blinded by gratitude. "And with Parliament. A victory now will make it so."

"One can only hope."

"England is bleeding." His brothers' deaths—especially in a time of such division and tension—brought a deep, unmanageable pain. Would that they had solved their differences—and England had achieved peace—before they had been brutally slain. "But I believe we're close to the end." Luke secured his notes in a leather satchel. He would do what was needed to get there.

* * *

Joya worried at the dinner table, surrounded by Luke's aunt and uncle, Degory, Hugh, and the older, scarred knight, Mace.

Luke had not returned for the evening meal. He had been seen at the money changing shop on the bridge in the morning, but not since. Hugh had found Luke's chamber empty of any clothes or possessions. She looked to the door once again. "Where is he?"

"Worry not, my dear," Luke's Uncle Benjamin said, casting a glance at Emma and Degory. "We've all seen how he looks at you. He will not leave you here, I'm sure of it."

"He knows my father is coming for me," Joya said.

"Well, he won't leave Hugh."

Worry etched into Hugh's eyes. "What if he does? What am I to do? Penryton is gone…"

Hugh's uncle patted his nephew's eggshell white hand. "You will not speak of this again. You will always have a home here."

Joya twisted her girdle, playing with the buttons. "I think Luke has left."

"For Ireland? They say York is there," Degory said.

"I heard something about the king's troops following Luke to Holyhead," Joya said. "But he came here instead."

"Holyhead?" Degory ran his hands through his hair. "That's just a short ferry ride to Dublin. One of York's castles, Denbigh, is not far from there."

"Egad." Mace scratched one of the scars on his neck. "Margaret's not been able to take Denbigh, but York's forces there are near depleted. Could that be part of Luke's plan? Bring reinforcements and reclaim the castle?"

"Maybe York is on his way to England. Easy to land in Wales." Uncle Benjamin said. "That would put York close to us." He cast his eyes down and sucked in his lower lip.

"Let's not fret over what may or may not be. Rumors are flying," Emma said. "I heard York was sailing to Calais. He can't be two places at once."

"We can hope Luke is going to Coventry," Joya said. "It's just fifty miles north. He said he would consider seeing Margaret."

"When pigs fly," Degory said.

"You said you talked with him," Uncle Benjamin said.

"I did," Degory said. "Several times. At the most, he was polite. At the least, he tried to draw me to York's side."

Joya forced one more bite of roast. It clogged her throat like sawdust, and she could eat no more. They had been guessing for too long, and it brought them no closer to understanding, or knowing of Luke's whereabouts. "Please excuse me." She rose from the table. "Is it safe on the deck at this hour? I would like to take a walk."

Deg bolted to standing. "I will escort you, if you'd like."

Outside, the aroma of dinners in the other houses on the bridge mingled. A touch of summer warmth softened the air. "I just realized it's June," she said. "Wasn't it just May Day?"

"Much has happened. It's June sixth," Degory said. He inhaled deeply. "It smells like it." He paused as they entered the main deck of the bridge and looked both ways. "Which way, north, or south?"

Joya followed his gaze. The bridge was long, over a hundred feet, she supposed, and wide to accommodate the businesses in addition to bridge traffic. Uncle Benjamin's home was situated closer to the north end of the bridge. "Let's walk south."

"So." Deg righted a broom by the hitching post in front of the haberdasher. "Do you really think Luke will see Margaret?"

Joya sighed, releasing some of the weight from her shoulders. It was comforting to worry with one of Luke's family members, knowing they cared deeply for him, also. "He may have said it to end our debate."

She knew she mustn't be too hopeful that he would meet with her. Degory's dark tale of the pickle barrel was shocking. She, too, had seen Luke's strong spirit. That his brothers couldn't have broken it was no surprise. That they had tortured him in trying to do so was shameful.

"I'm sorry I told you. About the pickle barrel."

"I'm glad you did. It explains some things for me, about Luke and his brothers." She thought for a moment. "Deg?"

"What?"

"Will you please share with me what you learn about Luke? If you discover his whereabouts or plans, would you consider—"

"Telling you?" He nodded. "When he comes back—"

"What if he doesn't?"

"Or when we find him," Deg continued, "We must work together to not let him slip away again. I don't think he's seeing Margaret. I do think he's seeing York and his allies. If he knows he can't escape without our following him, he won't lead us to York."

"If I could just have some time with him. He has been … receptive to me lately. If I could convince him—"

"Oh, I think you could, Joya. I've seen the way he looks at you."

"Well …" Her face heated, and she dropped her gaze.

"All right," Deg said. "We have a pact. We'll alert each other when he next tries to slip off in the night, and we'll make double our efforts to bring him back to the Bonwyk flock. And I'll help you find some time with him when he returns."

* * *

Luke rode out of the forest and into Rewley, an isolated abbey thirty miles from Redstone. Though it was almost dark, he could have found the hostel by the noise alone. Men singing slurred words, the smell of roasting meats and pigeons. The stables were busy with the currying and stalling of new arrivals. Maneuvering past the horses and wagons, he found a monk who sent him to Wagg's room.

Luke noted the fine linens and damask cover on Wagg's bed. He preferred comfort over coin, obviously. Luke announced himself with the guard at the door. Inside, Wagg sat with Lord Harmon. They offered him a flagon of wine and a stool.

"Godspeed, Lord Penry." Wagg slurred his words, deep in his cups.

"Godspeed." They toasted, and Luke started planning his exit. He had no interest in aimless, befuddled chatter. "Celebrating, gentlemen?"

"It's been a devil of a day," Wagg said. "My horse stepped into a hole. Couldn't run, blast the luck. Had to leave him in Winchester for stall rest."

"Unfortunate," Luke said. "Did you get another?"

"Aye, but his gait is awkward. My neck's plaguing me." He rubbed it and took another drink of wine.

"Sit with us, Penry, don't go skulking off by yourself again." Wagg rose, unsteady, and banged on the door. "Murphy. Penry here looks hungry. Bring him a rack of ribs."

Wagg turned to Luke and gestured again to the empty stool. "Was your trip without incident? Were you followed?"

With lack of a graceful excuse to leave, Luke seated himself. "I joined a group of bowyers and armorers traveling this way. No one was overly interested in me," Luke said. With every mile, doubts about the Red Bridge plan had haunted him. Why had York's plans changed so drastically? And not for the better. It would be more prudent to supplement the Irish troops with men from Calais.

Luke had sent word to York but received only a terse answer: "Follow Wagg's direction. He speaks for me while I'm here."

"'Tis good you arrived this eve," Wagg said. "We have started moving the troops. Been making fifteen miles a day, which means they'll reach Redstone by Saturday. And see." He pointed to a dozen canvas bags, each big enough to hold four geese. "We have your gunpowder." Wagg's eyes narrowed. "You seem troubled."

Luke glanced briefly at the gunpowder bags, a reminder of his grim, new project. Wagg had bought enough gunpowder to take down three bridges. Waste of funds, but it might turn out to be a useful surplus. "I'm concerned about numbers." Luke lowered his voice. "What good are a thousand Irishmen when facing over ten thousand Lancastrian troops?"

Wagg laughed softly. "'Tis good you're not commanding an army, Penry. You must have faith and be bold. We have recruited another thousand Englishmen who will help us defeat the Lancasters. We'll catch them unaware. The bridge is our secret weapon."

Luke considered that. "Are the English troops mustered?"

"Mustered and moving. They will rendezvous with us from the east," Wagg said.

"But it's been several days. What if Margaret's plans have changed again?"

"They haven't," Wagg said.

"They brought ten thousand to Blore Heath. Will they have that many at the Red Bridge?"

Wagg leaned forward and lowered his voice. "Think you we rely on one report? We have an entire family of spies in Coventry, and two members of Henry's own court report to us. Margaret continues with her preparations to march the southerly route that will take her to Redstone."

Wagg held up his hand. "I know your next question. How do we know this for sure? Because the royal army has been gathering provisions in large proportions, large enough to feed thousands, not hundreds. Several hundred pack horses are being held off the Watling route near High Cross. Entire storehouses of grain and hay have been procured, and pack wagons are being built." He sat up, chin raised. "We are informed, and strategy is more important than numbers – that was proven in Blore Heath, at Ludford, and at that French battle…" Wagg paused, a mischievous smile moving those big ears of his, "…what was it again, Harmon?"

Harmon laughed. "I believe it was Agincourt."

"Ah, yes!" Wagg grinned. "The French had three times the number of England's troops, yet it was France's biggest defeat."

Their laughter needled Luke. Yes, Agincourt was England's biggest victory in the war against France, but each battle had its own peculiarities. He ticked off points with his fingers. "The French had heavy armor. They fell from exhaustion wearing it in the heavy muds. We had longbow archers. And the French were overly confident. I don't want us to repeat that mistake."

Wagg's features darkened. "At this battle, we'll have the element of surprise, and we'll have your bridge. Once the king is dead, they could have twenty thousand men and it won't do them any good. Their cause will be dead, too."

"Not quite." Luke placed his half-consumed wine on the table, concerned about Wagg's line of thinking. "Kill the king, and they'll still defend his son. Prince Edward will be the new king, and Margaret will win."

Lord Harmon waved his hand, joining the discussion. "But our plan—Simon Wagg's plan," he corrected with a fawning bow to Wagg, "includes the queen and the prince. With all of them gone, York's way will be clear."

Luke leaned forward. "It's not York's plan?"

"Of course it's York's plan," Wagg said, casting a sharp glance at Harmon. "And we all see the opportunities in it, that's all Harmon is saying."

"So you'll have to face King Henry in person," Luke said. That would risk another military humiliation like Ludford Bridge, when Andrew Trollope, captain of 600 Calais troops, quailed at seeing the king leading his army and switched loyalties after the king offered pardon.

"We have secured Lords Ryland and Barlow, two experienced captains," Wagg said, finishing his flask. "They are fine strategists, and you, Lord Penry, need only take care of the bridge for us. We will do the rest." He reached in his satchel and handed Luke a small, folded parchment. "A message from York, for you."

Luke unfolded it and read. *Lord Penry, great sympathy for your family. Vengeance will be yours soon. Godspeed you to the bridge.* Luke looked up. "York will be at the bridge?"

Wagg's smile curved with the very confidence Luke feared, and he held his fingers up, indicating two inches. "We're this close. The end of the wars. A Plantagenet on the throne. King Richard. But first." He stood, pulled a parchment from a stack of them by the table, and rolled it out. "The Red Bridge. Let's go through it one last time."

Luke's sketch of the bridge filled the table. "The Lancasters will arrive at the bridge from the north," Wagg said. "They'll see or smell the campfires. Scouts will advance and report their estimate of how many troops. They'll want to take the Watling to St.Alban's—it's a better road, faster travel. But we'll block them."

Wagg traced the Redstone River. "It's too wide, too deep to offer any fording. And Margaret will be flush with the victory at Ludford Bridge, chomping at the bit to add another victory. She won't back down."

Margaret traveled with the armies she raised, staying close enough during battle to watch, as she had done at Blore Heath.

Wagg continued, outlining the formation of the Irish troops on the south end of the bridge.

"We'll parley. Henry will offer pardon, but it will be futile. The royal banners will be flying, red will be draped on the horses and the knights and archers and footmen, and they will begin their march onto the bridge. You'll be in a boat below where you'll light the fuses, Luke. When the king reaches the height of the second arch…" Wagg clapped his hands. He pointed to the support structure of the bridge, the stone and timber piers between the first and second arch.

"Based on your sketches and information, erosion from the river's current during the flood has weakened this pier the most. The explosions will compromise the piers, crack the timbers and boom! Here and here, and the full section of the bridge will fall.

The king's cavalry shall fall with it." Wagg's eyes focused past Luke, lost in his own visions.

"If any troops make it across the bridge before then, Lords Ryland and Barlow's units will cut them down. Once the bridge collapses, most of the troops will be bottle-necked at the north end of the bridge. Margaret is blood-thirsty. She likes to watch, so she'll be there. We will kill her, and her bastard son."

Luke's shoulders tensed. "You won't get near them." Luke said. "The minute the bridge collapses, the royal guards will be on them like bees, protecting them. Besides that, the bridge will be down."

Wagg pointed. "You take care of the bridge, and we'll take care of the rest. Mark my words. There will be no royalty but York left standing."

He tossed the map back on the table. "You need to get back to Redstone. I'm sending a couple of guards with you. They'll help you build the explosives and prepare the bridge. And you'll need to convince your family that you've abandoned York."

"They know nothing of the plan."

"Of course they do. The plans are how you got arrested in the first place. Good they were in code."

"They know neither when nor where."

"If you return after this trip, they will wonder. Tell the lovely Joya Ellington that she has finally convinced you. Tell them it's cost you too much already, losing your brothers, your lands. Beseech Margaret to forgive you, and send her a message."

Luke met Wagg's gaze. He had not mentioned Joya. "How did you know Joya was in Redstone?"

Alarm widened Wagg's eyes for a moment, replaced with an expression of proud annoyance. "We have a good network, Penry. Nothing escapes us."

"I will not lie."

Wagg studied him, eyes narrowed. "Which is precisely why you must. You've dedicated yourself to His Grace, the third Duke of York." He paused. "Our next king. You have sacrificed your lands and your brothers. Make it worthwhile. Convince

Tabor, your uncle, all those loyal to Margaret. It's how this plan will work."

Luke struggled with the urge to strike Wagg, to knock the self-important smirk off his face. What Luke wanted was to see York. What he needed was reassurance that this was the best plan, that Salisbury was convinced it was the right plan. Instead, Wagg sat before him, smug, drunk and unconvincing.

"So, Lord Penry, you leave for the bridge at first light. And we'll be two days behind you. Godspeed."

Wagg and Harmon watched Luke leave.

"He's reluctant. There's much that can go wrong," Harmon said. "This plan depends too much on one man, and he doesn't look reliable."

"He's such an annoyance, don't you think I would tap another man if I could? Penry knows the cursed bridge and, with his family he can move about on it—and under it—with no suspicion. But mind you I leave naught to chance," Wagg said. "Penry will get one last 'York' message from our man in Ireland. If that doesn't calm him, the guards will control the gunpowder at all times. If he fails to do his duty once the canisters are fashioned, I've ordered the guards to light the explosives."

"And what if Penry stops them?"

"If it comes to that, they are to kill Penry. He will not stand in our way."

* * *

From the sidelines in a hurling field in Kilkenny, sixty miles south of Dublin, the Third Duke of York jumped up from his seat. He cheered, adding his voice to the hundreds watching as his son, Edmund, ran to the grounded ball. He executed a fluid roll lift. His heir raced down the field, his young, muscular legs eating up the distance to the goal, expertly controlling the ball. He worked his way through the crowded middle of the field. He feigned to drive it home. He zagged to the right and swung the hookie stick hard, hurling the slioter toward the goal. The goalee dove desperately to block it and failed, and the white ball sailed home for the winning score.

York's heart swelled with pride. His son excelled at hurling.

The crowd roared, and the players threw themselves onto one another. Kilkenny Blue had won.

He was glad they had traveled south for the hurling contests. They had proven to be a pleasant diversion from the tensions in Dublin.

A man worked his way through the crowd, a messenger, his leather pack visible. His brown hair stuck to the sweat on his brow. "Your Grace, a message." The young man fumbled the metal hook free from the leather and produced a vellum envelope.

York examined the seal. The abbot from Waterford.

Carrier message arrived from Christchurch yesterday. Wagg reports spies in the channel. Moving Irish troops inland fifty miles to avoid detection. Next report from Ludgershall.

Wagg's enthusiasm seemed to pop from between the lines of the message. His young commander resembled an overly eager hunting dog.

Wagg more than made up for that failing with his talents, though. He had proven to be a gifted tactician, and relocating the troops was one of many of his good ideas. If Margaret discovered the Irish, it would be nigh impossible to sail in to Sandwich and join forces with his son and Warwick to complete their mission. They had all been attainted, their holdings and assets seized by the crown. This was the last chance to capture the throne. He had chosen the right man for the Christchurch leg of the plan.

Smiling to himself, he rose to congratulate his son for his victory.

* * *

Lord Tabor sat with Benjamin Bonwyk in his solar. He had arrived midday, earlier than anticipated. Five days on the road and he had finally arrived at Redstone with Peter, Fritts and Martin. Unfortunately, Penry had left before Tabor's arrival.

Joya was with Benjamin's son, Degory, shopping in the village.

Tabor studied Benjamin. He was around Tabor's age, softened in the middle with thinning, grey hair that still showed remnants of brown, more Christopher's coloring than Lord Penry's. A second born son, Benjamin had done well for himself as a merchant voted mayor.

Swords of many lengths and widths hung in the room, along with a tapestry of battle. "Did you serve at Ludford?" Margaret and King Henry trounced York and his followers there last autumn.

"No." He raised his sword hand, showing a disfiguring scar. "Injured my wrist before my fourteenth birthday." He rubbed his ample stomach. "That's why I got so wide."

"The older I get the more I collect there, too." Tabor patted his stomach and faced Bonwyk. "Lady Tabor and I appreciate your hosting our daughter. She left without our permission, and we apologize for her having arrived uninvited."

"We are beholden to her for bringing Hugh to us. We spent dark days, wondering if he was safe. Besides, Emma and I have had the pleasure of Joya's company. She is a winsome woman. She has enchanted our son and all of our household."

"Thank you, but it's time she return to her home."

"We were hoping you might stay for a few days. Rest up before you turn around and travel again."

Benjamin's invitation spoke to Tabor's fifty-five-year-old back. It had never fully recovered from the battle of Blore Heath. "I would appreciate that, Benjamin, thank you."

"Excellent."

"The purpose of my visit is twofold," Tabor said. "I came to bring Joya home, and I have also come with an important message for Lord Penry." Margaret's message included a full pardon and return of Penry's lands, and a statement that whoever had killed Luke's brothers had killed her troops and stolen their horses and livery.

"I'm deeply sorry for the problems my nephew has caused your family, Lord Tabor. Luke should never have run off with your daughter and placed her in such danger. I think of my own daughter, and …" He closed his eyes and shook his head. "We have been trying to get Luke to abandon this alliance. My family has been steadfast to King Henry." Benjamin leaned forward. "How is Henry these days?"

It was a question Tabor heard many times. Since his marriage to Margaret, Henry suffered spells of mental unsoundness that lasted weeks, months—even years. He couldn't speak, and would wander aimlessly.

Margaret had become with child during one of those spells, setting tongues to wagging about whether Henry had truly fathered Prince Edward. Luke had rudely mentioned it at Coin Forest.

He met Benjamin's gaze. "Henry is clear-headed and hale. He suffered some illness at Blore Heath, but it was related to the cold, not his mind."

Benjamin absently twisted the chain at his girdle. "What do the physicians think cause him to become so—um—disoriented, but still be able to spring back and become alert?"

Tabor shook his head. It was the root of England's troubles. "Margaret detests those episodes, to be sure." During his spells, Parliament would strip Margaret of her considerable power, and transfer the Seal and all royal authority to a Protector who would rule England in the king's "absence." The Duke of York had served as Protector, during which time Tabor had to admit England had recovered fairly well from the confusion the spells caused, for Henry absolutely could not rule during those times.

"Our king is strong," Tabor said. "He was devastated at the lives lost at Blore Heath, and furious with York and his followers. He has been active in battle strategies."

Benjamin settled in. "That's welcome news. Problem is, when the king is well, Margaret can meddle, and she does, especially with tariffs. The London merchants are angry with her—no wonder Margaret moved the court to Coventry."

"So what of your nephew," Tabor asked. "Where is Luke now?"

"I don't know. He recently traveled to Ireland, but he has shared nothing more."

"Could he be with family?"

"There are just Emma and me and our children, Degory and Joan."

"Where is Joan?"

"Devon, but Luke was never close with her. To be honest, he was never close with anyone but Degory. As children, he and Degory were great friends, but Luke has been distant for years. We were surprised when he came last week. "

Tabor rubbed his temples. "He must be with York. Joya is fond—too fond—of Luke. I'm sorry for her, and I'm sorry for your family, Benjamin. I see nothing but tragedy ahead."

Chapter 17

Joya met her father on the back deck of the bridge. The setting sun painted a glistening feather on the river, winking with the waves. He held her close, caressing her hair, silent for a time. "Good fortune has followed you, *Ves' Tacha*. I have been sick with worry."

"Forgive me please, Father. I know—"

"Remember the Ellington gliders you and Stephen played with when you were children?"

She and her father shared a smile. "Of course." For summer days on end, they had reached exciting speeds and taken many tumbles.

Eventually other children found out about it, and the hill was filled with winnowing baskets and young ones crying out with joy. "The speed was so much fun," she said. "Even the falling was fun, rolling down that big hill."

"I worried for you," her father said. "You tumbled so wildly when you fell, I thought you might break an arm, or worse, your neck. But your mother only laughed."

Joya laughed. "She's that way. All children should have a mother like mine."

"She was doting," he said.

"And happy. The other children envied us."

"Sharai is the most fascinating woman I have ever known," he said, his expression tender. "'Life is dangerous,' she told me, 'but it's also fun. The grass is long, their bones are soft and young so they can play and heal and learn the difference between fun and dangerous.'"

Joya realized he was sending a message. "You think I should not have come here."

"Your mother told me she gave you her blessing to do so. I wish she had not. You are precious to me. I would protect you from harm, always."

"You think I will break my leg."

He laughed softly, sadly. "If that's all you'd suffer, I would be greatly relieved." He took her hand. "This Penry affair." He paused. "I don't want you harmed, but this is not a children's race down a grassy hill. It's a royal matter. You have chosen a path that leads to imprisonment. Death. Do you not understand the danger you're in because of him? Have you forgotten everything about Blore Heath?"

It pained Joya to see the distress in his dark eyes. The years had faded his beautiful black hair to white at his temples and his face was lined with years, but he was still her father, and she had always wanted to please him.

But all was different now. Her life had shifted, and she couldn't return to that place. She still loved him—she wished against wish that she could please him, but Luke had become the center of her life.

The change unsettled her, but somewhere deep within, it made sense.

"No, I haven't forgotten," she said. "We almost lost everything at Blore Heath." Stephen. Coin Forest. "We owe much to Margaret."

"We owe her everything. And you have freed an enemy who is set to destroy her."

"He is not evil," she said.

"I didn't call him so. He's industrious, from good stock and he's brave. But he's wrong."

She straightened, summoning the courage to say it. "And might you be wrong, too, Father?"

His mouth fell and his eyes widened in sheer surprise. "Nay!"

"I have not given up on him."

He tensed and pulled away from her. "God's nails! Where do you think he is now? He's with York. He's gone. And so is your good name, but you show no signs of regret."

"I love him. Just as you loved Mother, but difficult as it was for you, it's worse for me. Can you not see?"

"I see that I have lost you, as we speak."

"You believe that?" Joya asked.

"I have tried to be patient, but you have deceived me. You have dragged your family through the muck for this traitor. What are you thinking? Can you think at all?" He tapped his temple, his voice tight with anger.

His words lodged deep, the cutting pain taking her breath.

Her father waited, watching her. When she said nothing, he released a strangled moan and quit her chamber.

Joya extinguished the candle and fell on her bed. Her father had condemned her as a fool. Her heart had turned numb, a lump of mud in her chest. The man she had risked her life to save had left her. Was he in Coventry, fulfilling her deepest hope that he would ally with Margaret, or was he in parts unknown with York, where he would empower York to destroy everything her family held dear?

Oh, if Camilla could see her now. And Pru, dear Pru, who put such stock in love. What good was it to lose the ability to think clearly, to sacrifice all, lose all? The ache in her chest grew so that she could scarce breathe, but still love for Luke pumped in her blood, leaked from her eyes in tears that turned cold with loss. She swept them away, angry at her failure to bring him back to Lancastrian loyalty.

Mayhap her father was right. She had fallen into a hopeless spell with Luke and had lost all reason.

She had promised her mother she would spend one day with Luke, after which she would return home willingly and forget him.

Anger flamed in her belly, and dark thoughts burned in her head about York, York and his peculiar, W-shaped beard and unspeakable greed, dragging England into war so he could steal King Henry's throne. She pounded the mattress. She had come so far with Luke, but hadn't made a tittle's bit of progress in her effort to save him.

All she had been striving for slipped through her hands like so much sand.

She thought of the apricot seeds, glistening with her mother's secret oil. Guilt knifed its way through her chest. She had freed Luke, which had given York the power to take Luke from her.

* * *

Luke arrived in Redstone well after midnight. He had left Wagg's guards five miles back in a camp sheltered in the forest. He had instructed them how to pack the canisters with gunpowder. To distract them he warned them of the severe injuries they would suffer if they handled the gunpowder recklessly. While they bent over the canisters, focused on compressing the explosive without losing a hand, Luke approached the overly abundant supply of gunpowder and canisters. He slipped two extra canisters and bags under the tent wall. Unnoticed, he quietly claimed them when he left. Now he walked the trail he used to take with Degory when they swam in the river. He hid the explosives in dense bushes. He had his own plans for them. After currying and stabling his horse, he climbed into the storage room window that Degory had left open for him.

Upstairs, he paused in front of Joya's room. Her closeness quickened his heart. No fire or candlelight shone, and disappointment stung him. Sobered that she could affect him thusly, he continued to Degory's bedroom.

Inside, Degory was snoring loudly. Luke undressed quickly and slid into his bed. His neck and back muscles ached from the strain of what he knew he had to do, of how, in a few days, he would destroy any feelings Joya held for him and shred the small fabric of family he still had left. The fur coverlet warmed him, and he quickly fell into an uneasy sleep.

Luke's dream placed him on the Red Bridge, standing beside York and his powerful allies, his brother-in-law, Richard Neville, 5th Earl of Salisbury, and Salisbury's oldest son, Richard, 16th Earl of Warwick. Energized by their presence, Luke became reassured, more confident that the risks he was taking were worth it. These men represented England's future.

The river steamed in the early morning, a swirling white blanket that concealed the fast current that flowed beneath it.

In the distance, a soft rumble grew to the noises of creaking leather, groaning wagons, and hooves thumping the earth.

The Lancastrian forces had arrived, and Margaret herself, dragging her reluctant child prince in tow to see the massacre of her enemies.

In the growing noise Luke's heart pumped, bruising his chest with its urgency. He saw Joya in his mind's eye, her dimpled smile that blinded him with love. After this morn, she would never speak to him again.

"You who would take my throne," King Henry cried, "Come forward. Let your insurgence be settled this day."

"We approach with love, my King," York said, patient to the end. "I wish not to slay you, nor any of your faithful men. I merely wish to exercise my rightful claim to the throne."

"I am your king," Henry replied. "Ambition clouds your sight." Eyes wide and wary, Henry's horse pranced sideways. "Show your fealty, and you will be pardoned."

The morning grew still as men from both sides strained to hear.

York took a deep breath. "I will not stand down." He glanced at Luke, as if for reassurance, and led his horse forward.

"Then you will die," Henry ordered his trumpeters to sound the call to battle. "Advance!"

Pulling a still-burning torch from its holder, Luke raised it, waving it three times, down, the signal to ignite the explosives.

The bridge called to him with dear memories of a carefree youth. Luke saw the shops and the swings and the river below it.

Luke slipped into the long-ago pickle barrel, its darkness a bitter relief. He would be alone again, but he would do honor to the oath that offered the most hope, the most good to his beloved England.

Henry charged.

Large booms sounded from below the bridge. It shook the houses and dislodged the stones that secured the piers. The bridge broke just south of the halfway point, collapsing just beyond the center support beams. Men and horses stumbled on the collapsing bridge and followed the falling stone in a ghastly shower. Uncle Benjamin's house shook. The old lamppost collapsed.

Luke woke from his dream. He heard Degory's uneven snoring, saw the soft moonlight from the window, and shuddered. Soon he would face the devastation.

* * *

The next morning, Joya tucked her hair under her veil, thankful she had dressed warmly in her travel suit. Grey clouds cluttered the sky like bundles of dirty sheets, threatening rain. She would work quickly.

Joya had renewed her vow to learn more about Luke. When asked about his childhood at breakfast, his Aunt Emma had talked of Luke's industry, reliability and loyalty. She hadn't mentioned a single shadow from his past, though she must have known about the brothers' cruel treatment of Luke, especially the pickle barrel.

Joya finally accepted that Luke must surely be Emma's favorite nephew, and turned to other sources to learn more. She approached the church, a modest structure at the north end of the bridge. She would gain a seed of news on this grey morning, no matter how small, that would help her understand him, maybe lead her to him.

The vicar had propped the heavy door open, either in welcome or need of fresh air. Joya entered. A few benches were stacked behind the rood screen, and two stained glass windows poured weak patches of blue and gold onto the rushes. It appeared the church could accommodate only two or three dozen people. The large church Joya had seen in the village must host the majority of the townfolk and travelers.

"Good morn." The vicar was bald, older than her father by ten years, she guessed, an ox of a man, still hale with a thick neck and forearms that bulged out of his black habit.

Joya introduced herself and explained that she was a guest of the mayor.

"Lord Tabor's daughter, I heard. Gypsy."

Joya filtered his comment, something she always did when people met her and noticed her darker skin. The vicar said it with an admiring eye, so she felt no hesitancy. "Yes. My mother is Sharai, the Lady Tabor." She reminded him that regardless of skin color and growing hostilities toward Gypsies in England, her veins ran with noble blood.

His eyes were warm, suggesting he held no such preconceived notions, and they sat near the stained glass. They visited about Coin Forest and Somerset, and he said he had met Father Bernard many years ago.

"He wed my parents," Joya said, remembering the generous priest.

"He was beloved and esteemed," the vicar said, "May he rest in peace."

She nodded.

"Benjamin tells me you have been most kind to Lord Penry," the vicar said. "Brought his brother here."

"Yes. What happened to his brothers was most heinous. These are dark days."

"I pray for our king's health and recovery," the vicar said.

"As do I." Joya paused. "I understand Lord Penry spent most summers here during his youth. Have you had opportunity, over the years, to get to know him?"

"His family spent many summers here. The boys loved playing on the bridge—swinging, swimming, and—to Emma's consternation, jumping off the bridge when she didn't catch them in time."

"Heavens. The bridge is so tall."

"Aye. Little Luke was almost as big a daredevil as Degory. They were like two straws in a haystack." He laughed softly. "They used to sit in the aisle seats during services and roll marbles back and forth to each other. I never did tell him I could hear the marbles rolling, though they tried to be quiet."

Little Luke sounded engaging, very much like the man with whom she had raced boats.

The rector sighed. "Something happened to him. Sometime when he was around ten or so, he changed. Oh, he and Degory were still friends, but it was as if he was an amusing rascal one summer, and a wizened, old man the next. It was tragic to lose his father and older brother."

Degory had not mentioned that. "How did it happen?"

"Fire. Haystacks, piled too green. It spread to the tithe barn. They tried to put it out, but the upper loft collapsed on them. The younger ones—Christopher and Humfrye and Luke, they got away in time. Luke was always more tender than the other brothers—like a spring shoot."

"Have you seen Luke during this visit?" Joya asked. "He left without a word, and I'm worried for him. He has unfinished business with the queen and I was hoping ..." She stopped, wondering how much she could say. Monks and priests loved to gossip as much as alehouse wives.

"Nay. Like I said, Luke keeps to himself."

The rector's smile was genuine, and he didn't seem to be hiding anything, so she proceeded. "I thought I might stop at the guardhouse and see if anyone knows where Lord Penry might be. Who's manning the guard house today, do you know?"

"George Anter or Thomas Brooks, one or the other. If it be George, tell him I haven't seen him for Vespers in several days."

At the guardhouse, Joya found an appropriately chastised George who had been missing Vespers. George had been given a large face, but his eyes, nose and mouth had not been informed, so his features seemed concentrated, a small hub on a large wheel. Those features were lively, though, animated eyes, bobbing eyebrows and mouth busy with information.

Janet Lane

Luke's father, George said, enjoyed great wealth. He had inherited the massive estate, but was a poor manager of funds. George was still gossiping when she bid him good day with a wave and quietly shut the guardhouse door.

The Redstone changing house was quite the opposite in atmosphere. Once she passed the scrutiny of several guards, she was brought to James Swift. James was so tall and thin that a good wind would probably push him off the bridge. But he was professional, whisking her into a private money changing room, prepared to receive a new deposit or change funds for her.

When her conversation changed to inquiries about Luke, James backed away from her physically, stiff and alert. "I do not discuss the business of others."

"I respect you for that. When I transfer my funds from Coin Forest, I will expect that of you, too," Joya said. After the turmoil she had caused her father, she suspected that her funds would consist of what she currently carried on her person, but she assumed what she thought would communicate an aura of wealth and concern for it.

"I am heavily invested in Lord Penry's activities," she said. That investment was strictly from the heart, although she could stretch the truth by including the loan her mother made to her for travel expenses. "I should like to know where he is. That location will tell me whether he is investing my funds appropriately," she continued, echoing her father's words from overheard conversations and hoping it sounded convincing enough to gain some information.

"Lord Penry did not divulge his travel plans," James replied stiffly. "If that is all…" He rose, signaling the end of their conversation.

"He is in danger. I'm trying to help him."

James stiffened more.

"He has offended the queen, and he is ignoring her," Joya continued, needing desperately to convince him of the danger. "Both can bring grave consequences."

"If he has offended the queen, it's not without good reason. Lucas Bonwyk is a fine man. He lives by his principles, and he is purely and totally dedicated to England."

Joya resisted shaking her head to clear it. Why was he suddenly spouting testimony about Luke's principles and dedication to England?

Like ice melting to reveal the lake beneath it, it became clear to Joya. If James so admired Luke's courage and convictions—and his rebellion against the queen—it meant they shared the same views about Margaret ... and York!

She placed her hands on the table, rose on tiptoe and leaned forward. "You know where he is. You know."

"Aye," he replied.

"Where?"

"Here. In Redstone."

Joya hurried to Uncle Benjamin's house and found Degory on the back deck. "He's here?"

"And gone again," Degory said. "He must have come home just before dawn, and he left before I woke."

Chapter 18

Luke oared his boat to the pier, working quietly in the darkness. To avoid interrogation, he had deliberately stayed away from his uncle's house, waiting for the deep hours past midnight. He had only two days in which to prepare, mayhap less. If the Lancastrian troops traveled over drier roads, if Margaret whipped them into a fury, if they traveled with fewer supplies—many unknowns could hasten their arrival to the Red Bridge.

He waved to Wagg's guards, who followed his every move from the shoreline. They had personally loaded the two canisters they had packed, and they watched him now to be sure he anchored them properly to the bridge support system.

Good that they couldn't swim and had paled when he approached the dock to let them board. They had backed away instead, choosing to observe from ashore. Luke quietly opened an inconspicuous panel below the center seat and using his foot, dragged free the two canisters he had packed earlier by himself. Reaching down, he slid the guard-packed canisters into the compartment and closed the door.

Taking a wide stance to balance in the small boat, he lifted a canister. He wrapped it in oiled canvas the same ruddy color of the rocks at the base of the pier. Once secured to the pier, he dipped his hand into a bucket of mud and flicked it in a random pattern on the canvas. Once he had blended it to look naturally worn, he moved to a second pier and repeated the process.

Working alone, he had no one to help steady the boat as he worked. His movements were awkward, his progress slow. Finally he was done. He waved again to the guards. After rinsing the bucket, he returned his tools to the floor of the boat, lifted the oars and floated downstream to a thick copse of willows. He lifted the rope, untangling it before mooring the boat to the dock.

* * *

Joya shut the front door quietly and found Degory waiting for her. It was well over an hour before dawn, dark and misty.

"I found him." Deg spoke softly. "He went to the docks. Took a boat out."

"Is that saggy-eyed man with him?"

"Wagg? No. He was alone."

"Let's see what he's up to," Joya said.

"Did you learn anything from the bridge merchants?"

"Nothing more than what everyone seems to know, already—that Luke has returned." She faced him. "You didn't mention how Luke's father and brother died."

"You're dear to him. He should be the one to explain such a loss."

"You think I'm dear to him?"

"One need only see his eyes when he looks at you."

The words soothed Joya. "I so want to help him."

"You can."

"How? Whenver I try, it ends up tangled and ruined. Everyone in my family is clever except me. My mother manages Coin Forest. My sister, Faith, designs jewelry. Nicole reads in three languages. But I—" She hesitated to confess, but it had become such a burden, and Degory's look of concern reassured her.

She lowered her eyes. "I have no such wit as they."

Degory laughed. "Of course you do. You saw through James. I had no idea he supported York."

Stupid. Memories of Mother Issabel's harsh judgment scorched Joya. "I was told long ago. I am … slow-witted."

Degory tilted his head and peered into her eyes. "Despair not for that which should stay in the past. I have watched you. You light up a room when you enter it, and 'tis more than your gowns and jewelry. You're always thinking, listening, observing. And you saved Luke's life. You fooled four knights to free him."

"'Twas bad judgment. I shamed my father, I—"

"Your friends helped you, I heard."

"I'm sure they're suffering from my judgment."

"You're missing the point. The outcome may not have been as you wished, but they saw the worth in your plan. They know how capable you are. They trusted you enough to join you in your effort to free Luke."

Joya stepped carefully as the riverbank path became more steep. In light of Degory's reasoning, Mother Issabel's judgment lost some of its long-lived sting. Joya had not given such thought to it as Degory had. Was she dismissing her accomplishments because they displeased her father? Her mother had condemned the apricot seed tactic, but she had smiled when she talked of Joya felling four experienced knights. Joya had been warmed by that smile, for it revealed that she had made her mother proud.

Joya stood a little taller. "Thank you, Deg. Let's find out what Luke is doing down here at this hour."

They reached the docks.

"Look," Deg said. "There he is." Luke was untangling a rope, preparing to moor the boat to the dock.

"Godspeed, Lord Penry."

Luke turned toward Joya's voice. The interruption made his heart seize and her voice made his pulse quicken. "Joya." How much had she seen? "What in devil are you doing out at this hour? Are you alone?" The thought both annoyed and stirred him.

"Of course not," she said. "Degory is with me. We have some questions for you."

"Godspeed, cousin." Degory stepped out of the darkness, and the thin moonlight lit both of their profiles as they stood together on the bank that led to the boathouse. "What might you

218

be doing this fine ... night?" Degory tipped his head to the left. "Or would you say morning?"

Luke licked his lips. "I couldn't sleep, and remembered how ..." He searched for a useful word, "... soothing it was to take the boat out on the river."

"Odd that I didn't see you at dinner, or in your bed, failing to sleep," Degory said.

Curse Degory for bringing Joya along. Curse him twice for interrogating him, and thrice for doing it with Joya present. "I didn't need to put my head to the pillow to know I couldn't sleep."

"So you won't mind if we join you." Degory gave Luke a mealy-mouthed grin. "We would like a soothing ride, also."

"Please?" Joya added.

Luke conducted a quick mental search of the boat. There was only a bucket and some twine left, nothing incriminating. He could only hope they hadn't seen Wagg's guards or come to the shoreline until after he'd finished at the piers. "Come on."

They boarded and he threw the rope back into the boat. Joya wore her travel suit, but regardless of what she wore after Crystal Lake, whenever he looked at her he always saw the thin chemise she had worn there, wet, revealing her exquisite nipples. Desire bolted through his groin and he mentally tamped the thoughts down, offering her his hand to help her get settled on the smaller front seat.

He pointedly offered Degory one of the oars, and they took the wide middle bench and pushed off. "Where to?"

"The inlet," Degory said. "So you won't get too tired to bring us back."

Luke gritted his teeth. Before retiring, he would put tacks in Degory's bed.

They oared downstream past the boathouse into the quiet inlet, a good fishing spot for those who knew.

"Yes, most relaxing." Degory took a deep breath in and let it out. "Have you heard about the knights setting up camp south of here?"

Wagg's Irish mercenaries. "No." The outright lie ground like dirty gravel across Luke's tongue. He abhorred liars. Like an illness with no cure, he faced the unhappy prospect of telling more in the future. "Mayhap they're merchants, heading for the fair in Winchester?"

Degory shook his head. "That won't start for a fortnight. Thought you might know something of it since you've been traveling recently."

Luke's skin prickled. The boat seemed to be shrinking along with his choices. "Why would I?"

"Word has it they're York's forces." Deg oared three more strokes in silence. "There's over a hundred of them so far. Irish."

Luke waited. In the front seat, Joya was oddly silent.

"Could be merchants. Trading copper or tin."

"No. Their wagons are full of munitions."

Had Joya lost her tongue? Luke scratched his neck, awkward in the silence.

"And who is that man with the big ears who's been frequenting the bridge? I've seen you talking with him."

"Met him at one of my bridges. He knows my work." Luke walked around the answer, trying desperately to limit the deception.

Degory quit rowing. "Has he hired you, Luke? For a special project?"

Luke bristled under the scrutiny. "I do not discuss my projects until they're finalized."

"And have your plans with this man been finalized?" Degory prodded.

Luke's neck heated, and ill thoughts formed of how he could lift his cousin from his bench and throw him overboard. "I think this ride has come to an end." He grabbed the oar from Degory and rowed quickly to a small dock. "Godspeed, and get Joya home safely," he said, dismissing them.

"Oh, no, please don't be angry at Joya because of me," Degory said. "Take her around to the end of the inlet, give her a nice ride."

"Yes, please, Luke. Won't you?" Joya finally spoke. "I would so enjoy it."

"She has come all this way to be with you," Deg said, driving the stake deeper, trapping Luke.

Joya's lips, full and sensuous, were drawn in a pout, and her brown eyes sparkled in the moonlight. "You can go, Degory," she said. "Luke will take care of me."

Degory jumped up to the dock. "Get home before dawn, you two." He strode quickly off the dock and into the darkness.

"Ah, just you and me." Joya leaned forward. "In a boat." She added silk and softness to her voice. "Want to race?"

Luke's eyes, blue and angry, followed his cousin as he deserted him. Joya fought to contain a smile. Degory had helped her corner Luke. Haunted by the visions of her dream, she would now, at last, find the right words to make Luke return to the Lancastrian side.

"We know what the Irish camps mean, Luke. These are the plans you had in your saddle pack. You are leading them."

"Nay." He shook his head. "I am not."

She shot a frown his way. "You're very much involved. And why? Is it really no more than one royal struggling against another royal? When you speak of York, you speak of absolute right and wrong. York is honorable and pure and good, while Margaret is dark and evil and selfish. Oh, yes, and French. Is it that simple then?"

Luke intensified his rowing. She placed her hand on his arm. "Let's float. Give me this time, please, to understand you."

"We haven't the time. I must—."

"Must what?" She sighed in frustration. "I helped you, Luke. I freed you to do what you plan to do. Now I need you to help me. Everything I hold dear depends on it." She paused. "Must you die for your principles, even when you may be wrong?"

"You're frustrated because you've a strong feeling that I'm right. What you're feeling is fear."

"Of what?"

"Change. You cannot imagine a life for your family that does not include the shelter of Margaret's favor."

His words stung and invited more thought. For many years, her family had enjoyed preferential treatment from the crown. Could that be? "We are not loyal dogs who lay at her feet and bite anyone who threatens her."

He cocked his head to one side, as if weighing her comment. "Forsooth?"

The troubling images of her dream fueled her resolve to convince him. "There's to be a blood bath. Thousands of soldiers must die so York and his issue can sit on the throne."

"Who supports this French Queen, Joya? Not the English! All of London despises her and rufuses to supply soldiers to the king. Does this not tell you something about your beloved queen?

"She leads an army of 30,000, forced to serve, not for love of England or the king but for fear of the queen. Or for love of money, taken from our own people and used to wage war against us. Ask my dead brothers about her."

Luke's face softened, and his penetrating blue eyes turned pleading. "Joya, loyalty is not a one sided affair. It must be nurtured from each side. If it does not, what is it? Blind following. Or dedication based on fear? Loyalty is a decision we make. You can ally yourself with one whom you respect, with whom you believe in, and trust—or you can tie your sail to someone out of sheer gratitude. And a healthy dose of insecurity. What is your loyalty to Margaret based on?"

"God's blood, Luke! King Henry sentenced my brother Stephen to death. She saved him. Does that not count for our respect? Our trust?"

"Mayhap she saw the tides in England turning toward York, and the prospect of gaining undying devotion from your strong and established family looked attractive to her?"

"So you distrust her."

"She killed my brothers in cold blood."

"We have talked this to death. She has sworn she didn't."

"Easily staged."

"Who's being blindly loyal now?"

"My loyalty to York is based on my opinion of him. My faith that he will do what's right for England. It's not based on an isolated, selfish act that happened to become a saving grace for my family."

"Selfish?"

"On Margaret's part, yes. I'm loyal to the Plantagenets because York has earned it. I see his integrity and willingness to serve for the good of the country, not because he wants, as you say, to sit on the throne."

"You're as taken with York as we are with Margaret." Joya could swear she felt steam shooting out of her ears. "So York is so good and pure that he's approaching sainthood. Fine. But what about the men he would appoint to rule England? Are they so honorable and good? What about this strange man Degory mentioned? The one with the saggy eyes and big ears? Is he honorable and true?"

Luke dropped his eyes.

"Well?"

He started rowing again, not meeting her gaze. Joya's senses sharpened. She had found a flaw in his armor. "I sense he has dangerous secrets."

Luke smirked. "Some of your Gypsy magic?"

Joya drew a sharp intake of air. He attacked her heritage. She remained outwardly calm, but the affront made her bristle. Until he said that, they had been exchanging ideas, not slurs. "No magic. Simply something you should have seen but did not. After all, your brothers called you a turtle."

He drew back as if she had slapped him. She had wanted to hurt him back, and she had. Remorseful, she touched his arm. "I'm sorry. I know it hurts you but I understand why they said that. You avoid people, as if you're retreating into your shell. When you do that, you miss signs. Like this man—what's his name?"

"I can't divulge."

"Of course not." She had hoped he would have shared the name with her willingly. "This man with the drooping eyes." She snapped her fingers. "I remember now, his name is Wagg. I saw him the first night I came here, in your uncle's house. He was spying, edging close to overhear conversations. And the look he gave me was chilling."

A thoughtful expression came over Luke's features, and again he broke eye contact. She hoped that she had planted another seed of doubt about this man. "You say I'm afraid of change. I think you have wishful thinking about this spy whom neither Degory nor I trust. Think about that."

Luke did not respond.

"Think on York, too. Remember Ludford Bridge? Instead of staying with his men and fighting, he abandoned them, his tail between his legs. Should such a coward be king?"

"He retreated because his commanders switched sides. York's troops would have been slaughtered, so they left. It was not dishonorable."

Joya shook her head. "It's one thing to have a strong spirit, Luke, and I admire yours, but it's another to be so stubborn that you can't see the truth. The pickle barrel was horrible, but there was a lesson to be learned."

Luke's eyes widened and he dropped the oars. Recovering, his lips thinned and a muscle pulsed furiously in his jaw. She hated making him so angry, but she had to somehow reach him.

"What kind of lesson was that?" He slashed the words her way, venom deepening his voice even further.

"A lesson to not be so stubborn. Please, please consider the possibilities. You said you'd save England for me, remember?" She rushed on, hoping to open his mind, terrified that she had gone too far. "You can't save England. But you can save my family, and your family, too. Think of Hugh, your only remaining brother, and your uncle and your cousin Degory. Save them." She choked, the tears stinging the backs of her eyes. "Save us. Please, Luke."

He picked up the oars and sank them deep in the water, pulling them back out to the river. The oars created ripples in the water that slipped away from the boat, so like the deep hopes she had held, now swirling out of her grasp. Each stroke drew them nearer to the bridge, nearer to the end of their meeting, the end of her efforts. If she could not convince him after all she had said, it was hopeless.

She would gather her things, wake her father and ask him to take her home. She could not bear to stay and see Luke tortured.

She watched his face, memorizing the blue of his eyes, the intensity and passion always shining in them, the way the moonlight played on his brown hair, the firm set of his sensual mouth. She had tried.

He neared the shoreline and stopped oaring, letting the boat's momentum take them in and slide onto shore. The earth scraped against the bottom of the boat, a raw and decisive end to their journey together.

He covered her hands with his own and faced her. His blue eyes seemed to reach into her soul. His touch was gentle but firm, caressing the tops of her hands, a look so earnest and tender that she could no longer control her sorrow. Silent tears slid down her face, cooling in the pre-dawn chill.

He wiped her tears with his thumbs. "Nay. No more tears. I will do as you wish."

She shook her head. Her ears must be fooling her. "What?"

"I will declare my full and undying loyalty to our queen. I will do it before the sun sets on this new day. I vow to you."

Chapter 19

"Luke!" Joya cried. Her mother could never have spun a spell so potent as this one, to know that Luke had come to his senses. The thought danced in her veins and burst from her in a giggle that grew into full-throated laughter. Weeks of refusal from a man more stubborn than winter rains. Endless failure and frustration, but now, finally. Acceptance, and a vow. She jumped up from her seat at the front of the boat, reaching for him. "Finally!"

Her footing failed. Staggering out of balance, she rocked the boat. It lurched, the water surging up the sides. It tumbled her stomach and threatened to capsize the boat.

Luke bolted up, taking a wide stance. He lifted her at the waist, steadying her, his deep voice reassuring. "We don't want to go swimming again." He stilled her in his arms, settled the boat and helped her sit down.

She cradled his handsome face in her hands, laughing in delight. "You'll do it! Thank God! Thank the faeries! Thank you, Luke!" She rained kisses on his cheeks and neck.

His face sobered into an expression of sorrow, and she tried to kiss it away. "Do not worry so. All will be fine now. You'll see. Oh, Luke! I love you!" She covered his mouth with hers, kissing him deeply.

He resisted for a moment, then gave himself in to the kiss and pulled her close. Droplets of river water clung to his skin and she relished the scent of him, of summer and moist earth and the tang on his skin that was exclusively Luke.

Her Luke.

Her Lancastrian Luke.

She moaned, delirious with relief and the first sense of peace she had ever felt in his embrace. His mouth slid against hers, she thought she heard the singing of angels as she entered heaven.

He kissed her eyes, her forehead, her nose, and hands. "But you must make a vow to me." His voice had deepened, thick with desire, and he swallowed. "You must leave the bridge. This morning."

"I will not leave without you."

"You must. There will be a battle here."

A burst of wind chilled her back. "Here?"

"Soon, yes. You must quit the bridge. Today. You, your father, my uncle and aunt. Degory, and my brother, Hugh. You all must leave. I will take you to Marston, east of here. You will be safe."

"And you can come with us, and we—"

His face steeled. "You will not naysay me on this. You, Joya Ellingham, must pledge to me that you will do as I say with this. Your life—my life—depends on your leaving."

Fear chilled her, burrowing deep into her bones. "What's happening?"

His eyes narrowed. "There is no time for explanation. You must promise me. Now."

"Will I see you again?"

"God willing. Now say it."

"I vow—" She choked, stricken with the sudden return to the familiar, gnawing fear that she would never see his face again. She wiped away the first tear and ignored those that followed. Finally she took a deep breath, gave a shaky exhale, and continued. "I vow I will leave the bridge today."

"And?"

"Go to Marston with you."

His jaw muscle twitched. "And stay there until I come back for you."

She nodded.

He kissed her again, his mouth soft and gentle on hers.

* * *

Luke waited for Joya and Tabor to join him in the solar. He had returned from the boat storage building and visited with his uncle and cousin on the river deck, explaining that they needed to leave the bridge. Uncle Benjamin refused, saying he would stay and defend his home and village. Luke revealed that thousands of troops were coming. His uncle finally agreed to leave, and he and his aunt were packing their keepsakes.

To the east, the sun broke through the grey ceiling of clouds, promising good travel to Marston.

An object on the far shelf caught Luke's eye, and he retrieved it. The model bridge Luke had built for Joya.

Joya. Embers from her kisses still warmed him. He thought of how the sun played with the color of her eyes, lighting them from the shade of cinnamon to the hue of copper, and her hair, black and shimmering to her waist.

She reminded him of the dark-winged butterfly. She had fluttered into his life, bringing at times sunshine, fresh air and beauty. At other times her impulsive nature and best intentions created unimaginable crises.

She had brought the bridge he built for her from toosticcas. Impulsively, she had packed it with her clothes when she traveled from Coin Forest, and somewhere during her trip it had broken almost in half.

With time on his hands, he strode to the cupboard and grabbed a handful of fresh sticks. He could, at the least, repair *this* bridge. In his uncle's workshop, he found a small jar of horse hoof glue. Back in the solar, he began rebuilding the model. Working in the tiny space, he replaced portions of the arches.

This is what I was meant to do. Build. Not destroy.

Her words had stung him with their logic and simplicity. She had tried to save him, and he had injured her and her family. Save her—'twas the least he could do. Save England for her—had he really said that? Had his confidence grown into such arrogance? Forsooth. He could not save her, and he could not save himself. How had he been so bold as to think he could save all of England? Was he not as bad as Wagg?

And she loves me. How could this woman, the most beautiful woman Luke had ever seen, love such a fool? He owed her too much, and he had not the resources to repay her, or give her what she wanted. He had stumbled his way into a nightmare, and there was no escape for him, but he could get her and her family to safety.

She'd called him stubborn. He shortened a stick and dipped it into the small jar. Too stubborn to consider the facts before him. Must he die for his principles, even if they were wrong? Were they wrong?

Her comments about Wagg were the most unsettling, because she had put words to the growing mistrust Luke had been feeling. Because Luke had avoided his uncle's dinner and all his uncle's guests, Luke had not seen Wagg, and Wagg had not mentioned being there. Why hadn't Wagg told him he was there? *Was he checking up on me?* Suspicions needled their way into Luke's thoughts. If Wagg didn't trust Luke, why should Luke trust Wagg?

York's absence stuck in Luke's throat like a splintered bone. His brief message from Ireland had been only slight reassurance. Wagg was hiding something, but Luke had no concrete evidence to support it. The man was too vague about critical matters. York would be at the Red Bridge, he insisted, but where was he now?

Joya had accused Luke of being a turtle. God's blood! The memory of that pickle barrel penetrated his lungs like an acrid smoke, taking his breath. He had never thought about the meaning behind the cruel name; he had merely hated his brothers for it.

He let her words in again. "Don't be so stubborn. Consider other possibilities." He shook his head. He liked being alone, but there could be some truth in her words. He must stop keeping to himself. He must reach out to others. A man came to mind, someone who may help him. He plugged the glue jar, set the small bridge back on the shelf to dry, and met his uncle at the front door. "I'm on an errand," he told Uncle Benjamin. "I'll be right back."

Luke greeted the guards at the changing house and found James. In the privacy of the accounts room, he regarded the old man. Luke had come to help James save his business, but he also needed information. Could James be trusted? Would his information be reliable?

At the least, he would be more trustworthy than Wagg. Hopeful, Luke ventured out of his shell.

He met James' gaze, ready to note his every expression. "You have been discreet and trustworthy with my affairs," he said. "I have appreciated that."

"Thank you. How can I help you today, Luke?"

"You must keep what I am about to say in absolute confidence."

"You can be assured I will not—"

Luke held up his hand, palm facing James. "Some of what I tell you will affect you. You must promise me that you will conceal any worry or anxiety that may draw attention to you. I promise you, you have time to protect your business."

James' forehead tightened into two prominent vertical creases. "I will be subtle. Tell me."

"We are on the threshold of battle." He took a breath. "It will be staged on this bridge."

James' eyes widened. "Here. York?"

Luke nodded.

"When?"

"Soon," Luke said.

"He can't be here," James said.

"I have been told he is. I have seen his Irish troops; they are a few miles away. Margaret and Henry are traveling south, for St. Albans and London. York aims to stop them."

James' expression suggested he suddenly thought of the repercussions to his business, and his lips thinned. "My records. My clients' accounts."

230

Luke knew well his worry. Wherever there were battles, to the victors went the spoils. If the residents at the site of the battle were unfortunate enough to be on the losing side, lootings and burnings occurred. Margaret didn't know of James' support to York, but she was known to allow her mercenary knights to plunder at will as payment for fighting for the crown. James was at risk of losing everything, regardless the outcome of the battle.

"Move your records tonight," Luke said. "You may store them in the Flinton tithing barn. I have prepared this message for Will Flinton." Luke handed him a sealed parchment. "Warn the other bridge merchants, too, but avoid panic, and move by midnight. Post only guards you can trust."

"I hope Margaret's head rolls," James said.

Florin jumped down from the high shelf and into James' lap. James petted him and put him back on the floor. "I am indebted to you. I must tell you, though. York is still in Ireland. He isn't to return for at least a month."

An iron ball dropped in Luke's stomach. "What?"

"York plans to pick up more troops in Calais, but he is still in Ireland. "

"Why would he stay over? He planned all this."

"York is here, now?" James paused. "Have you seen him?"

"Nay."

"Who is your source?"

"Wagg, York's second in command."

"Second only in Ireland," James said. "In England, Warwick and Salisbury are closest to York, crucial to his plans." He paused. "Are you sure about the Irish?"

"I've seen them. The plans changed." Luke's mind raced. Either York and his leaders had found an ingenious, infallible plan that would end the war earlier, or Wagg was a rebel leader, acting independently and secretly. Would Wagg be so daring as that? Would York make such a big mistake of trusting Wagg?

"I'm sure they'll both be here, tomorrow or the day after, at the latest. Wagg is sure of the queen's travels, and that she can be easily defeated." Luke shook his head. "York said he'd be here. We need to reach him, posthaste."

"I'll do it," James said.

"My thanks. I must go. I'm moving my family out of danger. But York or not, there will be a battle." He struck James' arm lightly. "Thank you for the information."

"And to you for the warning. Godspeed," James said.

Luke gave Florin a scratch on his massive head. "I'll be back before sunrise."

* * *

Luke adjusted his armor and eyed his uncle's wagon. Large and filled to overflowing, it would be burdensome and slow them down during the journey to Marston.

Uncle Benjamin shot him a warning look. "Say no more on it. 'Tis what we need if we're to abandon our home."

"I did not have a part in this decision," Luke said.

"But you knew of it, all this time." The look in his uncle's eyes revealed bitter disappointment.

Luke led them from Redstone, his party of the Bonwyks, Lord Tabor and Joya. The wagon lumbered behind and Tabor's knights and Degory brought up the rear. Armor clanked with the gait of the horses, disturbing the late morning quiet.

Hugh lifted his breastplate, grimacing from the fit. He was so thin it had been hard to fit armor for him at Coin Forest. The smallest suit sagged on his thin frame, and the helm, a size too large, had wobbled on his head until he finally ripped it off and crammed it into his saddle pack. His hair stood on end from the helmet, giving him the look of having seen a ghost.

They traveled through the Cotswolds, one of the most beautiful parts of England, lovely rolling hills and pleasant valleys, stretching hundreds of miles from Avon to the north, all the way south to Bath. The area was rich from the wealth of wool, a treat for the eyes. The green countryside was dotted with spring flowers, sheep and small villages built with honeyed bricks of limestone. Achingly beautiful in the sunshine, they reminded Luke of his love for England. He wanted was what was best for her. And best for his and Joya's families. Would that he knew how to accomplish both, and get answers to all the nagging questions about York.

The roads were dry, which would help. Luke could not take them all the way to Marston. He would have to rely on Deg to do so.

Hours into their trip, they crested a hill and a sobering view unfolded. The fields below were splattered with signs of war. Hundreds of tents stretched, far as the eye could see, with large fields roped off for horses, dozens of smoking fires, and lines upon lines of wagons, many filled with arrows, their points glistening in the sun like sheaves of metal. Luke recognized the banners—the English troops Wagg mentioned.

Joya gasped and clutched her throat.

Luke extended his arm, stopping her horse. "Go back before they see us."

They backtracked quickly.

"What is it?" Degory, with the knights behind the wagon, had been too far back to witness.

"Troops. A few hundred," Luke said. They would move through the night to the Red Bridge.

"At least five hundred," Tabor said. "White banners."

"Yorkists," Uncle Benjamin said. "You should know, Luke." His tone was sharp.

"I didn't think they would be in this area."

"Where did you think they would be?" Uncle Benjamin glared. "God's teeth, Luke, you need to tell us."

"They're headed to the bridge."

"You never told us it would be this many." His uncle's voice was dark with accusation.

"I would never knowingly put you at risk. There's much I do not know," Luke said. "The sooner we get to Marston, the better."

They traveled with more urgency. As they approached the Marston village gate, Joya turned to him. "I would have a word with you." She led her horse away from the group and turned to him.

233

He joined her. "What?"

"Did you send word to Margaret?"

Luke's mind raced. "I haven't had the time. I was planning to find a messenger here."

"You vowed. You say there's much you don't know, but there's also much you do. You need to get word to her. You will seek a messenger here?"

"Aye."

Anger distorted her features. "You don't meet my eyes. You lied to me to get me to come here, didn't you?"

The extended lack of sleep had left him weak-minded. His web of lies and half-truths caught up with him, dulling his senses. Had he avoided deceit? Had he—

She slapped him with her reins. "Leave me." She spun her horse away and returned to her father's side, her lip curled in contempt.

Her scorn was a dagger to his side. She had believed in him for so long; why now would she drop all faith?

"I'll check for a messenger," Luke said.

"We'll wait here," Tabor said.

"Hugh." Luke gestured to his brother to follow him and they entered the village gate. "I need to send a message."

Hugh made a strange, guttural sound and reined his horse to a stop.

Luke turned to his brother. "What? You look as if you've seen the devil himself."

Hugh angled his horse behind Luke. "It's him," he said, his voice a hoarse whisper.

"Him? Who?"

"The bastard who killed our brothers." Hugh's face was as white as his teeth.

A man was leaving the inn with a woman on his arm, an alehouse woman by the looks of her carelessly provocative dress. By his posture and movements, he looked to be around Luke's age, average height, but by the considerable development of his arms and thighs, he had spent time in the lists. Based on his black-stubbled scalp, he had shaved his head a sennight ago. His charger was hitched at the side of the building. He wore only a breastplate over his breeches and a short sword was sheathed on his left, a war sword on his charger.

Caution knotted Luke's belly. "'Tis some distance. You may be wrong, Hugh. Let's get closer."

"Nay! He's an ox, and see his hair. He was nigh bald when he took Penryton." His brother's voice was as raw as it had been in Tabor's solar when he first told the tale of the siege. Without his helm, Luke imagined Hugh felt vulnerable. "He called me Goat Boy. He'll kill me."

"I'll kill him first."

Hugh's eyes, wide with fear, darted back and forth. Luke wished he had time to soothe his little brother. He had always been sickly and underdeveloped and had barely escaped this man's sword. Luke grabbed his brother's reins so he couldn't bolt. "Think of your fallen brothers. Get control of yourself. Come behind this tree and wait for him to pass. You'll get a better look."

Covered, they watched the man kiss and fondle the woman.

She held him tightly, as if trying to capture him, pressing her body close to him. He wrenched free, mounted the charger and rode toward them.

Hugh's breath heaved, rushed out in shallow puffs. "'Tis him."

"You're sure?"

"Sure as my own name."

The man lacked armorial bearings—a mercenary. Fury made it hard for Luke to breathe. He would kill this butcher or die trying.

A curtain of white rage rose behind Luke's eyes.

Luke was no stranger to the lists. He had trained in Ireland most recently, and had proven his skill at arms. "Slow down," he told his brother. "He has to pass us to get to the gate. We'll bide our time for the perfect spot."

They followed him through the village, waited at a respectable distance as he passed the gate to leave. Luke noted

Janet Lane

with relief that Tabor had taken Joya and Benjamin's family away from the gate entrance.

Hugh and Luke turned down the narrow lane leading north out of town. They stayed far enough back to avoid detection until the knight reached the crest of a large hill. He had passed a timbered area, and happened to look back. He spotted Luke and Hugh. He spurred his horse into a run.

His charger was large and powerful, but Luke and Hugh rode horses from Tabor's stables, known throughout England for their speed. Luke closed in on the knight.

The man grew careless. He jumped a fence, entering a compound of sheep.

The compound included two large grazing fields, each about two acres square, bordered by two small shearing pens and buildings. The assassin had entered the largest field.

The herders ran from the shade of a large oak tree and chased the knight, whistling and calling commands to the herding collies. The men spotted Luke and Hugh in hot pursuit. Sensing trouble, they scurried off the green field to the safety of their shepherd's hut.

The dogs nipped the heels of the sheep, trying to draw them away from the horses, but the sheep scattered in a roiling chaos. The knight chose to bolt for the west fence, threading through the flock. He made good progress until an old ewe stumbled and fell, causing others to fall. The sheep behind them collided with those in the front. The killer's horse stepped on the sheep and there was the sound of bones breaking. The mercenary's charger stumbled and fell in the white sea of squealing wool.

Luke picked through the confused herd and reached the knight. He was dazed from the fall and lay on the ground, surrounded by the bloodied ewes. He shook his head, jumped up. Clutching his war dagger, he braced his legs for battle.

Luke closed in on him and slid from his horse, sword drawn.

The knight raised his sword against him.

Luke advanced. A primitive roar of revenge broke free from his throat. "This is for my brothers!" He lashed out with his sword, determined to cut the man in half.

The knight dodged the sword. "Who in Hades are you?"

"I'm Lucas. Lucas Bonwyk, you swine."

"Bonwyk. Oh! Nothing personal there. Queen's duty, you know." His lips twisted into a cynical smile.

So he knew it was Margaret. "You killed my brothers. It sure as hell is personal." Luke advanced.

Swords clanged. The knight's sword skimmed to the hilt of Luke's sword, jarring his shoulder and wrist.

The knight wore no vambrace, so Luke retaliated with a fast thrust, catching a quarter of flesh on the knight's forearm. The knight's face fell for a moment, and he laughed. "You'll have to do better than that, Penry."

"I did. I struck sinew." Luke swung again, shoulders rotating, feet dug in the grass for stability.

They struggled, each man measuring, pacing, attacking.

Luke took deeper breaths, trying to see clearly through his rage. He lunged again.

He struck the knight's armor in his midsection. The metal dented, knocking the air out of his lungs. He grunted and stumbled.

Thundering hoof beats sounded behind Luke.

Hugh came rushing toward the knight. "Kill him!"

The knight looked up. "Goat Boy!" He burst into laughter.

The look on Hugh's face melted from fury to fear, and he reined his horse sharply.

Hugh's horse stopped so short that Hugh flew up in the saddle, catching himself before he toppled over his steed's head. Hugh scrambled back in the saddle and turned tail, spurring his horse away.

The assassin sidestepped to his horse and pulled his sword, never taking his gaze from Luke.

A smile curved the killer's mouth, taunting Luke. He thought of Christopher, so accomplished in the lists. His brother would have emerged victorious from a fair fight, but this devil's whelp had used royal livery as protection and cut his brother down.

Luke bellowed and struck the knight's sword.

Anger boiled in Luke's veins. He lunged and attacked without fear, eager to kill. Blades collided. Steel clanged. Luke saw nothing but the killer's eyes and his sword.

The assassin moved smoothly with quick, precise thrusts. He moved well. A message fired in the back of Luke's mind, an urgent message that he douse his anger to better match his opponent.

A sensation of fire cut across Luke's wrist.

Luke looked down, saw the deep wound. He returned his gaze to the killer. He willed his arm to keep swinging, and an inner calm came over him.

The killer's focus shifted and he pulled back to attack.

Luke countered before the killer could strike.

Steel met steel and the killer's wrist collapsed. His sword fell to the ground.

Pain needled Luke's hand, and he sucked air into his lungs, pressing his sword to the knight's chest.

The knight placed his arms out in surrender. "Don't kill me."

"Wait, wait!" Hugh called out. "I want to see him die."

Luke poised his sword to run him through. "This is for my brothers, Christopher and Humfrye."

The knight panted, but had the ballocks to smile. "Think. Or you'll never know who hired me."

Joya's voice rang in Luke's head, "How can you be so sure it's the Queen?" He considered it for a moment, but promptly shut the door and glared at the killer. "You said it yourself, it was Margaret."

"I said it was the queen's business. She has enemies. It was not her."

Luke's breath came fast and short, the killer's words sinking in. Would he regret never knowing? By Jove, he would, for the rest of his days. "Speak now, while you still can," he rasped.

"Nay." The mercenary laughed softly. "If I tell you, there's a price."

Luke held his sword, considering. He could run this fiend through and avenge his brothers now, this moment. But he would never learn who sent this bastard to sack his home and kill them. "You're a paid killer. I will not spare your life."

"You will. You will vow to me—vow to me on the souls of your brothers—that you will spare me. Then I will tell you."

Fury blinded him. "You murder my brothers and expect me to pledge on their souls? Never. Show us how brave you are with your own life, you bastard. Tell me and take the chance."

The mercenary's lips curled away from his teeth, and he shook his head.

Luke stared at the paid slayer. Even in his compromising position, the man's eyes burned, cold and calculating. Luke knew at that moment that he would die before revealing his secret.

It tortured him to think of letting this man go free.

"Lucas." Hugh shouted from a distance. "Pledge. So we can know."

Wary of distraction, Luke resisted glancing at Hugh. After witnessing this murderer kill his brothers, if Hugh would spare his life to get the truth, how could Luke kill him?

Moments passed.

Blood had saturated the padded gambeson under the killer's armor. Luke flicked his sword by the knight's right ear, slicing him again. "I will give you a twenty-yard lead."

"Thirty. On horseback. With my sword and dagger." He spoke his words firmly, but the whites of his eyes showed his fear.

"All right," Hugh said, still maintaining a good distance. "Swear, Luke." He paused. "Pray do it now."

"The truth," Luke growled.

"The truth," the killer repeated.

"And if you deceive me, I will track you down and kill you and all you hold dear."

"You need not worry," the knight rasped. "The minute I tell you, you will know I speak the truth."

Luke tamped down the fury that boiled under his skin. "I vow, on my brothers' souls, that I will release you. Now," Luke growled. "What's your name?"

"That wasn't part of our agreement. I said I would tell you who ordered your brothers dead."

Fury distorted Luke's vision. He took a breath to clear his thoughts. "Who hired you?"

The killer met Luke's eyes and held them, his gaze purposeful and fearless, but his chest rose and fell like high tide at Tintagel.

Silence hummed. Luke found it difficult to breathe.

"Wagg," the knight said. "It was Wagg."

Chapter 20

The killer rode away. Luke and Hugh retraced their route the two miles back to Marston to rejoin Tabor, Joya and their family. Luke dabbed at a bleeding cut on his wrist—the killer's sword had found the space between Luke's vambrace and gauntlet and sliced him, barely missing the sinews.

And Luke had let him go. He shook his head. He had failed to avenge his brothers. Their murderer had slipped like dust through his hands, uttering lies as bald as his head as he rode to freedom.

God's bones! Wagg was secretive and arrogant, but if naught else he was loyal to York, and so eager to put him on the throne that he was taking foolish chances, but he would never ... York would never order Wagg to kill Luke's brothers. Luke was sure beyond doubt that the Duke of York was an honest man. He'd proven that at St. Alban's. His troops had defeated and captured the king, but never harmed him. York had served as Henry's Protector and always treated him with kindness and dignity.

Unlike the killer, who had no honor. He killed for the highest bidder, and who could be higher than royalty? Luke should have run him through and been done with it. Now all he held in his hand was a wound and an insulting lie.

Hugh and Luke returned to the Marston wall and the guard delivered bad news. Part of their uncle's party had left. Lord Tabor and Uncle Benjamin had headed east, back toward

Redstone. Luke's Aunt Emma, Degory and Joya had entered Marston and gone to the inn.

"Why would they go back?" Hugh asked.

"Tabor would prefer to die defending the king," Luke said.

"But Uncle Benjamin, leaving Aunt Emma?"

"It's his bridge. He's mayor. He likely had no intention of staying here. He rode along to make sure Emma was safe. Now he can defend his home." Luke turned his horse to the right, toward the inn. "Let's check on the ladies, and I would have a word with the killer's woman. We may be able to learn the bastard's name, at the least."

The inn was bustling, large for the size of the village because Marston was on the way to a market town. Its thatched roof, checker boarded with fresh repairs and its swept walkways suggested cleanliness, and a guard was posted at the front entrance, his expression welcoming but observant, all signs of a well-managed inn. Luke was encouraged that Joya and his aunt would be safe here.

He rested his hands on the counter. His glove had shrunk tight on the wound, which had started swelling, but it was best to keep the blood hidden. A young man guarded the keys, his eyes wary, his cheeks so doughy his mouth seemed to hide under the swells of skin.

"Good eve." Luke said, keenly aware that darkness had fallen. He had precious little time. He should be on the road back to Redstone.

The clerk's gaze swept over his armor and he glanced toward another guard, who came closer. "We'll have no trouble here."

"Rest assured, you won't," Luke said. "We're here to see our aunt, part of the Bonwyk party. They arrived this afternoon."

"From whence do you hail?"

"I am Luke Bonwyk, Lord Penry, Somerset. And my brother, Hugh."

"Abovestairs, second door to the left," he said.

"One room? There are two women and a man," Hugh said.

"Two women and three men," the clerk said. "Two knights and a man about your age. The men have the room to the left of them."

Luke pounded on both doors and received no response at either one. He asked the doughy youth at the desk for a key, but he refused to give one.

Luke could imagine Joya's big brown eyes as she promised her father she'd stay at the inn. Tabor may have forgotten the apricot seeds, but Peter likely hadn't. "Let's check the stables."

The stable boy delivered more bad news. "Aye, I saw them. The young lady is quite comely, she..." He glanced at Luke and his smile faded. "They wasn't long, even with all those bags. They no sooner went to the inn than they came back again, bags and all. Packed their horses and left."

"Unescorted?" Luke asked.

"Nay. A merchant and two knights were with them."

"Deg, Peter and Martin," Hugh said. "Did they say where they were going?"

The boy shook his head. "Nay." He cocked his head to one side. "Wait. They spoke of a bridge, but not by name."

Luke flipped the boy a penny. "Do you remember seeing a knight with very short hair, shorn almost bald?"

"Aye. He's big, isn't he? He's soft on Lizbeth. She's big, too. Well, I mean, her—" He cupped his hands at his chest, swaying them and grinning at his clever hint about her physical charms.

"Might you recall his name? We made a wager, and he owes me."

The boy sobered. "Winton Hawke. Lord Clavell. But he left for good this time," he said. "Lizbeth is vexed."

Luke flipped him another penny. "For your mum."

"My thanks!"

"What now?" Hugh asked.

Luke closed his eyes. The moon was rising. God's teeth! Joya and Aunt Emma traveling at night to Redstone. Accompanied by knights, but what good were they in the face of armies?

Hours later Luke and Hugh arrived in Redstone, not having seen Joya and her party. For once, seeing the bridge brought Luke no pleasure. Foresooth, the bridge that had brought him so much joy as a child now looked more like a gate to danger.

The sun was just rising, and Redstone had become a spectacle of war.

To the north, the steep hill that led to Coventry was red with Lancastrian forces. They spilled up and over the hill like blood, past the crest and beyond, and down the riverbank to the east and west of the bridge as far as the eye could see.

To the south, the gentle hill and the road that led to St. Albans and London was alive with horses, archers, foot soldiers, wagons, and glaring white banners. The white extended like a giant sheet to the east and west of the riverbanks.

I'm too late. Luke thought of a hundred paths he hadn't taken and should have—things he didn't say and should have, secrets he hadn't shared and should have.

Degory raced his horse up to meet them. "Where in God's name have you been?"

"Waiting to see you at the inn. Where's Joya?"

"She's in the boathouse with Aunt Emma."

"Why did you leave Marston? They were safe there."

"You know Joya. We could follow her or try to find her later after she sneaked out the minute we closed our eyes. I don't know that I could stay either," Deg added. "It's Redstone. I couldn't abandon my home."

"God's nails." It confounded everything, but Luke understood the compulsion to protect one's home.

"The king is here. Margaret, and the prince," Deg said. "Every soul from Coventry seems to be here. Tabor rode his men north to see how many troops. He says seven, eight thousand."

The Irish would be outnumbered more than four to one, precisely what Luke had feared. "York? Is York here?"

"I haven't seen him."

Luke absorbed that. Joya's words echoed, "Wagg is not to be trusted."

"Wagg is here with a small army of Englishmen," Deg said. "A handful of noblemen and several hundred Irish. They're all camped on the south side. No livery—all peasants or mercenaries. Methinks they'll parley soon." Degory's eyes darted. Tension seemed to pulse from his body. "And what will you do here, Luke?"

Luke ignored him. He was consumed with one thought: James. "I have an errand to do. Hugh, go with Degory to the boathouse. I'll be there shortly."

Luke raced his horse to the bridge and rode onto the deck to the changing house. It was boarded up, but Luke saw movement on the front step, something black and white with a huge head.

Florin sat, meowing to get in. Foolish cat. With those gleaming gold eyes, someone would get spooked and kill him. Luke scooped him up. No James meant no news of York, but he could get Florin to safety.

He approached his uncle's house. Lights shone in every window. From the rooftop and from the ladder swing's support pole, several red banners furled in the light breeze, making it clear to all that Lancastrian supporters would protect the north side of the bridge. York's forces would think twice before attacking his uncle's house.

Lord Tabor rushed out with Uncle Ben. "Tell us what to expect, son," his uncle said.

"Bloodshed," Luke said. "Why did you not heed my warnings earlier, when I took you to Marston? Why did you come back?"

"Your uncle will fight for our queen," Lord Tabor said, a look of sheer disgust in his eyes. "Something you should have decided to do." Tabor turned. "You're a traitor. Get out of my sight."

His uncle regarded him at a distance, his face tight with pain and disappointment.

It was too much for Luke. He backed away and hurried to the boathouse. The sea of red soldiers ended about twenty yards before the bridge. The men watched him, the space between them crackling with apprehension.

Guards lined the city walls and filled the towers at the village north of the bridge. In the weak light at sunrise, lights shone in every window of the guardhouse.

The cold air held the smoke of distant fires and an ominous silence.

The usher Michael and three knights guarded the boathouse entrance. He glared at Luke, his eyes narrowed with the look of a man who had been told a bad secret. "Luke." All of the usual affection in his voice had been stripped, replaced with a tone of dismissal.

Inside, the boats normally housed there had been removed and benches brought in to accommodate villagers seeking safety from the post-battle pillage. Those who could find no shelter at the church had come here, filling the small boathouse to the walls.

A fire burned near the window with a makeshift chimney that channeled most of the smoke outside. The residue tainted the air, causing some to cough. Joya sat with Emma and other women in the front row. She glared at him.

"Florin," Emma said. "I'll take him." She cooed to the cat, and he jumped out of Luke's arms and into his aunt's lap.

A group of young children huddled on the floor in the corner. His aunt followed Luke's gaze. "They had no other safe place to take them," his aunt said. "All the fields are filled with soldiers."

"Joya, I would have a word with you," Luke said.

She raised her chin. "For what purpose?"

"Please." He moved toward the door.

She rose and strode past him.

Outside, he reached for her hand, and she put both of her hands behind her back. "You lied to me."

"I meant my vow to you."

Her eyes sparked, dark and dangerous. Her fists were clenched, her mouth tense. "Oh, yes, your vow was earnest. And all this," she stabbed the air and swept her hand at the bridge, "is merely a parade honoring your fealty to the queen."

"You think I could stop this? You think I'm more influential than King Henry and the Duke of York?"

"I think you could have prevented this, had you lived up to your vow. You're so damned sure of York's right to rule. How many must die to please you?"

"Surely you don't think I want war!"

"Tell me you have not met with York or his men."

"And are you any better, Joya Ellingham? You and your favored queen. Do you care how many die supporting her? How many must die to please you?"

She gasped. "Our time is done." She veered clear of him as if he had grown blisters of plague, and strode back to the boathouse.

Wagg was waiting for Luke at the south end of the bridge. Luke threaded his way through the crowds. People, people everywhere. The dreaded heat crept up his neck, into his scalp, a malady from which he'd suffered all his life in the presence of large groups of people. The smell reminded him of the hoards in London, but worse. Wagg's saggy eyes were sharp today, watching Luke with the same intensity as Luke was studying him.

"Where's York?" Luke searched the bridge and nearby fields for the tall Richard, Third Earl of York with his proud posture, blond hair and split-trimmed beard.

"He's been delayed."

"I've been told he's still in Ireland."

Wagg's eyes narrowed. "You doubt my word?"

"Is he in Ireland?" Luke repeated.

"I swear on my first born son's life, he is on his way."

Luke considered. He had no concrete evidence, only James's claim, and James may not have the connections he thought he did. "Did you hire assassins to kill my brothers?"

Wagg widened his eyes. "Where do you get these thoughts? We are united for York's cause. We help each other. Whatever would I gain from killing off your family?"

Luke considered the question, but he was exhausted from travel, emotionally spent from being condemned by all the people he held dear.

Wagg put his hands on his hips. "Where have you been?"

"Protecting my family."

Wagg gestured at Luke's bandaged wrist. "What happened?"

"Someone underestimated me."

Wagg raised a brow. "Does he still breathe?"

"With more difficulty now. Where, specifically, is York? Is he on Irish soil or English?"

"He's sailing. He's on his way. It's not easy for him to travel and still avoid capture."

"You've forced me to lie to my family," Luke said. "What are you not telling me?"

Wagg's nostrils flared, and his face darkened. "Your suspicions paralyze you. Think not that York is trying to join us? Think! And yes. War is ugly business." He pointed to the Irish troops behind them. "You think those men don't have conflicts, too?" He pointed to the north side of the bridge, where royal troops covered the steep hill, thousands of them behind them, and to each side of them, a sea of red pendants and royal livery.

"They're no different from you, Luke. You're brooding because you believe in York, but your family supports the king. Those troops support the king, but they have brothers, cousins, friends, sons, even fathers who support York. Thanks to Margaret, England is torn down the middle. You're not the only one suffering in this war, Penry." Wagg glared at him. "But you are the only one I'm relying on right now, this morning." His speech appeared to have exhausted him and he gasped. "Are you ready?"

"Yes," Luke said. "I am ready."

"I need your assurance. I'm risking my life with this, too. Do you think I killed your family?"

"No."

"Can I count on you? On this day?"

No, you cannot. "Yes."

Hugh and Deg joined Luke on the bridge.

Hugh looked from one side of the bridge to the other and lowered his voice. "The king's army outnumbers them. How in Hades does Wagg think he can win?"

Aware of Wagg's proximity, Luke replied, slightly louder, "He must have a secret weapon."

A sobered Lord Harmon took in the size of the royal army and limped to the bridge. He and Wagg shared a lengthy, whispered conversation.

At the Lancastrian end of the bridge, people stirred and horses whinnied.

Luke's neck tingled. He touched his brother's arm and spoke with urgency. "Hugh, it's time for you to go to the boathouse."

The muscle at his brother's jaw worked, pulsing. "I must needs stand with my brother."

"I'm appreciative, but you'll be safe there."

Hugh shook off Luke's hand and stepped away. "I am a Bonwyk."

The sky seemed to press Luke to the ground, and he tasted death in the air, a bitter, sour taste of finality. That his brother also did was clear in his eyes. Luke struggled with a stinging in the back of his eyes. "I am proud to have you as my brother. Now go to the boathouse."

"I will go to my death as Hugh, and never by another name."

"Go to the boathouse," Luke repeated.

The hurt shone in his brother's eyes for a moment, quickly replaced with a new resolve. "I will die with honor, not cowering in the shade."

Luke took a step toward Hugh, prepared to drag him to safety if need be.

Wagg stepped between them, blocking Luke. "Yes." He gave Luke a penetrating stare. "Your brother will stand with honor. Next to me." Wagg's eyes flashed with warning.

He's threatening me. And Hugh. Outrage flushed Luke's veins, but he had no time to address it.

The mass of soldiers and horses shifted, forming three distinct companies to the north. War had come calling, and time, with its chance to bid farewell, had run out. He looked past Wagg and gave Hugh a steady gaze, one that he hoped told of his concern and of their bond. "Godspeed, brother."

"Godspeed," Hugh answered, his gaze just as intense and determined.

Trumpets sounded. The sun broke free, spilling gold down the center of the river. The sea of cavalry and archers parted, and one man rode forward. King Henry sat, tall and determined on his steed, both of them in full armor, resplendent in polished steel. He held his shield, bright with rampant lions and fleur de lis. Trumpets sounded again and a second horse and rider appeared, this one shorter, more diminutive.

Queen Margaret. Honey brown curls covered her head, contained with gold netting. Below a jeweled gold crown, a single suspended pearl trembled above her eyes. She regarded the troops at the other side of the bridge, her gaze turning to Wagg, and Luke. Her eyes dominated her delicate, round face, her nose long and thin, her mouth small, forming a cupid's bow. Her expression regal, imperious. She claimed the moment with her presence, and the force of her spirit touched all around her.

Murmers grew to a loud pitch on the south side of the bridge. Once she had been recognized, guards spilled in on both sides to protect her.

Another round of trumpets sounded, and a third rider appeared.

An audible gasp of hundreds arose from the south.

"The Prince!" someone said.

"Prince Edward!" another exclaimed.

The news traveled to the large companies in the south fields.

The prince, only twelve years old, sat stiff in the saddle, chin high, eyes straight ahead. He had gained the height of manhood but not the meat, obvious even with his full set of armor.

The murmurs grew to a soft roar through the Irish troops.

More guards slipped in to protect the prince, and they escorted him and the queen off the bridge.

Wagg grabbed Lord Harmon's arm. "The stars are with us."
He slapped Luke's arm repeatedly. "All three here. Exactly as I
had predicted."

"Where is the Duke of York?" King Henry asked.

Wagg mounted his horse and drew him to the bridge deck.
"York is not here, Your Majesty. I am Simon Wagg, Lord
Carston, in the Duke's stead."

Lord Harmon led his horse up to the deck, next to Wagg.
"And I am Joseph Bartholemew, Lord Harmon, and I stand with
Lord Carston."

"Bearing arms against your king?" Margaret asked from the
safety of the north edge of the bridge.

"You are committing high treason, both of you," the king
said. "You will be drawn, quartered. Your heads will be posted in
London for all to see. Your lands are hereby withdrawn, your
heirs bereft if you fail to let me pass and beg my pardon." Henry
signaled his knights.

They passed the king and entered the bridge, advancing three
feet.

"I do this for England, Your Majesty. I am under York's
command, not yours," Wagg said. Sweat slithered down his jaw,
but he did not wipe it away. He sat even taller in his saddle. "You
may not pass." He signaled the Irish troops forward.

King Henry advanced two more feet and ordered his knights
to close in behind him.

Luke's muscles tightened to the point that breathing was
difficult. All fell silent, waiting to see if Wagg would respond.

Wagg looked to Luke and wiped sweat that had dripped in
his eyes.

"These are trying times," King Henry said.

Luke swallowed an ounce of awe, instilled since childhood
for the royal family. The king was a good man, devout and
generous. Honest and true-intentioned. His only flaws were his
infirmity and his absolute trust in Margaret of Anjou.

There was an elegance to him, a dignity that emanated from
the man. The massive crowds fell silent, listening.

"In this time of uncertainty," Henry continued, "Many slanders are committed. Truth is blurred, becoming hard to determine, and loyalties are strained.

"Listen closely. What I say will affect not only your lives today, but your family's lives and your lands, throughout many generations."

Henry's horse danced, and he settled it. "Stand down from this shameful position of treason. Surrender your arms. Pledge your loyalty to the true crown of England. Do this and I will pardon you. Now. This day. This hour. Pledge to me and save yourselves."

Hoofbeats sounded from behind Luke. A rider passed, his horse large, a charger. Luke looked up as he passed.

The bald-cut killer. Shock clarified Luke's vision. His brothers' murderer, a look of humility on his face, his shoulders rounded in servility and submission.

"Sorry, my lord," the killer said clearly to Wagg as he passed.

He met the knights and surrendered his sword, and he was allowed to approach the king.

The killer dismounted and dropped to his knee. "I am Winton Hawke, Lord Clavell, Your Majesty."

The king peered at him. "Lord Clavell is over forty years old."

"I am his son. My father was killed on the battlefield at Blore Heath. I'm sure you will recall his valor."

Son? Luke shook his head. Rubbish. A nobleman didn't murder his fellow countrymen for hire. The killer probably murdered Lord Clavell.

The king looked skyward as if to remember Clavell's death. He looked to his nearest commander, who merely shrugged his shoulders. The king paused and looked down at the killer. "Of course. He was a good man."

" I have four hundred soldiers in my company," the so-declared Clavell continued. "I have ordered them to withdraw. We were deceived. Tricks and threats were used to get us to turn against you."

"Liar!" Wagg shouted. The Irish troops booed and protested, drowning the killer's voice.

"We wish," the killer started, and stopped to let the protests die down. "We wish to serve you and your queen in any capacity. Please spare us." He glanced briefly at Luke and shot him a faint smile before returning his attention to the king. "I do truly apologize. I profess and declare in my conscience before God that our Sovereign Lord King Henry is the lawful and rightful King of this realm, and no other. I am at your command."

King Henry studied the killer's upturned face. "For your humility and apology, you and your men are spared." They lowered their voices and conversed, and Winton Hawke, if that was his name, disappeared into the crowd behind the king, likely to be interrogated about the day's battle strategies.

The king turned his attention to the army at the south end of the bridge. "Who else will come forward and declare fealty to me?"

The Irish soldiers' comments rose to a loud buzzing, but no one else came forward. Resolve froze their faces and they looked one to the other, all knowing what it meant to be taken alive.

"So be it."

Wagg retreated to the riverbank, dismounted and approached Luke. "He'll wait for more to defect and beg his pardon, but we must be ready. He pointed to the supporting piers under the bridge. "Light them," he barked.

It was time. Cold settled in Luke's stomach, cold and a dead calm. A glance back on the south bridge entrance showed that his brother was now being held by an Irish soldier. Luke tipped his head toward the boathouse and mouthed, "Go."

His brother shook his head and turned to watch the king.

"God spare you." Luke whispered and strode down the bank and under the bridge.

Damp from lack of sun, the earth filled the base structure with a dense, green smell. He stepped over a large rock, round and so moist it had grown a crop of short, hair-like moss all over the top.

His last image of the killer's short-cropped hair flashed in his mind—the killer, fading into the crowd of royal soldiers at the north end of the bridge.

Wagg's words echoed to him from his meeting with Wagg at Rewley Abbey. "We will kill her and her bastard son."

The Prince!

Comprehension flashed through his mind, a punishing insight. He lost his footing and stumbled off the rock.

Joya's voice echoed, tightly strung words about Wagg. She didn't trust him. She had a good sense of people, spent a lot of time with them, unlike Luke. She had seen the signs.

The facts assaulted him.

The killer had kept his promise back in Marston. He had told the truth.

Wagg was the one who had ordered his brothers killed.

York himself had talked of Wagg's outstanding sagacity, his quick perception. Wagg had harnessed York's Irish and English soldiers. He needed Luke, but Luke was at risk of being swayed to Margaret's side by his family and one beautiful woman named Joya. What better way to keep Luke hostile toward Margaret than to have him think she killed his brothers?

James was right. York had to be in Ireland, or he would be here. There were no changes to York's original plan. This Red Bridge attack was Wagg's idea, his self-important means to become York's hero. Wagg could kill without honor, because he had none. That made him more dangerous than York to Margaret and the king.

Recent events became clear to him. He connected formerly unconnected events that he had been too distracted to see before when he struggled with the loss of his brothers and his conflicting loyalties.

Luke had paid no heed to Wagg when he said he would kill the king, the queen and the prince, all in one day. Even though the king's wife and son had accompanied him to the Red Bridge, Luke knew both would be well protected by royal guards. By Luke's reckoning, if Wagg's plan caused the king to fall with the bridge and die, Margaret and the prince would survive.

But place an assassin in the midst of the royal family, an assassin clever enough to pose as a faithful nobleman-gone-astray. Get him in close proximity to the prince, and the deed could be done! The king drowned, in the river, the prince murdered by the assassin and even if Margaret survived, she would be rendered powerless.

York would win, assume the throne—and someone would have to take public blame for killing the king.

Luke's stomach went cold. Besides himself, the only witnessses to Wagg's scheme were Wagg and his man, Lord Harmon.

They will testify that you did it. York would condemn Luke's cowardice and Luke's head would decorate the gate. Wagg would be privately rewarded for his coup. Luke slammed his fist in his hand. "God rot it!" He ran to the boat he had ready for the purpose and rowed out to the gunpowder-rigged pier. He lit the fuse, making sure Wagg could see it burning from his angle. The burning fuses would protect Luke's brother and keep Wagg on his course to disaster. Though he had lacked the facts until now, Luke had followed his instincts with Wagg. Luke wouldn't blow up the bridge and the king of England based on a weasel-mouthed braggard who couldn't give straight answers to vital questions. The gunpowder was loaded onto the pier, but Luke had secretly mixed mud with the gunpowder and fuse anchors.

Now, to get that bastard assassin.

Chapter 21

Luke rowed like a man possessed to the north shore, not bothering to beach or anchor the boat. He climbed the steep bank. He must somehow fight his way through the royal soldiers and save the prince.

"Luke! What are you doing?"

He turned to see Joya running toward him from the boat house. "Luke! It's not too late. Pledge to the king. He will grant you audience."

"I pledged loyalty to Margaret. There is no time for this. I must save Prince Edward."

"From what?"

"Wagg and his assassin. You were right."

"Let me help."

"Nay. Stay here where it's safe."

"Where are you going?"

Luke ran up the hill, hoping to outrun her. He reached the outskirts of the royal troops. A soldier stopped him, sword pulled.

Luke held up his hand. "I'm here to help. The prince is in danger."

"Aren't we all," he said, preparing to lunge at him.

"Stop!" Joya caught up, gasping. "Let him pass."

"Who are you?"

"Joya. Joya Ellingham. The Ellinghams," she stressed. "Lord Tabor is my father!"

"Tabor," the man repeated.

"We serve the queen, you fool!" Joya pushed him. "Now get out of our way."

The man chose to fight.

Luke kicked the back of the soldier's legs.

The soldier grabbed Luke's sleeve as he fell.

They rolled down the bank. Luke struck him. The soldier fell and Luke yanked the jacket from him, hastily slipping it on.

"Let's go," Joya said. She lifted her skirts and ran ahead. "Come with us," she demanded of a handful of soldiers. "Hurry. Where's the royal pavilion? We have urgent news."

The soldiers pointed and turned their attention back to the bridge, all straining to watch the tension between the king and Wagg on the bridge.

Luke and Joya hurried on. The men they passed gave no resistance because they, too, were pressing toward the bridge to see what was happening. Luke spied the royal pavilion twenty yards away, the size of eight tents, white, royal pendants flying at all posts. "There."

At the pavilion, they found the door unguarded. They approached cautiously, peering through a large slit between the wall and the door of the tent without showing themselves.

The queen, the prince and four guards surrounded a large table. They were gathered around the subject of their rapt attention—Winton Hawke, the assassin.

* * *

At the bridge, Wagg watched Luke squeeze his brother's shoulder and head down the bank toward the boat. Could he be trusted? Hell, no. No one could be trusted. He'd needed Penry's expertise with explosives and bridges, but he was no one's fool. He'd put guards on Penry from the moment he left Abington. The guards had built the explosives, and made sure they were mounted on the piers. And if Penry didn't light the fuses, the guards would kill Penry and light them, themselves. Wagg had planned too carefully to leave it to one stubborn bridgemaker, crippled by demons and clearly under the spell of a Gypsy tart. Killing his brothers had kept him hostile to Margaret, and Wagg had insured he'd light those fuses. Luke wouldn't risk losing his Goat Boy.

But the bridge would explode, and this battle would secure Wagg's future. They would speak his name respectfully in Parliament. They would write him into England's highest chronicles, alongside the kings and earls and dukes. He would become as beloved as royalty. He would be granted a holding, a castle, a country manor. A duke's daughter in marriage.

A hand tentatively touched his shoulder, and Wagg turned. It was the Goat Boy, his brows furrowed in question. "The king's cavalry are just waiting in their saddles, and you're waiting, too. Why?"

The stunted boy must have spent his life in the nursery. "When the king is ready, they will make the first move." Wagg peered past Hugh, bending down so he could see under the bridge. Three fuses were lit and burning. Good for Penry. He had lit several to ensure that at least one ignited the gunpowder. Wagg's heart skipped. He had never felt so alive. He watched the fuses progress. They had timed several lengths of fuse, and decided upon a length sufficient to goad the king into a charge. Wagg himself would manage the time. If Henry's troops started to charge too soon, the Irish would have to push the king's men back to slow their forward progress. If the king hesitated too long, the Irish would start the charge but feign second thoughts and back off, and the king would pursue. Wagg had placed a small white flag on the bridge rail to mark where the king had to be. His front cavalry would control Henry's progress so he would be at the most vulnerable point on the bridge when it collapsed.

Wagg assessed the length of the fuses. If the king didn't charge soon, Wagg would.

Goat Boy shook his head. "I don't understand why—"

More trumpets blew. Sheep's horns whined. The royal troops raised their voices in a deafening battle cry, and the front cavalry spurred their horses.

Wagg's heart dropped to his boots. It was time.

* * *

From his limited vision through the slit in the royal pavilion, Luke considered the risks to the royals.

The walls were reinforced from within with fencing, a good security measure. Clavell wouldn't be slashing his way through the tent wall to escape. Even with four guards, though, were they a match for a trained assassin? Had Luke wounded the assassin enough in Marston to gain an advantage?

Designed for royalty, the tent measured roughly twenty by twenty-four feet. Clavell stood before three maps, spread out on the top of the long, sturdy table. A royal guard stood to Clavell's left and another guard to his right, standing between Clavell and the queen and prince. Two more guards stood on the side of the table closest to the door.

The queen leaned over the table top, studying the maps. The assassin pointed out certain areas, describing troop sizes and two cannon, a detail Luke had never heard about.

"Why are we hiding," Joya whispered. "You said you declared your loyalty to her."

"Aye, but so did he, publicly. I won't risk arrest while she tries to sort out which man is telling the truth." He held a finger to his lips and they listened to Clavell.

As Luke had anticipated, the assassin was feeding them a platter full of lies about the Yorkist strategies. The queen and her men leaned toward Clavell, capturing his every word.

"Wagg plans a surprise attack," the killer said, gravity in his voice, his posture protective. He made eye contact with the guards and the queen as he covertly grew closer to the prince. "The cannon are hidden below the bridge, in the boathouse. They're going to wait until you charge, and they will shoot into your troops and—look, see this area right here. It's the weakest point of the bridge. The bridge will fall." He expanded his words with a huge gesture, crashing his hand down on the map. "You must save the king!" He looked to the two guards closest to the door. "Now!"

The two guards cried out, "The king!" and hurried out of the tent past Joya and Luke.

Margaret blinked her eyes and shook her head. "No, no. Lord Penry assured me it's not going to..."

"Listen!" Clavell put a hand to his ear. "The battle cry, my queen! The king is attacking." The killer shouted. He pulled a vial from his pocket. "This will help!" With a strong flick of his wrist he flung its contents in a wide arc. A fine powder sprayed in an aggressive yellow plume that defiled the eyes of the two remaining guards, and Margaret and Prince Edward.

"Now!" Luke pushed Joya out the door, pulled his sword and rushed toward Margaret and her son.

Everyone held their eyes, crying out in pain from the sting of the foul powder. The killer pulled the sword from the guard nearest him and ran him through, pushing him backward off the bloodied sword.

Luke pushed the second guard out of the way. He shoved Margaret to the ground.

The killer leveled his sword toward Edward.

Luke swung his sword over the table. It collided with the killer's sword, stopping it before it hit the prince. "Now you'll die, you bastard."

The boy put his arms over his head and fell to the floor.

The killer stabbed at Luke, missed, and flung the bench at him. It hit the prince instead. The prince covered himself with the bench as a shield.

"Not today, Penry." The assassin raised his sword and retreated.

Luke stumbled over the queen and prince. Hampered by too many legs and arms, he couldn't find his footing.

The killer rushed out of the pavillion.

Joya! She was still at the entrance.

"Let go. You're not on my list," the killer said.

Sounds of a struggle came from outside the door.

The sound of a fist striking flesh. A woman's cry.

"Joya!"

Luke broke free from the tangle of bodies on the floor and hurried to the door.

Outside, Joya was on the ground, and the killer was mounted on a soldier's horse, already racing away.

Luke lifted her gently. "Joya. Are you all right?"

"The knave," she sputtered. "I tried to hold him." She rubbed her jaw and uttered a string of shocking curses.

Breathless with relief, he relished the heat of her wrath, the anger flashing in the brown eyes he had come to know so well with their flecks of copper and life. He lifted her to her feet, taking her in his arms. He kissed her hair, her neck, her lips.

And to the south, trumpets blared and battle cries filled the air.

* * *

The royal forces charged.

Hooves thundered on the bridge deck. Cries and screams filled the air as cavalry spurred their horses into action.

Chaos reigned on the bridge.

Goat Boy ran behind Wagg, grabbing his cotehardie.

Wagg pushed him toward the Irish soldier. "Don't let him out of your sight." Wagg smoothed his jacket and straightened his fighting dagger. He would be seen brave and in control, even before the spectacle of Henry's army.

"Charge!" Wagg screamed the order, and the Irish cavalry advanced. Wagg reined his horse back to allow his men past and avoid the melee.

Henry's front line crashed into the Irish, horses screamed, stumbling, being pushed backward as the royal charges advanced.

Henry was even with the white flag.

Now! Wagg willed the gunpowder to ignite.

Henry's forces grew closer. Horses fell, screamed as they were pummeled by the horses that pushed relentlessly forward from behind.

Now! Now! But the god-forsaken fuses continued to sputter.

A destrier collided with Wagg's and he and his horse went down. As his horse landed, it crushed Wagg's leg. He heard a terrible snap, a pain that stole his breath and forced him into a curled up position to protect himself.

More pain sketched its way through Wagg's body. A horse's hoof pounded his foot, and fresh pain exploded in his leg. Dragging himself through the gravel, he crawled to the bridge and hugged his body close to the deck outside the railing.

Screams of the dying filled the air, a chorus from hell, and still no explosion. The royal forces kept coming, a stream of horses and swords and red banners and death.

God Rot it! "Now! Now!" Wagg cried the command. There was a break in the cavalry and Wagg caught a glimpse of the south fields, whole companies breaking apart, troops fleeing on horseback and on foot in every direction, royal forces in pursuit. A rout! And still no detonation. The perfectly sound bridge continued to offer passage to every stinking royal soldier. They advanced in a fury to crush the Yorkist and Irish troops.

Damn, damn Penry!

* * *

Luke placed the benches upright. Margaret had found her son and they sprawled together on the floor of the tent, the queen's arms wrapped protectively around him. Tears streamed down both their faces, and their eyes were closed.

"Here, Your Royal Highness. Sit you here." Luke helped Margaret and the prince onto the bench.

Margaret reached out, touching Luke's face. "Who are you?"

"Lord Penry. And Joya Ellingham is here with me."

"Penry?"

"We came to help you."

"My eyes. My eyes," moaned the queen.

What had the black heart done to her? "Can you see?"

She opened her eyes a bit, blinking pitifully, tears pouring from them. "Aye, thanks be." She turned toward the door. "Where's that sod-hearted Clavell?"

"Gone. He escaped. I'm sorry." Luke put her hands together and poured fresh water from the table. "Try to keep your eyes open and flush them clean." He handed the pitcher to Joya, and she sat next to the young prince, offering aid.

"We'll catch the bastard. He'll be the first executed tonight," Margaret said. "We were utterly deceived by him." She turned to her son, dabbing his eyes with her gown. "John, are you there?" she asked her guard.

"Aye. I only got it in the right eye."

"I can hardly see," Margaret said. "But I heard someone die."

"Harry," the guard John said. "Clavell killed him. Lord Penry saved you and Edward."

"Penry." Margaret splashed more water on her eyes. "When did you arrive?"

"In time to help you," Luke said. "Lord Clavell—if that's his name or title—was the man who killed my brothers and raided Penryton. And tried to make it appear that your soldiers did it. I apologize for thinking so. My brother, Hugh, survived the attack, and he reported that Clavell and his men were dressed in royal livery."

"Your brothers were loyal. Who is this rogue, Clavell? And why would he kill your brothers?"

"I doubt he's Lord Clavell's son. He's a mercenary. Wagg hired him," Luke said. "When Clavell accepted King Henry's offer for pardon and was welcomed among your troops, I realized that you and the prince would be in the presence of a hired assassin."

"We are beholden. And what of the king," Margaret asked. "How are things on the bridge?"

"As I told you it would be. The bridge is intact."

A soldier entered the tent with a messenger. "Your Royal Highness." They bowed.

"How is my king?" Margaret asked.

"Our cavalry have crossed the bridge, along with the archers. The enemy troops are dead, surrendered or fleeing."

"Today is our victory," the queen said, smiling in triumph through her tears. "Tell the king I must see him at once."

The men left.

Margaret turned to Luke. "Say naught of Clavell's attack to anyone."

Luke thought she wanted to tell the king first. "As you wish. I would ask a favor, if you will," Luke said.

"Pray what is it?"

"I would ask that you forbid the troops from raiding the people of Redstone. My uncle is the mayor."

"I'm aware," Margaret said. "You have protected us twice this day, Lord Penry. Redstone will be safe, and you will receive a boon." Margaret turned to the only surviving guard, John. "You will say nothing of this to a soul." She lowered her voice and they continued talking, but their voices drifted away and all Luke could see was Joya.

An inner light shone in her eyes, the copper flecks sparkling amid the brown. Her smile took his breath, beautiful as always, but now bright with barely contained relief and appreciation.

Luke's heart took wings and he no longer felt the canvas floor beneath him. Surely they must be breathing as one, the two of them, sharing this moment.

Gradual awareness grew of the queen's presence, and the moment passed. Too precious to be forgotten, he stored it in his memory and returned to Margaret, who had mentioned a boon and reassured him that the people of Redstone would be safe. "Merci," he said to the French-born queen. "Merci boucoup."

* * *

Luke gained passage from the layers of guards and approached the stables. With the total thrashing of Wagg's armies, the royal armies had found time on their hands. The queen had kept her word and forbidden plundering, instead setting them to the task of burying the dead. Mace, Luke's own crusty, scarred knight, had rescued Hugh, who was safe and waiting at the boat house.

The royal family had taken temporary residence in his uncle's home. In turn, James had made accommodations for Luke's family and Joya in his home. Beds had been set up for Tabor and his knights at the haberdasher's store, and Joya had been placed in the counting room with Florin.

Luke had given Tabor and his family an abbreviated version of Wagg's plan and briefly disclosed that he had sabatoged the plan to destroy the bridge.

"You saved the king," Tabor had said, his voice a mixture of awe and gratitude.

At Margaret's request Luke had not spoken of Clavell's attempted murders of the queen and prince. Now Luke responded to the queen's invitation to join her in the stables. After today, there should be no further repercussions to his earlier alliance with York. Still, he approached their meeting with caution. The queen was known for her heavy demands.

He rubbed the tight knot that had formed at the base of his neck. Luke had saved the royal family. For such significant service, he could expect an audience with them, and the bestowing of the boon Margaret mentioned earlier.

But the day had passed without either one, and now this, a summons to meet privately with the queen. In the stables. It did not bode well.

The late afternoon sun languished in the thin sky, and the chilling air had been made foul with the stink of death. Hundreds of bodies littered the riverbanks and surrounding fields. The many Irishmen who had survived, grateful to be pardoned by the king, had fled to the forest lest he change his mind.

Inside, the air improved with the smell of newly stacked hay in the feeding bins.

A fourth guard nodded to Luke and moved a respectful distance away as Luke approached.

In the next stall Margaret wore a cape to protect her gown while she brushed a fine black palfrey, its coat shining with good health and proper care. He heard it had been a gift from the Duke of Somerset, one of the few noblemen who had gained and kept the queen's favor over the years. Luke bowed and greeted her. "Favorite horse?" He asked.

She regarded him with eyes bloodshot and swollen from Clavell's attack. "His name is Saber. From the Spanish stock in Troyes. Multiple champions, both sides." Pride thickened her voice.

Luke observed his fine features and tack. "He's a beauty." He patted the horse. "You sent for me?"

"I'm glad you finally returned to the king's service," she said. "The Ellinghams were steadfast in their belief that you would."

Saber slapped her with his tail. She smiled, indulgent, and resumed brushing. "Reports on Penryton are bad. The Yorkists ravaged it." She sounded too pleased with her report.

Luke dreaded seeing the damage. "And Wagg? Did you find him?"

"Mauled by horses on the bridge. Still alive when our men spied him. Both legs broken. When they closed in on him, he mumbled something about being taken alive. Like the snake that he was, he rolled off the bridge into the river."

The queen held her neck and grimaced, as if she might have been injured during the struggle with the assassin. "Wagg's commanders, Lord Harmon and the other one, they were slain by our cavalry."

Luke reflected. Wagg, self-serving and deceitful, had been quick enough to escape being drawn and quartered, but still suffered a difficult death.

Margaret's face darkened. "Most unfortunate. Wagg's secrets drowned with him. We'll never know how much York knew of Wagg's plan, but we know this: York is in Ireland, and he'll be back to fight."

She stopped brushing Saber. "Which is where you come in, Luke."

At the intensity in her eyes, Luke's blood chilled.

"York's absence today confirms what you've told me, that Wagg acted independently. I've told no that Wagg hired Clavell to kill us. Only my guard, John, knows and he's one of my most trusted." She waved her hand, sweeping toward the bridge. "This incident will be recorded as an accidental clash, not a battle. Henry has won over the commanders and many of the Irish have pledged to join our army. Your part in this debacle is in no way evident to York."

Luke showed no response. *He knows. I sent him a message.* Caution kept him from telling her, though. The combination of treachery and sheer will behind those weeping eyes made him hesitate.

She paused. "Now is the time for you to help me. I want you to report to York posthaste. Join York. Learn what he has planned next. You will inform me and join our forces. I'll give you your own command."

Luke took an inevitable step into the quicksand, knowing the perils of refusing her. "Prithee no, my queen. I am no soldier or commander. I don't have the heart for battle. And believe me when I tell you I do not have the disposition for intrigue. I would hurt your cause, not help it."

Luke had seen the post-battle brutality, royal forces walking among the dead on the battlefield and running through those who had not already died, slashing their way through the human carpet of wounded until nothing but tortured flesh and blood remained. War was unimaginably ugly. "Nor do I have the tolerance for command. I have always been … solitary."

She straightened, every inch of her small body tensing, her countenance as alarming as the stories men told of her at court, facing her enemies. "You will summon the strength you need to serve your king."

Luke's mind raced, turning stones looking for other opportunities to serve her, searching for common interest. "I will build bridges for you."

"I don't need bridges. I need leadership."

The stones looked more promising. Luke turned a few more. "I can give you that, my queen. Not with intrigue, or on the battlefield. I will rebuild Penryton, and offer you my support from there, and at court."

Margaret slapped the dandy brush in Luke's hand. "Your brother then. What's his name?" Her eyes clouded with a growing impatience that hung in the air like a night draft.

Luke ran his thumb over the bristles. He could not avoid displeasing her with this.

"Hugh? He's—unnerved after Clavell's attack. He's not built for battle. Doesn't weigh much more than your son. We both simply want to return to rebuild Penryton. I hope my service to you today—and my loyalty—have proven my worth such that you can honor this simple request."

A mean-spirited smile contorted her face. "Mayhap you and your brother are queasy soldiers. So be it." She formed each word in controlled, overly enunciated anger, her eyes narrowed with a thinly veiled threat. "In view of your service, I would not have you be a reluctant commander." She tapped the gate with the brush, rapping the wood several times. "You will provide me with a proven commander. At your expense."

Luke felt the heat of her anger and the underlying threat of absolute power. It could annihilate him and all he held dear.

"And you will serve me. You will see York. You will learn his plan. You will report to me."

The door opened, and Joya approached. Upon seeing them, her smile faded. She lowered her head and held her hands, waiting for the queen's invitation to join them.

Margaret gave a terse wave acknowledging her. "You may enter."

Joya opened the gate and entered the side stalls. Her gaze flitted to Luke for the briefest of moments as if to read the situation.

Luke glanced down, hoping she correctly read his gesture as a warning.

Joya bowed to the queen, slightly lifting the skirt of her torn, dirtied gown. "Your Royal Highness. You summoned me."

"Aye. Margaret studied Joya, her gaze sharp, scraping across Joya's hair, tangled and uncovered, over the soiled bodice and her muddied shoes. "You freed Lord Penry before I could meet with him."

Joya blinked rapidly. "It was a mistake. Lord Penry himself has said the same, and—."

"Your father is loyal. He tried to explain about the—the what? Apricot seeds?" She shook her head. "Deceitful. Reckless." Margaret gave her a pointed look. "Think not that I didn't see right through it. You defied me. You had good fortune in that I have been otherwise occupied until you could prove this man was worth saving." Margaret's eyes narrowed and she pointed the mane brush at Joya's face. "I will not have you stain your father's good name. Do not ever do that again. Never challenge my order. Never."

Joya began to drop to her knees.

The queen grabbed her arm. "Stand. You're disheveled enough as it is. Swear to me now. You will never again challenge me."

"I will never again challenge you, my queen." Her brown eyes shone as she met the queen's gaze evenly.

The queen raised her brows, a trace of a smile pulling on her mouth. "Fortunately, you judged Lord Penry better than we did. Because of him, we are all here to tell the tale. Thank you for your part in protecting the prince. I trust you won't be rash in the future."

"Pray forgive me, my queen. I was so sure of him."

"You were right." She took a step toward Joya. "You have proven yourself." She removed one of the several rings on her fingers and placed it on Joya's middle finger. "To your king, and to me."

Chapter 22

Two sets of three soft knocks sounded on Joya's door. She and Luke had earlier agreed to the special signal before she retired to the counting room. His meeting with the queen was finally over.

Her chamber had no windows, but she guessed the hour was late. She rose from her small bed and carried a candle past the empty shelves, all cleared earlier, Luke had told her, to protect James' clients' funds should the bridge collapse.

Florin perched on the top shelf, his glowing cat eyes following her. Most unsettling, she thought, hurrying past him.

She slid the three bolts free and tugged on the heavy door.

Luke slipped in locked it. He cupped her face in his hands and traced its contours, soft as a whisper. "Some swelling. He must have hit you hard."

"I had a good grip on him. I wasn't going to let him escape."

The candlelight flickered in his blue eyes, his gaze tender. "How are you?"

"I want this to end." It had been the worst day in her life. She had suffered paralyzing fear for Luke, her father, Degory and the sea of soldiers on each side of the bridge.

Joya had tried to divert her gaze, but she had seen the dead in the fields, in the river; had heard the moans of the dying. It conjured thoughts of Giles, that each soldier had family and friends who would never see him again. She had spent the last several months resisting the signs of war. Villages, fields burned. Newly informed widows, eyes dulled with loss, returning soldiers missing limbs, eyes, any hope of ever providing for their families. Turn away, turn away, think of more pleasant times—but she had failed to escape the visions. Now they pressed on her heart and clung to her soul and she was trapped under a cloak of cold, leaden death.

"It must end." Many had died this day, but Luke had prevented hundreds, mayhap thousands more.

Taking the candle from her hands, he put his arm around her and they walked to the small bed and sat down.

She turned to him. "What does Margaret want from you? From the look on your face in the stable, it's not good."

He placed the candle on the nightstand, took her in his arms, rubbed the tenseness from her shoulders. "She wants me to command her troops."

Joya had lived in constant fear that Luke would face the executioner, and now that he had escaped that fate, Margaret wanted him to enter battle? "No!"

"I'm no stranger to the lists. I can face competition. Win most of times. I have good instincts. And I always enter the fields strong and well-practiced."

"But you saw, this morning. The death, the suffering…" Her throat constricted.

"Shh." He covered her face with his hand as if to shield her from the thoughts. "I would kill to protect you and my family. I have killed to avoid my own death." He was silent for a moment. "But afterward, I'm overwhelmed with a curse, a … darkness that I must overcome."

He took a deep breath, exhaled audibly.

She gripped his shoulders. "Please don't. I can't bear the thought, Luke."

"I refused her, moments before you arrived. She didn't take kindly to it. I can only hope there are few repercussions."

Florin jumped into her lap, circled and snuggled, purring.

"Sweet boy," Joya crooned, massaging the cat's big head. "I heard James thanking you for saving Florin's life."

"He narrowly escaped the royal guards this morning. His eyes will be his undoing."

"They are beautiful, but unsettling," she said. Luke's rescue of him spoke well of his compassion. She squeezed his hand. "Thank you."

Candlelight flickered across his face, occasionally lighting his blue eyes. They shone with a new softness, a sense of ease.

"You have been carrying Wagg's secret since we met," she guessed.

"Nay. York's original plans were for me to repair a bridge so York's troops could outrun Margaret to the coast. I was told of the new plans after I left Cerne."

"Why did you finally pledge loyalty to Margaret?"

"I gave you my vow."

"But why?"

"Not for my belief in her. We will never agree on that."

"I must confess, our discussion on the boat was enlightening. I placed too much faith in her."

"And I too much faith in York and his followers. You judged Wagg correctly and quickly. Your wariness helped me to think more deeply on the Red Bridge plan. As soon as I realized it wasn't York's plan—he would never kill the king and most certainly never kill the queen and prince—I knew I had to alert Margaret."

"But pledge your loyalty to her?"

"So she would believe me. Much as I trust York will be a better ruler, what Wagg schemed wasn't war. It was murder disguised as war. Honorable men don't murder women and children to make it easier to ascend to the throne. I was never able to confirm if the plan was York's or Wagg's, so in the end I had to trust my instincts. If I supported Wagg, I would be no better than the assassin."

She worked up the courage to ask the next question. "What happens now?"

"Your father is taking you back to Coin Forest," he said, stroking Florin. "And Hugh and I must go to Penryton. I dread seeing it."

They were taking separate ways. Joya blinked away the stinging of her eyes. "You've heard from William?" Her throat was tightening dangerously.

"You remember his name." He smiled. "I think I mentioned him only once."

She swallowed. Luke had great respect for his steward. "Is he safe?"

"His babe was born the night Penryton was attacked. It doubtless saved William's life, because he would have fought Clavell to save my brothers. I received word that he has a son."

"William was the only one I ever heard you say you trusted." Her voice wavered, betraying her.

"What's wrong, Joya?" He scooped the cat off her lap and turned her to face him. "What is it?"

"You don't know? My father said he would discuss the hand fasting with you. Did he?" The folding of their hands would seal their betrothal.

"He did. He said I was not welcome at Coin Forest until then."

"And?"

"And what?

"Will there be a folding of the hands?"

"There are things...certain things...to work out." He paused. "I asked Tabor for your hand. I want to uphold your honor, of course." He gave her a restrained smile that troubled more than pleased her. "I assumed he told you."

"Why didn't you tell me?" She worried that he was unwilling, merely saving her reputation.

His smile faded. "What are you about, Joya? The last remnant of his smile vanished. "After what we've shared, do you not wish to wed?"

"What's to work out about the hand folding? I want to know how you feel about me."

"After what we've shared, you know."

"I need you to tell me."

He pulled free from her, backing up to the very end of the bed, arms poised to bolt. His look was indignant, as if she had asked him to demonstrate hand spinning. "I know naught of courtly love and poetry." He spit the words out as if they were bad plums.

"I love you, Luke. I don't need a long speech. Can't you tell me how you feel about me?"

"Let me show you." Firelight danced across his features. His eyes deepened with tenderness, holding no fear or distance.

A tingling swept across her skin.

He licked his forefinger and thumb and snuffed out the candle.

They were together, alone, in darkness.

He had sealed them in a vault of sounds and scents and sensations. His breath held traces of the cherry wine from dinner, his hair sweet with a clean-smelling oil.

His fingers laced with hers and broke free to travel up her arm, over her sleeve, up to her neckline, where his thumbs dipped below the fabric, skimming the tops of her breasts.

Desire shimmered through her, a trail of warmth that licked under her bodice, over her breasts and to her core.

He touched his lips to hers, the kiss rich and relaxed. Did it not say love, she thought. Did she really need the words?

"Why are we in the dark?"

"I want you to feel how much I care."

"But I can't see your eyes."

"Nor can I see yours." He kissed her fingers. "It's easier this way."

Her heart faltered. Was he refusing the betrothal ceremony? "What? What is easier?"

"I'm ill at ease with it. I hope you understand."

A confession, then. Itching with a blend of curiosity and dread, she wondered what he had to say. She loved him, had survived the sting of his judgments, had seen glimpses of his emotions, huge doses of his passion, and yet still these frustrating moments of resistance and hesitation to get close to her. Whatever it would be, he could not bear to see her face when he said it.

"You're going to scare me back to get even with my Evil Eye story?"

He laughed. "Nay."

"Get on with it, because you're making me fearful. What haven't you told me?"

"You have been kind to me. You saved my life." His voice, the voice she had come to love, came to her in the darkness, deep, resonant, measured. From the moment they met, he had been reluctant. Distracted by the horrors of battle, she had forgotten. So desperate to be with him, she had forgotten.

"You have been steadfast in your support, and I am touched. No one has ever cared for me in that way."

The blade sliced, laying bare her hopes. 'Twas no wonder that he couldn't say he loved her. He didn't. "You've been tolerating me. Humoring me."

"No, I—"

"I made myself convenient for you. I didn't give you a chance to refuse me, did I? From the time I found you, I have been annoying you, pushing myself on you, forcing myself into your life. I have been pressuring you, and you really see me as you see Florin, a creature in need of saving. From the river, from my own, stupid impulses. You—"

He took her face in his hands and kissed her, mouth crushing, tongue claiming, his hand firm on her bottom, he slipped her under him, heavy against her with his lust, grinding against her.

The bed wobbled but held.

He ravished her, kissing her hair, her ears, her eyes, her lips. He fumbled with her tunic, finally pulling it from her shoulders, biting her nipples, her neck, sucking her arms, her fingers, probing her folds open, sliding his fingers in, massaging her.

She rose from the bed to meet his hands, wet and groaning. Still he suckled and played, driving her higher. She cried out for him and found release.

He entered her, moaning, and they wrestled together in a dance of sensations that left them breathless, struggling for air.

He anchored her hands above her head and straightened his arms, rising above her. "I lose all control with you." He panted, his voice raw with emotion. "You slay me with your beauty, your hands, your body." He fell back onto her. "With your affection."

"But you don't sound at all pleased with it."

"It's too much. Too powerful. I can't control it … or myself."

She lay beneath him, warm and pulsing inside, so satisfied, yet mystified with the man she could not resist.

"I dislike it when Degory looks at you," he said. "There was that moment outside the royal tent when Clavell had his hands on you. Unbearable. At that moment I thought I had lost you. I –I was—I can't lose you," he said. His breath tore from his body in the darkness, ragged. He squeezed her hands so tightly she felt faint.

"You won't," she said.

"I love you." It was a proclamation, firmly stated in his deep, resonant voice. "I love you," he repeated, softly this time. "I would take your hand before I go to Penryton."

His words were uttered without joy, with an edge of sadness. Her heart bolted as fast as Goldie did when she reined her toward the castle after a long day of riding. "But what?"

"I can't do ceremony." His voice wavered with emotion. "I can't do it."

"The hand folding?"

He didn't answer.

She dared to hope she knew what he was trying to say. "Do you mean you can't do the betrothal ceremony in front of my family and friends?"

"Not in front of throngs of people. I cannot."

Relieved beyond words, she laughed. Groping for him in the darkness, she threw her arms around his neck. "Such an insufficient obstacle, my dear. I will promise to you in a garderobe, if need be."

"There's more, and you must know this before you agree to the betrothal."

He took her hands. "Margaret is demanding that I spy on York. To do so, I will need to publicly proclaim my loyalties to him."

Joya wished she could see his expression. "That won't make sense after having saved her life."

"Which is why she's forbidden us to speak of it. She has also ordered the guard silent—the guard who witnessed Clavell's attempt to kill her and the prince."

"But you also spared the bridge to save the king," Joya said.

"She will scoff at that, and claim I only did it to save my family. I must pledge to York, and soon. It must be convincing, and the deception will last so long as it takes to get the information Margaret needs. You cannot share this with anyone. Including your family."

"York is in Ireland."

"I may need to go there to convince him of my loyalty."

"Or Calais. Or battle. This is dangerous. She would order you to do this, even after you risked your life to save hers? It's not just. How can she do this to you? To us?"

"She has been doing this for years. She has sacrificed entire armies and villages to advance her cause."

His words rang off tune, like an old song she had never liked, come back to plague her. He was again criticizing the queen, but this time, Joya understood. The silence fell in on her, and she struggled to free herself from the net with which Margaret had snared them. The floor seemed to shift beneath her feet, and she yearned for the simplicity of the life she had enjoyed before it had become entangled with Margaret's.

"What say you, Joya? Can you forsake your family and wed a traitor?"

* * *

Joya glanced sideways at the man who would be her husband.

They had completed their handfasting ceremony moments before in the orchard at Coin Forest. Joya had kept her promise

Janet Lane

to Luke, completing the ceremony with only four witnesses: the priest, her parents and Hugh. Later this afternoon, Cam, Pru and George would arrive for the supper, along with Nicole and Stephen. Alex, Maud, Effie, and many from the village would come to celebrate, too, but this moment was quiet, to honor Luke's request.

Father Jeffrye, his mouth slanted in disapproval, glanced at the surrounding orchard and left, mumbling something about the formality and sanctity of the church.

Sharai laughed, kissed her daughter's forehead and sprinkled a sweet-smelling oil on her hands. She plucked a hair from Joya, one from Luke, and folded the strands in a white linen covered with crushed tree bark and rosebuds.

She passed a small cup to Joya and Luke, and filled it with a golden liquid. The aroma suggested honey but Joya could not guess the energy behind the mist that sparkled on the surface.

Luke took the delicate vessel with his thumb and forefinger and gave her a questioning glance.

She had reminded Luke of her mother's Gypsy spells, none of which were evil, all of which were filled with love. She smiled, reassuring him.

"To our beloved daughter, Joya, and her intended, Luke, repeat after me and sip the nectar. True love born, promises sworn." Her mother gestured for them to raise the cups.

Joya and Luke repeated it, and Joya sipped. 'Twas a delicate fruit nectar with honey that tingled as it passed the tongue.

Her mother's eyes sparkled. "Pleasures sweet, life complete."

They sipped again. Luke gave an appreciative groan.

Her mother placed her hand on her father's waist, and her father dropped his arm over Hugh's shoulder.

"Sky above, endless love." Her mother's smile dazzled with happiness, and Joya and Luke finished the nectar. Their family surrounded them in an embrace.

"We wish you happiness," her mother said.

"Well done," Hugh said. His smile was warm and generous.

"Congratulations." Tabor kissed his daughter's forehead. "You were right, Sweetling. He is deserving of you." He shook

Luke's hand. "She's my precious daughter. Protect her." His voice faltered, and he recovered. "Always be true to one another."

Sharai tended to her tears and the three of them left.

Now she and Luke lay on a blanket under the vivid pink branches of a blooming apple tree. His eyes, made bluer by the sun, brightened with intimate possession as he regarded her.

She smiled, so comfortable with him that she didn't try to suppress the giggle that escaped, so happy that she could feel so womanly, yet touched with an excitement she had not felt since she was a young girl, like the sun shining all the way to her soul.

She wore a gown of deep crimson, a light, shimmering silk her mother had been saving for this day, studded down the back and sleeves with dozens of dainty black onyx buttons, Gypsy colors of ceremony. The sword-and-rings pin of her Ellingham heritage, gold rings from her parents on her right hand, engraved with words of love and good wishes. She wore a betrothal ring from Luke on her left ring finger. And inside, a growing sense of delight she could barely contain.

"I love you." A giddiness, a breathtaking lightness had come over her.

"And I love you." He kissed his way up her arm, sending darts of desire through her.

"Be wary." She kissed him, a long, smoldering kiss that threatened to melt both of them. "Lest we create a scandal."

The delicate scent of her mother's oils and the flowering apple trees enveloped them. They were sheltered in a pink and white world of blooms that almost obscured the blue sky beyond.

"Sky above, endless love."

"Gypsy magic," he said, teasing in his eyes.

"If luck be with you," she teased back.

Luke kissed her and propped on an elbow, watching her, an easy smile causing a hitch in her breath.

A colorful assortment of herbs and flower petals lay scattered in the grass around them, the physical proof of a spell whispered by her mother to protect them in the years to come.

Luke wore a tunic of blue that brought forth the color of his eyes. He had tamed his brown hair for the occasion, and he had borrowed her father's ceremonial sword for their exchange of vows.

He kissed the betrothal ring on her hand, and she kissed his. They would be engraved later.

"My friends will be angry." She could imagine Cam's indignance when she and Pru arrived to witness the handfasting a few hours from now, only to learn they had missed it.

"I agreed to the wedding. They will attend that," Luke said.

"You'll be able to cope with all the people?"

"They are your people." He tapped her nose playfully. "Rest assured, wine will be consumed."

She laughed.

Bees buzzed in the profusion of blooms, and they entwined their fingers, looking to the flower-laced sky.

They had been surrounded by people since Redstone, constantly under watch by her father, who was fiercely committed to protecting her mostly tattered reputation until they became betrothed. She could finally ask about his plans.

"What now?" She lowered her voice, feeling traitorous just asking the question. "With York, and your promise to Margaret?"

"I loathe this complication. I simply wanted to save England for you. Ridiculous, I know that now. I cannot save England any more than I can swim upstream. Parliament has failed to solve this without war. I could do no more than salvage some of England's honor."

"And you did. You saved the Lancasters, you saved many lives, and you saved Redstone. But what of York?"

"I made two vows. I will be your husband. I will support Margaret." He kissed her, soft as a whisper. "I plan to fulfill my duty to Margaret before our wedding. I will thereafter leave the struggle for the throne to others."

"How will you fill your days?"

"Restore Penryton. Make it beautiful again for you and our children."

She sighed. "That sounds perfect."

"And we'll schedule regular travel to Crystal Lake."

She noted the playful turn to his smile and her heart skipped. "Forsooth?"

He tilted his head, still beautifully connected to his shoulders. "Indeed,' he said, his voice deep, sensual. "I need to show you how to properly race seedpod sailboats."

"Such audacity, my lord." She laughed, a crude, Cam-like chuckle. "You know I shall win."

"Nay. I will always win."

"I shall look forward to claiming my prize."

"What?" His brows rose with mirth, playfully coy. "I thought I was the prize."

"No, my talented bridge builder," she said, making her voice purr. She touched his heart. "*We* are the prize."

IF YOU ENJOYED CRIMSON SECRET

Please consider sending Luke, Joya and the rest of the cast some love in the form of a book review.

Just go to amazon.com, search for "Crimson Secret" and scroll down to "Write a Review." It needn't be a long and/or detailed review—just a rating and what you have time for--and it will be much appreciated by me and other readers looking for new historical romance adventures. Thank you, and happy reading!

Upcoming book release news at:

www.janetlane.net

Join my newsletter - never miss a new book or a hot deal!

ABOUT THE AUTHOR

Janet Lane writes action adventures in the medieval romance and contemporary women's fiction genres. She graduated with honors from the University of Colorado, where she completed the creative writing program. She leads writer's workshops, serves as a writing contest judge, and is a staff blogger for the Rocky Mountain Fiction Writers' national writer's group.

Her debut novel, Tabor's Trinket, made the #1 Amazon best-seller list. Tabor's Trinket won the international IPPY Award and Next Generation INDIE award. Emerald Silk, part two in the Coin Forest series, won an EVVY Award. Traitor's Moon, part three in the series, won the HOLT Medallion.

#1 New York Times Best-Selling Author Lara Adrian calls Emerald Silk "..an enchanting medieval romance filled with passion, intrigue and vividly drawn characters that leap off the page. I loved this novel!"

Janet was a featured author in RMFW Press's *Tales from Mistwillow*, and co-chaired the editorial board for *Broken Links, Mended Lives*, which was nominated for the Colorado Book Award. Janet blogs at janetlane.wordpress.com and at rmfw.org.

AWARDS FOR THE COIN FOREST NOVELS

TABOR'S TRINKET – Book One
International Awards: IPPY, INDIE

EMERALD SILK – Book Two
National Award: EVVY

TRAITOR'S MOON – Book Three
National Award: HOLT MEDALLION

Author's Note

The Wars of the Roses consisted of many battles fought over England's throne between 1455 and 1487. It was fueled in large part by Margaret of Anjou, King Henry VI's queen, who refused to surrender the throne in spite of her husband's erratic and extended bouts with insanity. It was a war of bloodlines, and of the nobility's increasing frustrations with the myopic interests of the royal families. The battles were rife with instances of commanders switching loyalty on the battlefields. These acts of treason ofen swayed the outcome of those battles.

The first confrontation between the Lancastrian King Henry VI and the challenging Duke of York was the First Battle of St. Albans on May 22, 1455, a Yorkist victory.

The second confrontation, the Battle of Blore Heath, September 23, 1459, was a Yorkist victory in which thousands of Lancastrians died (including the fictional character, Giles). This was also the battle in which Joya's brother, Stephen, was accused of treason in Book 3 of the Coin Forest series, *Traitor's Moon*.

The third clash, the Battle of Ludford Bridge, October 12, 1459, was a Lancastrian victory. This was due in large part because Andrew Trollope, York's captain of the Calais troops, switched sides after accepting the king's pardon. York fled to Ireland and the earl of Salisbury fled to Calais, where England's largest standing army was headquartered.

The Battle of Red Bridge is my fictional account of Luke Bonwyk, Lord Penry, who allied with York to defeat the Lancastrians. After York's sound defeat at Ludford Bridge, Wagg, York's rebellious Irish captain, took matters into his own hands. He developed a secret plan to ambush and kill King Henry, Queen Margaret and Prince Edward as they attempted to cross the Red Bridge.

After Ludford, the armies clashed at the Battle of Northampton, on July 10, 1460. A Yorkist victory was sealed when a commander switched sides from the King's army to the Yorkist cause. King Henry was captured and the king agreed that the Yorks were the rightful heirs to the crown. Many thought this would end the wars, but Margaret continued the fight, which ultimately lasted twenty-seven more years.

Early Warfare

In this world of instant communication and technological sophistication, it's hard to grasp a world with no Internet, cell phones, or timely message delivery systems.

In a time when an unmanned missile or drone can travel thousands of miles and hit a target with accuracy, it's even harder to grasp a battle in which the two sides leisurely arrived, set up tents, and enjoyed meals and a good night's sleep before beginning battle. The opposing military leaders would parlay, during which time they would converse and agree on a time when the battle should start.

In the mid fifteenth century, gun powder and cannon were used, but guns as we know them did not find their way to the battlefield until later. Armor was still valuable, though the English longbow was known to penetrate it. Soldiers faced showers of arrows, cannon and boiling pitch. They may have been beheaded with a deadly sharp sword, bludgeoned with a mace, had their skulls crushed, drowned in a river from the oppressive weight of their own armor, or been trapped face down in the mud and suffocated in their helmets.

Regardless of the century, war is hell.

Janet Lane

Also by Janet Lane –

THE COIN FOREST SERIES

THE COIN FOREST SERIES
HISTORY, MADE PASSIONATE IN MEDIEVAL ENGLAND

Tabor's Trinket (Book 1)

Emerald Silk (Book 2)

Traitor's Moon (Book 3)

Crimson Secret – (Book 4)

COMING SOON!

Prequel – *Etti's Wish (working title) – Spring, 2017!*

ANTHOLOGIES

"It's About Time," *Mistwillow* anthology, RMFW Press

Broken Links, Mended Lives, an anthology

All available on amazon.com, Kindle, and other retail outlets

www.janetlane.net

Join my newsletter – freebies, new releases, hot deals!

https://janetlane.wordpress.com/

FOR BOOK CLUB READERS

Due to the length of the wars (1455-1487), the final victory of the War of the Roses did not go to York or King Henry VI. The Lancastrian Henry Tudor defeated the last Yorkist king, Richard III, at the Battle of Bosworth Field. Tudor assumed the throne as Henry VII and married Elizabeth of York, daughter and heiress of Edward IV. This united the red and white roses and their attendant claims to the throne.

In October of 1460, Parliament, in the Act of Accord, recognized York as Henry's successor, which disinherited Henry's son, Edward. Margaret and the former prince were ordered out of London, but Margaret formed a large Lancastrian army in the north and hostilities resumed.

Was Luke's assessment accurate that Parliament could have solved the struggle and saved tens of thousands of lives?

Though it required murdering the royal family, was Wagg's plan of value for that reason—that they would have saved thousands of lives—or was it simply evil ambition?

How do Luke and Joya change over the course of the story? What events trigger their growth?

Would you like to live on a "Living Bridge?"

Was there more than one villain in the story? If so, who was/were the other/s?

What was this book's message?

What moral/ethical choices did the characters make? How would you have chosen?

www.ingramcontent.com/pod-product-compliance
Lightning Source LLC
Chambersburg PA
CBHW022027240626
47154CB00007B/2305